THE COMMUNE

The Commune

A novel

by

ERICA ABEEL

BOOKS

Adelaide Books
New York / Lisbon
2021

THE COMMUNE
A novel
By Erica Abeel

Published by Adelaide Books, New York / Lisbon
adelaidebooks.org
Editor-in-Chief
Stevan V. Nikolic

For any information, please address Adelaide Books
at info@adelaidebooks.org
or write to:
Adelaide Books
244 Fifth Ave. Suite D27
New York, NY, 10001

ISBN: 978-1-954351-79-0

Printed in the United States of America

to Jasper and Otis who bring joy

Contents

Prologue   **13**

CHAPTER 1
The Drive Out   **21**

CHAPTER 2
Dinner at the Commune   **32**

CHAPTER 3
The Marriage Plot   **45**

CHAPTER 4
Morning After   **54**

CHAPTER 5
Edwina and Nadine   **77**

CHAPTER 6
Edwina and the Children   **106**

CHAPTER 7
The Party at Dragon's Gate   **118**

CHAPTER 8

The Party at Dragon's Gate Gilda **132**

CHAPTER 9

Party at Dragon's Gate Nadine **140**

CHAPTER 10

The Party at Dragon's Gate: Leora and Kaz **147**

CHAPTER 11

The Media Elite **154**

CHAPTER 12

Charades **161**

CHAPTER 13

Desire **183**

CHAPTER 14

Combustions **201**

CHAPTER 15

Fred Does Suicide **209**

CHAPTER 16

Mayhem **214**

CHAPTER 17

Reverberations **224**

CHAPTER 18

Crisis **240**

CHAPTER 19
Beverly Baboon   **260**

CHAPTER 20
Pox   **269**

CHAPTER 21
The Marriage Plot Reconsidered   **288**

Acknowledgements   **313**

Blurbs of previous works   **315**

About the Author   **327**

"*Without thinking highly either of men or of matrimony, marriage had always been her object; it was the only honourable provision for well-educated young women of small fortune, and however uncertain of giving happiness, must be their pleasantest preservative from want.*"

— Jane Austen, *Pride and Prejudice*

"*Since marriage constitutes slavery for women, it is clear that the women's movement must concentrate on attacking this institution. Freedom for women cannot be won without the abolition of marriage.*"

— Sheila Cronin

"*I want to see a man beaten to a bloody pulp with a high-heel shoved in his mouth, like an apple in the mouth of a pig.*"

— Andrea Dworkin

"*Most women are one man away from welfare.*"

— Gloria Steinem

Prologue

August 26, 1970

*"This is not a bedroom war, this is a political movement.
Man is not the enemy, man is a fellow victim."*

– Betty Friedan

They begin to arrive, with their signs, their excitement, their smiles. Women in big Jackie O sunglasses and dirndl skirts; students in leotards and bell bottoms, a few with Afros; the East Side matron in a Pucci toting a gold shopping bag. A lone man in a bow tie glances around, moistly eager for praise at having shown up. They all eye each other shyly. Two young women, breasts free in their tee shirts, hoist a hand-painted placard stretched between two poles: WOMEN STRIKE FOR PEACE AND EQUALITY! Behind it appears another: FREE ABORTION ON DEMAND.

Leora pivots and rises on her toes to look up Fifth Avenue: too much air between the smattering of marchers gathered uncertainly among the awnings and polished brass. Far from the critical mass they need. The numbers are crucial – *to prove the fact of our revolution*, Gilda has said. They've carpet-bombed the town with leaflets to get the troops out: "*You do not have to be a militant feminist or a man-hater or a bra-burner.* IF YOU DO NOTHING YOU ARE SAYING YOU ARE SATISFIED WITH YOUR INFERIOR STATUS."

Were the naysayers right? Leora pictures that movie where Charlie Chaplin marches down the street waving a flag with no one marching after him ... One boozy night at the commune, Gilda Gladstone confided to her, Leora – maybe since she was the only human stirring in the house at 3 A.M. – that when she first proposed a national strike to mark the 50th anniversary of women's suffrage, she got shouted down. The movement too small to get the numbers, barely qualified yet as a *movement*, four months not enough time to organize and anyway no fucking money ...

Hang on, it's early yet, Leora tells herself. Doesn't she have a history of arriving early for the party? Story of her life ...

Late afternoon, she'd taken Finn on the number 6 train to Columbus Circle (little sister left behind, indignant, with the sitter). They headed down 59th Street past the stink of the carriage horses and dank breath of a subway entrance toward the assembly point on Fifth. The Strike has been called for 5:30: less provocative then for women to "walk off the job," and they'll catch the home bound crowds of rush hour. A storm has chased the soul-sapping heat of late August and brought a promise of new beginnings. Fleecy little clouds sail overhead.

Finn, never idle, reads aloud from the marchers' signs: END HUMAN SACRIFICE, DON'T GET MARRIED. "Is that like the Aztecs?" Finn says. Dear God, where'd he learn *that*? As for the larger analogy, she can think of four explanations, none ideal for a six-year-old. "Sweetheart, I'll explain later," Leora says.

There's Gilda Gladstone, the parade's Grand Marshal, on the south side of 59th beside the Plaza Hotel. Flanked by Nadine and her other lieutenants, pressing toward the assembly point. Gilda looking, as always, as though she can't keep pace with herself. "*The feminist crusader was having her hair done at Sassoon and was almost late,*" a catty male reporter will write. "*A cross between Hermione Gingold and Bette Davis ...* "

During the hours of mimeographing, leafleting, phoning, Gilda hasn't had time to let herself think. *Suppose just a few hundred women turn out?* What an embarrassment! Women simply *have* to show up, every media outlet will see this parade as the test of feminism's credibility and scope. The *fact* of their revolution.

Leora cranes around. No sign yet of Monica Fairley, the rising star whose star has risen from nowhere, in Gilda's telling, siphoning attention from *her*, the founder, and "ripping off the movement for her own ambition"; the mere mention of Monica can trigger Gilda's asthma. Mid-battle over who would liaise with press, lead the march, deliver the closing speech, etc., Monica offered to step aside – she couldn't abide strife among feminist sisters ("horizontal" conflict); she'd address a rally for Cesar Chavez and the grape-pickers instead. Into the breach leaped Nadine to broker a truce. Gilda will lead the goddamn march, Monica will emcee the rally on 42nd Street at Bryant Park ... Leora sometimes wonders how a revolution – what Gilda calls a "quantum leap in consciousness" – can so resemble kindergarten.

At minutes past five it's as if floodgates open. They come streaming down 59th Street, women of all ages and persuasions, office workers, nurses ... Women in tie-dye schmattes ... Iron-haired veterans of anti-war protests, militant and wide in the beam ... Students with Susan B. Anthony buttons ... Mothers with babies slung across their chests ... Solemn, lank-haired girls — "*the* daughters," Gilda calls then ... A few guys with kids riding on their shoulders ... For a stupid moment Leora thinks, where are they all going? The crowd in the square in front of the Plaza slews down side streets, placards riding high. OPORTUNIDADES IGUALES ... DON'T COOK DINNER, STARVE A RAT TODAY ... With any luck, Finn won't spot END PENILE SERVITUDE ...

The horns of snarled traffic stutter their rage.

They've liberated the Statue of Liberty! Word spreads that a posse has scrabbled up to banner the good lady with "Women of the World Unite!"

Leora jumps for another check of Fifth. This time round a sea of marchers floods the avenue, color red popping, white signs shifting like sails. My God, the numbers! *Beyond our wildest dreams*, Gilda will write. Apricot beams of sunlight angle low between the buildings and glance off the windshields of bleating cars and taxis trapped in the crush. Across the street, the truck for CBS. Farther uptown, NBC. *Today marks the beginning of the most important social movement of the 70's*, Gilda will say at the rally in Bryant Park. *How did I have the nerve?* Gilda will write.

A pair of mounted policemen, boots shinola'd, clop along nearby, the muscled flanks of their horses sleek with sweat. Leora remembers they *never got the permit to march down Fifth*. What, block a major thoroughfare during rush hour? the mayor's people said. Weeks of lobbying and ass-kissing, and they've gotten one lousy lane. "I don't believe the mayor will persist in this insult to women," Gilda has stoutly told a reporter from *The Daily Beaver*. "After all, Irish, Italians, other ethnic minorities are allowed to parade up Fifth Avenue every month, every year. For women, not once in fifty years?"

An urgency roils the crowd. As if prompted by a central brain, it powers on, heaves slowly forward amidst chants and raised fists. Leora, Finn, and other marchers feed in from 59th. They feel invincible, a great peacetime army. WE DEMAND EQUALITY ... FROM ADAM'S RIB TO WOMEN'S LIB ... A chant goes up: *JOIN US NOW, SISTERHOOD IS POWERFUL!*

Whistles and catcalls from men on the sidewalk. A beefy guy yells "If you won't wear bras, I will." He looks about to cry. A cop places a hand on his shoulder and gently eases him from view. Marchers smile broadly and chant. DON'T IRON WHILE THE STRIKE IS HOT. They jump to look back, marvel at how the marchers keep coming – "*A band of braless bubbleheads,*" a broadcaster will say.

The crowd is bursting beyond the single lane granted by the mayor, linking arms and taking over Fifth, toppling barriers. Mounted police hang, stymied, on the outskirts. Leora sees a squadron of cops form a menacing line and adjust their gear. Somewhere marchers are getting corralled together against sawhorses ... An eddy of disquiet ... Word goes round that a woman was knocked down by a cop on horseback ... A towering horse moves in too close, Leora yanks Finn out of the way. The horse rears and whinnies – a soprano blast and several low after-snorts. Leora sees the flared nostrils and swatch of pale pink gum, the white of its panicked eyes. More cops close in, billy clubs dangling from belts. Will they use tear gas? Ride the women down like Cossacks? Any moment this could slide into mayhem ...

FOUR MONTHS EARLIER

CHAPTER 1

The Drive Out

"Single women have a dreadful propensity for being poor, which is one very strong argument in favour of matrimony."

— Jane Austen,
letter to Fanny Knight, March 13, 1817

That summer of 1970 when the women's movement went mainstream and put the world on notice that nothing would ever be the same again was the summer, too, she was introduced to the "commune." Her life had stalled on several fronts. Why don't you come out to the commune for the weekend? Fred Lustman said. The storied place loomed in her imaginings as an exclusive club of achievers on the far end of Long Island who would hardly be clamoring for her presence. Driving out there one evening in May, she could not have guessed that she was barreling toward one of those fateful stretches that shape a person's life; that in the shadow of History getting made her own little story would corkscrew in directions that even she, with her hopped-up imagination, could

21

not have foreseen. Nor would she have guessed that like a secret agent from no known country she'd violate the commune's law against writing about their "elective family." Though of course her account of that momentous summer would only be fiction ...

Fred drove – a "safe" ten miles over the limit. Beside him sat Edwina Scahill, WASP royalty, wisps of dark hair from her careless chignon kissing her suede jacket – ravishing. Leora tried not to gawk. They were headed for Islesfordd, the fabled town on Long Island's gilded coast, and home to the commune. Islesfordd was generally impressed only by Gatsby-esque displays of wealth – yet the commune had acquired a notoriety based on, well ... intellectual capital. To Leora the very notion of a weekend there felt ripe with possibilities to fall on her face. To quell the nerves she took deep breaths and did her postpartum Kegel exercises. This only served to pitch her above her normal resting state of unbridled randiness ...

Ridiculous name, commune, with its overtones of socialism and kibbutz. Fred, no stranger to preciosity, had hatched it with his cohort, Gilda Gladstone, who'd kind of invented feminism – well, the second wave. The name was fancy for what was simply a low life "grouper house," a rental with far too many "shares" that the Town Planning Board would have banned, but for members from Olde Islesfordd who lacked the mental resources to agree on a dog warden. Most maddening, no one on the Board had any notion what a "commune" might be – a band of hippies? Beatniks? *Communists*?

"It's sort of a half-way house for the divorced who miss the intimacy of marriage but aren't ready to jump back into a new one out of loneliness," Fred had offered back in the city. "Or maybe a summer camp for grown up delinquents."

While he and Edwina chatted up front, *ignoring her*, Leora amused herself by picturing Gilda Gladstone as *Liberty Leading the People* on the barricades, as in the painting by Delacroix. Except Gilda would be more a balabusta leading a "zap action" against the Miss America pageant, schnoz first. Gilda was planning, Fred had told her, the biggest zap action of them all – some sort of nation-wide "strike" and parade of women down Fifth Avenue right before Labor Day ...

Fred was chain-smoking over a cough. The fug of smoke mingled with the musk oil Leora had daubed at her décolletage (you never knew). She rolled down the window and peered out at the big sky over Long Island's flats. A chilly blast – spring arrived grudgingly out here – but she couldn't grouse about air quality on evening one. Since her husband had split, she'd slid into excuse-me-for-existing mode. She reminded herself of a dog that complies with a jerk to its leash before it's finished business. Or the sad old guy with ashen skin she'd seen waiting for the M3 bus on Fifth and 45th. He'd gently swooned to the curb, looking surprised and a bit embarrassed that, maybe dying, he should cause a fuss.

Up front they were yakking about a "communard." Pretty exalted term for a lowly grouper. But some group! Leora tried to remember the cast of characters Fred had rattled off in the city. The queenpin, of course, was Gilda Gladstone. She'd be hanging out with an icon, a woman who was shaping the course of history! Fred Lustman, no slouch, had written an almost-best seller about the shock of accelerating change. Gilda's court seemed weighted toward "scribblers," the cutesy term for writers. Who else might be there? Likely Gilda's sidekick, a hotshot sociologist named Nadine Kusnetz. "Gilda needs Nadine," Fred had said. "She's not the most *tactful* person and Nadine 'translates' her to the world,'" he'd added, pleased with his phrase.

Leora more particularly hoped to see a horsey fellow with burnt-blond hair she'd spotted at Fred's parties – "mixers for intellectuals" – in the city. Peter something with unpronounced letters in his name which meant money. In his innocently gossipy way, Fred had let drop that Peter was about to publish a book – *another* scribbler – and rode to the hounds with a Hunt Club in Boston. Gilda must like to spice up the mix of pear-shaped academics with socialite fox hunters. Leora's head thrummed with what lay ahead: women opinion makers who lectured with icy poise and punctuated points with the heel of their hands, shapers of history, Public Intellectuals (whatever that was), everyone "someone."

Well, maybe not Fred's wife. Meghan was sous-chef in an Irish pub and stuck working in the city tonight. She'd never finished high school and looked of an age to re-up as a sopho-more. And maybe not so much Edwina here, though perhaps any actual accomplishment added on to such beauty would be overkill. Edwina took "society portraits" for the *Islesfordd Herald*, photos of "attractive people doing attractive things in attractive places," as they'd said about Slim Arons, who photo-graphed jet-setters and socialites. Edwina had once done a story in the *Islesfordd Herald* about White Tea garden parties, where the ladies all wear white and the hostess lectures about some shit in white tea that can help you live forever. It was mainly the rich who planned, like the Greenland shark, to live pretty much forever, Leora had observed. The rest of humanity, unable to afford such a project, had more modest expectations. Leora wondered how Edwina held her own among the commune's intellectual heavyweights. Perhaps she got credit for being the girlfriend of JoBeth Mankiller, the feminist art historian. Or a free pass as the prettiest woman in Fred's coterie.

Fred himself was actually on somewhat shaky ground in the "someone" department – one of the "almost famous," he liked to joke, sourly. *Overload*, his break-out book, had appeared rather a while back in the land of what-have-you-achieved-lately. He had a lot riding on a new work about the future of sexual arrangements, which included not only group sex, but group marriage, "triads" and what have you that would consign the bogey-man of *possessiveness* to the dust bin. Possessiveness – unlike fear, anger, etc – was a bogus, made-up emotion that crippled the potential for a rich life. Meanwhile, *Overload*, he'd tell anyone within ear shot, was soon to become a movie by the director who'd made *King Kong 2*. A nitpicker might point out that the manuscript had merely been *optioned*; Fred's CV had a way of getting inflated. No matter, congratulations on Fred's latest success were in order. Men developed crushes on him. Women adored how he actually *listened* when they recounted their little troubles – and who *wouldn't* love a man whose default position was to marry you?

Fred sometimes confided in his semi-stutter – with lash-batting modesty – that he was burdened with more t-t-testosterone than the average guy. (Through some mysterious alchemy he transmuted obnoxious into charming.) Leora feared that she, too, was burdened by too much of whatever the female equivalent of t-t-testosterone might be. Sex was her main skill set. She must be some sort of mutant, at least in the world's eyes. It did make living feel like a luge plunging around turns in pursuit of the next rapture. Among men this was considered rakish and sexy. Women were simply sluts. That was fine by her. She'd thought of crocheting a sampler quoting Marvell's poem to hang on the leprous walls of her bathroom:

The grave's a fine and private place
But none, I think, do there embrace.
Now therefore, while the youthful hue
Sits on thy skin like morning dew,

And while thy willing soul transpires
At every pore with instant fires,
Now let us sport us while we may ...

"I wouldn't let Gilda bother you, it's nothing p-p-personal," Fred was saying in a bass deepened by all that testosterone; his stutter more Etonian than speech impediment. "Gilda doesn't exactly cotton to attractive women."

"Of course it's not personal – to her I'm *invisible*," Edwina said. "There's no more dangerous place to stand than between Gilda Gladstone and any man with a pulse. All 'Our Leader' cares about is finding the next guy."

She couldn't hang here like a carp. Leora leaned forward, thrusting her head between them. "Well, isn't that a bit ironic, coming from the mother of the women's movement?" Her voice raspy from disuse and second hand smoke.

Fred gave his faux laugh, a ha-ha designed to whisk-broom away a remark beneath consideration. "I don't think Gilda cares to be called 'the mother' of anything."

Edwina continued to ignore her. "The day Gilda is cordial toward me I'll know I've lost my looks!"

"Now now. Light this for me, would you? The commune is the family we all wished we'd had. A refuge from the cut-throat competition of New York. It's a place where we all root for each other," Fred added, voice cracking. He always went misty-eyed over the solidarity offered by the commune.

Edwina seemed unimpressed. "I think Gilda's chilliness toward me is also about JoBeth," she persisted, mumbling over the weed she was lighting.

"I hate that '*about*' stuff, it's psychobabble." Fred had de-creed himself guardian of English usage.

"Well, that's not my point, is it?"

"The point, it's nothing personal. Gilda's position on the lesbian thing is strictly political. Anyway, why would she be hostile? After all, you've put yourself out of competition."

"Chr-rist, Fred."

Leora felt a surge of warmth for Fred and his kindergarten efforts to get all the communards to make nice. Then she remembered reading somewhere about Gilda and the lesbian thing. Gilda feared that an influx of lesbians – what she called the "lavender menace" – into the movement might drive away mainstream women and paint feminists as man-hating lesbians who wanted to destroy "respectable" notions of womanhood and the traditional American family. She'd even claimed the C.I.A. had sent dykes to infiltrate the women's movement as part of a plot to discredit it. For all of Gilda's revolutionary fervor, perhaps there was something in her of a Tupperware hostess. Leora's palms felt clammy. The evening ahead suddenly loomed as a minefield.

The pair up front were now snickering about a sculpture some Islesfordd fat cat had stuck on his lawn. The wannabe Gatsby, they called him. Apparently the art work resembled a giant phallus and was visible all along the western end of Hooker Pond. There was talk of lawsuits: how could people have their grandkids visit? Leora hadn't caught the actual name of the offending party. Up front they might as well have slid shut the partition in a cab. *Me here, Leora Voss!* she wanted to shout. Clearly, Fred, her "sponsor" to the commune, had his priorities, which at the moment did not include her. Leora focused on feeling grateful to be invited.

"Have you heard the latest about Islesfordd's most notorious shrink?" Fred was saying. "Guy who runs those nude encounter groups?"

Edwina's suede shoulders jerked, as if she'd been jabbed by a cattle prod.

"He just managed to get himself disbarred," Fred went on. "Or defrocked – or whatever happens when they take away a psychiatrist's shingle. Guess it didn't help that the man actually boasts in his new book about fucking his patients. He doesn't watch out, he's gonna end up bludgeoned in his own bed."

Edwina abruptly swung around to Leora, as if just discovering her presence in the back seat. "So: what brings you out to Islesfordd?" she said, fake hearty.

Leora was focused on how to package herself, but she would later remember, after mayhem descended on Islesfordd, how Edwina had freaked at mention of Ilesfordd's most notorious shrink.

"Well, to be honest, I've scarcely been *any*where since my, uh, separation. I spend most weekends with the kids, window shopping at this new English design store, Conran's."

"*Window*-shopping," Edwina said in her throaty voice.

Leora had a sudden image of Edwina trailing her fingers in the water of an ornate fountain in some villa in Umbria.

"Or we rent a rowboat in Central Park." Skip the detail that Cara was successfully resisting toilet training. That her last date from Parents without Partners kept a snarling, killer-grade Rottweiler in a cage in his studio apartment, like what the Nazis used to sic on the Jews. That her winter had been given to hassling the slumlord of her 7th Street tenement for heat. She'd strung up a kite's tail of rags from her living room window to mute the drip-drip from a leak and a portion of rotted floor beneath it had sluiced away to the apartment below and its tenant, father of a toddler who'd almost been struck, had threatened the slumlord in the hall with a butcher knife. Leora would not soon forget his face, the purplish red of underdone sirloin.

"Guess, this weekend is sort of my 'coming out,'" she said brightly.

"Leora's too modest," Fred said. "She's written a novel, pieces for *Gotham*." A piece about those French maids who killed their employer."

In fact, *one* piece, and for the lesser rag, *Metroland*, not *Gotham*. No matter, Leora was grateful to have Fred apply his expertise at self promotion to her. As for her unpublished opus about debauched ex-pats in Ibiza, it had been dismissed as porn, worse, *angry – women didn't write that way* editors agreed, though women soon would, and as usual her timing stank.

Edwina switched on the radio. Santana, *You've got to change your evil ways, baby* … Pop songs seemed to lag a bit behind the moment.

Leora's hands went clammy again. If Edwina, with her social creds, was dismissed by the Mother Superior, how would Gilda react to a newly separated, marginally employed mother of two who hadn't, she had reason to believe, lost her looks? Leora badly wanted in to this club. The commune could serve as gateway to a better class of potential mate than anything she'd unearthed in her travels. She must take care to conceal her agenda, the way bobcats bury their scat. She suspected she was seriously out of phase with the commune's official rhetoric; some of its buzzwords, like what Gilda called "personhood," could give her hives. In fact, she was out of phase with what women all across America had suddenly discovered they needed, whatever the cost: autonomy and going it alone! Freedom from the oppressor! Marriage was slavery, and house-wifery had made women miserable and sick, etc. etc. In a recent article in *Pandora*, Hadassah Sarachild had just declared married women prostitutes.

The thing was, she'd already done autonomy and would now happily become a prostitute. In college and the years following, when the rest of her classmates were doing wife in the 'burbs, she'd followed her bliss, as Professor Ballocks had called it. More than ten years before women's lib. Summer of graduation she'd hitched around Europe and scootered along the Neckar with a blond German too young to have been a Nazi. Then, when more prudent girls sailed home on the QE 2, summer of wildness safely behind them, she defiantly stayed on as an ex-pat in Europe (the great dream of the class of '58, but only men acted on it). Hung with the Beats. Scribbled bad poetry in Sartre's cafe. She traveled with her French Catholic boyfriend on a boat carrying pigs to Ibiza – she'd not soon forget the screams of pigs protesting their fate. In Ibiza she began the novel that never got published. Following her bliss invariably involved a man allergic to marriage. Naturally, she rejected the solid tax lawyer for a languid boy who self-destructed between Tangiers and Mazatlan and ended up a bicycle bum in Manhattan where everyone said how sad. All this autonomy had got her *where*? In a fanged struggle for survival.

Now, as the first Great Wives Walkout was shaking up the land, women leaving their boring oppressor husbands to become their own person and fulfill their potential, she aspired to a domestic safe haven of the sort she'd once scorned. She could be a figure in a time warp, the impoverished cousin from a Jane Austen novel, only X-rated, who'd stumbled into the 20th century with the wrong agenda. She wanted Jane Austen and the Marriage Plot – she was swimming upstream against the zeitgeist. Her pursuit of happiness required sharing the great adventure with a mate. And if said mate were not destitute he'd hear no objection from her. Leora sometimes looked around her at the revolutionary fervor and wondered, after the band stopped playing and the banners were folded away and the marchers dispersed and a few flyers left blowing down the avenue, what were you then supposed to do with your fucking autonomy? Why was it cool to end up alone? You die alone; while still among the living, why not rub your solitude against a kindred other's? Leora also wondered how many of the sisterhood would actually stick it out for the long haul. Would they be turncoats like that Trotskyite friend of her father who was now a Bircher? She was haunted by an image of a woman left standing on the barricades alone, frantically waving a standard, while the others had jumped ship, reconciled with a reformed mate who was now – ideally, anyway – a male feminist.

Fred, she noticed, had turned off the highway and up a country lane. The trees formed a black Gothic arch. The car lurched up a rutted driveway. Fred maneuvered a curve, and there before them loomed … a version of the *Psycho* house in massive grey stone. Three stories high, sharp angles, pilasters and turrets, orange light in the odd window. Only part habitable, it looked like. Beyond the turrets, ragged clouds hemmed in grey scudded across the moon. Below the house, gleaming malevolently like the tarn from *The Fall of the House of Usher*, a mirror-smooth pond. What sounded like organ music drifted from a high window. Leora shivered. They'd arrived.

CHAPTER 2

Dinner at the Commune

*"Sentimentality makes one romantic.
The beauty of feminism, for me, was that it had made
me prize hard truth over romance."*

– Vivian Gornick

"If you should ever need my life, come and take it."

– Anton Chekhov *The Seagull*

"Well, you made it!" The gravelly bark came from a woman in a low-cut dress, wearing her nose like a piece of statement jewelry.

Gilda Gladstone. Leora inwardly saluted and clicked her heels. The other communards sat fanned around Our Leader in the guttering candle light at a large Spanish refectory table. Leonardo's *The Last Supper* but with both sides of the table. The dining room was a long narrow space with casement windows, forming an "L" off the baronial living room.

"Maybe the 'Marquise of the Mess' can scrounge up some leftovers," Gilda said. "But shouldn't someone clear first? 'Duke of Dishwashing'" – a royal sweep of her arm – "how 'bout it." She knocked back her drink, the faceted red goblet flashing shards of light.

Marquise of the Mess? Duke of Dishwashing? And Leora had thought *commune* was precious.

"I believe table clearing is the job of 'Countess of Cleanup'" – from a guy with serious lockjaw. Leora's heart fluttered as she recognized yellow-haired Peter from Fred's gatherings.

"'Marquise of the Mess' – your call!" Gilda bellowed. "Where's the fucking Marquise?" She glanced tipsily around, sending a fork pinging to the floor. "Oh, hi Edwina," she said with a signal lack of warmth.

Leora was unpleasantly aware that her presence had yet to be acknowledged. To the right of Gilda sat a man with sweet eyes beaming mischief from behind round wire-frame glasses. Leora startled: at the far end of the table a gray-haired guy slumped, dozing, in his chair. Maybe Elijah had come for Passover and forgotten to leave.

"Gilda, as Princess of Protocol, you do have tasks around here," a woman offered, fluttering an ornate fan though the room was far from hot. She looked older than the others. Her hair was smoothed in a peach helmet and her face set in puzzlement at the disappointments she'd drawn from the deck. Her mollifying tone told Leora she must be Nadine Kusnetz, Gilda's "explainer to the world." Leora instantly felt intimidated. Nadine had written a hot book about the unfortunate fallout of women's lib on men – like making them impotent. The book was considered treasonous by radical feminists because it respectfully considered the male point of view which deserved neither consideration nor respect and anyway MEN SHOULD WRITE THEIR OWN FUCKING STORY!

"Yes, Gilda, tell me, what *do* you actually do around here?" Edwina said. "Besides eat my raspberry sundae yogurt. The one I left on the top shelf? You could *replace* what you eat, you know."

"Wasn't me ate your fucking yogurt, I hate the stuff."

"Face it, you never pay for a goddamn thing," said Edwina.

"Gilda, I do think you maybe owe a f-f-few of us m-money," Fred murmured. "I'm on the Atkins diet and I've eaten hardly anything for weeks," someone said. "I think I'm owed a refund."

"Well, you drink enough Stoli to make up for it. I guess hiding it in the basement fridge didn't work."

Leora's head snapped back and forth as at a tennis match. She couldn't identify all the players. Nor could anyone identify *her* since she had yet to be, uh, introduced.

Behind her the kitchen's swinging door spun in a woman with long russet hair consulting a ledger. The Baroness of Bookkeeping? "Gilda, I'll tell you exactly how much you owe," she said, with a sprightliness that could shatter glassware. Her finger trawled down a page of the ledger. "It goes back a ways. And as Sultana of Shopping, I believe you were supposed to buy dinner last week."

"*Buy dinner?*" Gilda shouted. Her arms churned the air and she coughed phlegmily from the enormity of the thing. "D'you realize" – a fresh fit of coughing lifted her butt off the seat – "I was being interviewed by a reporter from *Time* and had all I could do to control my *rage* at his paternalistic tone. How could I *shop?*"

She had a point, Leora thought, trying not to feel too impressed. She'd seen on the hall table a dog-eared galley of *The Female Eunuch* by Germaine Greer, the new bombshell of a feminist everyone was talking about. Naturally, the communards read *galleys* of groundbreaking books long before the sheep-like public. Leora wasn't sure what Greer meant by a female eunuch – maybe that a woman became sexually neutered by traditional marriage? Leora suspected it would take more than marriage and a working furnace to neuter *her*.

"Gilda, the last time you supposedly bought dinner, you remembered the curry but forgot the lamb." "You clean the table by swirling one finger around in a tea towel." "We should just put you on flower arranging!" Laughter, they couldn't hold it against her, Gilda was sooo helpless about domestic stuff ...

The notes of an organ piped and chuffed from some distant region upstairs: Bach's Toccata and Fugue in D minor, the go-to score for horror movies. The piece always gave Leora the willies. She remembered the communards had rented this white elephant from a theater impresario; apparently he'd left behind a friggin' organ.

Edwina frowned and nodded toward the rafters. "Would someone tell me what *that man* is doing here?"

"What *man*?" Gilda said absently. "Y'mean Sebastian Nye?"

Yikes, the publisher of the *National Bugle*, a rag to the right of Mussolini. In the commune's circle, even the shits were someone. Leora's frail confidence took another hit. "Yes, *that* man," Edwina said.

Gilda waved her hand dismissively. "Oh, Seb Nye just comes by occasionally to play the organ." Topic closed. Apparently the commune was not a participatory democracy.

"Well, maybe Seb Nye should practice the organ in Islesfordd's House of God, Inc.," Edwina said. "Especially since he's a born again musical prodigy. He'd do better just to stick with his fascist magazine."

Leora spotted her chance and went for it. "I once heard Sebastian Nye called a 'crypto Nazi' on TV for defending McCarthyism."

She felt herself the object of several gazes uncertain they need land. Her cheeks burned. She'd never gotten the hang of slotting herself into the conversation without sounding like a gunshot at a concert.

"Oh, sorry – everyone, this is my guest, Leora Voss," Fred said.

Across the table Gilda scrunched up her face at Leora, struggling to bring her into focus, a pirate viewing some fugitive object through a spyglass, and growled. Leora decided to take this as a "greeting" – and sign she hadn't lost her looks. Fred ran through the intros, a tumble of names Leora hadn't a prayer of remembering. As she nodded dumbly round the table her eye skittered off the man with round glasses to Gilda's right. He was too pleasing a package to risk looking at.

"Yah, I remember that show," this man said suddenly, voice level as the flatline of an EKG. "It was Gore Vidal who called Nye a 'crypto-Nazi.'"

The glint of his glasses hid his eyes but Leora sensed friendly. She felt her neck doing its imitation of rosacea. "On William Buckley's show *Firing Line*, wasn't it?" she said. "Things got pretty ugly. Nye retaliated by calling Vidal 'a queer.'"

Leaden silence. *Ack* – hadn't she'd been alerted, driving out, that homosexuals were a vexed topic with Gilda? Gilda cleared her throat, or gargled, or growled, hard to know which.

Luckily, at that moment, the red-haired bookkeeper swung back in with three plates of congealed-looking stew. She was definitely guilty of attractiveness. Actually, all the women at this table looked good. They must have to sneak in the old feminine upkeep. You didn't want to be caught getting your legs waxed or under the dryer at Kenneth's, while telling women they could have calves like an ape and fright wigs like Bertha-the-pyro-maniac in *Jane Eyre*.

"*Soo*, Terry ... " Gilda pitched toward him, spilling out of her low-necked dress – "what's going on at your shop? Is *Gotham* really up for sale?"

Terry looked away, lips working. "You'll have to take that up with the editor-in-chief. I'm on extended leave from *Gotham*."

Leora had been too flustered till now to make the connection: Terry would be *the* Terry Cameron whose name lived high on the masthead of *Gotham*. Another *someone*. The hot glossy was essential reading for aspirational New Yorkers who enjoyed going bat shit with envy over the power players and high-status types profiled in its pages. Terry's wizardry as an editor had made him a minor celebrity. Leora had once caught a glimpse of his boss, a large fellow with dangerously kind eyes, known for bellowing his displeasure in a three-testicle voice at any underling who failed to deliver. Leora wondered what he'd pulled on Terry to make him so skittery.

Leora glanced to her left. Golden Peter might be a better bet. Up close he looked "distressed" like his threadbare polo shirt, maybe the work of too many mint juleps at the Derby. Kind of asexual, as if he'd reproduce by mitosis ... The package a fair exchange for a working furnace. It was high time to retire her fixation on male beauty – hadn't it flogged her up too many blind alleys already? For a woman, time was of the essence, though that view would not go over big at this table. Here you were supposed to *become the man you once wanted to marry*. She would happily become that man, but she also wanted to marry him.

Peter was busy staring across the table at Edwina. How did you *not* stare at Edwina? She was the face of love, an invitation to ruin. It was the eyes, grey-green, and the way they turned down at the corners, like a dreaming Florentine boy; her lips turning *up* at the corners, the dearest nose, whisper of dark mustache, the old ivory of her skin, medallion of fat beneath the shoulder cut by her bra strap. Delectable, all of it. Men must turn swine-like around her. Peter here might be sprouting cloven hooves under the table and a brindled hide and would fall, oinking, on all fours. Had he not gotten the memo about Jobeth Mankiller?

It must drive Gilda batty that Edwina took her seductiveness so for granted she couldn't be bothered using it on men.

★

" – so my plan is to organize a national work stoppage, a giant *STRIKE* to show the power and scope of feminism," Gilda was saying in her heartland gargle, leaving a trail of unfinished thoughts behind words that sprinted ahead. "We've got to focus on recruiting the mainstream. We mustn't get co-opted by the radicals, the crazies, the fringe."

Leora leaned eagerly across the table. Finally! Gilda was talking about this audacious plan for a national strike and massive women's march down Fifth Avenue. Already the papers had picked up on it – in the mocking, wink-wink tone they adopted when writing about the women's movement.

"Excuse me, this is hardly the moment to exclude people – we're trying to put together a Strike *Coalition*," Edwina said. "The press loves to portray the movement as a cat fight – the radical 'crazies' versus the 'hopelessly bourgeois.' Let's not play into their hands."

Leora saw her second shot. "Why not ask Monica Fairley to join forces with us?" – blushing at the presumption of "us." "She just gave a talk on women's lib at the Women's Democratic Club that's sort of put her on the radar ... "

She trailed off. Gilda's face contorted and her eyes kept blinking as if blinded by mace. *Ay caramba*, she'd stepped in it again ... She felt vacuumed backwards ...

"*Monica trying to rip off the movement for her own profit ... Sucks up to the media ... Who the hell is she? A front for the fucking CIA is who! ... A fashion plate ... I wrote THE book that launched the movement ... Germaine wrote ... Kate Millett wrote ... Simone wrote... And The Hair? The Hair writes 'The Summer Drinks Book'! ... With a foil cover for tanning! ... Seduced Henry Kissinger into doing the Intro ...* "

Of course Gilda would loathe gorgeous, thin, honey-haired Monica – a marauder on her turf. Across the table Leora caught her own reflection in the mullioned window, scrambled by the guttering candle light. Every group needed someone to hate, and as per usual she was the designated hate-ee. She was securely in her discomfort zone! Leora squinted past her own image into the darkness outside. Earlier, she'd spotted a garden shed where she might spend the night ...

"I think Leora's got a point."

She turned, slack-mouthed, toward Terry. She felt like Anne Boleyn eluding the blade. Time lurched forward again.

"Sure, Monica Fairley is a, uh, Joanie-Come-Lately," Terry went on levelly, "but in no way can touch *you*, Gilda. You *are* the movement – its founder, organizer, figurehead. Without you there'd *be* no movement. But Monica does have a gift – you got it exactly right – for attracting media. She can bring more people to the table, younger women, activists, black feminists to help us make the numbers for the march."

"Terry's right." Nadine Kusnetz worked her little fan. "And by the way" – she directed a sad, lovely smile at Gilda – "Monica said the *nicest* things in that talk about *you*."

"Nice" chimed with Leora's sole encounter with Monica. A feminist confab at some cavernous midtown hotel. A speaker observed that sitting closer together would help break the ice. Leora, taking the advice to heart, pulled a chair over to a table that included a famous columnist for the *Beaver*. The woman gave her the stink-eye and noisily shifted her own chair to close Leora out. Suddenly, there was Monica, with her smile and honey hair cupping her bosom, perfect. She motioned to the others to widen the circle for them both ... Then, feeding Leora's name through a mental calculator: *wasn't it* you *who wrote that piece on –* ? *Wonderful piece ...*

"In fact, we should invite Monica to join the Strike Coalition Committee, the red- haired book keeper was saying, voice too high by an octave. "I bet she'd be happy to join forces with us. We need critical mass to justify a permit to march down Fifth Avenue. Last we approached the city – "

" – they goddamn turned us down – *again*," Gilda interrupted, dropping her case against Monica as a terrier forgets a toy. "But this time we'll come back at them with the prospect of ten, twenty thousand women – and children and men – taking over the streets. Blocking thoroughfares! A national work stoppage! The way I see it, wives refuse to cook for husbands, waitresses stop waiting, and cleaning women stop cleaning and secretaries close their steno pads and telephone operators unplug their switchboards ... "

The table exhaled, as Gilda laid it out for them.

"Leora's quite an accomplished woman," Fred said, sidling into a pocket of silence. She wrote an article in *Gotham* about the new play *Murderous Maids*. It's based on a notorious case in France in the 30s about two incestuously linked sisters who killed their employers and gouged their eyes out."

"Mmm, sounds like a barrel of laughs," the bookkeeper said.

"I'm fucking tired of seeing women portrayed in a negative light," Gilda barked. "We should focus on the positive. Isn't there enough negativity and hostility toward women in the media already?"

"Actually, those twisted sisters also inspired Jean Genet's play, *The Maids*," Terry said in a coiled voice that commanded attention. "Something about that murder – maybe the class rage – resonates. Or maybe it's *female* rage. I can hear it rumbling in the distance, heading our way like a tsunami." He looked as though he were following the progress of a fly in front of his nose.

"So long as she doesn't write about *us* – house rule," Gilda said. "The commune is off limits."

Despite the rude "she," Leora was flattered that Gilda thought her clever enough to violate the house rule. Leora nodded demurely and thought of all the great material percolating within these walls. If she conjured up a *fictional* "commune" and peopled it with characters only loosely inspired by the originals, that wouldn't violate the "house rule," would it?

"We've got to focus on raising money for the march," Fred said quickly, before Gilda could return to the charge, "and fast. Four months is no time at all to pull the thing together. God knows, plenty of money floating around Islesfordd. There's gold in them thar hills – or behind the hedge rows."

At the word "gold" Elijah jolted awake from the dim far end of the table. He adjusted his tweed jacket the way a goshawk fluffs its feathers, and surveyed the gathering with the twinkly smile of a serial killer.

"So this stock I've been telling you about," Elijah said to the group, as if resuming a prior conversation – "it's a surgical treatment company for spinal disorders. See, they go in laterally – "

"Henry, please, could we wait till after dessert?" someone protested.

Modest shrug. "I picked it in March 1968 and it was at 37. In two years it's tripled! Friends, I'm giving you the insider tip of a lifetime."

Glum silence. The communards looked as though they'd taken him up on more than one insider tip of a lifetime and gotten burned.

"I've gone out of my way to court the wealthy matrons out here," Gilda groused, "but no dice, they're blind to their own interests ... Or they feel threatened, I dunno, 'cause the movement exposes their own lives as a sham. The way my housewife neighbors in Nyack felt when I wrote the book ... " Her chin made a pass at the table.

"Maybe we should cozy up to the Polish Gatsby," Edwina said.

"Great idea – in fact, why have we never thought of Kaz Grabowski?"

The name straightened Leora's spine. *Kaz? Here in Islesford?*

"He really does come on like the Gatsby of Islesfordd," someone said. "Swanning around in those eggshell linen suits and yellow ties. Wonder if he's got a Daisy out here. Does anyone actually know him?"

Leora kept her mouth zipped; this time she would wait on the right moment.

"Why not invite him for dinner?" the bookkeeper said. "D'you think he'd accept?"

"Of course he'd accept!" Gilda cried, indignant. "The money guys need us more than we need them. We're the most interesting people out here!"

"I'm not sure *I* need Grabowski," Peter said in his plummy drawl. "He bought that hideous property up from us on Hooker Pond – and managed to uglify it even more. I mean . . . a bathroom with a gold toilet? If you go out on the pond you can see the place, some kind of weird pastiche from Disney world."

"There's a vile 'sculpture' of a giant phallus on the lawn – a totem of male chauvinism," Gilda said.

So it was Kaz *Fred and Edwina had been mocking in the drive out ...*

Nadine fluttered her fan. "The residents along the pond are suing to have the sculpture removed. What's Grabowski trying to prove?"

"Oh, that he's a major collector, a de Medici of Pop Art," Edwina said. "Actually, that giant cock is a work by – " Leora didn't catch the name, pronounced with reverence.

"Well, guess we have to suck it up if we want to co-opt the fat cats out here," Gilda said. We need their money, they need our brains and cachet – it's perfect synergy."

"*Co-opt*": the commune's favorite word.

"Since no one actually knows this Gatsby, how do we best approach him?" Gilda wondered.

The table went silent, as an angel passed over.

Gilda nodded out on the hope of co-opting Grabowski, relieved that Henry would spend the coming week with his wife in Marblehead.

Fred pondered whether to fire his agent before the bitch unloaded *him*.

Edwina felt pissed at JoBeth for refusing to come to Islesfordd and shield her from the male predators behind every forsythia.

Terry contemplated garroting the man who'd stolen his happiness, and maybe garroting himself for inviting it.

Leora shot a sideways glance at Nadine, who appeared wrapped in secret sorrows and might be polishing her own obit. The night kept delivering surprises. If someone had told her that so many years later she and Kaz Grabowski would be inhabiting the same small corner of the planet in the same moment, would she have believed it? The great puppet master in the sky maneuvered them all according to his own inscrutable whimsy. Coincidence was a bit cheesy in fiction, but perhaps in life it could advance the plot.

Abruptly, Fred turned toward Leora, shattering the group trance. "It just occurred to me – didn't you once know Grabowski? In fact, why do I think you once had a *thing* with Kaz Grabowski?"

Gilda gazed woozily at Leora across the table. All eyes converged on her like the beam from heaven that struck Excalibur.

Yeah, she'd once had a thing with Kaz Grabowski. That could maybe prove useful around here.

"Oh, you know" – dragging out the words – "he was an old friend from college." Leora smiled. She might not need to sleep in the shed after all.

CHAPTER 3

The Marriage Plot

There was a crooked man, and he walked a crooked mile.
He found a crooked sixpence upon a crooked stile.
He bought a crooked cat, which caught a crooked mouse,
And they all lived together in a little crooked house.

The other communards had slouched off to bed and the two
of them perched on a sofa in the living room; they might be
shipwreck survivors on an ice floe. In the grate a fire smoldered,
but some genius decorator had set the sofa way back so the
warmth reached only the household deities. Wind banshee'd
through window frames, Leora glanced with a shudder at the
room's shadowy reaches. Fred had neglected to mention that
Cormorant Cove was a marriage of Charles Addams and the
Norman Bates motel. It appeared un-heatable and had likely
languished on the market till the commune offered to rent it.
At least the organist had knocked off.

The touch of Terry's hand sent lightning up her arm:
"Someone's here."

A form folded into a poufy chair in a far corner stirred and stretched. Elijah, the sleeper, awakes! Leora realized he was Henry Lyman, a stockbroker she'd met at one of Fred's parties. A flimflam man (as she'd come to suspect) who had relieved her of her meager savings to invest in an insider tip. Until dinner tonight, she hadn't seen Henry in a few years. Not since the party at Fred's ...

Henry Lyman – "ace stock picker," according to Fred – had backed her into a corner of Fred's kitchen to sell her on "a really hot tip." *Insider stuff, the next big thing. Stock called Piece 'o Cake. Today it's at 60. That's practically double in a few months. And this is just the beginning. I guarantee you this is a quadruple in the next twelve. We got a home run here.*" As usual, the mention of money had made Leora's eyes glaze over.

"Is Henry for real?" she'd asked Fred. "I just gave him all my savings."

"Well, Henry's a bit eccentric maybe, but he's got a good track record and this is an insider tip. *I've* given him money and so have Gilda and the others" ...

★

Henry twinkled down at her and Terry over specs set low on his ski-slope nose. Winked at Leora. "We got a home run here. I'd join you both for a nightcap, but gotta dash."

Leora suppressed a giggle. "Where's he dashing at this hour? What's the deal with Elijah?"

"Henry is Gilda's boyfriend – well, maybe more of a consort now. He's developed narcolepsy and keeps falling out, kind of embarrassing when Gilda takes him to an inauguration. I suspect she's in the market for a replacement."

Was Terry a candidate? She looked at him. He looked at her. They kept this up for a while. It was sweet to yield to what they both recognized they'd resisted with the others around. His hair side-combed across his dome of a brow, a maneuver she found touching. Behind his granny glasses one eye looked worried and round, the other beamed out at her. Her nether region came alive. She shivered and peeled her eyes off him. Hard to tell sometimes between desire and the flu. The first man she'd ever touched, the hard ridge on his jeans, ever so tentatively – afterwards, she spiked a fever. They were in a hayloft in Woodstock, New York. Like in the Swedish movies that mapped out the erotic landscapes of her teens, except in Swedish movies the hay didn't scratch. He must have been involved in Woodstock's summer stock playhouse, this man, she can't remember … Her fingers spidered around his denim crotch sheltering the living, stirring thing, but he lifted her hand away and pressed it, and maybe brought it to his mouth, one of the lovelier gestures she's known. Had it all been downhill from there?

★

"Terry, thank you."

"What for?"

"You kind of rescued me tonight." Sounding more distressed *damsel* than she would have liked.

"Well, to be honest, I'm surprised Fred didn't brief you. Gilda's worked up an epic hatred of Monica Fairley. Can hardly blame her. The movement's been hers alone. Then along comes Monica, gives that speech at the Democratic Club about her 'conversion' to women's lib – and it's treated like the Second Coming. Why? Because Monica's a celebrity – for being a celebrity. She moves in power circles. And she's smooth-as-cream – 'clouds men's minds,' in the words of my onetime boss. The figurehead the, well, male media might prefer to our Gilda."

Leora sipped from the faceted goblet she'd carried from the table. *Doesn't excuse "our" Gilda acting like psycho bitch.*

Terry laughed low in his throat, as if he'd heard her. "Gilda's actually called *herself* a 'bad-tempered bitch.' She's easier to take when you understand the commune's her 'elective family.' She's into groups, whether here or the communal hot tub at Esalen. For Gilda the commune's a way to ensure people will keep caring about each other."

"Why do I get the feeling she doesn't love women a lot?" (she needed to lose the nervous laugh).

"Gilda's more of a Big Picture person. Her concern for women takes a more abstract form."

Leora reflected, feeling a bit disloyal, that this Monica who was nipping at Gilda's heels seemed comfortable with both the Big Picture *and* actual women.

"I'm kind of fascinated by Gilda's contradictions," Terry said. "She hates being alone."

"Don't we all," Leora sighed.

"I dunno. Sometimes it feels better than jumping right back in."

Oh. Not available, then? Funny, women seldom talked about being unavailable.

"Leora: that's an unusual name."

"Leora was Martin Arrowsmith's wife in the novel by Sinclair Lewis. My parents must have forgotten that Leora was picked off by the plague her doctor husband is trying to cure. I cried when she died. She was a saint, that Leora" – a pause to imply this one wasn't. She would have liked to ditch the prelims and get right to the main event, root around in Terry's tobacco wide-wale cords, an excellent way to get acquainted, yet here they sat, in separate capsules. The look he cut her, he might be thinking the same.

Whooaa … Why couldn't she do slow and cock teasing, like other women? In theory, it was now okay – even compulsory – to drop the coy act. Maybe her M.O. had finally come into fashion: coupla Dewars, hustle hustle wham BAM, think later – *and how has* that *worked for 'ya?* She was willing to bet it *still* wouldn't, despite the new gospel of equality. Now it was just a lot more confusing, since no one knew how to read the signals or figure out their lines. When the horndogs of old just did their thing, at least you knew what you were dealing with. Oh, the horndogs of old! Of course she'd been as ready to do their thing as they.

She ought to go easier on herself. She was still in remission from the Cowboy of Wall Street. The Cowboy had come on hot and heavy and introduced her to the joys of Acapulco Gold (five years older than he, she preferred Dewars). Deep in and too late, she found she was the subject of an experiment in non-possessiveness conducted by the Cowboy and … whaddya know! – the fiancée he'd kept in the wings. The Cowboy and his fiancée were in an Open Relationship and testing the proposition that if he could fuck Leora – *with the fiancée's blessing* – they were good to wed. She'd done her part to advance scientific inquiry! Though she couldn't remember volunteering …

Post Cowboy, from deep within her funk, she picked up rumblings about the new self-love. To glue herself back together she enrolled at Betty Dodson's vibrator/self-love/self-examination workshop, which taught you to shed negative body images and take charge of your own pleasure. What better place to set herself to rights? In fact, why depend on some chauvinist scumbag for sex at all? The sessions were pricey but you got to take the vaginal barbell, whatever that was, home with you.

The hard part was getting past the silent film villain posing as a doorman, with his smirk and brilliantine'd hair in a widow's peak. A carpeted, dimly lit, incense-scented cave, the celebrants all in a circle, naked on their towels, the only sound Dodson's vibrator like a Phantom power boat coming into port ... Among the women was a plus-size, gloomy-eyed woman with a wen on her tit with hairs coming out of it and a negative everything image. A few sessions in, and she was a joyous new woman. Selfloving. Their little "All Woman Orgasm Army," as Dodson called them, marched off on a high. Just think, pleasure was yours to "access" 24/7, decoupled from men and all that bullshit that went down in the erogenous zone! Couple months later on Canal Street Leora spotted the woman she'd last seen peering up her zorch in Dodson's cave. Her heavy gait suggested an even heavier heart. She herself had relapsed. Clearly self-love was hard to sustain for the long term, maybe at some point you needed reinforcements from outside ...

Leora wanted to run all this by Terry – she was brimming with things she wanted to run by Terry. She loved his way around words. Words were a continuation of sex by other means (or however that went). She wasn't sure, though, her unexpurgated self was fit for consumption. She feared she lacked the emotional tool kit for what was commonly called a "relationship." Once Terry got his mind around that he'd take to the Islesfordd Walking Dunes. Or maybe not. Terry came on like the new breed of male feminist ready to go toe to toe with any woman in the empathy sweepstakes.

He'd lit a cigar. Its funky aroma evoked newsprint, rolled shirtsleeves, guy stuff.

"That was a nice gig you had at *Gotham*. All those terrific stories you ran on women's lib. What made you decide to leave?"

He shrugged. "Well, women's lib is *the* story."

Aware he hadn't answered her question: "Yeah, and you helped give it legs."

A moment, and Terry said, "when Clive Monomark became the new boss he promised to keep his hands off Editorial, but he famously can't resist calling every shot – and delivering nervous breakdowns."

Had Terry been a recipient?

"Around the same time I got separated ... Clive put me on a beat I had to turn down ..."

"Ouch, double whammy, I'm sorry." Curious about "the beat," especially as his mouth was doing that trembly thing again.

Abruptly, Terry leaned over and hugged her. Buddy-style, but hard. Quickly shifted away. "Sorry, I needed to do that."

"I'm glad you did!" They both exhaled loudly, laughed. It felt as though they'd traded bus exhaust for oxygen. She turned her face up. *Hey, hi ...*

"*So ...*" Terry groped for the thread ... "So ..." She wanted to place her palm on his hard-on. A steamy green continent, theirs to take, lay only inches away. "A lot of changes," he said faintly. "My wife lives in the brownstone on West 88th Street."

Leora pictured the famously gentrified block off Central Park: spiffy renovated brownstones, communal gardens, the works.

"I've taken a place in the Village. Horatio Street."

"Horatio Street!" Leora said. "I love Horatio! It's one of the loveliest streets in the Village."

"Yeah, and I got a great deal. I'm doubling as the building's super and live in the basement, so it's pretty much rent free."

"That *does* sound like a great deal." She wiggled a foot in its Capezio. She wiggled the other foot. "You're the super in a basement? And your ex wife lives in your old brownstone on the nicest block on the West Side?"

"Actually on three floors, she rents out the garden level. Yah, the place is pretty grand."

Keeping her voice neutral: "Sounds like *she* got a great deal. Uh, you didn't have a lawyer?"

"Didn't want one. I owed her ... everything. And more."

This was terrifically generous of Terry, or terrifically fucked up, and she wanted no part of it. Once again, she'd been poised to bowl down the wrong lane. She was done following her bliss, or hormones, or whatever dybbuk dictated her most disastrous moves. She was like men who think with their cocks. She'd had her fill of dreamy, tightly wound esthetes who had no clue how to maneuver in the world of health benefits and furnaces. Her father had longed to be a painter, neglecting the business to toil for hours in the basement of the stucco attached house on Butler Street. Every night after his second martini: *I'm going to sell that landscape for fifty thousand dollars ...* She conjured the glorious future. He never found a gallery ...

No, Leora, we won't do that again. She was no scheming climber like Edith Wharton's Undine Spragg – but she knew from basements. She'd embraced *la vie boheme* in the 5th arrondissement with the Beats, and Gyula, a Hungarian revolutionary from the Cite Universitaire, and the Harvard drop-out with such promise. She'd slept in the overhead compartments of trains, and on Ibiza's lava coasts; she'd been sick in a frigid outhouse strewn with hay in the Tyrol. She was twenty-one then and living poor came with a mission: to resist getting frog-marched into a woman's proper life. The life that all the women around her now couldn't flee fast enough.

Later, on 7th street in Alphabet City, *la vie boheme* lost its charm. The screaming matches about money ... The phone turned off after the third unpaid bill ... His closet she came home to with naked hangers ... The hole – perfectly round – drilled into the closet beside the front door (though the robbers were too high end to take her stuff: the Philco black and white

TV, the RCA phonograph with skippy needle) ... The unemployment for which she didn't qualify ... Hamburger helper ... Pop tarts ... Water bugs ... Heatless winter ...

The night of the firecracker ...

Well, good. Terry was a self-made down-and-outer. He'd given her fair warning.

Would it seem too obvious if she ... skidooed right now? She forged a yawn. Slid off the couch. "Soo, this has been quite an evening. Guess I'll check out the bedroom situation upstairs and hope I don't walk in on anyone."

She saw the muscle in his jaw working. He looked up at her with something resembling hate. "I'll say goodnight, then," she said.

Leora headed up stairs. How quickly they'd disappointed each other. And saved themselves a world of time and trouble.

CHAPTER 4

Morning After

"Love is like any other luxury. You have no right to it unless you can afford it."

– Anthony Trollope,
The Way We Live Now

Leora pushed open the French doors onto the sweep of lawn behind the house and breathed in the green and gold morning. An *Elvira Madigan* kind of day, Mozart's piano on the soundtrack languid and soaring, peeling back a vista of some paradise on earth ... Nearby the blown blossoms of a cherry tree petaled down pink confetti. Leora sipped at her coffee. The Countess of Caffeine had brewed high octane stuff to wake the dead, if not the fur-tongued communards snoring into their pillows. The night before, she'd managed to locate an empty bedroom on the third floor. She'd been too wired to sleep, running through her mind the cast of "communards." There was gentle Nadine, Gilda's sidekick; Peter, horseman and would be-writer, in love with Edwina like everyone else; Seb Nye, the invisible organist – she'd all but collided with the wretched organ on the third floor landing, its jungle of pipes both awe-inducing and monstrous. She tossed and tried not to think of Terry ...

She stepped across the lawn in her navy satin hot pants spangled with stars ("Further Reduced" at Filene's), trailing a cloud of musk oil. Leora suffered from *l'esprit de l'escalier*: weeks after the occasion she'd alight on the *perfect quip*. Toward dawn she'd come up with at least three witty rejoinders she could have tossed off at dinner ...

At the crest of the lawn she startled to see Terry Cameron brooding down by the pond, the wide-wale cords hanging off him. A kick of desire cut with regret. Something about him – his electric thinness, maybe – asked to be held, calmed, contained.

She shrank back out of his sight line. Just her luck to dig a guy who'd taken a vow of poverty and thought it cool to live like a troglodyte below street level with a view of feet walking. Terry was spacey and wounded in some way she couldn't decipher. She'd do better with an insurance salesman who read Rilke on the side ...

She'd been mad for Patrick Sweeney from the moment she saw him at someone's New Year's Eve in a blue work shirt and suspenders. Black-Irish, an architect. Architecture not the most lucrative job, exactly, except for a small pantheon of visionary starchitects, but who knew that then? And why would that have stopped her marrying him (she lacked the gene for "practical" the way some people are color blind). Patrick had been a star in his class at M.I.T. and landed a job at the hot New York boutique Porter and Eisen. With his trip-wire temper he managed in record time to offend the wrong person and joined the 53% of architects – *his* number – who were out of work, or underemployed. He'd always been a drinker – "whaddya expect, I'm Irish!" These days his only job, he'd repeat after his third Knob Creek, was marketing his own services. "Since M.I.T. I've had a vision of melding Modernism with classic architecture – and you're telling me to design *basement rec rooms* in Larchmont? Retail house wares? Drive a forklift?" He settled, eyes glassy, on the once-blue Queen Anne chair, disgorging its innards onto the floor.

She eyed the big *dracaena* plant by the window, one of plant-dom's uglier specimens that thought it was a tree. "Well, maybe just for now, so we can buy snowsuits for the kids at Morris Brothers."

"There you go again."

He was furious over the lack of recognition the world owed him. She *agreed* it was owed him! Only the world didn't work that way.

After fury, came sodden contrition, the blubbery regret: why was he beating up on her when none of it was *her* fault? Repeat whole routine following night, the space heater glowing orange when the boiler was out. They'd signed on for a two-hander in a long-running farce on 7th Street and Avenue A.

She had no talent for psychiatric social worker, the de facto trade of most women who "manage" difficult mates. And what about *her* vision? She was honing her skills as a magazine writer, learning as she went. She free-lanced for super market freebies. Wrote the occasional "service" piece for *Gotham*. The story on *Murderous Maids* for *Metroland* almost sent her into orbit. None of it added up to a living wage. She needed to land something fulltime with health benefits, now that Patrick's had expired.

Through his M.I.T. network Patrick found work at a cutting edge design firm. He worked late into the night, his team always on "charrette," acing a deadline. It was a relief to have his sulking presence out of the apartment. Leora worried slightly that the domestic calm was predicated on Patrick's absence. But the kids got properly fitting snowsuits that weren't from Goodwill. Evenings after their tubby she and the kids would watch the nature show *Untamed Kingdom* through a scrim of dancing white lines on the old Philco. The cantering kangaroos, the mating habits of Whydah Birds. The "mad March hares" boxing in fields during the month of March. Soon they'd be able to afford one of the new color TV's.

The rare nights Patrick arrived before the kids' bedtime he brought home wondrous toys. Melody, "a colleague at the shop," created interlocking plywood shapes that Finn could assemble and re-assemble into different "sculptures"; a toy kit that could turn into everything from workbenches to wagons. His colleague Melody was a "design genius, " Patrick kept repeating. "These toys draw on the insights of Carl Jung."

"Sure beats the insights of Fisher-Price."

"There you go again. Why must you denigrate what I find beautiful?"

At some point Leora guessed what else Patrick found beautiful, which might be allied to his ever later nights.

"Let's be adults here. Frank Lloyd Wright once said that two women are necessary for a 'man of artistic mind' —one as mother of his children and the other his mental companion, his inspiration. Wright believed rules are made for the average man and ... how did he put it? – 'the really honest, sincere, thinking man must live without them.'"

She boxed air, like the mad March hares on *Untamed Kingdom.*

"There you go again."

She pestled down panic ... *Keep this craft afloat, on account of the kids ... Cara still an infant ...* "That was a different era when Wright said that, times have changed."

Disgustedly, he left the room.

One 2 A.M. she found Patrick passed out dead drunk in the hall in front of the bathroom. She managed to get out of him that Melody had dumped him. For a Dutch "starchitect." He wouldn't come to bed. Leora covered him there on the floor with the threadbare army blanket.

A clash with the boss, and once again, Patrick was emptying his desk. Alongside Melody's defection, he hardly seemed to notice he'd been fired.

"Mom! dad's under the plant and won't come out," Finn told Leora, when she came home with the groceries. She found him sitting cross-legged beneath the spiky arches of the *dracaena*.

"We were each other's muses."

"Your talent – no woman can take that away from you."

"Our belief in each other helped us believe in ourselves. The rest is irrelevant."

The rest: would that be her and the kids?

Sometimes all the choices stink. She couldn't do this alone. Who would be there with her when Cara got an asthma attack? "You can be your own muse," Leora said. "You don't understand, it was the collaboration that drove our creativity."

"Why couldn't you keep just the collaboration – like Louis Kahn after he broke up with his lover, you know, the one with the Chinese name?"

"Now you're taking *Melody*'s side!"

A friend in mental health advised Leora that perhaps it did not serve her best interests to play Dear Abby to the husband who'd been balling his office mate.

Patrick rallied; architects were moving across the country and away from their families to help pay expenses, he said. He took the job, with her blessing, in Houston; returned to New York with a woman "not difficult and mocking" like her.

One night when Patrick was still in Texas, the boiler in their tenement, always capricious, chose a blizzard to go on the fritz. She and the kids could see their breath in the air. Cara had developed a cough with a "whoop" to catch the next breath; in this blizzard, little chance of getting her to the doctor that night. Leora tried to warm the room with the space heaters and candles, but wind stole in through the warped sills. She thought she could locate the switch that would kick the boiler on, it was only one flight down to the basement, she'd be back upstairs in two minutes. Enough time for Finn to find the old firecracker he'd collected from God knows where and light it.

★

Well, it wouldn't hurt to say good morning, would it? She floated down the lawn toward Terry, hearing the dreamy strains of *Elvira Madigan* again.

His eyes, grey ice, stopped her short. "I'll be catching a train back to the city soon."

"What, in this beautiful weather?"

He seemed about to offer something further; didn't. In morning light he looked scruffy, one head-piece of the round glasses taped together. "My life's a bit complicated at the moment," he said.

"Isn't everyone's?"

From a window in the kitchen came Fred's baritone rumble, then a piercing soprano, the unmistakable sound of a woman acquainting her mate with his manifold sins.

"Talk about complicated." Terry nodded up toward the kitchen window with a wan smile. "Maybe we can have coffee some time."

Leora shrugged and walked up toward the house.

★

"Whenever a friend succeeds a little something in me dies."

— Gore Vidal

At the threshold of the kitchen she hung back. She'd hoped to noodge Fred about becoming a member of the commune but this might not be the moment.

" – I bust my ass in the city all week, and you're out here fucking Sophia Merdle's colored maid? I mean, are you fucking kidding me?"

"Please – *Black* or *African American* maid. 'Colored' has gone the way of the dodo. How do you come up with such nonsense?" Fred had been expecting his wife on a later train.

"You're telling me you went jogging this morning," Meghan said, like a detective taking testimony.

"Yep, on the beach, like every morning. Bacchus Beach this time, where gays go cruising. And who should I see cruising around with them? Lester Annis."

At Meghan's blank look: "You know, the shrink who runs nude encounter groups and just got defrocked?" Fred prompted. "Lester certainly covers all the bases."

Meghan, not to be distracted, glared at his loafers. "You went jogging in *those*?" A disgusted groan. "Why is it never enough?"

"That's a p-p-profound philosophical question. Albert Camus asked, 'Why should it be essential to love *rarely* in order to love *much*? What Don Juan realizes in action is an ethic of *quantity*, whereas the saint, on the contrary, tends towards k-k-quality.'"

"Don't give me Albert fucking Cam-oo."

Fred clucked at the stupidity of this.

"You reek of sex. You even make passes at your friends" – which Leora could confirm, but no hard feelings, it was sloppy and alcoholic. "Gilda's *daughter*. You'd hump the garbage pail."

"I think we'd all be better off if you didn't always need to *personalize*. This is nothing against *you*."

Leora generally rooted for Meghan, a blooming Irish Rose of Tralee. Meghan was the commune's Queen of Cuisine and much lauded for her savory stews of fish, mussels, clams. Leora pictured her standing in a white chef's apron over a great pot ladling out *zuppa di pesce*, cheeks pinked by the steam. Meghan did indeed bust her ass in the city as apprentice to a chef. She was also writing a book on Scottish pub food – she must have caught the scribbling bug from the commune – which might be the first book of its kind. She was grotesquely young for Fred even with his surplus testosterone. He'd rescued Meghan from a boyfriend who pushed her to get the new silicone implants developed by a French medic that promised "the bouncy breast." Without undue pressure he'd married her (Fred married often, if not successfully, and the number of his ex wives was not known). Gilda had no use for a woman as lovely as Meghan who couldn't spell. Leora saw a kindred soul who understood what lack of money did to a person and craved a safe haven. Meghan had kind of blown the marriage plot, though, by choosing such a testosterone-addled haven as Fred. He didn't make babies: his sperm couldn't swim, or it had a short attention span and got distracted once past the fireworks. The world of food might be a better bet.

Leora was tempted to warn Meghan, beware the siren song of the Great Wife Walkouts. Don't leap till you've got your gig in place. She pictured her former college classmate Libby Fenwick Futterman ...

The previous summer Patrick had been occupied taking the two-women ethos of Frank Lloyd Wright for a test run. Leora took to wandering the grittier reaches of the Lower East Side, Cara snoozing in the carriage, Finn lollygagging behind, fishing treasure from garbage pails. In August the place became a runway for the detritus of humanity; anyone solvent fled the area like a plague site. Leora ached to see a woman approaching with a complicated, delayed-action gait, more spider crab than human. Leora steered around a red-eyed "Jesus freak," all but spraying her with his rant, one of a host of mental patients dumped on the streets by the city's fiscal crisis. Avenue A was lined with abandoned tenements with blown-out windows. From a dark hallway studded with garbage voices called *Hola, chica*! *Ven aqui*!

She veered west to safer pastures, scolding Finn to come along; as usual he was clutching some find from the garbage. She turned down Stanton Street toward Our Lady of Perpetual Help, where the homeless had queued up for a meal. Leora politely averted her eyes from this gallery of misfortune: folks in the wrong-size clothes, raw ankles, alkie tremors, faces with that terrible city tan baked in. A pregnant woman with a noble dark unibrow sat against a wall amidst possessions that included a stack of hardcover books and a spindly plant. New York's very own Dust Bowl!

Toward the end of the line Leora all but collided with – no, could it be? The fuschia lipstick overrode her lips, her greying hair stood up in witchy spikes, and she clutched two *shopping bags* stuffed with what looked like her worldly goods, one filled with empty plastic bottles. The Bag Lady! Female bogeyman of their college nightmares.

"Libby, I didn't recognize – "

"It's that bad, huh?"

"Of course not. I'm … nearsighted. I'm so glad to see you."

Leora flinched at their embrace. Libby Fenwick Futterman smelled like the person on the subway who requires you change cars.

"Why *would* you recognize me?" Libby swiped her sweaty forehead with her palm. Her fingernails were rimed in black. "Yah, so I left Elliott, had you heard? We grew apart and Elliot was just too boring. In bed – well, I never knew a man could be … sexually dyslexic." She looked pleased with her expression. "He was stifling my potential and keeping me from being my own person."

Leora wondered if the woman standing before her was Libby's own person.

"Then, well, it turns out I couldn't get a job because – well, you need to have *had* a job to *get* one. And then Elliot starts skipping support payments – And I couldn't pay for a babysitter while I was looking for a job that no one wanted to give me because I've never had one … " She'd kind of lost the thread. "There's always a long wait at the welfare office … And now, well – " The line was shuffling forward. "Oh dear, I'm hungry."

Her own hem was all but dragging in the lower depths, but Leora offered to stake them to lunch.

In the Parthenon Diner the air conditioning quickly sealed their skin in old sweat like sausage casing. Leora ordered a black and white ice cream soda for Finn and set him up with a coloring book. Cara, pink and sweet, was still napping.

"How are your kids handling the split?" Leora said.

"Well, for a while they stayed with Aunt Hester in Islesfordd, but she's gotten a bit dotty. And I'm on medication that makes me forgetful – sometimes I totally blank out. They say I'm 'unfit' to be a parent … The nerve! I think they may be in foster care."

"You *think*?"

"Actually, that was just a bad dream I had, they're with my godmother in Brookline." She scarfed her egg salad sandwich, oblivious to the schmear of mayo at the corner of her mouth. Leora slid a napkin and her own tuna on rye across the counter. "Now Elliot's hassling me for a divorce."

"Jesus, what will you *do*?" She pictured Patrick having a nooner with his design genius: what would *she herself* do? Her hand as she lit the Winston jumped.

"I dunno, maybe turn tricks? Over on 9ᵗʰ Avenue?"

Leora pictured Libby – "Cricket" in college – her heart-shaped face of a Homecoming Queen, her plaid wool skirt with the giant gold safety pin, about to leave for the Princeton Darmouth game. She'd come out at the Whatzit Ball when the term applied only to debutantes.

Finn stopped trying to spin the red naugahyde top off its stool. He fixed her with his good eye. "Mom, is the lady going to do a trick?" "Not exactly, dear, remember your book, *Amelia Bedelia*? How words can have several meanings? Let's see what I brought for you." Leora ferreted through loose tampons in her bag for crayons and a new coloring book – and in that instant the Eureka moment just ... frisbee'd in.

She handed Finn his supplies. "I just had this amazing idea. We've gotta tell your story. I've been free-lancing for *Gotham* magazine, writing these dinky roundups of the city's best yarn shops kinda crap. But this is a story that captures our moment."

"Wait a mo – what story?"

"*You*! What's happened with you! The piece would have such resonance for women – for everyone. My silly stories for *Gotham* have given me an in." *I'll make you a star*, she almost said. That was the slogan of *Gotham*'s fearsome editor Clive Monomark whom she'd heard bellow the phrase across the office cubicles.

Libby teared up. "Too cruel, I'd be a public spectacle for everyone to mock. They'll get off on thinking, thank God that's not me!"

Leora wavered. It *would* be cruel; Libby was no advertisement for mental health ... Ambition argued louder. *Gotham's* readers would take a prurient interest – the best kind – in the story of a woman much like themselves who'd gotten the promise of feminism so horribly wrong. A story everyone would be talking about over water coolers, at dinner parties ...

Leora said, "I think people would *admire* you – for the guts it takes to throw off a suffocating life in search of something better."

"The Fenwicks would turn in their graves."

No doubt, but that was part of the piece, wasn't it? She let Libby talk, occasionally inserting a counter argument. They ordered two more ice coffees. Leora was in no hurry. She was certain of the outcome. Bottom line, everyone wants to "tell their story" ...

She'd never written it of course.

★

"Why are you *lurking* there? Don't tell me you were *spying* on us." Fred glanced round the kitchen piled with last night's dishes; flicked ashes from his cigarette into a mug wearing a beige skin on its surface. "Can I help it if I have more t-t-testosterone than other men?" He looked to Leora, a fellow prisoner of sex, for sympathy.

"You don't stop with the Albert Cam-*oo* Meghan's gonna split."

"I'm more worried my agent's gonna split."

★

A yellow-haired man came striding into the kitchen in jodhpurs and riding boots. Peter Grosvenor pronounced *Grove-ner.* Peter kept his own horse in Islesfordd, Fred had said, and rode to the hounds at Boston's Myopia Hunt Club and other fancy shit like that. All this had greatly impressed Gilda, who'd once been on a pony in Central Park and at a socialist worker's camp in the Borscht Belt.

"Wait'll you hear *this*!" Peter waved a newspaper clipping at them. "The advance review of my book in the *Beaver.* A flat-out rave! I thought maybe my relatives and a few fellow members of Myopia Hunt would buy the damn book – but this review is really going to break me out. If I wasn't still schnookered I'd break out the *Dom Perignon.* "'Seminal study,'" he read from the clip … "'Brilliantly argued'" … "'Makes the obvious sound original …'"

"So happy for you," Fred mumbled, hoping the review was on a back page.

"Thanks, m'friend." Peter looked tearful. "That's what I love about this place,

we celebrate each other's success."

Actually, *makes the obvious sound original* was no ringing endorsement, Fred thought, desperate to find the bright side. And maybe the review was just a 400-word throwaway. Fred was too terrified to ask, though the clip Peter was waving about like a ditz looked promisingly small.

"My publisher is so excited about the advance reception I'm about to sign a contract for a new book. On the new men's liberation movement!" Peter ran a hand through longish hair with lighter streaks that might be salon-engineered, only WASPs didn't go in for that.

Fred was feeling quite dizzy, starting to see double, in fact.

"I don't suppose Edwina is up," Peter said, nasal drawl failing to conceal his eagerness. "I'd like to show her the review – " He flapped his clipping. He noticed the encrusted dishes adorning the kitchen's every available space. Dessert plates of a green leaf shape with alarming ceramic veins, such as his Boston relatives gave each other at weddings. "Christ, hey, was I Duke of Dishwashing?"

★

Fred's face had gone a color not associated with rude good health. He might joke that he was one of the "almost-famous," but Leora knew. She'd made envy into an art form. She envied the domestic bliss of Frog and Toad (Finn's current favorite characters) even though they were maybe gay; Babar and Celeste; Will Pig and Won't Pig, along with every other animal couple in Richard Scarry's books, including the ones who slept in separate beds. She envied all pregnant women since she'd had trouble getting knocked up (kinked Fallopian tubes); envied in her nightmares the (imaginary) achievements of people who had died. Her last ignoble emotion, she feared, might be envy of those who got to go on living.

Fred was wondering if a heart attack, the worst pain known to man, could feel this awful. Peter just a well-connected dilettante, related to the publisher of the *Beaver* ... That pointless WASP ebullience ... Instead of playing touch football with the ingrown Grosvenors, he wrote pap about "libertarianism" and how charity should replace "government handouts" ... The *noblesse oblige* bit ... And now some bullshit on male feminism – why, he was as much a feminist as Ernest Borgnine ... A project cooked up just to impress Edwina, who was the main reason he'd joined the commune. The worst, Peter was siphoning off the recognition owed a REAL WRITER, LIKE *HIM* ...

Fred's last thought: Suppose Peter got *The Today Show*? It was after that he must have blacked out. He opened his eyes to find himself on the kitchen floor. Was this another warning shot across the bow? What the doctor had once called an "ischemic *event*," like it was fucking opening night of *Aida*?

Leora's alarmed little face swam above him. "Fred, can you hear me? Should I call 911?"

Fred raised himself on an elbow and felt around for damage. "I think a shot of Stoli should set me right." He nodded toward a cabinet in the same Spanish Inquisition style as the Cove's other furnishings.

★

Fred had spent a bad week. His agent Cressida insisted his latest book predicting future social trends was essentially a retread of *Overload*, his earlier book about the shock of change. "I mean, you've written the same book," Cressida said. "You've even lifted whole passages verbatim from yourself! How can I go out and pitch this to publishers?" A clump of ash from the cigarette she never flicked dropped onto her enormous shelf of a bosom. Fred started to point out that a recent winner of the Nobel Prize *boasted* that he kept writing the same book over and over in an effort finally to get it right, but Cressida had to take another call.

Fred had wanted to be a player and go to all the best parties and meet everyone for as long as he could remember. He'd got a tantalizing taste of it with the hoopla over *Overload*. Critics applauded its "visionary flights," the way he'd conjured up hordes of people, all standing with their eyes fixed on a tiny electronic screen, a form of mind control the State in cahoots with business magnates touted as advanced technology. Atomized and separate, people would never unite in their own interest and became easy to manipulate. A few spoilsports dismissed

Overload as social science lite from a journalist who'd mainly written cheesy sci fi for the lad magazines. Never mind, it only mattered to be on the radar. Though he'd somehow failed to *stay* there. Was he a one-trick pony? He beavered away, chain-smoking Camels in his rancid little writing studio at Cormorant Cove ... What if your *best* wasn't good *enough*? He'd taken to tippling Stoli throughout the day – siphoning off that stash someone was trying to hide in the basement fridge of the main house. He invariably greeted guests to the commune with news of his latest "movie sale." After four P.M., between the mumble and the stutter, no one could quite make him out, but people cut Fred slack (invites to his "intellectual mixers" were much coveted).

Perhaps the galloping world that he himself had conjured up had overtaken him, Fred thought at low moments. Pink-slipped him. He was no longer *bringing the news*. Yet Peter Grosvenor got precious space in the *Beaver* for his pap about *charities*? Why couldn't Peter just raise a glass with Sons of the American Revolution and torture foxes like a proper overgrown preppy?

Compounding the injury were all the *women* claiming "their moment." The wretched women – this he had *not* foreseen, as too improbable – were dominating publishing, bombarding readers with their shrill feminist broadsides that in ten years no one would read. One woman had spun a whole Dante's *Inferno* out of getting ogled by construction workers. Another proposed cutting off men's dicks. Lilith Hornswoggle had just come out with a doozy about freeing up women by promoting childbirth in an artificial womb – an idea swiped from *him*, the witch. Gilda, Germaine Greer, and Kate what's-her-face could publish their goddamn shopping lists! Not that any of them deigned to shop these days.

Except for all the females hogging the literary landscape, Fred had nothing against women's lib. In fact, he was all for it. Basically he liked difficult, spirited women with high IQ's. Especially if they had great tits. He liked being around the engine of excitement that was Gilda Gladstone. The people she attracted. Indira Gandhi. The King of Sweden. Eugene McCarthy, who'd come for lunch the other week. Fred wanted to be part of the story and women's lib was *the* story. The reflected glory spotlighted his own projects.

But when feminists became puritanical scolds who hassled him about his appreciation of women – no, his *love* for women – it made him cross.

★

"Fred, m'man, what are you doing down there on the *floor*?"

"Oh hi, Seb," Fred croaked, "you here to practice the organ?"

Leora's antennae twitched. So here was Sebastian Nye, the invisible organist from last night. Dapper and haughty like a Jazz Age swell; gabardine pants – no trendy bell bottoms for him; a little *too* handsome for everyday consumption. That Edwina hated Nye pointed to an affair gone bad. Leora wondered what stunt Nye could have pulled that she'd dumped him for JoBeth Mankiller.

"Damn back's out again, L-4 and 5," Fred said. He produced a couple of pelvic thrusts. If he did get *The Today Show* Peter Grosvenor would be all over TV, they were copy cats, those idiot bookers. He'd be on *David Susskind*, yacking with intellectual superstars, full of himself and stupidly unaware the host's questions were sophomoric. He'd do *Phil Donahue*, forum for hot-button issues! Fred moaned softly. And then next year, when Peter's book came out in paperback ... *more* publicity ...

He'd have to live the whole nightmare all over! After that, the men's lib juggernaut ... Would it never end? "Sebbie, this is Leora Voss," he gasped.

Nye glanced at her with one of those male appraisals swifter than the speed of light. He occupied too high a price point for her to be visible. Leora flashed ahead to life as an older woman. She'd be like Teflon, no male gaze would stick. She'd have toenails like horn. Crepe-y upper arms like she'd noticed when Nadine was working her fan. She heard the women communards: *we're not on earth to please men* ... Leora decided to look on the bright side. There was something deathly in Nye's too-even features. And a guy who'd *praised Joe McCarthy on TV* fell beneath even her lax standards ...

Nye bent from the waist and fanned a couple of flyers in Fred's vicinity. "I hope you'll be well enough to come to my concert. I'm conducting the Bruckner 8th at Town Hall June 25th." Nye devoted himself to conducting a single work, Bruckner's Symphony No. 8 in C Minor, Edwina had mentioned at dinner. He performed the piece at a range of august venues, papering the house with friends and the ignorant, to the amusement and ire of the actual music world. "The Philharmonic has refused to play under him because he can't keep a beat," Edwina had snickered.

"Uh, perhaps you could, uh, give one of these flyers to Edwina?" Nye slipped a few under a green leaf plate.

Leora, still smarting from being so flagrantly unnoticed, kept polishing her brief against Nye. At dinner last night someone had cracked Nye was a self-hating Jew. That he was Jewish, self-hating or not, would have been news to Islesfordd's "restricted" Rottlesey Club, a need-not-apply country club on the ocean where Nye was a member. Gilda clearly had a thing for WASPy guys, even ones who were self-hating Jews.

Nye leaned back against the counter, one loafer (Ital-ian-looking, butter soft) crossed over the other. "Tell me" – faux casual – "is Edwina up yet?" His nostrils quivered, as if to pick up her scent.

So Nye was still hot for Edwina? To judge by her reaction the previous night to his presence in the house, the feeling was not mutual. Edwina must need an air traffic controller to direct all the male attention.

"C'mon Sebbie, you had your shot with Edwina," Fred said. "Edwina's moved on. She's a lesbian, bisexual, whatever. In case you hadn't noticed."

"Oh, what does that all mean, anyway? Trust me, I know Edwina. It's suddenly fashionable to be a lesbian, is all. Edwi-na's very suggestible when it comes to fashion. She's a walking repository of the latest trends."

"That doesn't sound terribly respectful," Fred said.

"What Edwina needs is to be protected – from herself. *That's* respectful." He checked in with his sculpted right bicep.

Fred said, "I'd keep such thinking under wraps, at least until after the Women's Strike."

"Strike? Oh, that ridiculous ... parade of Gilda's? If it ever comes together – kind of a long shot, I'd say. Feminists are just a militant minority, doing it *pour le sport*. Women are simply self-limiting and shouldn't blame it on men. Face it, so many libbers are just so unattractive, couldn't get a date if they were the last woman on earth. Gilda tried to hit me up for money for the Strike. I wouldn't give them two pesos. If not for the libbers, Edwina would never have decided to be a lesbian."

Leora wondered if Nye shared such ideas with Gilda, and would he be excommunicated if he did, even though he had a pulse. Non-resident communards like Nye must get special dispensations.

"Y'know ... you – *communards*." – Nye's mouth argued with the word – "you're slaves of ideology. You live according to what you think you *should* want. But the heart wants what it wants."

"Why do men always quote Pascal when they want to justify wanting something they shouldn't?" Fred somehow sounded authoritative even lying on the floor. "You can't let go because it's Edwina who shafted *you*. You're far more possessive than any woman I've ever known, c'mon, show a little self-respect. Anyway, as I explain in my new book, possessiveness is a bogus emotion, not real like fear or anger. Give it up! You're a walking delusion. You might be suffering from what shrinks call narcissistic injury. Or, you're simply a masochist – *flay me, flay me*," he piped in a soprano. "It's quite unattractive. In fact, you've become a stalker."

"Speaking of shrinks," Nye said, impervious – "hasn't Lester Annis just been disbarred for seducing his patients? Doesn't speak well for the profession, does it? Annis should be pilloried on Islesfordd's village square, that's what. Like they used to do with poofs in Merrie Olde England. Fred, old man, you don't seem in the best of shape. You'll catch cold on the floor like that. Take care of yourself, wouldja?"

★

"Fred, dear," Leora said, "I could be awfully useful around here as Boyar of Bathroom Cleanup, Chatelaine of Shopping, and maybe Nurse Ratched. I could also take out the garbage and perform back flips while reciting Frederick Douglass's 'What to the Slave is the Fourth of July?'"

He raised himself on an elbow. "Don't hate me, but ... Gilda says there are too many women in the commune already. The last thing she wants is someone lovely like you. And you are, you know, quite fetching. Especially in profile."

"But I thought after last night ... My 'in' with Kaz Grabowski and all – "

"I tried, believe me ... The thing is, you look too good in hot pants to get into the commune. And I'm not sure Gilda would *remember* last night."

"But what about the bookkeeper? That gorgeous red hair ..."

"But she's Florence Luker, a *CEO* – of the Maid Marian Foundation."

Oy gavolt, another *someone*; Leora's hopes plummeted.

"Gilda likes that Florence invites her board members out, deep pockets who contribute money to WOW and the Strike. She even puts up with Dogmatix, Florence's Jack Russell terrier. Even though he's always getting into the garbage." Sigh. "Oh, c'mon, don't look like that, you're making me feel terrible" – He collapsed back down on the floor. A Fred tactic. Whenever he delivered bad news, he made him*self* out to be the victim.

Gilda charged in wearing a low cut caftan. "Where's Terry Cameron?" she said, panting.

"Went back to the city," Leora said.

Gilda scowled, as if Leora were at fault. She tottered, fingers to her forehead. "What did they put in those whiskey sours last night? Where they hiding the coffee?"

"The coffee pot's out on the sun porch," said Leora, who hadn't been dignified with a greeting.

"This occurred to me around 4 A.M.," Gilda said to Fred. He lay flat on the kitchen tiles, nose pointing at the ceiling. Gilda appeared not to notice. Clearly, empathy was not her strong suit. "The Women's Strike will be a *strike* for *real*," she went on, standing over him. "We'll call a national work stoppage. Secretaries will put the covers on their typewriters, waitresses stop waiting, cleaning women stop cleaning and everyone who is doing a job for which a man would be paid more will simply STOP … And come evening, we'll sacrifice a night of love to make the political meaning clear."

Leora forgot she'd been barred from the commune. Even though she stood, nose pressed to the window, looking in, it was thrilling to catch the moment when History was being forged. She'd called her own strike fifteen years ago – but it was only *her* out there. She'd balked at joining the army of housewives in the 'burbs – damned if she'd wax floors in false eyelashes and chauffeur Cub Scouts – balked at everything prescribed for women, castor oil forced down the throat. She was off to the libertine life! She chased after Ivy fuck-ups wondering what stop they'd gotten off at, the dreamer on the bike, Gyula from the Hungarian revolution, the wise-ass zoning lawyer who said, you haven't had such a bad of a time with me (she would always remember the extra preposition *of*). What a difference fifteen years makes! Now she'd down the castor oil like ambrosia. Gilda had the brilliance to ride the zeitgeist. The timing was on her side and she knew it – hell, she'd semi-*created* the timing. The press and guys like Sebastian Nye could snicker at the movement all they liked. Leora sensed that Gilda's people were out there in force, in the cities and 'burbs, purple mountains and plains, just waiting to be tapped. Primed to board a new era.

"We'll co-opt the civil rights crowd, the anti-war protesters," Gilda was saying to Fred's upturned nose. We'll co-opt welfare mothers, PTA housewives, career women who used to be scared of being called 'feminist.' We'll show the country – and ourselves – how powerful we are. After August 26 this nation will never be the same!"

Leora all but pumped a fist in the air. Struck by Gilda's heartland vowels of Rockford, Illinois, August as Ah-gust.

"The big obstacle is still the damn pencil-pushers in the City. They've dug in their heels about letting us close down

Fifth Avenue. We need an enabler, a fixer in our camp who can co-opt the key officials."

Suddenly, Leora saw she could build on what she'd started last night and make herself essential to Gilda's great project. "I have an idea," she said, in her flute-y voice. "Kaz Grabowski is pretty tight with City officials. They say he makes the zoning board roll over for him. He may be your man."

Gilda, who had ignored her presence till now, focused on her like a wolf sighting an antelope.

"Since Kaz Grabowski's an old college friend," Leora said, flying by the seat of her hot pants, "I've taken the liberty" – meting the words out slowly, a-tingle at her own chutzpah – "of inviting Kaz Grabowski to dinner here the first Saturday in June. I do hope everyone's on board with that," she added earnestly.

A long moment. As Gilda absorbed this, Leora pictured a chain moving from one sprocket to the next.

"Well! Why isn't someone planning dinner with the Marquise of Menus?" Gilda barked.

A voice from deep within the house bellowed, "Gilda, phone for you!"

"Tell them I'm busy."

"It's Indira Gandhi!"

"Can't it wait?" Gilda yelled back.

"She says it's urgent."

"Oh all *right*, she growled, "be right there." She glanced down at Fred. "For Chrissake, Fred, what are you doing on the *floor*?"

CHAPTER 5

Edwina and Nadine

*"'Life' in this 'society' being, at best, an utter bore and no aspect
of 'society' being at all relevant to women, there remains to civic-
minded, responsible, thrill-seeking females only to overthrow
the government, eliminate the money system, institute complete
automation and eliminate the male sex."*

– Valerie Solanas, *The SCUM Manifesto*

*"And then I did not know her pleasure from mine, my body from
hers. We fell into and became each other."*

– Kate Millett, *Flying*

Edwina Scahill stood at a mullioned window on the second floor
of Cormorant Cove peering down at Sebastian Nye's yellow
Porsche. It was parked in the driveway at a careless angle, as
if slung there the way he tossed his Burberry over the sofa. It

was the damndest thing: someone's precious toy – shorn from the someone – made your palms ache, even if he was a creep.

She moved to a rear window overlooking the lawn that sloped down to Hooker Pond. A girl-woman was crossing the grass. Fred's friend Laura – or Lara? – had an airborne gait, like a mime on ball bearings, and did not inspire confidence in any direction. She wore star-spangled hot pants that tried too hard, and a dopey grin, as if she'd just pulled an ace from the deck. Close to the water's edge Nadine Kusnetz sat on a scabby Adirondack chair gazing out at the pond, the goddess of Melancholy.

Too annoying that Gilda gave free run of the commune to anyone with a dick. Had Gilda never heard Nye's cracks about "the libbers?" To put distance between her and Sebastian Nye, who must be lurking about the premises, Edwina decided to take the kayak out for a turn around the pond.

A quick nod hello at Nadine – the woman really was a downer, she seemed encased in a hair-drying bonnet of gloom. Even her smile was sad. The planes of her face evoked the glamour of some forties move star long forgotten – for a moment Edwina saw precisely how she'd want to light Nadine for a jacket photo. Generally, Edwina preferred to give the deeply gloomy a wide berth. She'd seen more than her share at that place kitted up to resemble a liberal arts college, with its oak wainscoting and wicker chairs and masses of white rhodies. Except no liberal arts college, to her knowledge, offered a required course where 220 volts dance through your brain. Edwina hated white rhodies.

She dragged the kayak into the pond and fed herself into the old wreck, which must have dated from the Inuits, but was actually a present to Gilda from publisher Barney Rosset. Water quickly squeegy'ed through the toes of her sneakers. Once she got paddling, though, it was lovely: she had for company a rather soiled swan and green darning needles, an irridescent hover above the water.

Coming up on Dragon's Gate, Kaz Grabowski's place, Edwina let the kayak drift. The house, too large for its plot of land, was a mongrel mix of 18th century French chateau by way of Disney, complete with conical turrets, crenelated windows, and colonial schmonial. Dumpster-ready. They said the former owner, an animal lover, had built a habitat for a Monitor lizard. Dragon Gate's much-maligned phallus-sculpture thrust skyward from a too-green lawn of grassy squares that appeared freshly installed. Edwina wondered about its owner, so comfortable with ugliness.

What was it with men and their Dr. Jekyll first act? Their Mister Hyde surfacing only after you were in up to your eyeballs? She'd met Sebastian Nye at an organ concert at St Ignatius Loyola on Park Avenue in New York. His walls were hung with 19th century drawings by Ingres and Manet. Nye played her a recording of the great E. Power Biggs playing the organ at Notre Dame. Nye's audio system – Garrard 410 turntable, Tandberg speakers – looked fit to fly a jet plane. His teeth were expensive and perfect. She looked at the slightly animal set of his ears and the way, when he bent to pull a record from the shelf, his hair flopped over his forehead, and she felt its silk brushing her collar bone. Nye was her first esthete. He inhabited a different universe from the anti-war marches and flaming draft cards, the freedom trash cans and bra burning and consciousness raising groups – all the exhilarating changes exploding around her. (In truth, some felt more alarming than exhilarating, like women pronouncing that "all men are rapists" and "a man is a walking dildo.") Nye "sponsored" young musicians at Juilliard and wanted to take her to the Salzburg Festival in Austria to hear "the world's best music" and maybe Bayreuth for Wagner's *Ring* cycle. If not this year then next. He charmed her with long term planning. To think past the last orgasm was so *novel*, such a turn-on amidst the sexual free-for-all. Women were gung-ho about the free-for-all but Edwina thought they might have been sold a bill of goods. Men were just getting license to do what they'd always wanted to do but without the effort. Experience had taught her that you needed to travel a ways together truly to become lovers.

Nothing was perfect, of course. Nye co-published a far-right magazine with William Buckley which her friends called "a fascist rag." But the Seb Nye *she* knew was passionate about Art capital A, not politics, Edwina told herself. Nye's political thing was just vestigial stuffiness. Anyway, Buckley wasn't such a bad sort: liberals gave him a pass for being a reactionary who talked like an Oxford don – kind of like a chimp who could dance *en pointe*. Also, on his show *Firing Line* he'd sparred with Germaine Greer.

Edwina hadn't known how much she wanted to feel safe.

★

When did it turn? How could she have missed the transition? She was that frog in its tank, oblivious to the water gradually heating to boiling. He started coming on like he owned her, demanded an accounting of every moment out of his presence; she could scarcely glance at the pizza delivery guy, for godsake. This wasn't garden-variety possessiveness – Nye wanted to set up house in her head. She'd once thrilled to the prospect of musical odysseys to Salzburg. Now she only felt invaded. She started to lie (badly) about where she'd been, what she'd done – lied just for the hell of it, just to punch out breathing space.

"After we're married ..." he'd start. Then he'd lay out plans for expanding his River House co-op by annexing the apartment next door. He needed more space for a new set of AR18s speakers from Acoustic Research. And his harpsichord. F. Scott Fitzgerald had talked a lot of hooey when he said American lives have no second acts. He was warming up for his "second act" as a musician. He added, she might think about creating a darkroom.

After we're married? Not so fast. Edwina now understood Monica Fairley better – not that *anyone* understood Monica Fairley and why someone that pretty had gotten so worked up about feminism when every other avenue stood open to her. Monica had gained fame around New York as a commitment-phobe – kind of flipping the roles on men. She'd made a habit of dumping New York's most eligibles by leaving engagement rings and Dear John notes on pillows whenever marriage threatened. "Marriage feels like a restriction, not an enlargement," she'd written in *Pandora*. "You become a semi non-person." It struck Edwina as kind of hypocritical to write men off when you had them coming and going like in a bedroom farce.

Still, with this marriage thing, Monica had a point. "Semi non-person" was pretty much the way she felt around Nye. He pressed her to wear her hair center-parted and draped back over her ears, like the harem women in his drawings by Ingres. She moved through the days bearing a mirror-image of herself, judging Edwina Scahill as something Nye would approve of. Or not. When she tried to tell him that she'd lost any sense of boundaries, that she no longer knew who she was, as distinct from what he wanted her to be – that she felt annexed, like the apartment next door – he dismissed that as "libber talk."

Edwina shuddered to remember their last months. How desire could pivot on a pinhead to revulsion. His thumb resting on the pulse in her neck – it freaked her out, the *intent* behind that gently resting thumb. He drew a heart with her blood on the bathroom mirror. He didn't like *her* to touch *him*, recoiled from being done-to –so pervy. His thing was to orchestrate her responses, play maestro in the sack, his baton his cock, fingers, tongue. Nye was the other extreme of the old in/out her women friends beefed about. She wasn't sure he ever came. She tried to conceal her arousal, which she fought, the resisting it almost part of the turn-on. She might be the only woman in zip code 10065 who faked *not* having an orgasm. Those last months she was all excuses, too tired, too crampy, too anything ...

She was too tired that night at the music festival in Verbier. She was afraid. Their hotel sat high up in the Swiss Alps, far from everything, and when he reached for her she slid away and ran barefoot in her white batiste nightgown down a carpeted hallway and a flagstone path to a graveyard and crouched to pee behind an angel beaming its sightless smile into the mist.

★

"Everyone who had ever cared to investigate the nature of human loneliness had seen that only one's own working mind breaks the solitude of the self."

– Vivian Gornick

"The curtain descends/Everything ends/Too soon Too soon"

– *Speak Low*, Kurt Weill

She will be sorely missed, her obit would read.
Sorely, a word suggesting antique lace ...

We are deeply saddened by the death of ... Her fucked up family by her side ... Lived life to the fullest ...

But *had* she?

Nadine Kusnetz flicked open the little fan she'd acquired during a conference in Indonesia. This spring the hot flashes had checked in big time for a last hurrah. Nadine hoped the wretched fan – silk with tangerine tiger lilies overlaid by silver butterflies and a tassel on the end – looked more Madame Butterfly than menopausal.

There would be language in the obit about her "landmark" books on feminism, her "distinguished" career teaching sociology at NYU. Her long marriage to Sam who died – when? – terrible, she couldn't remember (she hoped the obit writer wouldn't use "pre-deceased" when he could go with "dropped dead"). Her son Ivan, who "survives her." In her "final illness," her grandchildren would look at her in love and terror, impatient to escape and rejoin the sunny world and press their arms around it and seize their moment on the stage. Ivan would take the family to an Italian restaurant in Queens, nothing fancy but real Italian cooking, not too far. Who thinks about the dead, after all, except ritually at Yom Kippur, and those random moments when a hiccough in the brain rips a vent in the fabric of time?

She had a zest for life ... Forever in our hearts ... She liked clean bathrooms ... In lieu of flowers –

What *did* she want in lieu of flowers?

She wanted the music at her memorial to be *Jerusalem ... And did those feet in ancient time/ walk upon England's mountains green ...* wanted the most Anglo of hymns. She was half Jewish but hadn't they all longed to escape into the great American blandness?

Beside her on the splintery table encrusted with lichen the latest edition of *Luce Inc.,* its cover story *Growing Old in America: The Unwanted Generation.* Coming up on sixty, Nadine supposed she was guilty as charged. *Unwanted*, though? Who asked? Her hedge against futility had always been her work. Unlike the neighboring housewives in Maplewood rattling around in their too-roomy lives.

She missed her life ... Did they ever say that in obits? Because she felt that, she had missed her life. The life she should have had. As if all those years married to Sam Kusnetz were someone else's, a shadowy stand-in for *her*. She'd periodically planned to strike out in search of her life, always deferring, so profligate with time, paying it out and out and out like a rope without end. She knew it existed, the joy of the richly coupled; she'd glimpsed it here and there like some golden scene inside a Russian Easter egg. Her bond with Sam had congealed into what a colleague classified as "companionate marriage." Companionate suited Sam. Perhaps he was relieved not to have to mess with carnal mess. He was probably – the opposite of Fred – low on testosterone. Perhaps he was gay, but too frightened, because that was then. It saddened her to think that Sam might have missed his life, too. More than anything else, except raising Ivan, they had done *that* together.

Sam and Nadine – maybe their true bond – conspired to keep each other from living life full out, the obit would say.

That would toss a 7 Pot Chili into someone's bloody Sunday.

The thing was, she'd been so busy. Raising Ivan, the battle to storm the mostly-male academy... She'd toss her 3 x 5 note cards into Ivan's playpen to keep him amused while she was writing her thesis. She was always working – toward her doctorate, to nab tenure, promotions, make deadlines on monographs and books; editors always wanted it yesterday. She was at her desk by nine A.M. seven days a week. The living part of life could wait, she thought, while the rope kept paying out and out – not aware that work had *become* the living part.

She was more married to work than to Sam Kusnetz. Who in his mild way either didn't notice or didn't mind. So long as he could spend Sundays playing his violin in his pajamas.

To think that back then a husband felt entitled to "mind!"

Back then it was only men who were more married to work.

Nadine reached for another Marlboro. Filthy habit, but the best people indulged; at least, while shortening your life, it sharpened the mind. She thought of her beloved shrink friend, who got a laugh from ordering "a gin and tonic, hold the tonic." He wasn't laughing now.

Perhaps it was inertia that had kept her soldered in place. The seductions of habit, a fatal comfort. Fear of gambling on the unknown; her bump-free ride with Sam offered few surprises. Fear of solitude. Germaine Greer said that loneliness was more cruel when you were with someone who'd ceased to communicate. No, Germaine, loneliness all by your fucking self is more cruel. Though you'd never know it from all the Nora Helmer's slamming out of their *Doll's House*, at least in the tri-state area. "Living consciously is the business of our lives," a feminist icon had written. "Steady work is the answer to loneliness." But not everyone could stay holy 24/7, you needed a respite from steady work – in the form of a hairy, demanding, obtuse, non-communicating, horny (or not horny enough), farting, snoring, briefly-cute-in-its-youth presence.

She'd had opportunities. What else were all those conferences for? Chicago, late evening, the bar of the stately old Palmer Hotel. The man offering to order them both another round was a doctor, practiced in Chicago. Pleasant face, a gentleness. They purled out their histories, spurred on by the artful lighting and anonymity of a hotel lounge. A torchy singer doing Ella Fitzgerald, just for them, at this late hour. He'd shrugged free of an early marriage that fit him like a baggy elephant suit.

Nadine sensed the heel of his hand close to hers. She'd put that part of her life on hold for so long she'd forgotten it existed. Work excited him: I'm part of a team at Northwestern Memorial Hospital exploring new ways to look at the colon. She wanted to ask how doctors could still function as sexual beings, like wouldn't knowing what they knew demystify a body as an object of desire? He said, we're developing a procedure that will soon be standard that could reduce the mortality rate by 36 percent." One A.M. and the booze flowing and Ella's songs, it sounded romantic, crusading medics on the frontiers of research.

Dinner next night in a revolving restaurant atop a skyscraper, she'd never have guessed she could be charmed by anything so cheesy. Men don't need that much, he said; he indicated the length of his palm. When she glanced up it was a different view out the window. The restaurant had moved. After, they went back to her hotel room, she came, hard, astonished at her own sounds.

They met again later that year in Atlanta. Over breakfast, he invited her to a medical conference he was attending in Dubrovnik. After, they could sail the Adriatic coast. She stared into her coffee. She couldn't do this. Sam didn't manage well in her absence. Ivan had gotten a part as the "second cop" in a school production of *Our Town* that she couldn't miss; she was on deadline with a chapter for a new anthology. A pang of lust, as her body remembered their night at the Palmer Hotel and how the earth – well, the restaurant – moved. Her own version of Hemingway. She *could* do this.

She was buttering her toast, when abruptly he asked: have you ever had a colonoscopy? You look in the right age range. No, Nadine said, taken aback. Should I? He said, well, we can remedy that. In fact, I'm about due for one. Why don't we schedule them together! I'll set it up at Northwestern.

Apparently, the "procedure" he'd helped pioneer not only reduced mortality – it was a sacred bonding ritual!

Back in New York Nadine discovered she couldn't get away to Dubrovnik after all. Ivan needed help rehearsing his lines. All three of them.

★

Forgive yourself, Nadine's shrink friend once said. The words had stayed with her. Likely, she'd never left Sam because she'd never had it in her to greatly harm someone. She'd never felt her own desires were that super important; never worshiped at the shrine of her self. Now, of course, "my turn" had become a holy duty.

The truth was, a rupture would have left Sam a bloodied wreck.

The truth was, a terrifically nice woman would have appeared on the doorstep in Maplewood before you could say "casserole" ...

As for her son – the truth was, Ivan was a pain in the ass. That wife of his. Maya, a performance artist, believed traditional marriage was prostitution and the hooker who got paid for her services was at least honest. Maya and Ivan had agreed to put his career as an industrial designer on hold to care for their infant Fidel and toddler Christabel (after the suffragette). This while Maya retreated to her studio on Spring Street to make art, if that was the word.

The unwritten clause: grandma would pick up the slack. The last time she'd sat for Fidel, he'd barfed rancid milk down the front of the mauve silk blouse she'd had custom made during the Whither Machista? conference in Mexico – then bawled in rage – at *her*, she could have sworn. She'd never gotten the stains out. She lacked the grandma gene, starting with the title "grandma."

She'd done her best to dissuade her son from slacking off. "But Ivan, this is the moment to push your career to the next level, not play house-husband." Why couldn't Maya dream up her next "sex magic ritual" while she was making meat loaf?

"Y'know, mom, you and Gilda go on about how women have always sacrificed their work to a husband's ego and career. And here I'm a guy finally doing the Right Thing – and you attack me? What's with that? I'll get consulting jobs, work during Fidel's naps."

"But this, uh, 'performance art' of Maya's – it's hard to tell from pornography. She even says in the program notes that she started her career working in porn."

"I don't get it, you've made a career of encouraging women's self expression."

Nadine felt all bollixed up. What he said was right – yet something felt all wrong. "I mean, Maya's performance piece *Public Cervix Announcement* – it kind of crosses a line ... " Nadine couldn't go on. In the piece Maya invited the audience to "celebrate the female body" by approaching the stage to peer at her cervix with a speculum and flashlight. She called herself Maya Wet, it said in the program, because *I love waterfalls, urine, vaginal fluids, sweat, anything wet.*

And to think her only child had chosen this!

"The trouble is, mom, your public and private selves are wildly out of sync. Maybe you should write a book about it!"

★

Edwina paddled into view, dipping the oar now one side, now the other in a rhythmic weave. From where Nadine sat the kayak looked to be riding ominously *low*. Now there was an enigma: Sebastian Nye was any woman's dream – just not Edwina's, evidently. Maybe no man was.

Putting it together with a woman couldn't be easy, even today, even cheered on by the posse around Jobeth Mankiller. She had to salute Edwina, who had always struck her as rather fragile, a cat's whisker away from – well, there was some rumor about a crack-up, a season at McLean's, Rolls Royce of mental hospitals. A mother who'd jumped out the window. (She'd gotten all this from Fred, who had a way of absently dispensing gossip like someone shedding dandruff.) She'd always viewed Edwina as a trust fund girl, the dabbler she'd vowed, years before Gilda's book launched the movement, never to become.

Okay, she'd plead guilty to a certain impatience with women who'd never pulled a living wage – that would be most of the women, communards excluded, around her. She also felt impatient with the sisters just now discovering *Work*, like St. Pauline on the road to Damascus; she'd been *born* a believer, it seemed.

Nadine swatted at a skeeter; lit another Marlboro. A bit of attitude-adjustment was in order: as an organizer of the Women's Strike, it wouldn't do for her to feel superior to the sisters who were now claiming their rightful place. The real heartbreaker, of course, they had yet to discover: to go on working – to *persevere* – in the absence of acclaim or money. Like so many scribblers and toilers in the arts ... She herself had scrambled up the rungs of Academe, kissed asses and quite literally worked herself sick to get tenure, then make Full Professor. She'd traveled the country to research a book that had suddenly put her on the public radar ... The whole package more than paid the rent. She'd been ... she wouldn't say, *lucky*. She'd say, *clever*.

Or maybe not so clever as she'd imagined ...

Nadine zoomed in on Hooker Pond. The water, its clear sepia of an Old Master painting, astonished her, she might never have seen water. A clump of iris – when had iris been so purple, a psychedelic Tyrian royal purple, it knocked her sideways. The peaceful drone of bees steadied her. A breeze wafted a scent of honeysuckle ... A marine fart gurgled up from the sediment at the bottom of the pond, primordial, stinky, stirring ... The gorgeous stink! She tipped forward, a sob caught in her throat. She wanted MORE, more life, the life she'd missed, she wanted to claw back the years.

★

"I had managed to solve the Jane Austen problem that women have been confronting for centuries – securing a provider for your children, finding a mate to pass the time with, and creating a convivial home – in an entirely unconventional way."

– Ariel Levy

"Keep a tender distance/so we'll both be free"

– *Marry me a Little*, Stephen Sondheim

The lone swan fed among a flotilla of water lilies, dipping its gold beak and black mask; the serpentine neck the very line of beauty. Edwina paddled toward it for a closer look, keeping well away, though. Gilda and her posse had gone out on the pond one drunken dusk to "commune" with the swans. The swans were not amused. Why was this one alone? Weren't they said to mate for life? Maybe it was a widowed swan, or a renegade female that split from its male chauvinist mate.

Edwina banked her oar and sat rocking slightly, hypnotized by the scribble of inverted trees in water ...

In college Jo had occupied some outer ledge of her awareness. JoBeth – Nicholson then – had arrived freshman year fully formed, in a sense, knowing she liked girls. Strictly "perverted" *Well of Loneliness* stuff, and mighty daring for the class of '58. Jo, as she called herself, gained instant fame around campus with her paper arguing that Donatello's statue of David – naked but for a flowery hat and boots, foot resting on Goliath's head – had a homosexual "subtext." That she threw around the word "subtext" – and with distinctly male authority, when women were so fluttery, so tentative – added to her mystique. JoBeth was easy in her skin and handsome, with pale hair shorn like an English boy at Eton and the lowering gaze of a morphine addict – a generator of sexual excitement. Half the campus wanted something with her, though no one quite knew what the "something" might involve: a few rebels, naturally, eager to stick a thumb in the eye of propriety, but also the pageboy set from boarding school. It got ridiculous, the ziggurat of offerings piled high by admirers on the threshold of Jo's room in Throbbing Hall.

Her androgynous allure spoke to the preppies who came snuffling around the bucolic college campus, nose to the ground, in search of an heiress who put out. Jo, they decided, was too pretty to be a dyke, nothing that couldn't be set right by a good stiff prick. A Dartmouth jock in a crew cut and lettered sweater came on to her at the Winter Art Show. "Fuck off, boy," Jo said.

Edwina was too busy on the Ivy circuit to take much notice. Once, in a park near the college she saw Jo and Cindi, a debutante from Houston, kissing under the lilacs. A couple of local guys – "townies" – pointed and snickered. Edwina fled, frightened. Later Jo was booted from college and went off to study art history at the Courtauld in London, and Cindi would do time at the Menninger Clinic and later marry her shrink, a Jew with those icky curls, which her family agreed was better than being a lesbian.

★

Back in New York – after she'd made her break from Nye; after a second sort of hell landed her at McLean's funny farm – Edwina sometimes ran into Jo. Museum openings, Soho galleries. Jo looked pretty much as she had in college: short gosling-colored hair plastered to her head, freaky kimonos over the severe black-and-white of a seminary student. She taught at NYU, Edwina knew, and wielded a big reputation as a feminist art historian. They'd exchange those New York nods that waste no warmth on someone beyond the sphere of one's immediate interest.

One evening Edwina found herself on impulse at Jo's lecture on "the male gaze" at the City Museum. Male painters of the 19th century depicted women solely as objects of male desire, Jo explained to her rapt, mostly female audience. The women in those portraits are depicted *seeing themselves as seen by men* in a kind of double awareness, which even today is reflected in popular images, in advertising, say. She clicked to a slide of Titian's famous *Venus of Urbino* – "little more than 16th century porn. Everything about her panders to the male gaze, from her inviting smile to her soft features and idealized body. The anatomy exaggerated to better please the viewer. Follow her arm down to her hand in her groin. Is she covering herself up? Or, is she getting things started?"

Edwina felt lulled, hypnotized, almost, by Jo's low, mildly affected voice – was she aping an English aristocrat? Well, she'd lived in England, hadn't she. She watched Jo's arrogant strut as she moved away from the lectern and how when she gestured at some detail of the slide with the pointer the sleeve of her kimono slipped back to expose her white arm, and she lost track of what Jo was saying and only wanted it not to stop.

★

At the reception following Jo's lecture, Edwina, buzzed on champagne, wandered off through a series of dim galleries. She stopped before a large 19ᵗʰ century portrait of a woman. She bent to see the attribution: Francois Gerard.

"So you found *The Princess of Talleyrand*, one of my favorites."

Edwina pivoted, startled, to see Jo gesturing in her magisterial way at the canvas. She hadn't heard anyone come into the gallery.

Jo planted herself on a bench and sat, elbows on knees and legs akimbo; looked from her to the painting. Edwina was aware of her scent, something lemony, mingling with the airless, exhausting smell of museum.

"The portrait reminds me of you," Jo said.

Edwina eyed the elegant princess, the flush of her cheeks snatched from life, the gauzy Empire-style gown displaying her lovely arms. The artist had captured the pearlescent skin; her flesh trapped light. The princess looked down to one side, absorbed in her own coquetry.

Edwina said, "Why do I think that's not a compliment?" Then, when Jo, annoyingly, failed to respond: "How so?"

"I used to see you and Sebastian Nye ... around, and I got the impression you were a prized work in his art collection. Or rather, he regarded you as one, an idealized beauty from the 19ᵗʰ century. An *objet d'art.*"

What the – ? Pretty nervy, they hardly knew each other.

"You could have walked out of one of Nye's 19th century drawings by old masters," Jo went on. She narrowed an eye at Edwina. "An Ingres, actually – though I doubt he owns any originals. The way you wore your hair, even."

Edwina touched her fingers to her messy chignon: it was true that in the past (which she hoped to obliterate) Nye had wanted her to look like a harem favorite in an Odalisque by Ingres. Pressed her to wear Empire style dresses that showcased her tits.

"At one time Seb Nye and I shared an appreciation of the visual," she said coldly. "I'm a photographer after all."

"Oh, of course. Maybe you'll show me your work."

Edwina could detect no condescension.

"In any event, I no longer see Sebastian Nye and prefer not to speak of him."

A rapid nod. "I remember you at an opening – in Soho, it was. You walked across the gallery – *watching yourself* walk across the gallery. You seemed to see yourself through a filter of seeing how you must appear to the rest of us."

Maybe she'd quaffed too much champagne. She felt unable – or unwilling – to defend herself.

"Sorry, I shouldn't have said all this."

"No, you should have – I mean, no, you *shouldn't*." Christ, she'd lost her language ...

"It's just I find it troubling that women can be so ... compliant with the way men want them to be," Jo said. "Forgive me, it was not meant as a put-down of you."

Edwina couldn't peel her eyes off the painting, something about it enthralled her: the princess's nacreous skin, plumped with light – why, it was *Jo's* skin. Of a different grain than the honest hairy flesh of men. It was her *own* skin.

★

She began attending Jo's talks at the Women's Art Collective. One evening a group of them went out for coffee after in a nearby greasy spoon. She sat in a cramp, churned by feelings she couldn't sort out; eyes fixed on photos of the Statue of Liberty and other tourist attractions laminated onto her plastic place mat. She wondered if she might be tacking back to something placed on hold twelve years ago that she'd meant, without knowing, to revisit. She clutched onto the Statue of Liberty, as if to resist the magnet of Jo tugging her in like iron filings. She now saw the co-eds of '58 as ladies in Victorian bathing suits with bonnets and bloomers. The formerly unthinkable was now not only thinkable – many women thought it the only honest choice.

★

A party up in Rye, in Westchester. A softball ball game is in progress, somewhere a radio tuned to Herb Alpert, "*This Guy's in Love With You*" ... *My hands are shaking/Don't let my heart keep breaking ...* It's hot as hell. Edwina wears a tank, hot pants, topsiders, which she knows show her legs to advantage. She loops slowly around the field, shooting pictures with the new Polaroid Land Camera she's blown $200 for, the heat drumming through her tennis hat. Jo shows zero interest in sports, she sits at some distance in the fork of a tree reading a tome about Jacques-Louis David. She wears a while silk Nehru shirt. Her skin of a shocking pallor beside all the health and freckles and shoulders schmeared with Bain de Soleil. Edwina shoots her from multiple angles to capture how the sun through leaves dapples her body, making her part tree, part faun, wanting to capture the lavender shadows under her eyes and the blue ones she imagines behind her knees.

Jo leans in to look at the pictures Edwina has pulled from the side of her Land Camera and spread on a picnic table. Edwina goes light-headed at her sweaty musk ... To think they'd all once lived in terror of Body Odor ("B.O.") and most things betraying ownership of a body. "How did I get to be the star of the show?" Jo says, laughing. *Aren't you always?* Edwina thinks irritably. Jo rests a hand on Edwina's bare shoulder, the better to lean in. Edwina jerks forward under the hand *please don't*. "Why you so jumpy?" Jo says. "I'm not jumpy." Jo props her elbows on the table, butt aloft; the sun fires up silver highlights in her close-cropped hair. "I like this shot, the way you framed it." Edwina's mind has gone AWOL, she's nothing but a craving for the hand to return. She'll jump out of her skin. Please. Please *do*.

Edwina has never felt so merged with someone. She's woken up in an exotic country that feels like home. It's a delirium, intoxicating, the silkiness after men's rough stubble. A new book has come out on male/female relations as combat. She and Jo are on the same side – yet with air between them, bound together and free. She has no thoughts about what sex Jo is or how it could matter.

Nothing's tidy: there's another woman. She fears Nye has spoiled her for love.

I think I was attracted to you in college but I didn't dare.

You should have.

Too busy being bored out of my skull at the Yale-Harvard game.

When I first saw you, I thought, my God, Merle Oberon.

But I'm pure-bred. Mother never had it on with a Maori, or whoever the fuck Merle's father was. I wish she had, it might have brought Mother into the human fold.

Think of all the time we've wasted.

Back then I wasn't up for volunteering to be a witch in Salem. Besides, you were awfully full of yourself. That paper of yours on Donatello's gay David ...

It was right on the mark, that paper! And back then I didn't even know what we now know about sodomy in Florence, so famous that in France it was called "the Florentine vice – "

Back then I don't remember you as pedantic ... Pretentious, maybe, with all that "subtext" stuff, but not pedantic.

It wasn't just Jo-and-Edwina, like the two-headed hydra of straight pairs – she'd acquired a community, joined an army of activists. So much work to do! The marches against 'Nam, rallies for welfare rights, protests against Miss America contests, speak-outs on abortion. The press conference to defend Kate Millet – the media had piled onto her for declaring herself bi-sexual. The battles with Gilda Gladstone, who wanted to "purge" NOW of "mannish, man-hating lesbians," "disrupters of the women's movement" – as if butch lesbians weren't women too! Gilda had stirred up a fuss by telling the *Beaver* that lesbians were ruining the movement, that a member of Daughters of Bilitis had tried to seduce her.

Jo's friends made edgy feminist art that prodded Edwina to put teeth in her own timid photos. Her friends were out to dismantle art that cast women purely as objects of desire for men. "We need to reclaim our own bodies, the flesh and fluids and mess," Jo said. Hannah Wilke made terra cotta sculptures of vaginas. A topless self portrait pocked with wads of pink chewing gum folded into origamis mimicking tiny vulvas ... Brilliant! what better image of woman chewed up and spat out? Artemis someone wore a "theater stage" she'd crafted and invited passersby to stick their hands inside and cop a feel – the message eluded Edwina but she would never have admitted it. A hell raiser in farmer's overalls wrote broadsides bashing intercourse: "There is never a real privacy of the body that can coexist with intercourse ... The vagina itself is muscled and the muscles have to be pushed apart. The thrusting is persistent invasion. A woman is opened up, split down the center. She is occupied – physically, internally in her privacy."

The next great moment belongs to women, the *Village Voice* trumpeted. Edwina loved running with the girl gang. When she thought of Nye at all she thought isolation, loneliness. He'd made the body and its hungers shameful. Now Jo had blown through all the confusion, helped her understand how she'd been complicit in her own objectification. Men and women together felt uninteresting and tired to Edwina. Here at the margin she was at the white hot center.

★

How strange that it was dear old Peter Grosvenor she could talk to about Jo. Peter was a distant cousin; they'd learned to sail together on Lake Tashmoo on Martha's Vineyard (along with Peter's currently estranged wife). At ten Peter got on a pony at Netherfield Farm and never looked back; won the silver medal for dressage at the junior Fontainebleau championships. After St. Paul's and Yale he made a brief pass at law school, before embracing the family trade of conspicuous idleness. He gathered with Sons of the American Revolution at the Somerset, his club on Beacon Street – a Brahmin bastion since forever – rode to the hounds, lived the sporting life of an English gentleman, and could expect to keep company with the very best people in Mt. Auburn Cemetery.

Eventually the renegade spirit of the '60s penetrated even the ivy walls of the Somerset. The '60s had made High

Fatuity embarrassing. Peter had once taken a writing course at Yale with Robert Penn Warren, who'd encouraged him ... He cranked out a book proposal about charitable giving as a solution to poverty; snagged a contract through his Old Boy network. Edwina thought Peter's book a bit musty, when everyone was calling for Revolution and women wrote tracts about clitoral orgasms and eliminating the male sex – but it beat dressage and forcing horses to walk sideways against their better instincts. At one of Fred's coveted parties Edwina introduced him to Gilda.

"Bet you're tired of being called 'the mother of women's lib,'" Peter said.

By evening's end, Gilda had invited him to her audience with the Pope.

Edwina felt she could talk to Peter because he had the great good manners not to *judge*, the way most people felt it was their sacred duty to do. Surely he knew about her misspent sophomore year in Rome ("the calamity in Rome," as she named it to herself). Who in the family didn't? Peter never let on. Their other game: she knew he was in love with her, he knew she knew, and they pretended it wasn't there, the way you'd politely ignore a loud fart in church. Once – just once, he'd said, "Darling we need to talk." She said, "No we don't" – and that was that. She simply couldn't put Peter and sex together in the same frame. Peter was sort of, well, too *genial* for sex; *jolly nice*, he'd say in bed. In/out, Christ, hey, *whoopee!* He'd presumably consummated his marriage – but if you stuck him in front of *The Origin of the World*, Courbet's painting at the Musee d'Orsay of a great hairy vagina, vulval pearl peeping out, she suspected he might faint dead away.

For now, she and Peter had a high old time laughing to-gether at the British names and Anglophilia so dear to the new money moving in on Islesfordd. "Have you heard the latest? They're calling a new restaurant Wankers. What does all the Brit stuff do for these people?"

"Maybe they want to be David Attenborough on '*A Life On Our Planet.*' There's a fellow out here with the name Lifshitz or Lipschitz who's started a clothing line of tennis shirts with polo mallets on them. For guys who once played stick ball."

While Gilda remained willfully blind to Peter's life beyond the commune, it troubled Edwina. Why, oh *why* must he torment his girl-wife? She talked in the wispy mew of Jackie Kennedy and appeared oblivious to her sisters out there realizing their potential. She wanted only to realize her potential as a housewife. He was taking a "hiatus" for the summer at the commune, Peter said, while his wife "enjoyed the place on Martha's Vineyard" and they gave each other "space" to "sort things out." Yeah, right.

Bottom line, Peter was a peach – the way men were, until you needed to count on them.

★

"It's not that I'm attracted to *women*." It was early morning and they were walking the ocean shoreline before breakfast. "It's *Jo* I love. Just Jo, this one individual. Who happens to be a woman. She could as easily have been a man." (Was this true? sometimes she wasn't certain.) "Jo feels like both and neither. And why can't the sexes be a little porous?" (thrilled with her own advanced views). "Maybe we're not all so rigidly male/female." Edwina toed the foam riding in on the tongue of a wave. "Boundary-less love, it's mysterious, you can't dictate the terms. It's so hard to explain. Peter, thank you for listening to this madness."

★

What she hadn't told Peter, for fearing of encouraging him and hearing him say, *We need to talk;* what she hadn't told him was that at six A.M., in that semi-conscious murk dangerous to self-deception, certain qualms about her life with Jo had a way of scuttling in.

Six A.M. and she understood she would *not* go with Jo to Fire Island Pines, a gay mecca with all-night revels at the Boatel, queens conga-lining to *Hello Dolly*. (Jo went without her.) In the hard light of 6 A.M. treasonous thoughts about some of the radical dogma bubbled up. Marriage is "state-licensed rape" (*really?*) Sex with a man means "yielding to patriarchy" (what did that even mean?) The thrusting is "persistent invasion" (if you insist). Having an orgasm with that man is to "collaborate with the patriarchal system" and "eroticize your own oppression" (was there such a thing as a bad orgasm?) It was Puritanism stood on its head.

★

But maybe that's what turned so ugly with her and Nye: they were a textbook case of a woman "yielding to patriarchy."

★

Maybe it had nothing to do with "yielding to patriarchy," maybe Nye was just a fucking creep.

★

Jo's friend Germaine Greer said, if you're "emancipated," you should taste your own menstrual blood – and if that sickens you, you've got a long way to go ... "

★

Crossing the playground in Bethune Square on her way to Jo's loft, Edwina saw the women pushing toddlers in swings. A carriage with a mobile of frolicking seals. Another bullet to dodge. Though she'd never felt the pull of making babies. Children made her nervous, their abrupt movements, sticky hands, talent for mayhem. To have a child was to make you a hostage to fortune and set you up for suffering. Her own family was the best deterrent. Mother had never Moved On, as you were meant to, she jumped from their 14 floor living room window and landed on an awning and snapped her neck.

★

Edwina became abruptly aware that the kayak had drifted too close to the solo swan. It let loose with an avian braying, exposing an eerie black-striped *tongue* – then *hissed*, raising sections of muscular wing. Suddenly its lovely swanny neck looked mean as a python. Edwina seized the oar and tried to maneuver the kayak away ... Something obstructing the oar. The boat was caught on an undercarriage of rope-y stems. She knew their roots reached deep into the bottom mulch, forming a dense tangle beneath the surface. The lilies, color of blush wine with gold corollas, innocently glowed at her. Fucking *nymphaea odorata*, named for nymphs who seduced gorgeous young men into pools of water and drowned them. Monet hadn't known the half of it ...

The kayak kept shipping water. Edwina rose in a semi-squat to reconnoiter. She must have leaned too far to one side, the kayak tipped her into the brackish water. She felt the rubbery embrace of stems that snaked downward toward dim green chambers ... Remembered reading a thriller about a killer on the lam whose craft gets trapped among water lilies ... She clung to the kayak's gunnel.

Nadine frantically gestured from shore. "Should I get help?" Her voice sounded far away.

Edwina called, "I'll swim the damn boat in." It was three quarters submerged ... She put her weight on the kayak's gunnel to maneuver the thing on its side and tip out water but it was stuck ...

Peter appeared on the lawn in riding boots. He waved something at her – what the fuck, shouldn't she be the one waving for help? He crashed into the pond in his boots.

"Stay back, it's not good out here," Edwina yelled. The excitement brought Florence Luker's terrier to the water's edge. Dogmatix set to yapping in the infernal soprano of small neutered dogs.

The fickle June sun was swallowed in cloud. Edwina was shivering. She clung to the rotting kayak, kicking at the slimed roots wanting at her legs and feet. She could see the heels of Peter's riding boots break the water as he swam toward her. He heaved himself onto the kayak, sinking it deeper. Waved a piece of water-logged paper at her. "My review in *The Beaver*! You're the first person I wanted to show ... Couldn't find you ... And darling, here you are!"

Jesus fucking Christ. "That's lovely, Peter" – her feet were tangoing with ropey stems – "but it couldn't have waited? We could die together out here."

"I'd rather live together. We need to talk."

Christ, not that again. We need to talk: the last words she'd hear on earth. "This fucker is about to go under – and it's a present to Gilda from Barney – "

"Listen to me, this business with JoBeth, it's just a phase. I know, I had one too. Way back, of course, at St. Paul's. We thought we were being English."

"Thanks for not sharing."

Nadine was shouting from the shore. "Hang on there, I'm gonna call the Coast Guard!"

A splash. They both looked toward shore. Edwina was not happy to see Sebastian Nye cutting toward them in a powerful crawl.

The kayak went under with a sucky sound. They rested their feet on the bottom, briefly hammocked. She'd read in the *Vineyard Gazette* about freak drownings of swimmers who got tangled up in roots. Okay, no need to panic, they'd both grown up around water, the tides in Chappaquiddick were more treacherous.

Edwina said, "Let's try to breast stroke in, keep it super shallow – "

A few strokes, and Peter was in trouble. "Damn boots," he spluttered ... ... filled with water ... can't get 'em off." His head went under as he jack-knifed to yank the boot off with one hand. The other still clutched his *Beaver* review, riding above the surface like Tristan's sail on the Irish Sea.

Edwina cupped Peter's chin and attempted to haul him, side-stroking, toward shore. Suddenly the pond's Loch Ness monster reared up beside them. Nye reached for Peter's head, palmed it and shoved him under. Edwina screamed, "What are you doing, you crazy bastard?"

Fred had joined Nadine at the edge of the pond. "This is no time for horsing around," he called out. "You're kind of on your own here. The Coast Guard refused to come. They said they don't do ponds, only oceans."

Peter resurfaced, but he'd taken in brackish water and was wheezing and fighting for breath.

"He's trying to drown Peter!" Edwina screamed.

"Fred, we should call the *police*," Nadine said.

Nye looked poised for a second lunge – then abruptly dove under the kayak and maneuvered it onto its side. Water sloshed out. The thing was semi-afloat.

"Hang on, and I'll tow you both in," Nye said.

★

It took two sets of hands to get the boots off Peter, who lay, head turned to the grass, heaving up pond. In one hand he still clutched a soggy scrap of newsprint.

Fred felt relieved. After hearing about the *Beaver* review, he'd conjured up a variety of "tragic" fates for Peter. If Peter had actually drowned he would have been tempted to blame himself. Fred knew that was just magical thinking, but even so ...

Nadine stood by in a trance. The idiot had come this close to "a tragic accident." Forget tragic, how about cretinous? She could hardly fathom that he'd throw it all in – for *what*? She wanted more, and after that *more* more. She wanted to stick around for the what-next, the denouement of their little dramas, the wealth of tomorrows. She lit a cigarette and smoked it all the way down.

Fred glanced her way. "I think we could all use a drink."

Edwina shook her head as if they were incorrigible children, and headed up toward the house.

"Look at you, you're shivering," Nye said, coming abreast. He grasped her arm above the elbow. "We need to talk."

She was uncomfortably aware that her nipples were taut under the soaked tee shirt. Nye stood above his slightly erect cock, visible under the chinos, a weaponized male primed for action.

"Darling," he said, "be a little nice. I got us out of a tight spot."

She shook off his hand. "Who asked?"

CHAPTER 6

Edwina and the Children

"It is a truth universally acknowledged, that a single man in possession of a good fortune, must be in want of a wife."

— Jane Austen, *Pride and Prejudice*

Cara's crying jag showed no sign of winding down. Leora hung over the antique crib they'd hauled from the attic, and trundled out the ammo: *Mommy back soon … Here's big brother* (Finn ignored them, nose in a book) … *Who are the finest children on all of Avenue A?* (a routine that reliably amused Finn, it echoed a line from his *Lilac Book of Fairy Tales*) …

Let's all sing: Puff the magic dragon lived by the sea/and frolicked in the autumn mist in a land called Honalee …

A duet of Cara's yowls and Leora's reedy soprano. Leora, knuckles white on the bar of the crib, fought an urge to shake it. She saw deep into her own ugly mother. *Flesh of my flesh, blood of my blood* — but dammit, I need to get to Kaz Grabowski's party. For nothing so frivolous as fun. She lay her cheek against

Cara's silky head, scalp hot with rage over the arsenal of affronts endured by babies.

Finn sat on the floor hunched over a water-damaged *Babar and Zephyr* that he'd plucked from a garbage can on 7th Street and Avenue A. He was fascinated by Zephyr's Monkeyville, a village of monkey dwellings fitted into a canopy of trees. Leora was proud he'd learned to read way before other kids. She noticed he was working an unbent paper clip in his ear.

"How many times have I told you not to do that!" Cara started up again. Leora on the verge. She sometimes caught the children dubiously frowning at her, as if privy to some Platonic ideal of Mother she'd missed by a mile. This reliably happened when their balky old Dodge Dart refused to start up and she burst into tears.

"Leora Voss, phone!" a voice hollered up the stairwell. It echoed the hollered "phone!" in the dorm at Foxleigh College. A call that promised a "clean-cut" boy from Princeton and a session in the back seat of a car parked outside the coach's ivy-clad cottage, spots from the porch shellacking flagstones wet with yellow gingko leaves. They kept each other good company, she and Harry Dawes and his hard-on. Aerodynamic. It could launch him into the soggy night like Apollo 5. Then he was pushing insistently at her head and the party was over ... He'd become a gynecologist, she heard.

"My sister can't come tonight, she has cramps," a voice said on the phone. Sister? That would be her baby sitter for tonight.

DAMN! the flakey girl had thrown a wrench in phase one of her plan. Leora groaned. To think it was she who'd co-engineered tonight's party ...

Couple of weeks before, she'd told Gilda that Kaz Grabowski was coming to dinner at the commune, unable, even as she spoke, to believe her own chutzpah. Then she had to deliver! She hadn't seen Kaz in years – except once on line at MOMA – and their parting had not been amicable. Would he even take her call? Did he hate her face? She sensed something dangerously unpredictable. Was she poking at a hornet's nest?

Kaz came on the line with a speed that suggested something to do with his groin.

"Leora Voss, it's been a while," he said, voice thick.

"It has indeed – and now it turns out we're neighbors." She stammered out the dinner invitation she'd rehearsed, garbling words. "We're just south of you on Hooker Pond."

Silence, as if a new optic had scissored open. "Dinner at the commune?" Super casual: "Don't tell me you're part of that commune crowd at Cormorant Cove."

"Well ... semi-part."

"I'd love to, but – (she steeled herself) – "I'm throwing a party myself that same evening. Why don't you and all your" – (she heard him breathe out) – "friends ... come to my place instead? It's just up the road, you know. Dragon's Gate, better view of the pond than your place. Got a Botero sculpture of a nude by the driveway, can't miss it."

Leora Voss," he added. "You never took your husband's name."

★

She realized she was sharing the living room of Cormorant Cove with a man who was diving his hand to the elbow behind the cushions of a sofa. Henry Lyman, Gilda's consort and "ace stock-picker." He triumphantly fished out two coins and twinkled at her over his half-rims. "Amazing what you find back there! Stuck here for the evening, are 'ya? Listen, put some money in farmland in Adair, Iowa, and you'll soon be traveling about with a nanny."

"Thanks, Henry, count me in," she said absently. Too distraught over the sitter's no-show to remind him she was already counting on that back surgery outfit he'd put her into, "the insider tip of a lifetime" that would soon quadruple, ha-ha ...

Gilda charged in, muttering, in a red Empire dress with little puffy sleeves gathered beneath the bosom. She ricocheted off furniture like a bumper car. "Henry, see if you can find my goddamn contact lens behind those cushions." A fresh round of bawling from upstairs. Gilda recoiled, as if the anal glands of a skunk had let 'er rip. Rounding on Leora: "*The commune was not designed to accommodate YOUNG CHILDREN.*"

"Really sorry ... This my ex-husband's weekend ... last minute crisis ... "

"A teen-aged girl came cantering down the stairs. A cloud of dark hair, oversize tortoise shells – a prettier version of Gilda. "I'm fed up with being sent to a school that's like Bar Mitzvah Central. Why did you send me to that place?"

Leora felt like a prisoner in a hellzapoppin' farce; she half expected to hear the slam of plywood doors.

"Becca, what are you talking about? Buckingham is non-denominational. Isn't there a giant crucifix in the auditorium?"

"Another bummer. D'you realize all the over-the-top bar mitzvahs I had to go to? This kid Fitz-Lloyd Mitnick, his family rented out the Museum of Natural History for the night, with Andy Williams singing Moon River in the African Mammal Room ... Oh, and the one at the Plaza? Everything in fall colors, with fall-themed tablecloths and napkins, gourds, pumpkins with straw. And the 'centerpiece' is live scarecrows standing on the table while you ate. They kept silent and hardly switched positions. I distinctly heard Mr. Mitnick say –

"Okay, okay, you've made your point." Gilda hiked up her low-necked dress; a large WOW button had pulled it south.

" – and the RSVP asked for your shoe size because, surprise! every kid got a pair of high top sneakers and the Harlem Globe Trotters were there to perform and sign sneakers."

"For heaven's sake, Becca, that was all ages ago – "

"That's the point, I've been traumatized. Shit like that you don't forget." She went over to the fireplace and stood with her back to it. "Bryony Cruttwell told me this is what the English do when they fart. Bryony said her mother saw you after a fight with dad, lying in an alley with the toes of your shoes sticking up. I'm sure he had plenty of provocation."

Gilda looked unhappy. But Leora caught a bat-squeak of impatience to get on with the evening's pleasures – or, rather, business. It struck Leora that she and Gilda had something in common.

"Becca, listen, why don't we spend more time together this summer? I'd love it if you moved out here." Leora had never heard this ... *conciliatory* voice of Gilda's ... "I was thinking we could fix up that little apartment over the garage. We could do stuff together, like – I dunno ... shop."

Becca softened, but only briefly. "A little late for that. At those bar mitzvah's the kids always made fun of my hand me downs that never fit ... Anyway, you'd cancel, there's always some bullshit Steering Committee thing that comes up. All you care about is your goddamn March." A disgusted sigh. "I guess you've forgotten about my summer internship at the Queens Detention Center? Of course you have, you're so busy being famous and telling the world how liberated '*the* daughters' will be you never notice your own goddamn daughter. If you weren't Ma Feminism, Family Court would have put me in foster care for gross neglect. Anyway, why would I want to be around your horny old communards? I mean, the other night, Fred ... *eeww* ... made a pass at me."

Fred tripped in, nose first and pigeon-toed, in white ducks and a blue-striped shirt. "Becca, I hope you're not coming to the party tonight in *that*." He motioned at her khaki cut-offs and a tattered grey tee that said, "I Put Out More Than Anybody."

"Why would I go to a party where everyone sucks up to my mother, and wishes she were Monica Fairley instead?"

★

Fred said, "Guess I'm lucky I don't make babies."

Gilda, morose, shook her head no. "You don't understand. Even with all the crap" — she waved her hands about — "I feel *blessed*."

★

Leora sneezed; the sea damp and mold had triggered her allergies. She eyed the sofa where she'd fooled around with Terry that first night. She longed to share a good laugh with him about Henry, get his thoughts on Becca as the daughter of a household name, and much else ... Terry would doubtless be at Grabowski's, along with the Islesfordd poohbahs. But her main business at the party would not have been Terry.

A piercing shriek from the second floor.

Leora took the steps two at a time.

"*Drop* it! *Drop* it!" Florence Luker, the commune's bookkeeper, stood over her Jack Russell terrier who was having his way with a diaper. The dog shook the diaper from side to side, shit flew. "*Dogmatix, drop it!*' The terrier merrily eyed Florence and shook.

Leora whipped out a Pop Tart cracker from her kiddie stash. The terrier dropped his booty and snapped it up.

"You're not supposed to give dogs sugar, it can make them very sick," Florence scolded. Leora scuttled around, cleaning up as best she could. "And why would you leave dirty diapers strewn around?"

Leora observed that Dogmatix had pulled the diaper from the trash and moreover had invaded her space.

"Well, what do you expect, with the smell?"

Becca flounced in brandishing a mason jar filled with a viscous lotion. It gave off a sicky-sweet scent of skin lotion, cologne, and a reassuring after-note of Noxema.

"Anyone know who might be responsible for this?" she said, indignant.

Oh brother. Leora's involuntarily glance at her son gave the game away. Finn was fond of mixing up gooey concoctions with soy sauce and leftovers at Chinese restaurants – "magic potions," he called them. How and when did he get into the guests' cosmetics?

Edwina appeared in the doorway, a vision in a Marimekko jump suit patterned in yellow and charcoal disks, her lower eye lids pearled and mysterious as a Leonardo. Owning all that beauty had to be a full time job. Given that Edwina was neither an actress nor a courtesan, such loveliness seemed superfluous, like a creature's gorgeous plumage that had no function.

Edwina eyed the mason jar Becca still held aloft, Lady Liberty with her torch. Sniffed. "So *that's* where my Erno Laszlo moisturizer went. It only cost me five hundred bucks."

"Finn, what have you been up to?" Leora scolded for form's sake. May as well pack it in here. She could see it: the old Dodge Dart wouldn't start, she would cry, and the children would turn their too-wise gaze on their disaster of a mother.

Edwina was surprised to hear herself laugh. "Maybe you've got a budding chemist on your hands." She looked at these children and her throat went tight. Finn appeared greyish and old for his age, as if he'd been farmed out to the workhouse; the teeth of some small animal had done a job on his shirt. Edwina wondered at the lavender splotch beneath his eye, a birthmark or maybe a burn scar. The little girl's onesie, way too large, puddled around her feet. They were urchins out of Charles Dickens. A little left-over sob escaped Edwina, she must contain a cupboard-full of old sobs. She cut a glance at Leora as if she fed the kids Hostess Cupcakes. Edwina said,

"Finn, dear, that's a lovely shirt, but did something kind of nibble it for lunch?" She crouched beside him for a better look.

"Yeah, my gerbils."

"Oh, I used to have gerbils, they're so dear, the way they curl up together into a fur ball when they sleep."

"Yeah, but the rats ate mine."

A silence stretched. "Does that boy have conjunctivitis?" Florence said loudly. "Do you realize how *contagious* pink eye is?"

Edwina was about to give her what-for, but Finn was staring at Florence with his skewed gaze. "Mom, she looks like Zephyr's aunt in *Babar and Zephyr.*"

Leora, now in a fugue state, recognized that Florence did in fact weirdly resemble Zephyr's red-haired, purse-lipped aunt from the trees of Monkeyville.

A dimple blossomed on Finn's cheek. He was well aware of his own mischief, Edwina thought, charmed. Such a beautiful child. Surely they could do something about that blemish. "You're quite the reader, aren't you."

Cara, no longer amused by the visitors, started to bawl.

"Oh, you little darling!" Edwina crooned, tearing up. "What must you be thinking? Here you are in this funny ole' house with funny people running all around."

She liberated Cara from the crib and nestled her, indifferent to the banana puree on the baby's onesie. Cara pulled her head back and fired off the great super-awake-stare of babies. Edwina walked to the window, rocking and bouncing. "Now let's see, what have we got out here? Tulips." She pointed to the curved driveway below. "Don't you love tulips? See the purple ones? Finn, come look. How many colors do you see?"

Cara only stared in wonder at Edwina. Edwina wondered back at Cara, the mysterious precious weight of her. She'd never had much use for children. She applauded the French for basically ignoring them.

Jo had refused to come out to Islesfordd for Grabowski's fundraiser – "the combination of old money prigs and capitalist pigs would turn my stomach." JoBeth despised everything about Islesfordd and its "smug hetero vibe." Even though Edwina had explained that Fred was her good buddy and only managed to get her into the commune after plying Gilda with whiskey sours and now she felt obliged to show.

In principle Edwina agreed with many of Jo's objections to Islesfordd, yet she sometimes found her lacking in solidarity. After all, she herself struggled to embrace the less attractive aspects of Jo's world. Like Rita Folkenflik's cunt coloring book. Like Jo's buddies the GutterDykes, a band of itinerant lesbians, who sometimes crashed at her pad on Bethune. As Jo had explained, the GutterDykes said to hell with demands for equal pay for equal work, blahbedy blah. To hell with trying to convince guys there was such a thing as a clitoris. "The GutterDykes live as separatists in an alternate, penis-less reality."

Edwina tried to be a good sport about it. Not hard. She had only to picture the way Jo held a cigarette – in her left hand, thumb curled, fourth finger extending just so.

★

A complaint in her gut reminded Edwina that Sebastian Nye might be bringing his dubious keyboard talents to the fundraiser at Dragon's Gate. Gilda and the communards would be there in force – who would notice if she sat this one out? She'd done her part by designing the ad for the benefit in the *Islesfordd Herald*; they'd already raised a hefty sum from the sale of tickets. Enough to print flyers for the benefit that assured potential takers, "*You do not have to be a militant feminist or a man-hater or a bra-burner*" ...

"Leora," Edwina heard herself say, "I gather there's some sort of nonsense with the sitter not showing. Why don't you go to the fundraiser? I mean, Grabowski's your old buddy, isn't he? I'm happy to mind the kids. We'll have fun, won't we, Cara?" She jounced the baby in the crook of her arm.

"Oh, I couldn't possibly ask that."

"You're not asking, I'm offering. Wouldn't surprise me if the sitter shows later, but I'll spell you for now. I suspect it'll be the usual menagerie at Grabowski's, even though it's an event for the Women's Strike – people out here hardly know what cause they wrote a check for. Frankly, I could use a break from the whole scene." She'd avoid not only Nye, but a second, scalier predator, a fixture of Islesfordd evenings.

"Yah, the scene doesn't vary much," Edwina went on. "You generally get a mix of nouveau riche and old Islesfordd at these shindigs. Old Islesfordd means the Rottlesey Club." She rolled her eyes. "You can't apply for membership, they have to find *you*."

"So, in the first camp" – Edwina warmed to her subject – "you get a Milt Merdle. He's a venture capitalist with the most appalling laugh you can hear from Ronkonkoma. The Merdle-esque wives have skinny quads of steel from workouts at the Liesl Butz Studio, the better to grip their husbands with and keep from getting traded in. Quads of steel equals status in Merdle-land – their first wives had thunder thighs."

Florence threw up her hands. "For this Liesl Butz fled Nazi Germany!"

"In the second camp, you get the stiffs from the Rottlesey. That gargoyle Elsie Van Otten – catnip for the tabloids – lives in a derelict mansion with a hundred cats. I think of her as Islesfordd's very own Miss Haversham. Years ago her fiance, a doctor, I think, forgot to show up at the altar. Quackenbush, Elsie's man servant, caretaker, whatever, does her every bidding. The whole town is besotted with things English. Think of the names: Islesfordd, Shittington Grange, The Spotted Dick. English equals *class*. Islesfordd used to be named Poopatucks for the original Indian settlers ... "

Edwina sniffed and eyed Cara. "Oops, speaking of which, better get you changed." She lay Cara on the window seat cushioned in chintz and set about cleaning and re-diapering, wondering how she knew how to do this. Cara, who usually set up a squawk, watched Edwina, mesmerized.

"All spiffy now! Let's see, children, do you have any lovely books we can read together? To Leora's dismay Edwina lifted off the bed a stained and battered item titled *Russian Folk Tales*. Another of Finn's trash can finds. It featured stories called *Fomushka the Village Idiot* and *Ivan the Imbecile*. Leora had checked them out; as the titles promised, the tales offered a perspective that would not go over big with Mister Rogers and "Welcome to my Neighborhood."

"Ackshually, mom doesn't like that book." Finn shot her a sly glance and his cheek dimpled. " Let's go with *Babar and Zephyr*."

A peal of laughter at his precocious "go with." "Of course, dear," Edwina said. "First, why don't we all take a look at a very strange instrument, like a giant piano, called an organ. It's on the stairs one flight up and Finn, dear, you must promise to hold my hand."

Finn jumped up and down. "Oh mom, can we?"

"Edwina, you're so kind to offer, but really, I couldn't – "

"Stop with the Cinderella bit and wear something fabulous." She eyed Leora and sighed. "Forgive me – but when you get to the party, try not to act blown away by it all. So *not cool.* It's a bad idea around here not to have money, and I'd hate to see you chewed up and spat out."

CHAPTER 7

The Party at Dragon's Gate

Women's Liberation is very much a minority movement. It's evangelical. It's a movement that makes people feel good, and there will be a lot of people reading these books who won't do a thing to change the conditions of their lives; still, they like reading about revolution. In one sense it constitutes a kind of pornography; it's a fantasy about the different ordering of things without individuals really doing anything about the ordering.

— *Time Magazine*, August, 31, 1970

"Reading [*Sexual Politics* by Kate Millett] is like sitting with your testicles in a nutcracker."

— George Stade,
professor of English, Columbia University.

"Food comes first and then morality."

— Bertolt Brecht

★

"Deal! Let's shake on it! You may want to shake this hand because I masturbate with the other."

Leora pivoted on the grass to see a devil man with silvery hair, too-black eyes, cruel lips – a plume of sulfur rising off his toes would not have surprised. She suspected she was looking at Lester Annis, Islesfordd's felonious shrink.

Leora was all aflutter to find herself at this distinguished A-list event. Ilesfordd in summer offered big-ticket benefits behind every hedgerow. But this had become *the* must-attend benefit of the young season.

Over a single phone call Gilda had managed to *co-opt* Kaz Grabowski and persuade him to turn his soiree at Dragon's Gate into a fundraiser for the Women's Strike for Equality. No lead time at all. A flurry of planning sessions, jammed phone circuits, mimeographs working overtime – and maybe smoke signals from the Islesfordd Walking Dunes – and the event got cobbled together. Leora's view of Gilda kept flipping between dismay and awe. A nasty-tempered bitch who preferred Big Ideas to actual women (though Nadine and a few actual women could count on her devotion). Yet she'd changed the way people think – with a book that had "sung out" of her, Leora had heard her say. She'd *bullied* this party into being. Gilda in action had so much energy gusting through she needed to be battened down ...

Predictably, a few Old Islesfordd stiffs forbade their wives to attend a party for Women's Strike with "those bra-burners." But many of the town doyennes who had long eluded Gilda were here in force. These "communards" were so *original.* The most exciting thing to happen to Islesfordd since the Commodore of the Rottlesey got caught, pants around his ankles, at the Ramrod Social Club with his brother-in-law. To write a fat check for the Strike was to ride the wave of the revolution that was changing up all the terms, and purchase, with a nice tax write-off, your niche in history. One woman in a Lily Pulitzer thought she might actually *march in the parade*. After, she could meet the husband for dinner and theater, maybe catch that naughty show *Oh Calcutta*, though did she really want Chip gawking at all the pubic hair?

★

Leora lifted a flute of champagne off a passing tray, determined to stay focused on connecting with the host. Every moment brought an influx of guests, but no sign of Kaz. Leora wondered how the valet guys could park the cars fast enough – unless they pulled the whiz-bam parking stunts of Dean Moriarty that Jack Kerouac had exalted in *On the Road*.

She wandered into a room with high-set ogival windows like at Oggsford. Mounted on the wall was a giant pair of lacquered red lips by some Pop Artist. She'd never known "eclectic" could make you nauseous. Henry Lyman dove his arm, elbow deep, behind the cushions of a sofa, and winked at Leora. It struck her as faintly obscene. Omigod ... she'd given her life savings to this clown?

She hurried on to what she supposed was the game room. Elk heads sprouted from the wall displaying spiral antlers. Some poor beast had been butterflied into a rug, head raised and fangs bared. A little yip: a woman's stiletto heel had caught in a fang.

Leora reflected that the only game in Kaz Grabowski's past would have been a Madagascar hissing cockroach.

Outside, torches on bamboo poles tongued the darkening sky. Long tables covered in white damask were set with platters of lobster salad, nova scotia, and prawns of predatory size, each table presided over by a giant pink ice swan to rival the ones on Hooker Pond. Guests converged on the nova, frenzied as a shiver of sharks feeding on menhaden, forking great salmon-colored slabs onto their plates. Framed by a stand of dark green holly, Sebastian Nye sat hook-shaped over a little piano playing *Mack the Knife*. Out toward the pond, resplendent in the dusk, rose the much-maligned sculpture of a plaster cock. Actually, from this angle it appeared to be ... not one at all. Had all the fuss been about a colossal *lipstick*? Mounted on a ... caterpillar track?

Leora's heart flutter-kicked: there was Kaz, greeting guests a ways off by a wrought iron gate. He wore an eggshell linen jacket with pocket handkerchief and a yellow tie. Nye had segued into *The Age of Aquarius* ... The torches flamed ... A *shriek* of laughter ... Kaz had spun all this glitz from nothing ... She might have slipped through a portal into *The Great Gatsby*! Leora pictured Jay Gatsby displaying his *schmattes* to impress Daisy *such beautiful shirts, she sobbed* ...

Of course it was *she* who was kind of pursuing *Kaz*, not the other way around. And the only green light around here glowed from gray metal power boxes with nasty gills and voltage to shock you to kingdom come.

She'd first seen Kaz in less fancy circumstances. A spring evening of junior year in college over ten years years back ... She'd been guzzling Mai Tais at Trader Vic's with her date, an Ivy prince from Princeton. He suggested a carriage ride through Central Park. The black carriages reminded Leora of Chopin's funeral and she pitied the weary horses lifting their tails to take a dump, but the date wanted to play boorish tourist, ironically, of course. Their driver had white-blond hair on a round Russian schoolboy's head and looked too young to drive anything. He kept swiveling on his high perch to glance back at them – her? – with a sly sleepy smile. Flanking their seat, two vials of fuschia and orange flowers made of sateen, plus a gold maple leaf. It made her heart ache, this effort to beautify the carriage, which smelled of stale smoke and the bottoms of tourists from Azerbaijan.

He was moonlighting for his uncle who'd just had his gall-bladder out, the kid said. A vaguely Slavic accent. He seemed eager to convey that he was above driving a horse-drawn carriage. Maybe, like in Cuba, he was a neurosurgeon trying to earn a few extra bucks. Where did she go to college? he asked, turning full around. Her date, placing a warning hand on her knee, said to the kid, "Hadn't you better steer the horse?" Leora had been raised by Lefty parents to be polite to those who serve you (and didn't even like to be served) – so she answered the boy. The wretched horse plodded ahead on autopilot. It was too cruel, she and the preppie blitzed on Mai Tais with tiny parasols from Trader Vic's, and the forbearance of this creature, the bones of its shoulders laboring under the scabby hide.

Later that term the kid appeared backstage at her arty college on the Hudson after her performance in a student operetta called *The End of Humankind*. He thrust a bouquet of roses in wax paper at her. He must've bought them on the subway or something, because the roses were budded up tight and never opened after she put them in a vase with water, just drooped their buds down. In the hall backstage someone said, I could swear I smell horse manure.

His name was Casimir. Originally, Kasimierz. A Polish name, he said. "Call me Kaz." His "r's" were soft, dwelled in the front of his mouth –"exfoliation" would come out "ex-ful-iation." "Ing" became "ink."

"But we don't share a workable frame of reference," she said. He'd pestered so, she finally agreed to meet him at Kettle of Fish cafe in the Village.

"What does that got to do with anythink?" Kaz wondered in his slow sleepy style. He scratched his brush of colorless hair, genuinely puzzled. She might have said, It's raining frogs. Perhaps he hadn't understood?

"We don't have a whole lot in common," she translated.

She put him at maybe four years younger than her and wondered the bar didn't card him. "I live for literature, music, the arts. Those whooping horns in the overture to *Der Rosenkavalier!* They perfectly convey Octavian coming."

Kaz's eyes bugged out in his round head. He'd never heard a nice girl talk dirty.

"I'm going to write a book about George Sand and Chopin at Nohant, Sand's country manor near Bourges. That's in France. Delacroix painted this gorgeous double portrait of them there, but some moron cut the painting in two and it was sold as separate parts."

Kaz scarcely knew what to do with all this. He felt overwhelmed. He felt turned on, like when his step-mother beat him. "Chopin is Polish," he said hopefully, mispronouncing the name. "Just think, if my uncle still has gallbladder, we might not meet." He looked awed that they'd managed to escape this terrible fate. "Tell me what to read."

She was taking a Senior Seminar on Henry James. "Well, you could start with *Washington Square*. It's short. And a great revenge story. This cat called Morris betrays the heroine, an heiress – he was only after her money. Then he has a change of heart, and she turns the tables on him."

The following week: "I saw the movie – they call it '*The Heiress*' – at the Thalia. When Morris comes back to marry Catherine, and she walks upstairs while he pounds on door and calls her name – and she just keeps walking – I clap!"

After Princeton switched her out for a debutante from Virginia horse country, Leora distractedly agreed to go with

Kaz to the Jersey Shore over Memorial Day weekend. She had a monster cold and the rain never let up. They checked into the Seashell Motel. The room's maroon carpet was pocked with cigarette burns and stained with maybe ejaculate. The loneliest motel room in the universe. "Like something out of Edward Hopper," Leora joked. Kaz just looked at her from under his sleepy lids.

The thing about short guys, the anatomy fits to a T. It touched her that Kaz knew how to make love, that somewhere along the line he'd learned this.

It's sometimes hard to distinguish lust from love.

"I'm going to marry you," Kaz said, "you'll see."

She ran her fingers over the pink medallion his scruff had raised on her chin.

Kaz fell into the slot of filler-date; since her amours rarely ran smoothly, she saw rather more of him than she'd expected. Her classmates dated preppies from the Ivies whom they'd known from boarding school. At bull sessions about the meaning of life, they'd decided the ideal man would be an architect, that rare being who made art and also made money. Leora kept Kaz hidden from her friends. As a full scholarship student, she was uncomfortably closer to him on the economic food chain than to her fancy classmates. She often treated him with a distraction that would have driven any sane person away.

Winter weekends of her senior year they roamed the canyons of Manhattan. There was a light-heartedness and ease; no pressure to trot out an ideal version of herself because it wasn't, at least on her side, *serious*. Kaz wasn't of her world. Her current passions – *The Threepenny Opera* and Kurt Weill ... The Beats and *On the Road*'s Dean Moriarty and "the ones who are mad to live" and "burn, burn, burn" – she'd never be done trying to construct her world for him.

She wondered if she were a little in love with Kaz.

One evening Kaz took her to dinner at Little Poland, a community center with a restaurant, where they ate steak and potato dumplings for three dollars.

"Som thinks you don't never forget," he said abruptly, his pupils two hard points. "I used to muck out stalls for my uncle. That's polite for shoveling horseshit, pardon my French. The smell stays in your hair. The worst, I had to clean sheath of male *horses. Sheath is —* " She asked him please not to go on.

"You watch me, I got rule: you earn dollar, and the first person you pay is *you.*"

Leora had stopped listening; any mention of money and her mind glazed over. She was thinking of Strindberg's play *Miss Julie* and how her servant Jean has to flee an outhouse from the bottom through his master's *merde* and comes upon Julie and falls in love.

"Some day we go to George Sand's house in France," Kaz was saying. "You'll see."

One arctic night Kaz took her to a New Year's Eve party thrown by his new boss, a contractor. An Irish architect in a blue work shirt, green wool tie, and suspenders named Sweeney turned everybody in the room, and her life until that point into a blur. He was talking architecture with the resident genius at Penn, second only to Louis Kahn, about his vision of melding Modern with classic architecture, talking so heatedly he forgot to notice the passing of the year. Leora had only ever seen such high color on a girl.

After she got married, some detail about Kaz, his slow, taffy-pull style of speaking, his brush of wheat-colored hair, a moment of motel love, would wave at random from some back alley of her mind. Years later she saw him on a queue for an opening at MOMA of the Frank Lloyd Wright show. He wore a good tweed blazer over an argyle sweater and the same inward smile, rich with secrets. He never made eye contact. Patrick had just gotten "laid off" from the second firm after Porter and Eisen. She prayed that tonight he wouldn't get wasted like the last time.

★

Leora startled: a donkey must have crashed the fundraiser from that farm up the road. She spun around: no, the braying came from a human. Leora guessed from Edwina's rundown that she was hearing venture capitalist Milt Merdle. Every fourth second he cut an explosive hee-haw, as if someone had yanked a cord. One eye was regular, the other bulged out larger and was set on a different axis, as if he'd been formed to cover all the angles. Merdle had built a spread on the Atlantic like an airplane hangar, Edwina had said, with twelve bathrooms, bowling alleys, movie theater, and helicopter pad (the town was suing for noise pollution). He apparently found everything hilarious. The skeletal woman in pink and black Pucci must be his wife, Sophia.

Leora kept an ear tuned to the conversation. The Commodore of the Rottlesey Club was telling the Merdles about the need to curb further development in Islesfordd (code: keep out the "undesirables"). "I hope" *harrumpf* – "to be a good steward of the land," the Commodore said.

Milt Merdle laughed.

★

"Here, hold the goddamn baby, could you? I can't think straight when I'm holding an infant." A woman with a low hairline handed off a bundle to a pale, slope-shouldered man with a pacifier strung round his neck. Leora recognized Hadassah

Sarachild, author of the new book about the male plot to fill the loony bins with "inconvenient" women. Hadassah turned toward another woman and Leora caught only fragments: "We're going to see a day when technology is so strong that women don't have to have babies from inside themselves" ... "I never said, 'all sex is rape.' What I said is that penetrative intercourse is, by its nature, violent" – she paused to seize a passing Belgian endive with crabmeat and caviar – "and that sex" – she crunched the cool white endive brined with crab – "shouldn't put women in a subordinate position."

Infant Sarachild started fussing. Hadassah rounded on the slope-shouldered man. "Where'd you put the damn Enfamil?"

Leora was in a tizzy. She rarely got out, and mainly to go to Daitch Shopwell, the pediatrician, or Rexall for her Valium, where the busybody pharmacist went *tsk tsk*, you don't wanna take *that* ... And here she was in this happenin' place.

She recognized Elsie Van Oppen from the tabloids, the freaky heiress who lived in a mansion with all the cats. They'd called the County Fire Department on her to cart away the cat shit and hose the place down. Elsie wore a Maharajah turban with a shiny red pendant dangling off it, the whole affair tacked at the neck with pipe cleaners. On second look, Leora saw the pendant was a red flying fish, maybe an actual fishing lure.

The hulk positioned deferentially behind her must be Quackenbush, her man-of-all-trades. He was lantern-jawed, with eyes sunk deep in his head, and appeared more Elsie's appendage than a free-standing being. Quasimodo, the man behind Leora called him. Apparently the poor guy also did yard work around Islesfordd.

Elsie gazed at Leora, eyes shining with vampiric rapture. Effing certifiable. If she herself walked around the world looking like that they'd cart her off to the county Bedlam she'd seen on the Expressway, its windows flaming orange in the sunset; an Elsie van Otten was just "eccentric." "Islesfordd's very own Miss Haversham," jilted at the altar Edwina had said. The shock of getting jilted at the altar must have scrambled her brain.

"The host is a nouveau with appalling – *Greek* taste," Elsie said to a fellow guest, glancing round, fish-lure swinging.

Leora had checked her esthetic standards at the driveway with the Botero sculpture, and she wasn't sure where "Greek" came in – but the style here, she thought uneasily, was definitely dog's breakfast.

"They say Grabowski made his money running a string of ho-houses in the Orient."

Well, that had a certain louche appeal. But why trust anything Elsie Van Bonkers might say about their host? Yes, she'd love more champagne. Amazing! You need only stick out your hand and whatever you desired landed in it! Leora caught a scent of honeysuckle, innocent and bucolic, an emissary from a gentler world.

"It's *impossible* to find good help out heah," a woman said.

Sophia Merdle, wife to the laugher. She spoke in a quavery, self-enamored warble that could single-handedly bring back the guillotine.

"Tell me about it," her friend said. "I'd settle for someone who won't raid the liquor cabinet."

Sophia nodded, her face a map of commiseration. She inclined toward a waiter, sticking out her butt in deference, to capture a flute of champagne. Leora wondered if such body language could be acquired, or did it require a certain net worth. "The wu-u-rst is my mother's helpuh. She doesn't get up till noon. There I am in my studio with the weur-k – "

The work? The friend drew a blank. Oh, of course, Sophia made "art" from colored strings reminiscent of hair that collects in the shower drain ...

" – and I'm thinking Lolita is parading half-naked around Milt – like the girl who ran off with Gertie Chasm's *ancient* husband ..."

"I wouldn't worry, Milt is besotted with you."

"Actually, he wants to buy me an island off Virgin Gorda. I'm thinking of creating an art work by building a little oasis in the middle of the sea with three palm trees on it."

The friend leaned in: "Frankly, I came tonight mainly to see what the fuss is all about. 'Cuz I don't really get it. Why would I want to go on a Women's *Strike*? I *love* the idea of looking gorgeous and having men whistle at me."

Leora stopped listening. What a trove of stories and characters here! The mother's helper helping herself to mother's husband ... The *Islesfordd Herald* regularly reported pitched battles between warring interests – like the sugar baron with forty acres on Hooker Pond, who claimed the kayakers were "pepperazi" come by to gawk. He'd bought up all the kayak rental stores, and now the Tourist Board was suing him. Meanwhile the swells with houses overlooking Bacchus Beach had their knickers in a twist over the "fagalas" who left condoms in the dunes for their children to find. Hell, they'd gobble this stuff up at *Gotham*!

Leora had beavered away for the magazine on "service pieces" (*The Best Place in the City to Buy a Vibrator*), filler that had gotten her north of nowhere. She itched to write one of those "lifestyle" pieces on the hustle for power and status in New York that was Gotham's calling card. She could persuade Terry Cameron to edit her, fat chance.

Bottom line, though, combing the Want Ads for a full-time job and posing as a normal person at interviews was itself a full-time job, especially with the city now mired in a financial crisis. She could ill afford the life of a free-lance writer. Free lance was for people who didn't need health benefits for their children. The great heroines of fiction never worried about health benefits. Except, in Jane Austen, where, in a sense, everything was about health benefits. Come to think of it, the Marriage Plot was at least partly the Health Benefits Plot.

Sophia Merdle moved in too close and Leora had to resist backing away. "When is Gilda Gladstone going to speak?" she warbled. "I hear she's a *fiery* speakuh."

Sophia's skin was ultra creamy – how many wool-bearing mammals had died to keep her in lanolin from their sebaceous glands? Her whippet thinness rebuked the peasants who took solid nourishment. Her own bod, Leora fretted, an exercise in bad design, starting with the scoliosis, and what about her mind, chasing itself in circles and slaloming around like the dog with rabies from her old neighborhood in Queens ...

"Casimir needs a woman to show him how to spend his money," Sophia purred.

Oh really? How did Sophia know his name?

Her own agenda here made her suddenly queasy. *Was she a gold digger?* She couldn't live with herself if she were. She lifted another flute of champagne off a passing silver tray and examined herself on this point.

Actually, she was more of a tin digger. A pig iron scrap digger. She glanced around: damn, *must* Kaz be so conspicuously consumptive? He was kind of overdoing it; like a six-year-old repeating the same lame joke. She administered a mental slap: she'd checked her scruples in the driveway along with her esthetic standards, remember? Scruples were a luxury beside the need to survive. Scruples were a cul de sac in the evolutionary chain ...

Hell, didn't Jane Austen's Lizzy dig Mr. Darcy more after viewing his humongous estate? She could learn to adjust upward.

It might be kind of a novelty to adjust upward, since she'd already had much success adjusting downward. If she ever managed to put it together with Kaz, she'd suggest doing something really cool with Dragon's Gate. They themselves would live in the caretaker's cottage. The rest they'd turn into a summer retreat for kids from Harlem and her slum in the Lower East Side, rotate in whole busloads of children every week. Old Quasimodo could teach weight training or bell ringing. She laughed out loud to picture the reaction along Hooker Pond.

CHAPTER 8

The Party at Dragon's Gate Gilda

"There is only one happiness in life, to love and be loved."

– George Sand

"Marry me a Little"

– title of a song by Stephen Sondheim

Leora spotted Kaz down by the garden gate and decided to make her move. She was distracted by a fracas nearby. A figure in a scarlet dress elbowed through a clutch of women to open a path, God parting the Red Sea. Gilda Gladstone: was she about to speak?

No, she was streaking toward Kaz.

The women stretched out hands toward Gilda: "Thank you thank you" ... "You changed my life" ...

Gilda flicked her wrist their way. "Oh, people tell me that all the time."

"Now I know why I've been asking myself, 'Who am I?'" ...
"Yeah, yeah," Gilda muttered.

A woman in flowered bell bottoms stood directly in her path: "I am never going to forget that I am not my husband's other self – I am ME!" Gilda kept barreling toward Kaz, clipping the woman's shoulder. The woman teetered backwards. "Heavens, she almost knocked me over!"

Leora suspected Gilda had never located that wayward contact lens. Even without 20/20 vision, though, her radar locked onto the desirable men. Maybe she used echolocation like a bat.

By the time Gilda made it to the garden gate Kaz had been danced away by host duties. Gilda scanned the party for who else. Terry, maybe? A woman with a dark glossy beehive seized her arm: "Gilda Gladstone, I'll bless you as long as I live. I've been dying to ask: could you keynote our Women's Temperance League next month?"

"Join us, sister, join us," Gilda said, moving off.

She spotted Henry in a huddle with two ladies in Farah Fawcett shags from the Village Improvement Society. Sure enough, he was trying to hornswoggle them into investing in – what was it this time? Oh Jesus, that farmland in Adair, Iowa? "Expect to post returns of 4,200% over ten years ... Farmland is where it's at .... As the saying goes, they just aren't making any more of it ... "

For a second Gilda was tempted to warn the women off. She suspected she'd never see a penny of the hefty sum she'd forked over for the farmland deal – the "insider tip of a lifetime" – an investment triggered less by wisdom than lust. At least she'd had the wits to pull her money away from that dud "set to skyrocket" involving cutting edge, uh, back surgery.

She'd met Henry at the Fund for Empowering Empowerment, where he'd been trolling for clients. The conference ran late and she put him up in her apartment, an aerie with balcony high above Lincoln Center. The next morning Becca left early. Gilda lolled among her pillows – satin-encased to prevent wrinkles; hypoallergenic for her asthma – nursing her second Espresso, all but forgetting her guest was still there. Nadine had complained that once she was in shouting distance of fifty, caffeine – practically *anything* – would trigger monster sweats, turning her slick all over. So galling when she was on a book tour. Gilda had given menopause the slip. No time. How could she be bothered when she was jetting around the globe to give talks, working on the new book, laying the groundwork for the Women's Political Caucus, etc. etc.? She'd just turned forty-nine. An age she planned to remain for the duration.

Henry appeared in the door to her bedroom – to say his thank you's, she supposed. His blue eyes twinkled at her over his low-set glasses, as she lay propped up on the pillows, newly streaked hair waving about her shoulders, peach nylon negligee framing her decolletage. He appeared to reflect for a moment. Then he shucked his clothes and stood with his furry chest and cal-iper-shaped legs and cock at attention and climbed into her bed.

She had feared physical love might be done with her, though she felt far from done with it.

It had been lovely, the first couple of years with Henry. His eyes behind the specs riding low on his nose could turn amorous in a heartbeat – and it was off with his baby blue cashmere crewneck. He wrote to her: *I want to breathe you in ... I want to get a little drunk with you tonite ... Your energy and vision and SPIRIT turn me on ...* They traveled. She took him to the conference on New Leadership in Copenhagen, on World Gender Equality in Mexico City, on the Paradigmatic Paradigm of Whatsit in Oslo. They'd retreat to the local Hilton, order up champagne, wreck the joint (except in Mexico, where the dysentery they breed there made it advisable to take separate rooms). He was a frequent weekend guest at the commune.

One minor complication: Henry had a wife. Gilda-and-Henry were an open secret; she was photographed everywhere, sometimes with Henry in full view. Even cuddling with Henry. The wife, Tinka, ensconced in a Greek Revival house on Boston's Beacon Hill, appeared not to mind, or at least voiced no objections. Gilda guessed that at some level Tinka was rather *pleased*. It reflected well on *her* that this otherwise dullish husband, with his carefully curated pleasures – like the P-rade at his Princeton reunion: should he go as a Roman legionnaire? a toreador? part of a 50-strong "centipede"? – had managed to attract a household name.

He and Tinka slept in separate bedrooms in the house on Beacon Hill. Still, Henry became wracked with guilt over his off-duty life (though not so wracked that he stopped pursuing it). The guilt became a third presence, like his spinal stenosis. When Gilda invited him to go with her on a speaking engagement on the QE2, or fly first class (always in her contract) to a conference in Anchorage, where they rode in sleighs and ate cranberry venison stew, the guilt receded.

One Sunday Henry rolled out of bed and pulled on his plaid bathrobe. "I love and admire you and I love us, but it's killing me. And it's not fair to you. You've understood all along I could never leave my wife."

"Of course I have," Gilda said, alarmed. "And I'm not asking you to. I have no wish to be a home-wrecker."

He looked wounded. "But we can't go on this way."

"I don't see why not."

He needed to choose, Henry said.

Gilda had no desire to choose, or be chosen. She wanted to ... go on this way. The violence of her marriage – a *dual*

violence, they'd been like a match to kerosene – and the tortuous
divorce – had wrecked the wife thing for her. She had trouble
seeing herself fulltime with any man. He'd leave the toilet seat
up and nose hairs in the sink and insist she spend Thanksgiving
with his dreary relatives, the aunts with cat-eye glasses, gramps
who read the "funnies," the alkie brother with purplish hands
whose wife would ask for her autograph – *NO*.

She needed to see daylight between her and Henry. She
liked the freedom of part-timey. The mix of sex, companionship,
work; the occasional luxury of (a very brief!) stretch alone – why,
it was perfect. She'd fly with Henry to the conference on The
Goddess in Every Woman and they'd knock around Stockholm
for two days – and after, she'd wave Henry off and turn the
key to her apartment (oh, that satisfying click as the cylinder
turned over). The fridge would be empty except for cottage
cheese wearing a green yarmulke and maybe a bottle of Chablis. She'd unhook her bra and sit on the sofa covered in puce
sailcloth with the pink and orange pillows from Marimekko
and put her feet up on the cracked leather ottoman and write
the hell-raising speech for WOW she'd jotted notes for on a
cocktail napkin. She might take a goblet of Chablis out to her
26th floor balcony looking south over the city's turrets. Henry
was afraid of heights.

The commune, the elective family she'd long dreamt of,
had become an essential cog in this life. That you were no damn
good at marriage didn't mean you needed to live in quarantine
or jump into another hellish union. At the commune she could
shed "Gilda Gladstone" and schlump around in her fuzzy robe
over breakfast – there would always be someone around to
make a cheese omelet or brew up another pot of Colombian.
She could take refuge from the coupled world without being
judged. The commune, like family, had to take you in. Too bad

Fred brought around good looking women – like that Laura or whoever – what *was* her damn name? Not really pretty, actually, but *younger*. Predatory. Lying in wait to snap up a guy she herself might enjoy.

At the magic hour of dusk the communards often gathered round the pond, kvetching about who was Kaiser of KP that week or celebrating their "family of choice" over a third round of vodka gimlets – Gilda thought of them at such moments as characters from Chekhov in a once-grand country house. One evening she'd caught this *Laura* sitting on the grass in her infernal hot pants, knees hiked, offering a crotch shot up one side. Terry Cameron had almost fallen out of his Adirondack chair. She sensed Laura was no feminist, either; Gilda smelled a heretic. The girl might have been sent by that John Bircher Phyllis Schlafly to infiltrate the commune. The way the butch lesbian had been sent by the FBI to wreck the movement. Schlafly might want revenge for that debate where – well, Gilda had called the wretched woman a witch and hissed, "I'd like to burn you at the stake." Not her finest moment, Gilda thought.

Maybe she did want Henry to choose. *Her.*

★

"Tinka suggested you come spend the weekend with us in Marblehead. We'll go for a sail in the Catalina 16, always a good stiff breeze …"

What? "Henry, that's very kind of her, but I don't think so." Open relationships were now all the rage, and Henry had once let drop that his wife was interested in a threesome of some sort. How did someone with the name Tinka even *know* about threesomes? She herself, Gilda reflected, was pretty meat-and-potatoes and perfectly content with a twosome. Of one thing she was certain: she didn't want Tinka horning in on what was her and Henry's. She'd begun to want more of her and Henry. She'd underestimated Tinka's emotional IQ. Why fight your husband's mistress when you could *co-opt* her?

Late that summer Henry developed shortness of breath and was rushed to surgery. The operation on his aortic valve was a success (at least for the doctors), but it left Henry the unwanted door prize of narcolepsy and a weak sex drive.

Gilda felt betrayed. Henry had loved her, genuinely, loved her body and the way she looked. She thought she'd found her person, to wake up with and have coffee and read the Sunday *Times* with and travel to the world's exotic locales. Now he wasn't holding up his end. His investment schemes had turned so wacky, people fled at his approach. She wondered if surgery plus the meds hadn't unhinged him. He grew so tight he roamed the commune after nightfall turning off lights to reduce the electricity bill they all paid a share of. He wanted to monitor the number of squares of toilet paper used by each communard and charge accordingly. He insisted on wearing the "sticky socks" the hospital had supplied for his surgery. Where he'd once been New England-eccentric, Henry was now an embarrassment, nodding off in the bouillabaisse at the French Consulate's party, plumbing sofas for escaped change. She kept him around like her cracked leather ottoman, a doze-y consort to ward off the perception that she was desperate. She *was*. The most decrepit guy could be dusted off and propped up and re-purposed as a plausible mate by a resourceful woman. Sort of the way they repurposed cars, and just about everything else, in Havana. When it came to women of forty-nine – even world-famous ones – men did not return the favor.

Gilda checked some notes she'd scribbled on a napkin for her speech. "*It is easier to live through someone else than to become complete yourself.*" Well, she'd become complete herself, and more. Like Bella, Florence, Nadine. Monica Fairley, that bitch, played the double game of preaching self-sufficiency while sleeping with New York's most desirable men.

Even complete, Gilda reflected, she felt *more* complete with a man. With any luck, posterity would never be the wiser.

CHAPTER 9

Party at Dragon's Gate Nadine

I was a bride married to
amazement ...
I don't want to end up simply
having visited this world.

— Mary Oliver

A sudden splash – then a rush to the pool, the way people on a beach move as a herd toward a shark sighting or casualty of the surf.

Someone had jumped in naked. Milt Merdle's hee-haw exploded above the melee. It was perfect! Way more fun than the evening's competing event, the Gala for Recovering Wife Beaters.

And just moments ago, someone had been dressed down for using a gold toilet that was Pop Art! Poop Art, people were joking.

Through the crowd Nadine spotted Hadassah Sarachild frolicking in the pool, her melon breasts bobbing.

She stepped away from the crush into a little gazebo mimicking a "folly" at Versailles, in no way compatible with Dragon Gate's design statement of a chateau in the Loire Valley on LSD.

Nadine had spent an eventful couple of weeks. Her restored appetite for the things of this world, unlike so many impulses, had legs. Maybe she should thank Peter Grosvenor for almost doing himself in. She could hardly bear to think now of all she'd miss after she passed off the scene and the world went on, unforgivably, without her. She missed it already, the things of the world going on without her. She missed things she could still have. The books she had yet to write, July nights in Avignon, guacamole, the next eclipse ... Brainstorming with Gilda about the Women's Strike. She missed love and all the fucks she'd missed. The fucks she might still have ...

She'd recently sighted herself in Bonwit's window in that upper-body *clench* ... the hunched posture adopted by older women, as if they feared getting snatched away any moment by death. She put herself on Fogey Alert. Shoulders back, heart out, chest proud ... *Don't waddle* ... No more sleeveless ... She continued smartly down Fifth.

She had actually, well ... checked out the Personals in *The New York Review of Books*.

★

She'd never reveal such a defection, a regression to the old man-centric crap. She owed herself, her image as a feminist figurehead. She'd just published her article, *Does Marriage Have a Future?* and was working up a landmark paper about a matrilineal culture in which men would become non-essential. Nadine was especially eager to conceal her flirtation with the Personals after the drubbing from the sisters over her latest book.

Damaged and Confused argued that the new sexual equality had turned men into wrecks, boats bobbing about the open sea with no steering mechanism. Nadine's misplaced empathy was undermining the feminist revolution, the sisters said; whatever shit is bothering men, let *them* the fuckers, worry about it .... Others dismissed the book as pop psychology. Even Gilda had kind of held her nose.

The truth was, they were envious. After a long career belaboring points in academic jargon with only a passing resemblance to English and proof-reading pages of footnotes, she'd written a short, nasty book that – just this summer! – had climbed onto the *Beavers*'s Non-fiction Best Seller list ...

★

"*WIFE WANTED: intelligent, beautiful, 18 to 25*" ...
Scratch that one.

"*FOXY SENIOR, 84, seeks woman, 50 to 65, to share walks from parking lots to doctors' offices. Must like detailed descriptions of illnesses and grandchildren's pictures. Limited flatulence, clacking teeth ok.*"

How much flatulence was "limited?" Nadine wondered.

"*ANTEDILUVIAN MARINER (M) seeks attractive coxswain (F) to put in at terra firma amidst coming torrents.*"

That was more like it. "Long-term relationship inevitable," Nadine would have added.
"*PORTLY, HANDSOME MAN, 71 summers, some hair and teeth, ample supply Spanish fly.*"

Nadine circled that one.

"*WORN-OUT HUSBAND*, seeks wealthy, titled, childless widow of an unentailed estate to swap podiatry, colonoscopy, and dental stories; knowing "Mairzy Doats" a plus. Large type for response."

"*DISPROPORTIONATELY BLESSED GENERALISSMO, deposed by an ungrateful peasantry, seeks a talented contortionist with low morals and high pain threshold for long-term relationship, satori, and maybe a little narco-crime on the side*" –

Sense of humor, that one. But "high pain threshold?"

★

She arranged to meet PORTLY/HANDSOME in the bar of The Library restaurant on Upper Broadway near her apartment. She'd mailed him the only picture she had on hand: a jacket photo with a resemblance, people volunteered, to Faye Dunaway.

She felt the laser-beam of an appraisal through the double-paned window as she walked to the entrance of The Library; willing herself to move briskly *heart out*! in spite of the sciatica shooting pain down her flank. A quick glance around the restaurant: no one here she knew, thank God.

A few pro forma exchanges, and the ensuing chill made Nadine wonder if she should have contacted the flatulent Generalissimo or FOXY SENIOR.

Nadine, you are not the woman in the photo, PORTLY HANDSOME said, his voice reasonable and sweet. Tell me, Nadine, do you really think that's fair? Is it fair, I ask you, to expect me to ride my motorcycle all the way across Central Park when you have so mis-represented yourself? I mean, from your photo I thought – I mean, to be honest, I'm only attracted to women who menstruate. I would have thought better of you, an authoress who writes a book about the fallout of feminism on men. I tell 'ya honey, it's just this kind of BS that can really mess a guy up!

★

FAT ASS UGLY, You have the worst nose job I've ever seen and your plastic surgeon's license should be revoked; your hair implants resemble dune grass seedlings to prevent erosion; and in the interests of public safety you should be driving a motorized chair, not a motorcycle. This speech came to her only after she'd safely closed the door of her apartment behind her.

Even with her funky hip, she'd moved fast. She'd spotted at a back table in the restaurant *oh my God* JoBeth Mankiller. She'd once attended JoBeth's all-female seder, along with the notorious Viola Liposkaya-Rothbottom, who'd attempted to murder Andy Warhol.

Her last view of PORTLY he was sitting at their table flossing his teeth.

★

A chance encounter upended her world.

She'd just wrapped a talk on *Damaged and Confused* in Islesfordd's Bullhampton Hall. Her spiel incited the usual attacks from radical zealots, in particular a posse that called itself GutterDykes (especially unpleasant as they were friends of Edwina's partner, JoBeth). Nadine had done feminism a disservice, a GutterDyke said, by suggesting it put men's balls in a vise. That was an okay thing! the woman said. The problem was Nadine didn't seem to think so, in fact, was altogether too empathetic toward men and their well-earned woes. (One of the posse had written about "not only divesting men of 'cock privileges,' but – *why not say it?* – divesting them of cocks.") Nadine trotted out the canned rebuttals (she'd grown skillful at this). As the crowd was dispersing, a man approached the little stairs to the stage. Dark gold skin like Nehru's, thick brows that hunkered over his eyes, rumpled striped shirt with a tie, no jacket. The sight of him stirred up something she'd forgotten she could want.

"Dr. Kusnetz, I want to thank you for your generosity in writing a book that finally gives men a voice" (eyes dark grey). "Men are royal jerks and we've had it good, too good, for too many years" (such a big fellow, bit of a gut). "At the risk of sounding even jerkier" (a panda/bear of a guy) "I consider myself a male feminist" (boyish, it was the full childish mouth). "But men have paid a price for buying into some of the new trends" (the diction Ivy, no regional marker) ... "Like the house-husbands who've accepted the role of baby sitter and home maker" ... *You've captured men's psychic and physical distress ... I admire your courage in defying .... your empathy in this wonderful ... this wonderful ...*

The sense of words hardly mattered. She felt a mighty letting go of the ligatures that pinned her together, stood there emptied out and opened up. The man talked and talked and Nadine nodded at what she guessed were appropriate intervals. His skin would feel rough-smooth, with the warmth underneath of a human man's, and taste of salt from her tears. On rare occasions she'd seen such men. Once during a vacation in Antigua she'd hiked up a hill with an English doctor. Another beamed a lost smile from the Obits. They presumably existed, such men, in the same time space continuum that she occupied, but might as well inhabit Pluto ... Yet here was this man.

A little shell-shocked. As if his missus had just checked off a laundry list of his worst offenses against womankind. Perhaps his interest in her topic was more than academic?

His rumpledness said academic, but had he mentioned he "worked in finance?" Would she ever find him again? She distractedly thanked a woman who said, You stick to your guns, honey, and she watched the man melt into the crowd.

That's the life I should have had, Nadine thought.

CHAPTER 10

The Party at Dragon's Gate: Leora and Kaz

"Can't repeat the past?...Why of course you can!"

— F. Scott Fitzgerald, *The Great Gatsby*

The moment Kaz saw her his eyes changed. He detached himself from his group and walked toward her over the grass. His toe caught on some low-lying Pop Artifact and he stumbled. A flicker of anger that went out like a firefly.

"Leora Voss, I thought you'd never come, I'm so happy to see you. What a lovely dress." She smoothed the skirt of a lavender cotton number borrowed from the girl in *Cristina's World*. She felt happy, too, his sleepy eyes, pale brush of hair, Polish "r" that hadn't changed. They stood there, hands hanging, smiling and stupid from the pleasure of it.

She said, "I was held up by, you know, babysitter problems."

He nodded, suddenly serious. He appeared to know she had kids. *She* knew he hadn't married. He'd followed her, as she'd followed him.

"Do you manage okay? I mean with two young children?"

Swatting away the condescension: "'*Manage*'? The children are the joy of my life."

"You never thought about marriage and children," he said, as if suddenly back in 1960. "You were the only girl who didn't, you always wanted something different. You didn't need women's lib. This march they're planning" – he arced his hand toward the crowd – "you were already there."

She'd been so alone. "Who could have imagined the women's movement back then?" Leora said. "In those days the only way for a woman to 'live all the way up' like Hemingway's damn bullfighters was to resist: everything they wanted for you. But you couldn't just ignore the rest of the world" with impunity." A moment. "You couldn't refuse to follow the crowd," she prompted, "without getting roughed up a bit."

"You look like ... like Leora, same as always." His eyelids heavy as a dreaming lizard's. The air went wavy between them. "Y'know, you opened up the world to me. Chopin, George Sand. Henry James and *Washington Square* – well, the movie, anyway."

"Oh, right, '*The Heiress*.' With Olivia de Havilland, such a movie star-type name. We're such different people now, don't you think? They say we change all our cells every seven years ... " She rattled on, flinging out words to avoid *going back*. She didn't care to go spelunking in the past, she wanted certain events in the past to be sealed in a cavern with a rock jammed into the entrance.

"The other week when you called, it felt like life throws me geeft," Kaz said, lapsing into the familiar accent.

"The serendipity of finding that we're neighbors – it's pretty amazing." A moment. "A happy accident," she translated.

"*You ordered a perfect night, Kaz, must have been your little rain dance.*"

From within their bubble they both turned to stare at the interloper: Lester Annis/devil man. A flick of anger from Kaz, swift as the one she'd seen earlier.

Kaz introduced her, an "old friend." Leora nodded, rather than shake, because she couldn't remember which hand did what.

"How do you two know each other?" Annis said, satanic eyes scanning something flammable between them.

"We met on account of an uncle's gallbladder operation," Leora blurted, breaching her own advice to herself.

Kaz frowned. Clearly, he didn't care to be reminded of his first life, seeing as he was on his 4th or 5th. "Please excuse us," Kaz said to Annis, I must show Leora something."

He guided her by the elbow to a pond gouged into grass the kelly green of astroturf. Leora looked down at the bloated golden koi weaving about, propelled by fish desires. Kaz said,

"This is not the moment tonight, I need to be host – but perhaps we could meet again so we can talk?" His voice burred. "We have lot of catching up."

"Yes, perhaps we could meet again." She was almost inaudible. That night in the Edward Hopper motel on the Jersey shore ... Kaz just a kid ... The body remembers ... She focused on a fat fish that hung in the pond alone, unmoving. *Tell me when, tell me where ...*

She was still waiting on Kaz to advance the plot when a server rounded on them swinging a silver tray. Kaz held him off with the flat of his hand.

"Are you happy?" he said.

She shifted her head back, disconcerted. "Is one ever? I mean, *completely* happy? I sometimes wonder if we were even *meant* to be happy. If that doesn't sound too much like *The Three Sisters*." Chekhov, Russian playwright she refrained from adding.

"Another book I must read." His eyes fixed on her as if seeing the portal to Chopin and the rest. "I get everything I need," he said.

A weird ring to that; something around the edges suggested more than just a statement of fact. They might be reading lines from different playbooks. She only half-listened as he told her about a cache of "valuable artifacts" and a painting from the 19ᵗʰ century that he'd long coveted, discovered at auction, and "snapped up." "I think this stuff would interest you," Kaz said.

★

Gilda came barreling toward them. A woman trailed her, tottering in her strappy sandals and out of breath: "You've given us a new world, where the daughters no longer have to play games – "

A second woman stepped forward: "And men no longer have to play supermen!"

Gilda kept on course. "Do it, sisters," she threw out, "you have nothing to lose but your vacuum cleaners!"

The women looked puzzled.

"Gilda Gladstone, it's an honor to have you as my guest," Kaz said, "I'm delighted we could put this evening together" (the "r's" at the front of his mouth). He inclined slightly from the waist. The kid driving the horse carriage had come a ways. "Of course you know Leora Voss."

Gilda grunted and waved a dismissive hand that just missed striking Leora's chest. Gilda hadn't remembered the lord of Dragon's Gate as this ... magnetic. "I'm thrilled at the way you've thrown your support behind the Strike," she gushed.

"It's such a pleasure to be neighbors. We've been admiring your outdoor sculpture, we get a great view from Cormorant Cove. Such original work! You're a De Medici of Pop Art."

"You're too kind."

"I hope you'll join us next week at the commune for a brainstorming session about the Strike. We would value your, uh, input."

"It would be honor to contribute any way I can."

"And after the meeting, I hope you'll stay for dinner – and maybe a round of charades," Gilda said, giddy as a young girl.

Gilda in high flirtation mode was not a pretty sight. From what Leora knew of the commune's style of charades, Kaz might come up short. The communards liked to one-up each other, picking esoteric titles and topics impossible to act out. The president of Grubb Fidelity – notorious around Islesfordd for ordering his girlfriend to mail herself to him in a carton – had drawn "Antidisestablishmentarianism." He was not amused.

"Tell me," Gilda said, "how did you develop your taste as an art collector? You have what a fellow collector I know calls 'an educated eye.'"

Leora tamped down the laughter gathering force like an impending sneeze. The moment had arrived to surrender their host to Gilda. The crowd was getting restive, itching to hear her speak. A committee member was pushing toward them. Leora shot Kaz a little horizontal wave. The initial contact, rich with promise, had been made; there was sure to be a sequel.

And then Gilda was hustled to an improvised podium against the house. A snick snick of flashbulbs, the cold lights of fireflies. Gilda stood up there, breast-y in the red Empire dress, neckline dipping low, streaked hair in feathery waves, and started speaking to the crowd in a natural voice, rushed yet peppered with hesitancies, the rhythm of speaking with a friend. She spoke in a lower register than Leora had heard at commune dinners, a warm contralto with broad vowels from the heartland. *We're about to take the next step forward ... The reward is in the here and now ... Our ability to be alive and be ourselves .... Millions of ordinary human women for the first time are changing the course of history ... Changing the agenda for our sons and daughters ...* She waved her hands about, pulled them to her chest, thrust them out. *We're making* HER*story* –

Yikes! Was that a boob half-popped out? The neck of Gilda's dress had moseyed down past her shoulder ... A few murmurs and snickers, people craned around to see ... Gilda somehow shrugged it all back together and went on with her spiel, never missing a beat.

The guests assembled there forgot for a moment to be good stewards of the land; forgot for a moment to wonder where they could launder their next gazillion; or whether the mother's helper was maybe welcome to her husband, the lousy bastard; or how much flatulence was "limited;" or how to nudge the marriage plot forward ... With consummate skill – because no skill showed – Gilda was flying without a net, no notes, improvising, speaking as she always did, yet maybe sober. Gilda conjured up the new peaceable kingdom *sans* the battle of the sexes – no more of *that* tired shit ... *Men are saying* NO *to masculinity,* NO *to the need always to be dominant and never show any softness,* NO *to that brutal, sadistic, tight-lipped Ernest Hemingway* – [a passing plane garbled her words] ... *There are no bears to kill ... Men will welcome their liberation and the end of their loneliness ... They'll live longer! And welcome a woman who can come out from behind that simpering mask that hides so much impotent rage ...*

And you and your generosity will be part of Herstory. The Women's Strike is planned for exactly fifty years since the suffragettes marched ... On August 26 women doing menial chores in the offices as secretaries will cover their typewriters and unplug their switchboards, and waitresses will stop waiting, cleaning women stop cleaning, and everyone who is doing a job for which a man would be paid more ... Stop!

And when it gets dark, instead of cooking dinner or making love we will assemble, and we will carry candles symbolic of the flame of that passionate journey down history.

CHAPTER 11

The Media Elite

"There has come into existence, chiefly in America, a breed of men who claim to be feminists. They imagine that they have understood 'what women want' ... They help with the dishes at home and make their own coffee in the office, basking the while in the refulgent consciousness of virtue."

– Germaine Greer

"Even the brightest movement women found themselves engaged in sullen public colloquies about the inequities of dishwashing and the intolerable humiliations of being observed by construction workers on Sixth Avenue. (This grievance ... seemed always to take on unexplored Ms. Scarlett overtones, suggestions of fragile cultivated flowers being "spoken to," and therefore violated, by uppity proles.)

– Joan Didion

★

"So what happened with your marriage? You don't have to answer," she added.

"Thanks."

She couldn't put a foot right with Terry, and it was somehow he who made it so. She'd run into him here at her own secret place: Little Harbor, Islesfordd's small boat alternative to Megalomantic Marina (so named in recognition of the Indians who'd got there first). Apparently, it was Terry's place, too. The fog had socked in, chasing the fishermen and boaters. They'd fallen into step together because it seemed more awkward not to, and maybe from a mutual urge to annoy.

"Isn't it weird how we reify 'marriage,'"? Leora said, to fill dead air. "Make it into a concrete thing? It's like 'he, she and some third baggy monster: '*The Marriage.*'"

"You don't need to define 'reify' for me," Terry said shortly. "Maybe you hang out with people unacquainted with the mother tongue."

Fuck you! She was about to split, when she noticed the putty-colored shore up ahead was ... *on the move.* "Oh, my God, the kingdom of fiddler crabs!" Tiny, scuttling crabs beyond counting had colonized this section of shore. They were comical, with their hyper-claw carried horizontally up front like mini-knights a lance. Touching, to think how tiny they were and how plucky with that one weapon mounted for business.

"We're interlopers here," Terry said, his voice awed, inviting her in. "When you think of the industry of critters around us we never give a thought to. Fish that make their own light. Humpback whales singing – complex songs with patterns. It's like we live amidst a series of parallel universes like concentric rings and we're completely oblivious. These crabs are busy little buggers, mating, eating, digging. The male uses that big claw as a mating claw to wave at females."

He squatted in a fluid motion, lean thighs straining his chinos, to watch a crab vamoose down the portal to its marine chambers. It was always telling to observe a man around animals, even if it was only critters scarcely bigger than the water bugs surprised by a 2 A.M. visit to the loo. For a moment Leora thought happiness might be a man who would explain the crustacean world to Finn and Cara.

"And when a mating claw is lost, it's replaced with a small, feeding claw – while the remaining one expands into a new mating claw," Terry went on. "Ingenious, huh?"

"A pity humans can't repair the damage to ourselves. Figuratively."

Terry, still squatting, looked up at her. He seemed about to cry, it was unnerving. Men were now required to come on all emotional and vulnerable. It made you miss John Wayne.

He stood, mouth working. "What happened was I had an affair."

A moment as she rewound to square one and The Marriage. "Oh. You couldn't, like, be more original?"

"She looked like Kathryn Grayson."

Leora pictured a singer from the 40s with eyes set wide as a cow's, spit curls, the plummy little mouth askew as she trilled *Make Believe I Love You* in a wobbly soprano. "I see. I guess that explains everything."

"Have you ever been told you're rather tart?"

Well, *a* tart, she murmured – but he'd started up the trail toward the peak of the dune. His back told her he didn't care whether she was following or not. She followed, disliking herself. She noticed a dark blue stain on the side of his chinos where a pen had exploded. How sneakily men broadcast their desire to be taken care of. She'd never shown a talent for man care and over the years found that psychiatric social worker type women were up for the job – even if the man happened to be your husband. She kept such unsisterly thoughts from the commune, of course. She would have liked to run all this by Terry, if only they could get less angry.

She joined him at the peak of the dune, a bit breathless. They stood looking out over a wide swathe of bay hemmed in the distance by a spit of land with a deserted lighthouse at its point. Gauzy strips of fog whizzed across a sun that looked sucked back into space.

"The affair was not why Claire split. She wanted to work all the time and it pissed me off."

"Aiee, you tried to *keep her from having a career*? That's become *the* capital offense. In the 12th century you'd have burned at the stake for less!" She wondered what other nasty stunts had Terry pulled on himself.

His eyes were hooded, stubborn. "She and a friend from her consciousness raising group" – grimace – "started a little bakery business. Just a hobby at first, but it took off and then all she could do was obsess about the business and becoming a 'woman executive.' I'd come home to an empty house, piles of dirty dishes and laundry ... Of course her business pulled in less money than what we paid the housekeeper."

"C'mon, it's the principle of the thing. Why am I telling *you*? You're, like, Mister Male Feminist, the pieces you ran in *Gotham* ushered in 'the next great moment.' That story on work as the new romance for women, how life is 'do-able' only without romantic love. The tirades by Estha Outrage on becoming 'the agent of your life.' People joked next up would be a piece called 'My Period.'"

Leora heard Gilda banging on in her heartland twang about women "reclaiming their personhood" – a slogan she herself couldn't get her mouth around; she was allergic to any word with "hood" in it, except maybe Red Riding Hood. How could Terry be tuned into the zeitgeist and so clueless about a single human?

"I guess gut feelings sometimes trump 'principle,'" he said coldly.

They started down the dune toward a beach that stretched to the narrow mouth of the harbor. Leora breathed in the good marine smell of low tide and dried seaweed. A breeze carved the water into tiny metallic fish-scales.

"Naturally, Claire was egged on by the 'sisters' in her masturbation slash self-examination workshop," Terry said.

Seemed like half the city's college-educated women had signed on with Betty Dodson's coven to peer up themselves through a speculum. A story for *Gotham*? She wanted more of Terry's story. A mustache of sweat had blossomed above his lip. A forty watt bulb lit up in her brain: "Terry, excuse the dime story psychology, but do you think maybe you *meant* to drive your wife away?"

"I guess at the time I thought we should give each other, pardon the cliche, space. Then Claire met someone – "

"A guy who didn't do a number on her and *supported* her ambition, right?"

" – and I fell in love with my wife, the way it was in the beginning. She got to have the beginning again."

"Unh, maybe you fell in love with your wife again because she found someone else. A someone she found because you tried to clip her wings. Reminds me of that Jewish joke about chutzpah, only I can't remember the joke." It never failed, when men opened up about their troubles, you ended up sympathizing with the woman.

"There's a little wrinkle that makes it not so funny," Terry said. "The new boyfriend's a writer who can't publish a column without singing the praises of my wife. It's the 'Song of Solomon' with Claire switched in for the 'Shulamite.'"

"Whatta bummer. But can't you just … avoid his wretched column?"

"Well, I am in the business. And Asa Dribble is hard to avoid."

Ouch, the writer who'd invented the New Journalism.

"Clive Monomark has decided to make Asa's column *In Private* a regular feature of *Gotham*. I'm back at the magazine only part time and can't very well question the boss's editorial judgment. In the subway the other day, what do I see but an excerpt from *Gotham* about Asa's passion for Claire on the tile wall."

A hallucination, surely?

"The fact is, Clive has good instincts," Terry went on. "Asa writes like an angel, even if he gets tangled up in his own wit and wordplay. Every writer could use an editor but Asa more than most. Especially when he's rhapsodizing about the Shulamite."

How could Terry be so objective about Asa's 'wordplay' when the guy was screwing his wife?

"Want an even funnier joke? Clive asked *me* to edit Asa."

What? Suddenly Leora heard Terry that first night on the sofa: *Clive put me on a beat I had to turn down …*"

"I tell him I have a conflict of a personal nature. I didn't need to spell it out, the media world is gossip central, people knew about my wife and Asa long before I did. And Clive says, 'but you're the only editor in town who can make Asa Dribble intelligible for the average reader.'"

That Clive would require Terry to untangle the prose of the guy balling his wife – it struck Leora as civilized torture, of the sort only the media elite could dream up. A hoot of laughter escaped her. *Damn*, so wrong of her! "Oh, sorry" – she tamped down another splutter. "I also laugh at funerals. Sorry" – shaking her head against another eruption – "it's just so ... fucked up."

Light glinted off Terry's round glasses so she couldn't read his expression. She doubted it was friendly. Then, suddenly, he was laughing, too, sexy-low in his throat in a way that made her suspect she was going to miss him.

"Well, no one could accuse you of being sweet," Terry said. "But I guess tart is better than bullshit."

Not a compliment, exactly, but – he'd waved his big claw at her.

CHAPTER 12

Charades

"Everyone has their reasons."

– Jean Renoir

A warning growl, Thor clearing his throat. Lightning silvered a road map through the velvety black sky, bleaching the grass beyond the French doors. A freighted pause. Then the ear-drubbing boombuh boom BOOM, trailed by distant grumbling and a volley of crackles, like careless moving men throwing boxes around. Rain beat the ground so hard it jumped back up.

The great front door of Cormorant Cove swung open, and there in a black cape with red lining stood Mephistopheles ...

★

The communards had been hard at play. They didn't kid around when they played. Their goal in charades was to flummox, embarrass, *pulverize* the fellow communard who was "up" by choosing a title, name, expression, etc. that was impossible to act out – while displaying their own cleverness in choosing it.

Tractatus Logicus by Ludwig Wittgenstein (thank you, Fred) had so far been the evening's most sadistic pick. The poor soul who'd drawn it was Papacristou the real estate baron, who had last read something by Dale Carnegie and knew a developer named Wittenstein who'd stiffed him. He hadn't felt so demeaned since the kids at Holy Trinity called him a faggot. He left in a huff to retreat behind hedgerows tall as an elephant's eye and consult his lawyer about suing those cocksuckers. Better yet, he'd report them to the Town Board for violating Islesfordd's rules barring "groupers."

Fred's wife Meghan took refuge in the role of "timer," standing by with her smile and a cooking timer from the kitchen. Runnels of inky hair, skin like paper whites – freshness spilled off her. Her gingham pinafore was a grown-up version of one of Cara's rompers from Goodwill.

Leora had not been invited to play. Rebuffed again: would she never graduate from her status of "Fred's guest" to card-carrying communard? Sometimes, though, nonentitude offered advantages: safer to hug the sidelines in case she drew some doozy impossible to act out, like that real estate guy, and Kaz would witness her humiliation. He'd escaped into a far corner with Milt Merdle, perhaps to discuss their manufacturing venture in a city in Southern India. A beauty spot, no doubt, on the order of Calcutta where people lived inside cast-iron pipes and kids played together on live train tracks. – *No, Leora, we won't hoe that row, the Marriage Plot calls for discipline ...*

Leora marveled at the size of the crowd packing into the living room and jockeying for a view of the "stage" in front of the fireplace. Charades at the commune had become a major summer entertainment on the Islesfordd social calendar. A bit like the spectacle of lions mauling Spartacus and his fellow slaves in ancient Rome. Certainly more appealing than tonight's Fundraiser for Landmines and Leprosy (open bar, soft shell taco station, sushi station, BBQ and Popcorn stations). Even reclusive Elsie van Otten was here, tin fish dangling off her turban, legs the white of Wonder Bread between her miniskirt and green wellies. In the latest *scandale* the cops had swooped in to minister to the raccoons who shared her ramshackle mansion and had fallen sick from the foie gras Elsie fed them. Elsie's minder, the giant cruelly nicknamed Quasimodo, hovered, poised to fulfill her least need.

Most players this evening had gone down in defeat. Unless they'd been rescued by Terry, who sat cross-legged on the floor up front, beaming a laser-like focus on their frantic efforts. Nadine had only to roll her eyes heavenward (a mannerism that came easily to her), and Terry said: *City of God*, St. Augustine. Peter Grosvenor mimed a knife and fork cutting ... "Meat," Terry called out – "uh, '*Meet me in St. Louis.*'" Leora stitched through the crowd, the women in hip huggers or space-age dresses by Courreges, the men in Nehru shirts, a few Rottlesey types in Nantucket red pants. She took a proprietary interest in Terry's brainpower, even as she recognized that was absurd.

She watched Fred's wife Meghan stoop to whisper in Terry's ear, hair spilling over him. Doubtless they were discussing the fine points of charades, but bloody hell, why would he want all that hair in his face? Leora rubbed at her inner eye to expunge the image.

Gilda was up. She frantically signaled "book," gave a count of syllables. Her arms churned, fingers crawled over her flowered caftan. The players pelted her with guesses. Terry watched. Desperate, Gilda dropped on all fours. She rolled onto her back, all but cracking her skull on the coffee table, lay there, short legs treadling air, an arthritic beetle ...

At that moment, the giant crack of thunder made the room jump and Mephistopheles, or somebody, filled the doorway framed by sheets of rain: Lester Annis, the outlawed shrink.

From the upper reaches of the house sounded the sinister opening bars of Bach's *Passacaglia and Fugue in D Minor.* Leora shuddered. Sebastian Nye might be summoning the demons of the night.

"So sorry to interrupt the killer charades," Lester Annis said. He stepped in and shed his dripping cape, shaking his silver curls. "I'm just up the road, after all, and I was wondering if I could borrow a corkscrew. Something told me this might be the perfect place to find one. The sound effects" – he glanced upward – "are perfect for a dark and stormy night. What's Gilda doing down there, *'The Murders in the Rue Morgue'*"? He nodded toward a form on the floor scrabbling its feet at the ceiling. "Or a cockroach"?

Terry, undistractable, had never taken his eyes off Gilda. *Cockroach* ... "Oh, of course," he said quietly, "*Metamorphosis* by Franz Kafka."

★

"So, I'm all set to celebrate and raise a glass to myself, when I discover there's not a corkscrew to be found," Annis said. "Blame it on Esperanza, my new girl. Though Esperanza has other virtues." He looked to Leora more like a necromancer and master of the dark arts than a shrink.

Nadine's fan went into action. "Esperanza is not your 'girl' – she's 'a housekeeper.'" Scarcely bothering to conceal her dislike. "In fact, one reason we're marching next month is to make the world safe from calling a woman 'my girl.'" Annis was not hugely popular around the commune. The women communards regarded the style of therapy he'd once practiced as a front for male piggery, pure and simple. They would have banned him from the commune, but there was no convincing Gilda that a man needed other virtues beside a pulse.

"Well, 'housekeeper' wouldn't quite cover Esperanza's other talents, Annis said. Eyes glittery with insinuation to let that sink in. "Not to worry, I'll get my nomenclature in order – in time for the great Women's Strike!

"What, exactly, are you celebrating, Doctor?" Fred Lustman said.

"I just finished the first draft of my new book *The Future of Sex*. This evening, not two hours ago!"

Fred felt a scimitar twist in his gut. Hari-kari could not feel much worse. *Steady on.* "Tell us more about your new b-b-book."

"As the title indicates, I hope," Annis said, "the book's about the future of human intimacy. The world beyond the traditional couple, monogamy, and all the other fetters laid on us by the Puritans, may they rot in hell. So we're talking open marriage, group sex, swinging, polyamory in all its forms – "

"What is polly-ameree?" Meghan said.

Fred grimaced. Well ... if you wanted gorgeous it usually came with a downside. "Polyamory means being romantically in-volved with more than one person at the same time, dear." Nadine smoothed her tea-colored hair and smiled at no one in particular. Lately she smiled more than she had in the past two years.

"Excuse me, but why are these alternative lifestyles consid-ered new?" put in Leora, who had hung with the Beats before they became notorious. "I mean, Allen Ginsberg and William Burroughs were talking about open relationships – 'expanding the circle of intimacy,' Allen called it – back in the late 50s."

"So you actually knew those guys," Nadine said, "I'd love to hear more – "

"Well, thanks to me, their thinking is about to enter the mainstream," Annis interrupted. His eyes licked Leora.

"Your body turns me on," he said.

"It turns me on, too," Leora said.

Fred was trying to beat down panic like the fire warden at the Big Burn of 1910. *Annis's book way too close to his own ... A first draft finished ... focus on sexual arrangements ... Why, the book would fly off shelves!* If Cressida knew about *The Future of Sex* – and publishing was a small, gossipy village – the witch would fire him!

Fred reached for a bottle of ... something and splashed it into his vodka. Come five P.M. he laid down an early buzz with a double Stoli on which he could platform the commune's rotgut chardonnay and stay blitzed till he passed out under Meghan. The advantage of being a seasoned boozer, a corner of his mind stayed alert, as if sequestered in a small orderly corner within a dorm room mess. Over by the French doors he spotted Terry. He was chatting with Quasimodo, who looked flustered, as no one ever talked to him. Wheels spun within wheels. Perhaps he could massage Annis's unwelcome news to his advantage.

It wasn't the most kosher plan, but once the mind rounds a certain corner, and then the next corner, and the next – well, it's like the thing takes on a momentum of its own and you kind of need to keep the forward momentum, don't you? Especially when it concerned a sleaze like Lester Annis.

"A toast to the new b-b-book!" Fred said, in the earnest manner that never failed to disarm. "Lester, I have an idea for you. Terry Cameron, a new member of the commune, is the best editor in town. I'm sure you'll agree that even the most polished first draft could use a bit of t-t – *tweaking* by a crackerjack editor. Why don't you hire Terry to look at your pages? He wields a wicked blue pencil. As a favor to me he might agree to work you into his schedule.

Wow, this was damn thoughtful of Fred. Leora wondered if there might be a darker strain to his generosity. A mirror to her own worst impulses. For all its misty-eyed talk of supportiveness and solidarity, the commune sometimes seemed to Leora a tank of sand tiger sharks that eat their siblings in the womb. She wondered exactly how far envy and ambition might drive its members.

Again, Leora saw the story opening in her mind like a Japanese flower ... She heard Gilda's rude remark over dinner *so long as she doesn't write about us.* But this would be fiction, largely. The heroine would be an outsider, a female Candide minus the optimism. Hallie, her name would be, sort of hapless like her own. Start with the night she drives out with Fred and Edwina – swapping out the actual communards with her own players. At the first dinner Hallie gets ploughed under by the communal snottiness ... But she regroups, helps engineer a lavish fundraiser for a march down Fifth Avenue thrown by the area's newest Gatsby – Who would be Hallie's former boyfriend ... Hallie herself marching the wrong way down a one-way street; pursuing precisely the sort of domestic haven reviled by the newly liberated women around her ... Leora felt dizzy at the prospect of setting this Hallie in motion. The character would also be an aspiring scribbler, who in turn is writing about a writer struggling to join the commune, in a receding hall of mirrors, Escher-like, a seemingly infinite construction ...

The killer charades had started up again. The crowd pressed forward toward the arena in front of the fireplace. Leora dreamt on amidst the frantic calls and claps of laughter, picturing how she might set a scene here. Tease out the sense of impending violence. The air was rotten with it.

★

The duck pate! Nadine rushed to the French doors and flipped on the outside spots. The sight on the garden table made her stomach flip over.

She'd bought up every duck liver on the East End, spent the morning toiling in the kitchen in honor of the evening's charades – then, in the heat of the game, no one had thought to rescue the platters of pate from the storm.

Tonight Gilda was Countess of Cleanup; no percentage in reminding her when two such viable men as Terry Cameron and Kaz Grabowski were in house. Anyway, Gilda was hopeless about chores: she would start to set the table, then wander off to organize a zap action. They needed to keep her on flower-arranging ...

Nadine fetched several green garbage bags and a trowel from the garden shed and cheerfully set about shoveling slime.

Nadine had given up planning the music for her memorial. She might have booked a ferry trip on the River Styx and then bribed the oarsman to swing back around toward earth's sunny green banks. She'd taken to smiling at no one in particular, riding the unfamiliar wave of well-being that had buoyed her the last few weeks. This must be how most people muddled along. Maybe you could expect a little more happiness from life beyond hearing the doctor say he "wasn't concerned" about the shadow on your X-ray. A little more joy than what the Flatulent Generalissimo might have on tap.

She kept gyring back to the image, like a giddy teen, of the man who'd approached her at Bullhampton Hall. Bearish and boyish, the beetling brows and classy diction. "Panda Bear," as she'd named him, must surely be married with five children, which would disqualify him as a lover because how could she love someone oblivious to zero population growth? Of course, if *four* of the children were refugees adopted from Vietnam ...

No woman need wait around for life to happen any more. Christ, she herself had written that somewhere (it was harder to put into practice than on the page). She must engineer a "chance encounter" with Panda. The zeitgeist was in her corner: Lester Annis's *Future Sex* was about to feed polyamory or whatever the hell you called it into the mainstream. What did it matter if Panda had a wife? As Fred like to point out, some of us are built to love more than one person at a time.

She'd chivvy him out of his burrow with the honey of another lecture about the toxic fallout of feminism on men. The issue apparently spoke to him. Perhaps he considered himself a casualty? She was kind of burned out on the subject – she'd just turned down an invite from the director of Shitterton Grange for a panel called "Is *This* The New Man We Wanted?" She could tell the director she'd reconsidered. She'd stride onto the stage, shoulders back, gut sucked in, heart out.

★

Edwina normally enjoyed the commune's take-no-prisoners style of charades. Now Lester Annis had come crashing in out of the storm like something retched up from Hell. Edwina inwardly fumed at Gilda: as long as it had a dick it was welcome here, and any disqualifying objections – such as maybe the dick was attached to a psychopath – were moot.

Edwina had also to contend with *the other one*: Sebastian Nye rarely missed charades at the commune. Whenever Nye was on the premises she felt stalked, even if he was up in the rafters, pumping away on Cormorant Cove's creepy organ. At times she felt she could scarcely go anywhere without at least three guys wanting at her, popping out like malign jacks-in-the-box. Confide such a problem to a woman, and she'd get, Yeah, honey, *I* should have such problems. Complain to Jo and she'd get a lecture about the societal structure of male supremacy and stats on all the women murdered by male partners. Leora might offer a sympathetic ear. Leora lacked the survival skills native to most women Edwina knew; she'd leaped into a boldly visioned life but hadn't stuck the landing and felt she had no business judging others.

Hell, she could confide in Monica Fairley, the "intellectual's pinup;" she'd turned fending off men into an art form.

Edwina suddenly sensed Nye somewhere in the living room, the way an elephant picks up vibrations of a coming earthquake in its feet. Why couldn't he goddamn keep away from her life?

Rain let down in a vast rustle. Were it not such filthy weather, she'd be tempted to drive back to the city ...

"I have a proposal for you."

Edwina recoiled, as if scalded.

"Hear me out," Nye said.

He talked in her ear – and talked and talked. He still wore the same woody aftershave.

"Think of it as righting the scales," Nye murmured. "The world would be a better place without him. He's the source of all our troubles. It's Lester Annis who drove you into JoBeth's clutches."

Edwina backed further away, trailing the pads of her fingers along the lace runner on an oak table. "No one '*drove*' me into anything. Why is it so hard to comprehend that I love someone who isn't you? As for '*our*' troubles – what part of 'it's over' do you not get?"

She folded into the crowd. Rogue thoughts came and went, somewhat diluting her outrage. No sane person would come within a ten mile radius of Nye's homicidal "proposal." Of course, when it came to sane, as an alum of McLean's nuthouse, she had tarnished credentials. Nye's proposal offered an operatic grandeur – he would go *that* far for her? From another angle, it offered a tempting simplicity. Lately, nothing in her life felt simple.

★

Edwina pushed open the French door and breathed in the good smells loosed by summer rain: the green smell of wet grass; a rich, secret ichor rising off the bushes, glistening and still; a ghost of lilac. She headed down toward the pond, where tree frogs were piping up a storm. If Leora's darling children were here she would tell them, Listen to the frogs going RIBBIT, RIBBIT. Even if they didn't actually go that way. Ribbit, ribbit ... *Jung, Rado, Fenichel* ... Even the briefest contact with Nye flushed out hateful memories ...

She'd stayed long after she'd stopped feeling safe. Nye hadn't abused her in the way women were all talking about now – he'd devised his own version by making her a sex junkie. Making pleasure shameful. She dreamt he'd cut off her arms and legs and kept her in a box. Someone told her about Lester Annis, a "progressive" shrink with a "creative" style of therapy. Not one of those deadly Freudians who never spoke and thought any woman who didn't transfer her center of sensitivity from the clitoris to the vagina was frigid. In a former life Annis had lived in Islesfordd, then abruptly left. Now he ran nudist encounter groups in the Catskills that sounded kind of cool ...

Annis helped pry her loose from Sebastian Nye, yes. Then he started in with "transference love," meaning everything she expressed was, ahem, sexual desire for *him*. Often it was helpful to "physically act out" what she'd felt for her stepfather Nigel, he said. "The patient's development of erotic interest in the therapist is a useful part of the psychotherapeutic process," he said. During Freud's time analysts routinely had affairs with their married female patients, he said. Like Jung, Rado, Fenichel ...

It happened the night of "agua energetics," the night they shared a joint in his office. On the nubby sofa. After, he jumped up and washed his cock in the bathroom – he'd left the door cracked open. He sat brooding over his typewriter. He'd come in a jiffy. Was she now supposed to worry about *him*, too?

She needed a shrink to recover from her shrink.

She saw no point in bathing or changing her clothes. Something about her turned men into horrors. Every last one of them. Nye, Lester Annis. Nigel. It had begun right out of the gate, sophomore year in college, bleeding into the time in Piazza Santa Maria in Trastevere. Fall semester, her stepfather Nigel drove to the college to see his birth daughter, but all Nigel could see was Edwina. Soon she was spending weekends in his pied a terre on East 84th. The spring before Nigel left for Rome and the place in Trastevere they walked among the pink dogwoods on the college campus. She must come with him, Nigel said, they could do this, love chooses *us*, not the other way around. To live fully – *honorably* – you must live ruthlessly. The people inevitably damaged –"collateral damage," as he called Mother, who still loved him, Edwina suspected – would in time pick up and soldier on.

Only some didn't. A fortune's worth of shrinks argued that Mother had stepped out the window on the 14th floor because she was clinically depressed. They could say what they goddamn pleased. Edwina knew better.

She would mortify her body like those monastic Christians she'd once studied in Readings in Early Christianity who went into the desert to live in a cave and purify themselves. She found a pair of garden shears. Start by hacking off your hair.

McLean's could have been an Ivy college dorm or upscale Vermont country inn, with woodland paths and a pond and masses of white rhododendrons. When she recognized one of her doctors, any remaining confidence in the healing profession faltered. The doctor was a busty blonde she'd met at a resort in St. Lucia, where the woman was the go-to fuck for randy, married Brits. One morning she was waiting for the elevator on her way to breakfast, when across the hall a door opened and the cutest of the married Brits, one she'd fancied herself, slipped out of the doctor's room.

She was privileged, she knew. The less fortunate ranted in the streets.

Lester Annis and his brand of "psychotherapy" had been taken off the market – for the moment, anyway. At some point he'd traded the Catskills for Islesfordd. Now – she'd heard from a colleague at the *Islesfordd Herald* – he was about to rise phoenix-like with a book about the future of sexual arrangements. The *Herald* planned to run a story on Lester Annis in their Arts section as a "resident notable." Well, fuck that!

★

Elsewhere along Hooker Pond Leora and Kaz walked a path edged in skunk cabbage. Over the summer it had grown bigger than elephant ears – even the plant life here went in for overkill. The storm had driven out the fog and damp and installed a newly clarified night; voguing clouds unveiled the moon's indifferent glow.

"You could have married anyone in New York back then. After you came back from Europe."

"That was your fantasy. I was floundering and broke. I wanted to be a journalist. Guest Editor at *Mademoiselle*, like Joan Didion and Sylvia Plath. I wanted to be one of the cool ones. Confident. Composed. Joan Didion! She could turn depression into lovely sentences: 'We forget all too soon the things we thought we could never forget' – that kind of thing. I had a nervous giggle. I didn't have a daddy who could get me a job at *Time, Inc.* – and I was a crackerjack typist! I wanted to be a woman who kept just two limes and a bottle of Perrier in the fridge, and maybe a wilted gardenia. Instead, I stood over the stove schlurping Uncle Boyardee's Spaghetti-O's from the pot." *I fell in love/lust too much. Though not too much for me. I was too "fast," though not fast enough for me. How glorious that such delights were available to humans. A guy I was mad for said,* you ruined it: you jumped over the beginning. *I said,* why can't we begin right now?

"I still like Chef Boyardee – only now I eat it off Royal Copenhagen," Kaz said.

"Bet the stuff doesn't taste as good! And you, why haven't you married?"

"Sometimes we get stuck." He smashed his foot down hard on something in the grass.

She pictured one of those little moles, or voles, she'd seen about. They were cute, with black button eyes and tiny whiskers, but everyone seemed to have it in for them. "Stuck? You've certainly moved on, and up."

He shrugged. "Anyone can make money."

Oh really? Her father whom she'd adored had found such ingenious ways *not* to make money, she became convinced he was descended from aristocrats.

"I want to buy a magazine. I hear *Gotham* magazine may be on the block." Her breath caught. The potential synchrony here was almost too neat. "I want to be influencer. Get into politics and run for Congress. I want to give back and *serve*. Like Joseph Kennedy."

"Uh, Joseph Kennedy referred to Jews as 'kikes' and 'sheenies.' You'd do better to 'serve' like Jack or Bobby." She wondered what Kaz's relatives in Poland had been up to in 1940.

"You're right, you usually are." A large butterfly flitted by, or was it a bat? "I moved on alright, but maybe not in the ways that matter most," he said, voice burred.

"If the ways had mattered to you, you would have moved on, don't you think?"

"The truth is, I got stuck with us and what we had. I wasn't sure what I could offer any more."

What *we* had was more what *he* had. Perhaps everyone had their story, the one that became their only story, life-shaping – or warping. She suspected that through no particular talent of hers she'd become Kaz's story. Maybe his only story. "I guess back then," Leora said, "all I wanted was to wander the world."

Kaz grasped her arm and stepped in close, *I longed for you for years*, he said, and she remembered everything. They rested their foreheads together, like fond horses. His taste felt like home.

Someone was coming along the path, the quick step spelling agitation ... Edwina, her dark head down. They drifted into the shadows beyond the garden shed. They stood there in the gleaming dark, trees sighing rain off their leaves and cooling their arms. They could see through the French doors into the living room, where silhouettes of people chatted animatedly as on a stage set. For a moment the two of them looking on from outside felt as insubstantial as the drawing room comedy within.

"Why don't we meet someplace far from here?" he said. "Away from all the gossip and bullshit."

Was he trying to hide them? Well, they couldn't very well go back to her place on East 7th, its peeling walls a geological chart exposing layers of colors from other people's lives; the tenant perhaps lying in wait for the landlord with a butcher knife. But what was wrong with Dragon's Gate? Of course, "far from here" could signal a new beginning ... *We could begin right now* ... Why could she never believe in her own luck? Maybe her life to date had been a rehearsal and now, finally, she was about to get it right.

"I have to go to Charleston, South Carolina, on business. There's hotel I love, the Belmond. We could go to Magnolia Gardens."

Could you go backwards in love? Like Gatsby? If you thought about it, Gatsby could just as well have enjoyed his fortune and found a fresher Daisy not yet tarnished by life's deceptions and baby-less – did they have episiotomies back then? A Daisy without the baggage. But maybe it was the backwards thing, the return that made it so sweet.

They'd dreamt of a trip, once, she and Kaz. It had never worked out.

★

" *– the feminist critique of heterosexual sex seemed crazy to me. It denied my own experience, certainly.*"

– Betty Friedan

Three A.M. Leora shot upright in bed, parched; she'd never learned how to meter out the sauce. She pulled on a cardigan over her nightgown and made her way down the grand staircase thirsting for a gallon of water. Post charades, the living room looked as though a natural catastrophe had whirled through.

Gilda lay stroked out on a sofa in the flowered caftan, short legs akimbo, toes pointing at the ceiling.

Leora approached crabwise. "Can I get you something?"

Gilda opened one eye and growled. Leora returned with a bottle of club soda and two glasses. She set them on a coffee table littered with half-filled glasses and overflowing ashtrays.

"The Women's Strike," Gilda muttered into her glass – she levered herself up to semi-vertical – "I'm afraid it's gonna be a bust. It's too big an action to fail. When I put out the idea of an actual *strike* at WOW, everyone hated it *hated* it. We're hardly a movement yet, blah blah, just a few of us here and there, women won't stop working – they'll be scared of losing their jobs and won't show ... Now the thing's been set in motion, how embarrassing if it flopped. I dreamt it up, so the blame falls on me! The press will treat the movement as even more of a joke."

Leora went amazingly alert. Nothing like the confessions of a household name to get you sober ...

"The craziest part, I came up with the idea of a Strike kind of last minute," Gilda went on. "At a meeting of WOW they organized a putsch to rig the ballots and I got cheated out of a seat on the board. So during my farewell address, I just sprang this idea on them of a Strike – you know, as a way to grab back the reins. I truly believed we needed an action big enough to make national headlines. Now it feels like hubris ... "

"Suppose you simply call the Women's Strike a Women's *March* for Equality," Leora said. "That way women would only have to show up, without walking off the job. Much less intimidating."

Gilda's hooded eyes widened *swock*. "Solidarity without confrontation! I'll run that by the Coalition Committee."

Leora hoped she could claim a little credit here, but she wasn't sure Gilda knew her name.

Gilda took a swig of club soda. "Hmm, wouldn't mind some brandy with this. Y'know, Gay Talese or someone said, Every year there's a pretty girl who comes to New York and pretends to be a writer, and this year it's Monica Fairley." The mere name darkened Gilda's face.

Leora had sobered up enough to understand the need to tread cautiously. She herself was in awe of Monica. Her composure. Her freedom from gluttony. Monica seemed to cringe at the male media drooling over her, turned it around on men to expose how they thought with their dicks. Monica might have hatched on a different planet. And she was bringing Black activists to the table. Like balls-y Flo Kennedy, who drove Gilda up the wall with quips like "There are very few jobs that actually require a penis or vagina."

What Leora didn't get about Monica was the sex part. How could you truck with the mess of sex and desire and walk around with a broth of apres-love in your crotch and be so blithe and serial and *neat* about it? Leora was more in tune with the magenta realms of passion and that heroine of a French short story who'd dropped dead from an ecstatic night of love. Love dismantled your life, love was opera, the high note that exploded chandeliers. Monica was clearly not one of history's *grandes amoureuses*. Otherwise, she was kind of perfect. How could Gilda *not* hate her?

"She's trying to move in on us, rip off the movement for her own agenda," Gilda was saying. "The media eats it up."

The truth was, Monica had her own problems with the media, Leora thought, keeping her lips pressed together. *Screw*

Magazine had run a full-page nude pic with the caption "Pin the Cock on the Feminist" ... David Susskind had recently cracked, "I just wish Monica Fairley would find a good chap and relax."

"The media likes to think feminism is only for ugly women who can't get a man and how can someone that pretty care so goddamn much about the movement?" Gilda said. "I wonder that myself."

They'd all wondered. "I wouldn't worry about Monica Fairley. You're the movement's heart, soul, spokesperson. The movement is *you*, your brainchild."

Gilda nodded her agreement. "I just ran with what was about to explode into the open. If I didn't exist, someone would have had to invent me."

The truth was, Leora had picked up rumblings of Monica's rise. The press was itching to find a face for women's lib that wasn't Gilda's. Hadn't the *Beaver* just called Monica "the quintessential liberated brainy beauty?" At her last visit to her gynecologist, the doc had offered, unsolicited – while Leora was in no position to respond – that Gilda Gladstone was a loud-mouthed harpy and terrible role-model for women's lib. This did not seem the moment to bring any of this up.

Gilda flopped back among the pillows, arms outstretched, and coughed productively, Violetta with allergic rhinitis. "D'you know what it's like to be desired for your access? Your fucking *access*?"

Leora didn't, actually.

"Men want me for the perks! The parties, trips, flights first class, the all-expenses-paid ... I'd give it all up just to be ... loved and desired – for real."

Leora wasn't quite sure what Gilda meant by "all," but doubted she'd give it up. "Who knows what goes into the making of love anyway?" Leora said. "It's an impure mix at best, a sausage of

fantasy, delusion, admiration, lust ... a resemblance to his mother
... And, yes, desire for access." She felt remarkably eloquent given
the hour and the frightening mix of alcohol traveling her system.
Kaz had loved her as a conduit to a world of culture he'd never
imagined. From shoveling manure to ... Chopin! Henry James!

"At least Henry loved me for myself, we had a great time
in bed," Gilda mumbled. "Okay, he liked the perks, too. He
starts in with the guilt about his wife, then we fly first class to
Monaco for a conference – and *voila*! no more guilt."

Gilda's swerves were giving Leora whiplash – and the mention of Henry gave her worse. Florence Luker, finance maven,
had counseled the communards to pry their money loose from
Henry, or risk never seeing a nickel of their investment again.
Leora hadn't gotten round to it yet, the mere thought of "investment goals" and an "underwriting spread" God help her,
and she went brain dead. Every time she tried to nab Henry,
he was "dashing off" somewhere.

"I barter fame for love," Gilda said, "and I pretend not to
know. I *pretend not to know*." Something creaked deep within
the innards of the old house, a dybbuk at large in the night.
Gilda went on,

"Fame works the opposite way, too. I went away with this
guy for a weekend in the Catskills. So we're hiking in the woods
and run into a troupe of goddamn Girl Scouts – and the leader
asks me for my autograph! Back in the guy's cabin, the phone's
ringing off the hook. It's Indira Gandhi, needs to speak to me,
and *NO it can't wait*. God knows where they got the number.
You can imagine how all that went over with the guy."

Gilda stuck out her glass for more club soda. "I have a
horror – *terror* – of being alone. Even with everything" – Gilda
waved her hands around – "the commune, the Strike, invita-
tions to everywhere."

Leora nodded vigorously. In the Age of Autonomy Gilda's admission could send you to the gulag. Hadassah Sarachild had made a career of insisting loneliness was next to godliness and romantic love could never cohabit with work and self esteem. Leora had never bought the movement's exaltation of solitude. When Patrick was off with the kids for the weekend, she opened the bathtub faucets full throttle — triggering a panic of water bugs – to feel less alone.

"I guess it doesn't help that I'm such a bad-tempered bitch," Gilda said. "Tell me, why does the press always print the most unflattering shots of me? I'm not quite so ugly."

That killed her. She'd scolded Finn for saying, Gilda looks like a kind witch. All this shit about Gilda's looks ... Long noses were very Italian Renaissance. *Cleopatra* had a big aquiline nose, *Pascal* said so, and he was never wrong. Not every woman needed a kitten-y nub. Leora said,

"The culture's stuck in some dumb pinup ideal of feminine beauty. The fact is" – she felt inspired – "you have a ... a *haunting attractiveness*. I mean, your passion, vision ... *cojones*. You're an Amazon! The new desirable woman. And your fame – let's face it – your celebrity is part of who you are. So, yes, of course men are turned on by your access! As a marvelous, unique aspect of you."

Gilda looked interested.

"It's true a few men might find you threatening," Leora powered on. "But the 'new man' who's shed the old macho model, who wants equality in love and could embrace the totality of what you offer" (gah! she sounded like a screed by Hadassah) – "that man could be at the very next party."

"Why don't we go cruising together? We'd make a good team. My name, your body and youth."

Gilda slumped sideways, mouth open, and began to snore. Her own loud snort shook her awake. "In fact, I think I may have met this guy. What do you think of the squire of Dragon's Gate? Kaz Grabowski is quite charismatic in his way. Short men make good lovers because they try harder ... "

"Napoleon," Leora murmured. "Alan Ladd."

"I sense Kaz is very responsive to me," Gilda went on. "And not just because of the usual crap. Maybe because he's not really, y'know, one of us. Kinda macho ... I find that refreshing, male feminists can be a bit wimpy. Did I tell you? I invited Kaz to a conference in Swaziland in mid September."

"*Did* you? What did he say?"

"I don't want to get my hopes up too much but he seemed – *quite* enthusiastic."

CHAPTER 13

Desire

" — given wedding fetishization, I wanted to make clear that getting married wasn't validating my life; my life was very valid on its own. Falling in love was ...in fact enabled by the life I'd made on my own ... "

– Rebecca Traister

"The strike will prove our revolution as a fact."

– Betty Friedan

"And where the words of women are crying to be heard, we must each of us recognize our responsibility to seek those words out, to read them and share them and examine them in their pertinence to our lives."

– Audre Lorde

★

"*The Strike will be a boycott against advertising that depicts women as playthings, inferior, or frivolous. We'll create a world where no one will dare make an ad for Silva Thins that says, 'Cigarettes are like women, the best ones are thin and rich.'*"

Hoots, whistles, thumps – they could be at a call-and-response church service in Harlem. Gilda presided from behind an oak rollback desk. Before her women of all ages and sizes sat haunch by elbow on every available seat, cushions on the floor, they hung in clusters from the kitchen, they jammed doorways. Men were not welcome at the Steering Committee. Yoko Ono had walked in with John Lennon. The women had raised hell until they both left.

The packed space defeated the air conditioning. A smell of something overripe, stale perfume perhaps, a vegetal rotting. Sofas with throw pillows in fuschia and orange swirls, a high-backed rattan chair, red love seat, a lamp wearing a purple scarf. Pretty cool that Gilda could make an inviting home like this while making a revolution. Leora was miffed she'd not actually been *invited*. She'd crashed the meeting with Fred, who'd conceded with mournful eyes that Gilda still balked at her joining the commune. Even with her new status of cruising mate! Leora saw herself as a weed furtively trying to put down roots among the commune's perennials, only to get rudely yanked. Gilda must smell the competition for Kaz. They'd kept their burgeoning liaison – or reunion – in the shadows, but women have a nose for such things. What *was* Kaz's deal with Gilda anyway? Would his "enthusiasm" extend to accompanying her to Swaziland? Leora saw a nice *quid pro quo*: Gilda gets a handsome check for her projects; Kaz gets to rub up against these fancy-talking intelleckshuals who were shaping Herstory.

Leora decided to regard her boycott by the commune as a sign she hadn't lost her looks.

"*Our action is a responsibility to history, to ourselves, to all who will come after us,*" Gilda thundered on.

And on.

She was well and truly driven by a vision – the Joan of Arc of zip code 10023. Gilda was improvising, no prep, it seemed, no notes that Leora could detect. Moments before, she'd been a mess, scrabbling around for numbers jotted on shopping lists, cocktail napkins ... where the hell was that matchbook ... she seemed unacquainted with address books ... Now she filled the stale air with slogans, ideas, strategies, her thoughts outrunning words, butts of sentences left behind in the scrimmage ... They "ahl" must drum up support for the Strike, "*ahl*" of them (she'd kept the broad vowels of the heartland) ... Get out leaflets to secretaries in singles bars, mothers in playgrounds, women in the garment district, commuter stations ...

Caught up in Gilda's aria, Leora truly saw her as a desirable woman – yet one the world wasn't ready for, one who *men* might *never* be ready for, and she peered deep into the ugly truth of how a man could have a face to scare the horses, like this *macher* from Union Carbide she'd met on Megalomantic Beach, who had carbuncles and toenail fungus and some disorder that had cost him his hair, including *down there*, she assumed, and had made a bloody fortune off the misery of others, and all the girls wanted to sleep with him.

Leora pondered her coming rendezvous with Kaz. It felt treasonous to fall into the old man-obsessing amidst all this movement fervor. They'd meet someplace far from Islesfordd, he'd said, as if the place were a plague site. Leora flashed back to dinner with Kaz the previous week at the Old Sodom Inn, the gemstone glow of Tiffany lamps, walls papered in dark green

William Morris, smell of lemon oil on wood, the arch of her bare foot snugged against his ankle. No room at the inn upstairs, but just the thought ... The waiter affronted that they'd barely touched their *canard a l'orange* ...

"And now I want to share a crucial change with you," Gilda was saying.

"I'm afraid most women will be too fearful of a literal *strike*, and won't dare stay away from work ... We simply won't get the numbers. And what could be worse than a few freaky fanatics from the New Left who'd incite violence? Or stragglers from the lesbian fringe ... "

Nadine scowled from the wings of the big rattan chair; hadn't she told Gilda to stay off the damn lesbian thing?

"So I've decided to call the Women's Strike a Women's *March*. And we'll take to the streets at 5:30 or so *after* working hours."

Leora grinned around at the crowd – *me! my* contribution! – and clapped over the medley of yea saying, objections, confusion. Gilda's voice sliced through the noise.

"Another change. Of course men have thought of women as sex objects for too long. And yes, women have been oversold on love as the end of life. And I know I've said women should 'sacrifice a night of love to make the political meaning clear' and so on. But this is not a battle to be fought in the bedroom. Much as the press would love to see our March as a replay of *Lysistrata*, with wives refusing to have sex with their husbands."

"How much more fucking bourgeois can you get?"

Eyes swept like a lighthouse beam toward JoBeth Mankiller, standing hip out-thrust, before a couple of fan-leaf palms. Her lids at half mast, thumb curled over her cigarette, Brit schoolboy's hair. The room swooned.

"You take the teeth out of the march if we don't protest against centuries of oppression and male violence against women. We need to call men on their shit, not make nice. This is nothing short of *appeasement!*"

Yeas, boos, a smattering of applause. "It's not as if we're Nazi sympathizers," came a plaintive voice.

"Gilda, sounds like your ex was a prime example of the violence perpetrated by men."

"Cheap shot, Hadassah," someone muttered.

"This is just what the media wants, that we personalize the revolution and turn it into a catfight," Gilda said, without missing a beat. "Let's not give them the satisfaction."

"I'm with you there," Jo said. "But drop the 'lavender menace' shit. And keep your phobia about homosexuals to yourself. You sound like that Phyllis Schlafly talking about 'radicalfeministlesbians.'"

Gilda held up her hand over the dissenting babble: "There's nothing personal in my position – it's a simple fact that enemies of the movement claim we're pushing lesbianism and hatred of men." To Jo: "Of course you know that the CIA sent around a lesbian who tried to seduce me as a way to wreck and discredit the movement."

"Sweetheart, that's either A) a fantasy; B) your own twisted rationale for excluding women who don't fit neatly into your super square middle class heartland world; C) both of the above."

Leora could absolutely see why Edwina dug Jo – that superb arrogance, so unexpected, so sexy on a woman. Leora's mind vogued away from Jo and Gilda's feud, which raged on, back to Kaz. Did she really know Kaz? All those cells changing every seven years ... Who the hell was he now? Fred, ever a major conduit for gossip, had let drop that one of Kaz's factories in Southeast Asia might qualify as a sweat shop.

Leora thought of Balzac: "behind every great fortune there lies a crime."

★

Cormorant Cove. The Saturday after the meeting of the Strike coalition at Gilda's Fred Lustman went tippy-toeing about the sleeping commune. He pushed open the door to Terry Cameron's room, wincing at the groaning hinge. Waited: nothing in the house stirred. Saturday at nine, Fred knew, Terry always gave Peter Grosvenor a great game of tennis on the grass courts of the Rottlesey, where Peter was a member.

Fred made a thorough search: desk, drawers, closet, under the unmade bed ... Nothing. Where would Terry have put the damn thing? Fred padded, pigeon-toed, out to the glassed-in sun porch. His heart lurched: there beside a well-used ashtray lay two piles of typescript: the manuscript of *The Future of Sex* by Lester Annis. One pile was virgin pages. The other was so marked up in blue pencil, Terry might have been rewriting the whole damn book. Fred merely planned to borrow the manuscript and weave some of Annis's research into his own work. After all, with his first book *Overload*, it was *he* who'd put the whole topic on the radar, it was *he* who'd gotten there first. In the larger scheme, always the superior perspective, it was actually Annis who'd been pilfering ideas from *him*. Fred checked to ensure the coast was clear and skidooed with his bounty out the kitchen door and over the grass to his writing studio.

★

Leora hadn't eaten in two days so her stomach wouldn't pooch out. They sat beside the black-bottomed pool of Dragon's Gate beneath an umbrella in the shape of a pagoda. She looked around at the Italianate faun with pan pipes leering at them from the lawn; the white bougainvillea spilling out from urns, its thin crepe-y blossoms a match for the cheeks of Islesfordd's matrons. She took in the folly of the house: a stepped roof from Amsterdam; conical turrets borrowed from a French chateau; leaded windows from Oxford. "The height of hideosity," a reporter for the *Islesfordd Herald* had called Dragon's Gate. Leora seriously doubted any hideosity would trouble the ghetto kids she and Kaz would bus out here; hell, they could imagine they were at Disneyland-sur-Mer. She and Kaz would act as camp counselors from the gatehouse and put his bucks to work creating other recreational spaces in Islesfordd as well as New York's forlorn outer boroughs.

The previous week they'd arranged to meet at The Fairmont Royal York in Toronto. Friday morning, at the phone's first peal, she knew. A voice crackling across long distance ... he couldn't get away, he had "fires to put out, literally," she couldn't be more disappointed than he, etc. etc.

She'd knocked herself out persuading Patrick to switch weekends with the kids – but before her anger could fully ignite, Kaz was saying would she like to come to lunch at Dragon's Gate?

The gods of summer had smiled on her. Lunch would protect her from herself. These days she collected reasons to rein in the old libido, since once it galloped off, the affair went down the toilet ... *but we jumped over the beginning* ... Leora heard the apostles of the post-pill paradise: how Victorian could you get? Fine, ladies, feel free to leap into the sack, no strings. See how that works for ya ...

Kaz stood in the pool and watched her swim laps. She swam to show off her crawl and she swam because she couldn't vouch for what might evolve if they started messing around in the water (actually, water sex did not live up to its rep, the chlorine messing with lubrication and all). His chest hair was darker than his white-blond head. Body hair, she reflected, working her flutter-kick, was an under-celebrated feature of male allure.

★

Wilfredo laid out a first course of lobster salad on gold-rimmed plates. ("My houseboy," Kaz called him; your "domestic assistant," Leora had corrected.) Kaz surveyed the spread with satisfaction. "They get $100 a pound for this lobster salad at Loafs & Gippers."

Nerves, she'd noticed, flushed out his Puhlish accint. It touched her that he was nervous – but his fondness for quoting price tags would have to go. After they'd eaten, he beckoned at Wilfredo, who stood by, compact aloft, gluing on a set of spidery lashes. Kaz circled the air with his hands around their plates – a curious gesture to telegraph, she supposed, "make all this disappear."

Wilfredo ignored him. Damn, Kaz should treat his employee with more respect, even if Wilfredo appeared mainly interested in his beauty regimen – was her checklist getting out of control? Perhaps she could get Kaz to underwrite Wilfredo's tuition at Miss Vera's, an academy for drag queens recently written up in *Gotham*.

"Come, there's som-think I show you," Kaz said, excitedly. They entered the cool of the house. His hand on the small of her back guided her through the big game room, flanked by Napoleonic obelisks, the only sound their flip flops. Leora, matching stares with an elk head's glass eyes, stumbled on the fangs of the beautiful beast butterflied into a rug. They moved through a room sporting a chandelier with real candles – a fire hazard, *must go*, check – moved through a blur of gilt, brocade, leopard carpets (not real, she prayed), frescoe'd ceilings, ogival windows, a Babel of styles and periods. No wonder the Islesfordd elders were throwing a shitfit ...

A dim room that must be Kaz's study. He rummaged in a giant mahogany wardrobe. Drew out a large padded sleeve designed to hold paintings and placed it on a table of onyx marble inlaid with gold filigree. His hand shook as he slid the painting from its sleeve.

Leora gasped. Before her on the table, a large canvas of the famed double portrait by Delacroix of George Sand and Chopin – the one that got cut in two. Whoever had reunited them was no Delacroix. Leora pictured the sublime original of Sand at her sewing, head tilted and deep in reverie, face framed by hair smoothed into 19ᵗʰ century *bandeaux*, while above her Frederic Chopin sits at the piano, eyes dreamy, head slightly angled to catch the sublime melodies God is ferrying to his ear.

In the travesty before her Sand could be a Spanish hooker and the great Pole playing chopsticks. The picture didn't even aspire to forgery. It was the cheesiest of copies, a notch above painting on velvet, an oddity you'd find in a garage sale by a fledgling artist who hopefully now sold insurance.

"The first night I saw you at my fundraiser party," Kaz said, "I told you I bought somthink at auction that I search for long time. And the amazing think, I bought it before I know we are neighbors and will find each other again. Like these two," he added, tapping the painting with his index finger.

She shuddered to think how much he'd paid. Some auctioneer must have had a good laugh at his expense ... What was wrong with her? The money, the ugliness, none of that mattered. He'd cherished this memento of her. The love this revealed ... She steepled her hands in front of her nose.

"Kaz, I'm just so ... touched. I must have told you about that painting, what, fifteen years ago? In college? And you remembered. You actually went and found" – she wiped at a tear with her knuckle – "this."

He leaned in under her face like a curious child. "Don't be sad ... "

Another tear welled, he *couldn't see the thing was ugly.* "It's just so lovely ..."

He pulled her in, one hand on her ass. She opened her eyes and saw him blindly watching her, lashes fluttering. Stuff flew off herky-jerky. Lunch not safe at all ...

The sound grew louder. Someone knocking at the door? They clung to each other like the last refuge on earth. Someone *panting* at the door? Two bolder knocks.

"*Damn* Wilfredo! Just a moment," Kaz called hoarsely, struggling to get all of himself back in his trunks. "I told that fairy never to bother me here – "

He scooped Leora's cover-up off the floor and draped it around her. "Please forgive me, I forgot to mention Milt Merdle was stopping by and I didn't expect" – He opened his hands. "We have business problem, little fire to put out, and need to do it yesterday. Maybe you have chat with Sophia? You'll enjoy dessert. My cook makes blackberry cassis sorbet, very delicious."

Sorbet? "You really ought to be nicer to Wilfredo."

"I should fire him first, he only *pretends* not to understand – "

Leora held her cover-up away from her between thumb and index finger, her bathing suit swinging from the other hand, and headed for the door.

"Where you going? You can't go out like that! Put on something, I tell you I have guests ... And Wilfredo – "

"Oh, he won't mind!" she said gaily, pausing at the door. "Can't *wait* to taste that sorbet. And I'd lose the word 'fairy.'"

Wilfredo, who must have had his ear to the door, jumped back. She brushed past his bugging eyes – and gigantic hard-on – and found her way back the way they'd come and marched on out to welcome the guests. Sophia and Milt Merdle were seated by the pool. When he saw her, tits taking the breeze, Milt Merdle laughed.

★

"Meet me at 11 A.M. 'Our spot.' Urgent." Terry had scribbled the note on the back of a list of commune expenses and left it on her pillow in her little room behind the kitchen.

The list made clear that Gilda was wildly in arrears.

Her own condition felt more urgent. Without the marriage plot to offer ballast she was floating weightless, Neil Armstrong in his lunar module. Now, in the harsh after-light of reason, she regretted her tantrum at Dragon's Gate. Yes, Kaz was a workaholic – and maybe pussy-teaser? – but the other scale was tipped, after all, by the way he'd searched far and wide for the Sand/Chopin painting, a token of his devotion. That was men for you: assholic behavior in one scale, enduring love in the other, a teeter board bound to land you with the crazy ladies in Bedlam or *aiiee*! Bertha in her flaming attic.

Terry nowhere on their beach. Leora walked toward the point. A giant stood casting his rod out there. Elsie's Guy Friday, Quasimodo. She flinched at the name he'd acquired. Over the summer she'd glimpsed him here and there in Islesfordd. Shee once spotted him lying on the roof of Elsie's ancient wood-sided station wagon in the pose of Snoopy atop his doghouse – this while Elsie ran errands in town. She'd seen him again at some benefit, a performance art slash Happening. Quasi was the Happening, buried up to his neck in sand. He had not looked happy. A woman crouched down to offer him a sip of her g & t. He was treated around here like a combination object/servant/pet.

Leora approached and watched him fish. His cartoonish lantern jaw, eyes sunk deep in his skull.

"Any luck?"

He swiveled a meaty hand to indicate so-so. The line jerked and he reeled it in. He stooped to unhook the fish with great care, tenderness even, and gently tossed it back in the bay, where it zigged off, apparently unharmed.

"Soo – that's an unusual way to fish."

"That fella's still got some growin' in him."

You had the feeling it would do him violence to actually catch something.

"I could sell these here stripers in New York City, but they're under-sized, so I let them go. My granddaddy used to be a bayman. Can't make a living fishin,' clammin' these here waters no more. I mainly do yard work out here."

Leora conjured up the Islesfordd no one talked about, the vanished baymen, indigenous people, the Wilfredo houseboys and Black maids who used the Service Entrance. The Bulova maidens who'd worked in the old clock factory in the village. She could sense the invisibles, the bit players and servers and background noise who'd been there since the Rottleseys, before the new money came, before the commune. They stood in a huddle in the blanched light, reproachful ghosts, across the wavelets on the opposite shore.

Leora caught the flash of an object in Quasi's tackle box. A red flying fish, a lure of some sort. It suggested something she'd seen before.

"Miss van Otten give it to me," he said following her gaze. "A good luck charm."

She recognized one of the fish lure doo-dads dangling from Elsie van Otten's turban. Leora wanted to ask Quasi about his life before Elsie and how he'd become her go-fer and whether his baymen forebears had ever found better waters. But there was Terry appearing around the rushes and walking toward the little beach.

★

He had the sort of body tennis whites were created for. Except closer up, the "whites" were more a greyish yellow, and his shorts shrunk from too many trips around a dryer so his balls looked squeezed. Terry, as always, a walking Want Ad for women who still did men's laundry.

"I've somehow *lost* Lester Annis's manuscript – you know, for his new book. I was practically rewriting the damn thing from scratch ... Could have sworn I left it on the sun porch ... I've looked everywhere ... Whole thing's got me smoking again." He stubbed his butt in the sand, then reached down and put it in his pocket.

Leora swallowed hard. Shit. So her good buddy had gone and done it. She flashed to the charades party and how Fred had cunningly engineered the manuscript's transfer out of Annis's hands. She wondered how much farther Fred might go.

"Annis came looking for me at Cormorant Cove," Terry went on – "we'd arranged to discuss the manuscript. I couldn't very well say, sorry, I seem to have *lost* it. So I dodged him. Had to climb out the basement door like a thief."

"I'm willing to bet the manuscript will turn up before too long."

"Now why would it turn up just like that?"

They'd arrived at fiddler town, but the crabs, according to their own arcane calendar, had packed it in for the summer and disappeared. "The commune promotes a certain chaos, but things that need to be found eventually surface."

"What kind of bullshit is that? I like you better tart."

She let it pass. Someone had convinced men that you were put on earth to embody whichever person suited them at any particular moment. But if each time you called men on their shit you'd be spinning your wheels and never move forward.

Terry took a match to a mauled cigarette. "Meanwhile, Clive Monomark's offered me a raise to come back fulltime to *Gotham*," he said through an exhale.

"I love it, they can't manage without you!" She chuckled to think of a comment she'd once heard: *Terry Cameron can turn the most dismal piece of writing into Vladimir Nabokov.* "You don't look happy. Why are you not happy?"

"Well, for one thing *Gotham* may be back on the auction block. Whoever buys it, I doubt they'd keep Clive on. And during this 'hiatus' I got to thinking. I'm not into the *Gotham* schtick any more. Stories about hustling for power and status that play to readers' worst instincts ... 'How to Survive Eating in a Snob Restaurant' – I don't think so. There are better ways to avoid thinking about death. I want – corny as it sounds – I want to be of use. Anyway, I don't have the temperament to butt up against the likes of Clive. His bullying and emotional violence."

Leora heard Fred cracking that Terry was a sheep in wolf's clothing.

"I started out at the Boston Free Press, an underground paper, stories on radical workers, the sexual revolution, the price of marijuana in Amsterdam ... Salary in the high two figures. I've helped organize migrant workers in New Hampshire apple orchards. Refused to pay taxes to protest 'Nam. That's more my thing."

Well, that was of a piece with living in a basement. "We tend to outgrow our youthful idealism."

"Stendhal once said the superior man grows *more* idealistic as he ages."

She stared at Terry with a kind of hunger. The man *quoted Stendhal!* Stendhal had also written, "Love has always been the most important business in my life; I should say the only one."

196

Leora smiled to think how that would go over with the women writers churning out broadsides about the incompatibility of love and self-respect.

"I'd like to do an expose on Nixon's secret invasion of Cambodia," Terry was saying. "The whole operation is designed to provide support for the right-wing military junta that just seized power in Cambodia. Think Clive would go for that?" He cut her a sour look. "I suspect you don't have much use for that sort of thing either."

"I grew up around idealistic, my family and their friends were wed to the Cause. They got booted out of work for taking the Fifth, their lives were up-ended, some never recovered. The McCarthy period, and all. I don't have the privilege of playing do-gooder and martyr. I want a decent life for my children."

To her surprise, Terry was nodding yes and going *mmhm, mmhm*. She would have liked to tell him about Finn's encounter with the firecracker while she was tinkering with the boiler that deep-freeze night and how he had somehow come out of it with only that blemish beneath his eye, but Christ what a close call, and how since that night *freaked out* was her middle name, since she'd never stopped blaming herself, and how she'd been obsessed ever since with having enough money to give the kids a working life.

"You know, that piece you wrote about the sisters in France who killed their employer – "

"Yes, *Murderous Maids*."

"That was a damn good piece. I remember thinking, I want that voice in the magazine. Why don't you write for *Gotham*? You're not gonna get rich, but we do pay well."

I want that voice ... "I've got a few ideas that are just right for *Gotham*," she said, forgetting she'd blown it with Kaz, or he'd blown it with her. Trying not to sound over-excited. "Islesfordd's a goldmine of stories. The mother's helpers making off with the man of the house ... The sugar billionaire on Hooker Pond who claims the kayakers are spies, so he's bought up all the stores that rent kayaks, and now the Tourist Board is suing and sugar man has hired the lawyer who defended The Boston Strangler ..."

Mmhm, mmhm ...

"Elsie van Otten, Islesfordd's Miss Haversham, dumped at the altar thirty years ago by her fiance and living with a hundred cats ... "

"That one's got a lot of press already. But I love your other ideas."

Leora laid out the saga of her old classmate, Libby Fenwick Futterman, who'd split from her husband Elliott, "the worst lay in New York," and ended up at a soup kitchen. "A cautionary tale about women fired up by the movement who jump ship without a game plan."

"Yah, that one's a cover," Terry said. "Once you've got a draft, I want to see it. Lemme think about how best to approach *Gotham*. I'd go with the sugar gazillionaire on Hooker Pond first, nice window into Islesfordd. Call it 'The Kayak Caper.' I'll give the Managing Editor a heads up."

Leora drew slightly ahead, wanting to savor this novelty in private: a guy who bolstered her ambitions, as if what could be more natural. Though he'd managed, go figure, to do the opposite for his wife.

"Of course, the *commune* is a goldmine of material just begging for a writer," Terry said, coming abreast, mischief in his voice.

"Oh yeah, I've been making notes for a novel – well, mental notes – since the moment I arrived."

"*Mmhm, mmhm.* What you need to anchor the story is a nice murder," he said. He looked blissed out, as if downing a Blue Point oyster. "With all the intrigue and envy, Islesfordd feels ripe for it, don't you think? In fact, some sort of violence feels inevitable. There are too many clashing vectors of desire out here to avoid a collision. People want things harder. *Too* hard. And they feel entitled to just grab what they want, any way they want it, exempt from the normal rules, like Nietzche's *ubermensch*. Except they ain't never heard of Nietzche."

"Or *ubermensch*."

The vertical rays of the sun beat down. High tide, the bay swelled, tumescent, beyond the tidal mark. "The water wants us," Leora said.

Terry glanced around. "No one here – what the hell."

"Actually, I've gotten rather skilled at that." She stripped down to bra and pants and turned, happy she had a nice ass, and went sloshing into water the green of sea-glass. Terry followed in his tennis shorts.

The bay silky and extra salty, with a spank of cold, re-membering a recent storm. They swam parallel to the shore, swam a long ways and then kept going, locked in the rhythm of a matching crawl, cutting through the water, breathing and stroking in unison like a double-pontooned creature, till they reached the Point. They tread water. His thinning hair was slicked back in the style of German swimmers from the forties, his eyes without glasses water shot. Out beyond the boats riding at anchor the neck of a black cormorant broke the surface. Dived back down. They kept a measured distance, she and Terry, and she wondered what his cock was doing in the water, would it be floaty and soft? A marvelous fat sea worm that made its own light? She wanted to dive down like the cor-morant. They treadled the water with their feet and smiled at each other across the water and smiled and smiled as if they'd pulled off a major heist.

CHAPTER 14

Combustions

★

"Canned goods swell when hydrogen gas is produced by the interaction of acid in the food with the metal of the can. Pressure is exerted on the can ... If the sealed can is left on the shelf indefinitely, eventually it may explode. Do not wait for that to happen."

In August, season of big ticket benefits, Islesfordd leaps into over-drive as if time has slipped its gears. The *Islesfordd Herald* dispatched Edwina to photograph the swells at The Gala for Hookworm in Sub-Saharan Africa. She would have been happy to camp all summer at the commune, where she'd cobbled together a little photography studio in a third floor turret. She'd grown up around the coastal towns of New England; larking about Islesfordd with Fred she felt like a kid sprung from school. (His philandering with Sophia Merdle's Black housekeeper, while Meghan toiled in the city, kind of violated the ethos of the commune, but the philandering part of Fred was inoperable.)

Problem was, Islesfordd held few charms for Jo. She couldn't smell the Rosa Rugosa adorning the bays for the stench of patriarchy.

"The commune," Edwina pointed out, "was dreamt up by the mother of feminism" – how Gilda hated that frowsy moniker! "So that would make it a *matriarchy*." "That's what the communards would like people to believe. But Gilda's still in cahoots with the patriarchy. She's basically arranging deck chairs on the Titanic, when what we need is a major structural overhaul. We all know her ruling passion is to please men. She'd sell herself and the movement down the river for some guy." "I'm not so sure. She wants it every way. And where's the harm in that? Besides, we could really use your input at the Steering Committee. Gilda's been alienating too many allies with her homophobic stuff."

To Edwina, "patriarchy" was an abstraction. Except for outlier pervs like Seb Nye or Lester Annis, Edwina was hard put to see men *as a class* as the oppressor. They were more clowns. All that *stuff*, the pipe-like appendage like a donkey's swinging between their legs – so balky and unreliable, too. (An image of Nye from behind, bending naked over a suitcase at the hotel in Villequier, made him harder to hate.) And that Peter Grosvenor had almost drowned to show off his silly review – how pathetic was that? Dear Fred, pigeon toed, stuttering, blurry with booze, would stick it in central vacuuming. No, men were just fellow bumblers on the road to nowhere, though more transparent and helpless than women. Little boys accoutered with pubic hair and baritones.

★

They'd worked out that Edwina would spend weekdays in the city at Jo's place on Bethune. Leora – perpetually job hunting in a city chronically about to go bankrupt – lacked the funds to send her kids to day camp. Edwina jumped into the breach. Afternoons, stun-gunned by the city's summer heat, she took Leora's children to the public outdoor pool on St. Luke's Place. On their outings Cara sat proudly erect in her stroller that wouldn't stroll, wearing her white pique sun hat. She tipped up her bottle of apple juice like a trumpet. Pointed at the filthy pigeons and called out *wook*! And the Pakistani guy in the newsstand, dark-eyed baby beside him – *wook*! Finn had undertaken her schooling by teaching her to read street signs. DEAD END, Cara repeated. Finn's hand, when Edwina grasped it to cross the street, was always sticky, something she might have greatly minded in an earlier life. In fact, she was madly drawn to Finn, a strange child with an old soul vibe who would sit on Jo's futon by the window, head tipped to catch strains from an invisible world the way dogs hear sounds beyond the human scale. He had the "quiet eye" and laser-like focus of elite athletes, though on what he focused Edwina couldn't have said.

"When you grow up you're going to be an important man."

"You think so?" He shot her an awed look.

Sometimes Becca Gladstone came to the pool with them. She sat framed by a white Afro that seemed a form of aggression, yakking about her romance with an inmate at the Queens Detention Center where she was a summer intern. With plans for the Strike gearing up, Becca had kind of slipped Gilda's mind (again) – though her daughter's new love interest might have snapped her to attention.

"You won't catch *me* at my mother's goddamn march," Becca said. "I don't resent her fame, not at all. And it's not the march

I object to – it's her as a mother. I refuse to have anything to do with her."

Edwina sighed. "The truth of it is, makers of history don't always make ideal parents. When did a male maker of history, a Trotsky, say, ever get slammed for being a lousy dad?"

"You sound like *her*. Anyway, who's gonna show at the damn march? A few communards and the bourgeois types from WOW. She's alienated young women, gays, the radicals she calls 'the crazies.'"

"Can me and Cara come to Gilda's parade?" Finn said.

"Of course you can, dear."

"I'm going to make a sign: Down with Sexism."

"Perfect!" She was continually surprised and amused by how Finn was beamed to the culture at large beyond the ex-pected for a boy his age. Edwina felt needed by these casualties of driven mothers – her "foster children." Becca's mom had a revolution to tend to. Leora could be the woodcutter in a fairy tale, out to seek her fortune so she could buy Cara a working stroller. She'd consulted a pediatric plastic surgeon about removing the blemish under Finn's right eye, Leora had confided. The doc charged something exorbitant and she was holding off for now. Leora had never revealed how Finn had acquired the scar.

It came to her so naturally, Edwina rarely wondered at her love for Leora's kids. It was easy when you wouldn't have to bear all the disappointments they might face down the line, the wrong paths taken, the self-inflicted pain, none of it anything you could ward off or fix. Maybe by caring for Finn and Cara she was trying, through some weird inner calculus, to set to rights her own twisted history. Fred, of course, would dismiss that kind of thinking as *pap psychology*.

★

Early August, Jo surprised Edwina by announcing she wanted to spend the weekend at the commune. They had lunch at Therapeutix, Islesfordd's trendy new health food cafe. It nestled in the brick courtyard of The Watch Dial, a condo risen phoenix-like from the ashes of the Bulova watch factory. In its profitable prime, the factory had killed off half the town's blue collar women with radium poisoning. Local activists insisted the site was still saturated with heavy metals, including mercury and arsenic, but Merdle Properties had scratched the palms of some EPA goombahs to "de-list" it as a toxic waste site.

A mother in tie-dye bell bottoms herded her brood of four into the cafe. Edwina thought the older boy resembled Finn, something about the coltish legs. A surge of love at the thought of Finn's always grimy knees. Edwina hoped the family's arrival wouldn't trigger one of Jo's tirades about zero population growth, or how the world was suffering from "testosterone poisoning" (here at Therapeutix it was more likely arsenic).

The mother kept cutting her furtive looks. Edwina, accustomed, usually flicked them off as a buffalo's hide repels flies. Now she endured them patiently – then smiled full out at the gawker ... *I know*. People inevitably gawked at Jo, too, her insinuating eyes, pale boy's bob, monkish shirts, all of it ... *subversive*. What in blazes were they looking at, a girl or a beautiful boy? Some kinky divinity student? An *impersonator*. It seemed to bother people no end. Edwina adored the way Jo slipped wide of the usual categories, she might have dreamt herself up.

The mother-of-four's expression turned sly and knowing, the usual crap. Edwina sighed: okay, so this was how she would live in the world and she'd bought in. She leaned across the table and, keeping mom in sight, closed her mouth around Jo's full upper lip. Ahead stretched a golden August weekend. They'd drive out toward Montauket and lie topless on a deserted patch of beach, she'd taste the salt on Jo's arm. They'd eat fried clams in a roadside joint. Though women couples sometimes hung out on Bacchus Beach, Edwina shied away from the "gay beach," where the guys strutted their sculpted bodies in Speedo trunks. She balked at falling under the rubric of "gay" – or any rubric – as if she and Jo were a *species* like the piping plovers out here; she and Jo just *were*, their own continent, a world unto themselves. She had managed to find them a room in one of those sexy motels crouched in the dunes – cottage-cheese-ceilings and antiseptic-smelling, yet always fully booked in high season ... They'd fix a batch of vodka gimlets ... Jo would sit out on the deck and proofread her monograph on Baubo, the bawdy Greek Goddess who liked to hang out, legs akimbo, flaunting her vulva. She herself, drunk on sea light, would roam the "double dunes" with her new Canon F-1 camera. The example of Jo's steady discipline spurred her own ambitions ... Abruptly, she wondered, was she trying too hard? The previous week she'd overheard Jo refer to her photo gig at the *Islesfordd Herald* as "Edwina's little project" – a phrase reeking of male condescension. Lately she'd find Jo nose deep in some fire-breathing, humor-free feminist screed. *Nobody Needs to Get Fucked* urged women to "free the libido from the tyranny of orgasm-seeking." Edwina leafed through another pamphlet lying face down on the futon: "The nuclear family must be destroyed... Whatever its ultimate meaning, the break-up of families now is an objectively revolutionary process." Lately Jo couldn't stop fighting with editors about spelling women "womyn;" feuded with academic colleagues who weren't "woman identified." When had she gotten so doctrinaire? One night

Edwina arrived at Bethune Street to find the Van Dykes, or GutterDykes, whatever, camped out yet again at Jo's apartment. They traveled the country in vans, spoke to men only if they were waiters or mechanics, and stopped only on Womyn's Land in what they called Lesbian Nation. The leader was a jolly giant with a shaved head, large ear lobes, and tattoos. The talk that evening was all of "radical empowerment" and "lesbian separatism" and defying male supremacy. Swell. But did they have to soak their grimy denim and tie-dyed threads in both the tub *and* sink?

★

"I hang out with you in the city all week, yet you never come to the commune." Fightin' words, yet out they tripped. "I'm here now, aren't I?" "This once. It's too ... unequal. Where's the reciprocity?" "You know I work better in the city." The implication was that Jo's work on the male gaze and Baubo was of more importance than "Edwina's little project" – an assessment with which Edwina sourly concurred.

"I'm just not into that Duchess of Dessert/Prince of Pots stuff," Jo added.

"Bottom line" – anger rising – "you want it all your way. If we're to be together, I have to live *your* life. If you really care for me, you shouldn't get hung up on the commune's preciosity, it's trivial."

"It *is* trivial, let's drop it."

"That's not my point!" Edwina poked at her marinated yogurt cheese; it resembled something shat out by the mourning doves at Cormorant Cove. "These articles: Pam Whozit's 'Nobody Needs to Get Fucked' – where she says, 'Sometimes hugging is nicer.' She's kidding, right?"

"I believe Pam Wunderlich is arguing in that piece that 'polit-ical lesbianism' is morally superior to the sexually active variety.'"

"'Morally superior?' Sounds like a way to make yourself miserable. D'you get points for being a martyr?"

Jo shrugged. "Pam's just exploring celibacy and friendship as a new model for female relationships." She'd assumed the patient tone you'd hear in nursery school. "She believes we need to stop valorizing the male model and free the libido from, in her phrase, 'the tyranny of orgasm-seeking.'" "*Tyranny*? It's a tyranny now?" A snort of laughter. "I'd call it the new Puritanism. The tyranny of *ideology*. And by the way, it really bugs me when you go all ... *academic* on me." She was talking too loud; she caught their neighbor's little boy looking their way. She pictured Finn, with his skewed gaze and books he foraged from the trash and precocious phrases and air of hearing music no one else heard – she could whoop for joy at the thought of him. She said, "What could be lovelier than a little boy with grimy knees?" "I can think of a few things," Jo laughed. "We've been so conditioned by the patriarchy and male-identified reflexes, it's hard to wrap your mind around these new ways of thinking." "Mmm." Whenever Jo used words such as male-identified or ... *valorize*, and talked of a "collective oppositional consciousness," Edwina felt she was hearing catechism in Sunday School. Instead of a person. *Her* person in the world. "Never mind Pam Wunderlich, she can get overly dogmatic. We can honor these new ways of thinking about women in the world without getting hung up on them personally." Jo beamed her low-flying gaze. Reached across and grasped Edwina's hand. "I came out here to tell you about an exciting new project – and I want you to be a part of it."

Hope ballooned. Behind lay her life in men, a junkyard of twisted scrap metal ... They'd work things out. With Jo she was in for keeps.

CHAPTER 15

Fred Does Suicide

"The reward of art is not fame or success but intoxication..."
— Cyril Connolly, *The Unquiet Grave*

The gods were with him. A low-hanging sky, an angry sea at war with itself. Perfect! The tall motherfucker riding shoreward got whupped by waves scissoring in sideways, hustled back by the undertow with a sucking rattle – then bopped by the next swell in a mess of troughs and runnels spurting geysers of foam. From a lifeguard stand, ghostly in the fog, a red flag warned off swimmers.

He shucked his clothes, folded them neatly. He stared down at the knuckles of his toes. Such care had gone into making them. Why had he *folded his clothes*? That would be just the telling detail to include in a suicide scene ... Too late for all that, he'd soon be freed from the life-shortening struggle to make sentences.

He would keep his bathing suit on. He'd once seen some poor bastard hauled naked from an autumn surf, his dick shriveled from cold and overexposure to a pitiful knob. No, even in death, pride counted.

Should he do a Virginia Woolf and load his trunks with rocks? Not a stone in sight, just his luck; Islesfordd's fine white sand beaches were what drew people here, second only to the chance of sighting a celebrity. He couldn't very well drive back to the bay across the highway to collect rocks, stopping for three red lights, likely getting stuck behind old Farmer Brown's pickup truck, and maybe *losing his impetus*.

He waded in, fjording the waves, then gave himself to the cold glaucous swirl and kicked and dove beyond the first line of breakers. The sea churned him with an almost personal animus.

He'd left no note. He'd been unable to get it right; draft upon draft of balled-up paper overflowed his waste basket – Christ, his drafts would be discovered, why hadn't he shredded them? You'd sooner expose dirty underwear than an early draft ... He tread water beyond the breakers. He mustn't be too hard on himself, the multiple challenges posed by his suicide note would have defeated even Asa Dribble.

He had struggled to make perfectly clear that his wife's desertion had played no role in his final act. That Meghan had split the *moment after* she had contracts in hand for both her cookbook and TV show – well, such steely control, such command of the long game inspired only respect. He'd underestimated Meghan and wished her well. Especially as the topic of her book in no way infringed on his. Even semi-literate – or maybe *because* of that – Meghan was the new go-getter, unburdened by ideas or the moral dimension or grammar, and better equipped to navigate the convulsing world around them than he.

Yet how could he expose his true motive? Peter Grosvenor's lame treatise had gotten *Book-of-the-Month Club*. Not just as an Alternate – but a *Full Selection*! Which would ensure an appearance – a nightmare Fred had already envisioned – on the Today Show, etc, etc. To go on living in that limbo of the almost-famous – people at parties saying *how do I know your name?* – worse, to wake each morning, *still unrecognized* by the *Daily Beaver*, when Peter's mediocrity brought full page reviews, BOMC, fawning journalists; when in the latest interview Peter himself humbly acknowledged he'd never suspected his work would hit such a nerve – no, it was too much to endure. Every man has his breaking point.

He flinched to remember how he'd struck out in his scheme to borrow material from Lester Annis's book. The research was too imbedded in the text to lift out. He'd have had to appropriate the whole goddamn book. Take a contract on Annis and have him killed off. Maybe hire that Quasimodo guy, who worked for Annis as a yard man and knew the property ... To his shame Nadine had spotted him lurking at the kitchen door, waiting for an all clear to slip Annis's manuscript back to the sun room ... What a sorry business ... Let his disappearance remain a mystery to be woven into Islesfordd myth, and his thigh bone wash up on Megalomantic Shores.

They'd looked smaller from the shore, this second line of breakers. Harder to get the purchase out here to dive under and swim toward the horizon ... No sooner did he surface than the ocean kept throwing more at him, endlessly giving of itself ... Fear gripped him.

He was *supposed* to be scared, all was going well ...

But maybe not; why should he be scared of the very thing he wanted?

Suddenly, electric stings tattooed his skin ... Fucking *jelly fish*? They had no business in the ocean, he thought, indignant, the jellies worked the bay ... Ach, in August all bets were off ...

This ocean variety was *ocean-strength*, the stings kept burning harder ... The bastards got him in the eye lids, he was bobbing about half-blind. He tried to stroke to un-infested waters, but each wave showered down a fresh batch. If jellies had made it here, could they be chaperoned by a Portuguese Man o' War? He pictured the lucite sail cresting a fat blue blimp dangling a mess of pink and purple stingers. Those mothers could do serious damage ... Didn't they live in Florida? He'd never imagined suicide to be this *annoying*. Thrashing about was bad for his health, he might be looking at another ischemic attack like the one that laid him on the kitchen floor ...

A jelly got him in the balls, he breached like a porpoise – and in that moment he got it. How to crack open the suicide note! He'd always brought his writing up to snuff by polishing drafts ... The way to finesse it had come to him, *finally* ...

The shoreline was still visible. Unfinished business beckoned: he must rework his last words for posterity ... And there was Ethel Scull's fundraiser next week, thanks to Gilda, even an almost-famous such as him could crack A-list parties ... Busloads of press expected – surely someone from the *Beaver* he could sweet-talk. The Women's Strike! All the moving parts finally coming together and he would miss it? The thought of Gilda brought on a sudden lust for a whiskey sour ... The jellies were stinging to light him up like a Christmas tree ...

He ducked under a towering rogue wave. Each time he broke the surface, a new one pounded him under, wagged and rotored him ... Then the next ... and the next – He felt furious at the fun the waves were having at his expense. They came in sixes, he knew ... When he was up to number nine he stopped counting and tried to swim shoreward ... He made no headway ... His best crawl, and he was paddling in the same place, exhausted ... The roar of the surf was doubled by a roar inside, his own hoarse breathing ... A rip, he was caught in a rip ... He went under again, water rushed in through his nose, his mouth. *I need to get to the surface.*

He pictured those signs on the lifeguard stand: *don't fight the current, swim sideways parallel to the beach* ... Arrows on the signs pointed sideways, presumably for idiots who couldn't read. Shit, which way was sideways? A giant wave curled over on him, he was whip-sawed beneath ... He brought his knees to his chest and in one giant kick propelled his body upward only to get pounded by another ...

★

Toward eleven A.M., in a commune still sleeping it off, Leora received a phone call. It was from the Islesfordd police. A man had been found wandering naked in the rain along Montauket Highway, mumbling and incoherent, unable to locate his car, eyes swollen and half shut. He'd given the officers her number and name.

CHAPTER 16

Mayhem

*"The night was a time for bestial affinities,
for drawing closer to oneself."*

— Patricia Highsmith, Strangers on a Train

That same week Midas Close flirted with a second near-disaster.

The Islesford Herald:

On August 9th Dr. Lester Annis, a controversial psychotherapist and author, was found bleeding profusely from a head wound in the master bedroom of his home at 7 Midas Close in Islesfordd, Long Island. He was apparently bloodied from being bludgeoned with a weight used for workouts. Sgt. Waski of the Islesfordd Police Dept. said a 911 call came in the morning following the assault at around 7 A.M. from the victim's housekeeper, Esperanza Lopez. She found him collapsed in a

beanbag chair wearing bathing trunks, wrapped in a
bloody white rug. She called the Islesfordd Village Police.

Sgt. Waski tentatively determined that there had
been an altercation and the victim had suffered the
blunt-force trauma of several blows to his head, none
fatal. Burglary appeared not to be the motive.

★

Even the New York tabloids carried the story. Islesfordd had not had an assault case on the books in twenty-two years; the fabled playground was considered immune to the violence that plagued New York, where the homicide rate had doubled in a single decade.

Questioning of the victim by the Islesfordd police yielded little about the assailant's identity. Annis claimed a man had entered the house by the basement door, and then sprang out at him in the dark bedroom. There was a scuffle with a five-pound weight and Annis got clocked on the head. It was a moonless night and he couldn't identify his attacker. On further questioning it was revealed that the victim's head wounds were superficial, mostly incurred when he slipped on a flokati rug and struck a stationary bicycle near his bed.

★

The Islesfordd police quickly zeroed in on the commune. Lester Annis's house, a modest "contemporary" near Bacchus Beach, was just up the road from Cormorant Cove. He'd been known to attend the commune's charade parties; he'd recently been spotted at Ethel Scull's fundraiser for some whacko march Gilda Gladstone was planning; the communards were potential suspects.

Gilda went ballistic. The non-stop interruptions, squad cars coming and going in front of the house – could the timing of Lester's assault be worse? The whole business – so klutzy and clownish – was deflecting attention from the march! Usually, what meager space the male-dominated media devoted to the movement was monopolized by stories trashing feminism. A river of copy about Gilda Gladstone's "abusive marriage," how she used never to go on television "without a black eye," how her husband, "desperate with rage and envy" at her success, tried to throw her out of a moving car. (That this was somewhat true made it worse.) The latest garbage in *The Monitor* had dismissed Women's Lib as "an evangelical, feel-good movement with no power to actually change women's lives." Culture reporter Eric Throbbing had called the feminist movement an "infectious disease" and the women in it "a band of braless bubbleheads." Now Lester Annis was hogging newsprint by getting himself mugged!

Whoever dunnit was irresponsible in the extreme. She and her sisters were poised to unleash something so major it would make *national* headlines, show the world that the second great wave of feminism was about to rock the planet on its axis. As far as Gilda was concerned, the perp would be *doubly* guilty: (1) of creating a distraction at this pivotal moment; and (2) recklessly endangering the supply of Islesfordd's available men.

★

If Gilda was put out, the Village police and detectives who swarmed Cormorant Cove to question these commune-ists were having a shit fit. The weekend people who treated you like their new Hydrostatic Gas Front-Engine Tractor – that you could deal with. But the commune-ists – you couldn't hardly get a straight answer, you couldn't do your freakin' job. They kept throwing questions back atcha.

This blue hair Henry Lyman – called himself an "ace stock picker" – tried to sell Detective Neary on a stock for miracle spine surgery. "Insider stuff, the next big thing," Lyman said. "Practically doubled in a few months."

"We're here to question you as a possible suspect in the assault on Lester Annis, not buy stock," Detective Neary said (making a mental note of the stock's name and planning to look in on his bank account).

A few minutes in, and Henry Lyman had fallen asleep.

Adios Motherfucker. They should throw the whole bunch in the slammer.

★

"The night of August 11th ... where might I have been?" Nadine said, putting her fingers to her forehead.

Sergeant Waski was getting a hinky feeling about the suspect, the way she was staring into space like that.

In fact, the sergeant was witnessing Nadine in the grip of a Eureka moment. She'd suddenly seen the shape of a new book whole: the impact of the movement on blue collar women. She fanned herself wildly. "You know, women's lib has been criticized for focusing primarily on the upper middle class – white girl problems – and neglecting a key segment of the population," she said. "Rightly so! I'm researching an article about working class women in marginal 'McJobs', which will be a chapter in a larger work. Can we talk? At your convenience, of course. We could do lunch at Therapeutix. I'd love to know how your wife and daughters feel about feminism."

"Ma'am, my daughter is two years old – and I'll tell you how *I* feel about you libbers and your bullshit pardon my

French. The wife gets an assured lifetime income – why should she complain? I don't think you realize that you and the other communists here are potential suspects and I need you to tell me exactly where you were the night of August 11th."

"Yes, of course. I might have been giving a talk on 'The New Fathering' at Shittington Grange. But no one at the commune" – she indicated the sun porch dotted with half-filled coffee mugs and abandoned drinks – "could have physically assaulted Lester Annis. Frankly, they don't have the mental and emotional wherewithal. We bludgeon with *words*. When it comes to actually *acting*, writers become paralyzed by 'what-ifs' and nightmare visions of being someone's bitch in prison. '*Sicklied o'er with the pale cast of thought*' sort of thing. So: this book I'm contemplating. I know it's not yet under contract, but rest assured I have an excellent track record. My current book has been on the List for six consecutive weeks."

List? *What* list? Fuckin' city people. Miz Kooz-in-etz here might enjoy making wallets in a prison camp in Ossining.

★

"How did you know Lester Annis?"

"Well, I knew him mainly by reputation," Fred Lustman said. "I can't say he was wildly popular around here."

"Can you name any of his enemies?"

"Well, I for one thoroughly disapproved of his therapeutic methods, if you must know."

"Enough to assault him?"

"Now there's an interesting question – but a misguided one, if you don't mind my saying. 'Dislike' of his methods is too cerebral to inspire a physical attack. Bludgeoning with a five pound weight needs to come from passion, from the gut."

Someone driven to an extreme act to remedy an intolerable situation, he scribbled in his little notebook for a future novel. *Also persuaded he could act with impunity.*

"Say, *I'm* the one taking notes." The suspect's face looked like ground chuck – signs of an altercation? Like a struggle involving a five pound weight? "What happened to your face, sir?"

"Got stung by jellyfish. In the ocean."

Instantly suspicious: "Ain't no jelly fish in the ocean."

"Yeah, *really*, that's what *I* said! Put it down to ocean warming around the Galapagos." Fred lit a new Pall Mall. "Then I was attacked by a Portuguese Man 'O War."

"Impossible. Ain't never seen 'em this far north."

Fred wasn't sure if he'd actually fought off the Man 'O War or whether, half-drowned, he'd begun to hallucinate out there. "Say, I wonder if you could help me with a bit of research. I'm working up a book proposal about a latter-day robber baron, a fugitive criminal financer, who bilked a fortune from investors in the United States and is now on the lam in Latin America. As a law enforcement official, I bet you could explain how in those countries he always manages to evade Uncle Sam."

"Simple. He bribes the local authorities." The detective pulled himself up short: "Dammit, *I'm* the one asking the questions. You still haven't told me: Where were you the night – ?"

"I must've still been in Islesford Hospital."

"Why were you in the hospital?"

"Uh, you don't really wanna know. In fact, I'm compelled to remain silent since I plan to use that material in a novel at some point and can't reveal spoilers before it's even written!"

★

In his many years on the Force Detective Kevin Neary had never come up against anything like this. A dame with a Jimmy

Durante schnozzola and motor mouth, words coming atcha so fast you couldn't hardly understand. Waving her arms around ... Running to the phone on her short legs, yelling at the poor slob on the other end ... He could have a fifty-one-fifty on his hands. And she seemed to be the boss here ...

"You're asking me to remember the night of – of what, August 11th?" She threw up her hands in exasperation. "How would I remember? I've been swamped with details about the Women's Strike. I might have been at the Coalition Committee ... or the Steering Committee. We've been lobbying the Mayor to give us *all* of Fifth Avenue, not just the damn *sidewalk*. Would you believe he's worried about rush hour disruption? When we're about to *disrupt the entire world*? I don't mean to be impolite, but this, uh, investigation of yours is sucking up media attention better spent on the Strike."

"Madam, perhaps you don't realize: we're dealing with possible attempted homicide – here in *Islesfordd* – and you and the other members of your, um, com-*mune* are suspects."

"Me, are you kidding? I'm way too busy to try to kill someone. Think of the *aggravation* ... I'm calling for a 'paradigm shift' embracing the entire world of work, family, and community. So I ask you, where would I find the time? We need to look at the impact of corporate downsizing on working wives who suddenly become their family's sole provider." She cocked her head at him. "I just had an idea – talk about synergy! Perhaps your wife would like to join the march?"

"I'm separated."

"All the more reason she should come on board! Your ex could co-opt the local women for a sister action. The Women's Strike – I mean, march, we're calling it a *march*, strategic reasons ... is planning actions nation-wide. Transform society ... we are all Karl Marx ... all housewives, but '*housepouses*' a better word ..." (This dame impossible to follow, yes a fifty-one-fifty.) "Women out here could assemble at the windmill, take over Route 27, disrupt commuters from Islesfordd to Wapakoneta."

So he was available. Gilda had not failed to notice Detective Neary's small mischievous eyes, his sideburns, the dimple that came and went. The start of man-boobs, the beer gut – a *guy* guy ... He'd call his ex "the missus." The "wife-beater" undershirt beneath his uniform not the classiest garment, but it showed his chest hair to advantage, and she'd had it with the New Men who hung around, the feminist dads with burp rags; the namby pambies with their empathy and flay-me-I'm-the-oppressor voices. They'd petition their local assembly woman for permission to make a pass at their date. She was pleased she'd just had her hair layered in the Farah Fawcett look at Kenneth's, and put on the blue ruffled blouse with V-neck from Saks.

"Y'know, this assault case must be pretty exciting compared to the usual DUI stuff out here," Gilda said. "In fact" – she giggled, flashing a bit of decolletage – "maybe it was *you* who pulled me over the other night?" She'd been drunk as a skunk and lost a fender to some sculpture sticking out of Kaz Grabowski's driveway on Midas Close.

Detective Neary would have preferred to interrogate, and more, that dark-haired honey he'd seen on the premises, whatta knock-out, that tube top thing she had on, bazongas to launch a thousand ships ... This leader of the libbers was an old battle-axe ... The honker, eyes like his neighbor's Basset Hound ... Kinda ancient to be a Badge Bunny. Yet damned if she wasn't ... what was it? *Magnetic.* With the separation, he hadn't gotten laid in weeks, a manatee would have looked good to him.

"Well, if I had approached the vehicle and ordered the suspect out, I'm sure I would have remembered," Detective Neary said gallantly. "Especially if the suspect failed to comply."

"And if the suspect failed to comply?"

"For safety reasons, I would have physically removed the suspect from the vehicle – "

"Physically removed," Gilda breathed. "And then what?"

"Well, in the past, I would have used the Three Point Lateral Embrace."

"*Lateral embrace* … "

"But that's in the past. Now I would go with The Curled Angel or Flowing Triangle hold."

Why did this sound familiar? Then Gilda remembered she'd heard Becca and friends snickering about positions in the Kama Sutra with those names. Was Neary trying to tell her something?

"See, I'm into the writings of Dr. King and the application of nonviolence to conflict management. I'm convinced it's possible 'to win your opponent over' and not 'to win over your opponent,' which is the goal of Kingian Nonviolence. I keep experimenting with the concept in every phase of conflict."

"Right," Gilda said excitedly. "'Win your opponent over' – *Co-opt* your opponent! I try to apply the same philosophy myself."

"Anyway, not much attempted homicide in Islesfordd, the usual is more like the theft of a gas grill off of someone's deck. Or a raid on Elsie Van Otten's place to cart away the cat manure. Elsie has been running the place down for years, lucky she's got that handyman. The other day she asks for help repairing her car, an old LaSalle touring sedan. But the thing's been sitting there in the driveway so many years, bittersweet vine was growing into the motor casing and crank case – through the whole vehicle! Repair wasn't going to happen," he added, laughing.

"Bittersweet vine!" Gilda convulsed with laughter. "Growing in the motor casing!" (whatever that was). "And the crank case!"

She wiped her eyes. "Tell me, what's the status of that sculpture on Mr. Grabowski's lawn? The folks on Hooker Pond have been suing to get it removed."

Neary described the barrage of phone calls from "the weekend people" who didn't want the grand kids "exposed to porn."

Gilda leaned in. The commune should not be confused with the weekend people, she confided. Their "elective family" was in residence at Cormorant Cove pretty much year-round. "We're sort of a support system for divorced people who didn't do marriage right, but crave *community*. Y'know, it's not just sex people miss – it's sitting around the kitchen table in your bathrobe and letting it all hang out. I think you'd really add something. The communards would love to hear about your approach to conflict management. Why don't you stop by for a drink when you have a moment? Or come to dinner."

The sun porch was an oven. Neary swiped the back of his hand across his forehead. This Gilda gal – it would be like flying into a tornado.

"Would you like some ice tea?" Gilda said. "Oh my God, I should have offered you some earlier! I made it from scratch with fresh mint."

Gilda bustled back in bearing a tray with two sweating glasses. "Tell me, have you ever been to Swaziland?"

CHAPTER 17

Reverberations

"All this fuss about sleeping together. For physical pleasure I'd
sooner go to my dentist any day." Nina Blount, Vile Bodies

                                        – Evelyn Waugh

Like the rolling thunder of late summer's storms, the bludgeoning of Lester Annis continued to reverberate through Cormorant Cove. Leora amassed a fat folder of clips from the local
papers and New York tabloids – *"what you need to anchor your*
story is a murder," Terry had said. True, it was a pretty klutzy assault, more buffoonish than homicidal, but it would have to do.

    She prowled the grounds of Annis's spread farther up
Midas Close (modernist flat roof, lots of glass, she scribbled).
She was swiftly rousted from "the crime scene" by the cops.
However, they'd ignored her as a suspect, correctly sensing she
was not a proper communard, merely one of many hangers-on;
perhaps they'd bought into the commune's haughtiness and
thought her too insignificant to be a murder suspect ... Back in

her squatter's quarters at Cormorant Cove – currently a little maid's room behind the kitchen – Leora typed up notes and chapter outlines on her Olivetti. She was creating a fictionalized version of the signal summer of '70 before the Women's Strike; moving her characters around a mental chessboard, pondering which one might have the most pressing motive to attack Annis. Already she had four chapters.

She would have loved Terry Cameron's eye on her pages. The prospect of his querying, questing blue pencil seemed better than sex, or maybe an extension of it. She would have also liked to speculate with Terry on the actual perp – the real one who existed outside her novel (and who would take on a second life within it). Not for a moment did she buy Annis's claim that he'd been unable to identify his attacker.

Terry, though, hadn't come out to the commune lately and they weren't on any terms she could describe. A twinge, as she wondered if, as Nadine had hinted, he'd found some compelling occupation in the city. Like the super-stimulating job of editing *A Wee Taste of Scotland*, the cookbook of Fred's estranged wife Meghan. Terry could blue pencil a recipe, say, for haggis. Leora wondered many ways you could say, "Mince the lungs, heart and trimmings, add the finely chopped onions, and spoon the mixture into the sheep's stomach"? Time had not yet set its tracks on Meghan. Leora pictured her curtaining Terry with those runnels of hair the night of charades ...

Keep the focus, she ordered herself. Shortly after their aborted lunch at Dragon's Gate, Kaz had called, all but begging her to meet him for a drink. It felt like a reprieve, that call (a throwback to when as a little girl she needed her father to forgive her for ... whatever girlish sins – before she could sleep). She was on board again with the Plot, the joystick piloting her days. She agreed to meet Kaz, feigning reluctance. He picked her up in his blue Jaguar convertible, risking the jealous wrath of Gilda (who happened to have a committee meeting in the city that day) and whisked her off, hair to the wind, to The Three-Legged Mare. They sat in the pub's garden among rustic artifacts of a faintly sinister cast.

"Lookit, I've been bachelor all these years, so used to making work the priority. That afternoon, I fell back into my old ways. I made mistake. Big mistake. I should have given you head about the business crisis – "

"I think you mean 'heads up.'"

" – real emergency. Fires to put out."

"Merdle just happened to, like, *drop by*?" *I get what I need*, Kaz had said that first night at his party. The words had lingered in her mind: a form of positive thinking? Or a threat? She noticed a wooden antique in the garden that looked designed to inflict harm.

"I didn't know he'd come early. I didn't expect what happened – well, almost – in bedroom. It went out of control. It's effect you have on me. When I first see you at my party for Gilda I felt such a burst of love for you. I've been dying to show you George Sand painting. I wanted to surprise you and see your face ... I wanted the afternoon to be perfect. I had it all planned!"

He really was a variation of Gatsby, playing out the dream he'd held close all these years. "Well, you'll agree it turned horribly awkward. That can mess you up, to be interrupted at your most naked. I don't mean literally. Why didn't Wilfredo run interference?"

"I told you, he pretends not to understand. Anyway, I fired him – "

"Oh, you didn't! I hope you gave him generous severance pay and benefits."

"Right, well, I'll see to that ... The thing is I was too eager for us to be together again ... And I forgot to give Merdle – 'heads-up?' I can't stop hating myself ... "

He continued in this vein for long minutes. She smelled his fear that he'd lose her again, as he had years ago. She didn't want him to lose her. They'd reached the point where they were both in and she was giving him a hard time purely for form.

"I want to take care of you," Kaz said. "When I think how you're living in that ... slum."

She glanced around the tavern, fearful he'd been overheard. In enlightened circles such language had been abolished. Stricken from the lexicon. She realized how innocent about the women's movement Kaz remained, as if he were back in 19th century Krakow ... She wondered what that creepy object in the pub's garden was ...

After Kaz dropped her back at Cormorant Cove, Leora missed Terry, their prickly rapport. His word-smithery, the way they grooved into each other's thoughts ... A worrisome thought: Could he really be getting it on with Meghan? They seemed to hail from separate planets. Since when was that a deterrent for men? Terry's male feminist come-on had suggested he might be different.

Well, she couldn't have it both ways. Why the hell not? In a better world she would have Kaz and Terry both and cycle them in and out of her life with the moon's phases and as the spirit or flesh moved her. The French did this routinely, Mormon guys were absolute pigs, and surely most men above a certain income level enjoyed the varieties of amorous experience. She heard her husband Patrick going on about Frank Lloyd Wright, his claim that two women were necessary for a "man of artistic mind." Maybe two men were necessary for *her* as an aspiring artistic *woman*. Now *there* was something to add to women's demands for equality. She wasn't sure Gilda would go for it.

Leora would later learn that the artifact she'd seen in the pub's garden was a "Three-Legged Mare," named for a medieval gallows that could hang three people at once.

★

Lester Annis recovered from his wounds but was so traumatized by the aftermath of the assault, he slunk off to his mother's place in Boca Raton. What rankled was the snide, almost gleeful tone the press took in covering the attack – when *he* was the victim! The media response had rudely acquainted him with, well, how *loathed* he was. And this after he could have pocketed millons from Mercky Pharma for pushing that abortion pill as a cure for psychotic depression. Instead, he'd devoted his life to advancing medicine and the art of healing! The world's incomprehension, the rank *ingratitude* left him too demoralized to finish his book. His publisher announced that *The Future of Sex* by Lester Annis had been withdrawn from its spring list.

Fred sat in a fug of smoke in his studio at Cormorant Cove and drank a toast of Stoli to the mysterious workings of fate. Thank heavens the workings of fate had seen fit to abort his effort to drown. He'd almost deprived himself of his comeback! A clear field lay ahead. Without the specter of Annis's opus sucking up all the oxygen in media world, Fred could tranquilly complete his own book. He'd found a way to "weave in" some of the material he'd poached from Annis. Which Annis had originally poached, broadly speaking, from *him*. As Fred saw it, whatever contributed to the greater good of his own work justified any "irregularity." The commune, taking its cue from Robin Hood, created its own standards.

He peered out the door of his studio to ensure the coast was clear. From here it was a straight shot across the lawn to the main house and the Stoli sweating prettily in the basement fridge ...

To think he'd almost deprived himself, too, of the Women's Strike! If they managed to bring it off – still a big "if" – it would be one for the Ages. The major TV networks would likely cover it. He'd work the march so he got interviewed and quoted. The event would bring Gilda's fame to a pitch, some of which would rub off on him. After all, he was co-founder of the commune. It was here at the commune, summer of '70, that the impossible dream of the Strike had come together – a nice detail to include in the publicity for the new book. He'd decided to call it *Future Sex*. The spirit of Lester Annis's title shouldn't go to waste.

Fred wondered if many men would turn out for the Strike. They might prefer to guard their privileges, barricade themselves in their bars behind a brewski or doze off in a club chair and trust the whole uproar to blow over. "Women don't know how good they have it ... guaranteed income for life," a detective had said one afternoon at the commune. The detective might find himself on the wrong side of history ... Men would show up for the march if they saw it as a way to display their feminist bonafides and meet cool chicks. Not the purest motive but it was the numbers that mattered. He himself planned to lubricate the way down Fifth Avenue with a flask. Gilda was set to address the crowd at the closing rally and when it came to endless speeches Fidel Castro had nothing on Gilda Gladstone.

It troubled Fred that he'd messed with Terry Cameron's head by making off with Lester Annis's manuscript. Terry was easily the nicest person in the commune, if a bit spacey; he might fear he was losing his mind. He owed Terry, as a fellow communard, the solidarity that was the bricks and mortar of the commune – Fred felt his eyes go misty at the notion of their supportive spirit.

He recalled that a friend in Islesfordd, a wine maker with media dreams, was about to publish a new magazine, a more Left-leaning version of *The Atlantic*. They'd be staffing up right about now. *Gotham* was desperate to have Terry back, but Terry had given signs he was ready to move on. He must get on the horn *immediately* and drop the name Terry Cameron in the wine maker's ear.

Favors have a way of generating return favors, Fred thought, reaching for his Rolodex. He was not unmindful of the fact that at some future point he might want to tap Terry and his editorial wizardry to whip the reborn *Future Sex* into shape.

★

"Jo asked me to come with her on this 'grand adventure,'" Edwina said, voice choked. A tear coasted down her cheek to her chin and baptized the watercress sandwich on her plate." "She wants to sell the loft on Bethune and leave New York and join a *'real'* commune – an all-women commune in upstate New York called The CLIT Collective."

She and Peter Grosvenor sat on the raised dining section of the Rottlesey Club overlooking a pool the size of three soccer fields, among chittering young mothers in pink and green Lily Pulitzers and their yellow-haired kids. Edwina's was the only dark head. After the devastating afternoon when Jo had laid out her "exciting new project," Edwina had barely made it back to Cormorant Cove. She holed up in her room for two days, pleading migraine. At some point she managed to phone Peter in Boston, speaking in the voice of someone very ill.

He immediately hopped the shuttle from Logan Airport and whisked her off to the Rottlesey.

"We were having lunch at Therapeutix," Edwina went on, "and I saw this dear little boy who reminded me of Finn – Leora's son, Finn – and suddenly this ... *lust* came over me: baby lust. I said, what about kids? Jo says, of course kids can be a part of this. But she refuses to raise a child according to the 'patriarchal model.' She says there's this collective called Dykes & Tykes for communal child-rearing. We can adopt a baby from Guatemala, Vietnam. There are also new ways to have children. She starts talking about turkey basters, or some such. Surrogate sperm-givers. 'You could make a baby with Fred! I'm sure he'd be happy to oblige.'"

"No doubt of that," Peter Grosvenor said, thankful for the shades masking the hope in his eyes. Mesmerized by a dark tendril that had slipped loose of Edwina's chignon and feathered her collar bone.

"Every cell in me screamed NO! No to the whole package! I don't want to make a baby with Fred – or any goddamn 'surrogate.' I want my child to have an actual dad around and I don't care if that makes me 'complicit with the patriarchy.' No to Dykes & Tykes, no to communal this, collective that ... *No to the fucking CLIT COLLECTIVE.*"

A young mother peered over her sun glasses to ascertain whether she'd heard right.

Edwina glared at her. "Besides" – addressing the woman – "FRED'S SPERM DOESN'T SWIM."

Peter had never seen Edwina this unstrung. "You do have to give Jo credit for trying to accommodate you," he said. Reveling in the delicious position of defending a rival who was no longer a rival. He wondered how Edwina's sheets would smell.

"That made it even harder! The thing is, sitting there at Therapeutix I realized I couldn't live in the world that way."

"What way?"

"No more leers and whispers," she went on as if she hadn't heard. "You have to get up for it, all the time, armor yourself against the straight world's obscene fascination with it all – and probably envy, oh yes, *envy*! It'll all be fairly normal one day, but not yet. I never asked to be a pioneer." She pressed her fingers to her forehead. "Too much shit has gone down with me and men – Right from the start, with the old goat in Trastevere ... "

Peter refrained from nodding. He'd long ago resolved never to go within a hundred miles of that family scandal of his cousin's lost sophomore year of college. A year with her mother's former second husband in his Roman villa ... A "curettage" in Basel – unh unh, no way ...

"Men and I were jinxed after that. I was being punished, I suppose, for what we did to Mother, me and the old goat ... Then along comes Jo ... I'd never loved anyone before. I didn't know a thing about love!" She smoothed back her brow with third and fourth fingers. "Now I just want to buy Tupperware and live wherever the 'action' *isn't* and plant a perennial border and have Thanksgiving with family who never heard of 'Hello Dolly,' I want to walk in the park pushing a carriage with mobiles of frolicking seals and come home to a place with no tie dyed rags in the bath tub. I'm played out, Peter ... Y'know, Jo accused me of just 'experimenting' and wanting an 'exotic experience' but that was never true. Jo is my great love – my *last* love. I still want to be with her in every way you can be with a person and I can't imagine not wanting that – always." She tucked a stray lock into her chignon. "Say nothing. People mustn't know yet."

★

The following day Peter told his wife he was leaving her.

★

Edwina sat by Hooker Pond in her Marimekko dress, working on a g & t and semi-hearing the sizzle of summer cicadas and accordion twang of frogs singing their love. The creatures seemed in synch with a move she was contemplating ...

In the days since splitting with Jo she lived under a bell jar, the world's busyness and noise barely seeping through. She lived with a sense of everything to come as epilogue. She'd kept the breakup with Jo a secret from the communards. Once they found out, she didn't know if she could bear their snarky reactions and self-satisfaction at "calling it right" – "she thought it was cool to play at being a lesbian for a while," etc. (Even Jo had said as much.)

How wrong they would have gotten it. The truth was, she adored Jo, she fell asleep and woke to the memory of Jo's skin, her smells, their tangled legs. Her commanding way of moving through the world. Anything she saw or did or learned felt incomplete without her; when someone spoke Jo's name it hurt beneath her breastbone. But she'd been sundered from Jo by a magnetic force that she lacked the power – literally, *physically* – to overcome. Doubtless the younger women now making the scene – Fred's estranged wife Meghan – could walk the walk. She herself was stuck in an untenable middle: heart and mind and body she belonged to Jo – just not *with* Jo. During those truth-mongering minutes between sleep and waking, she'd fallen hostage to images of a man riding his kid around on his shoulders and making him blueberry pancakes in the morning and getting him on his first pony at Netherfield Farm, a kid with grimy knees and a faraway look who called him "dad." The next rest of her life would act as balm to soothe the damage she'd wracked up. She'd slammed up against her ordinariness.

★

At the sound of gravel crunching in the driveway, Edwina swiveled in the Adirondack chair. Sebastian Nye, in a striped shirt and salmon-colored pants, hair combed wetly back over his shapely head and ears, appeared round the corner of the house. He strode toward her across the lawn and down to the pond with a wolfish grin.

"So. It's done. Symbolically, if you will – better than an actual *murder* which would have been too sordid."

A beat before she understood, horrified, that he was referring to the assault on Lester Annis. He'd come to claim to her! Edwina rose slowly, gripping the back of her chair.

Nye extended his hand: *and now, the next chapter …*

"Who asked?" she said.

He drew closer. "What do you mean, who asked? *You* did. I mean, I thought you – I thought we had an understanding. That night at charades – "

"You thought wrong." She was about to escape to the house when she saw the raw cut on his cheek, probably from shaving. He looked older, the lower lid of one eye rimmed red. She saw him from behind bending over the suitcase in Verbier and the way his parked car looked without him and something like pity stole into her. It was not a nice feeling. "Seb, you need to give it up and let me be. Why won't you? Do it for me, do it for yourself."

"It's not in my nature to give things up."

"You're not a *scorpion*, chained to its poisoned sting, for Chrissake. You're a man. Believe me, I understand how fucking hard it can be to give up what you want. But sometimes there's no other choice. I have nothing *for* you, Seb."

"You did, once."

233

"You held me too tight. What once turned me on started to creep me out. Or maybe I just got tired of you, the way men get tired of the woman who loves them and move on, for no reason, of course reason has nothing to do with it." She'd run out of breath. "Keep making beautiful music, Seb. Come to our Women's Strike. Bring your buddy, William Buckley, and greet the new world." She moved around him, plucked her dress to raise its hem, and walked up the lawn toward the house.

"Dammit!" he yelled after her back – "*It wasn't even me who clobbered the bastard!*"

She stopped at the door and slowly turned. "I know. The way it was done – it's not in you to be so sloppy. Anyway, that night I heard you playing that wretched organ upstairs."

The sky blushed peach. He moved toward her, eyes tiger-yellow in the half-light. "Don't you see, darling? It's providential. Someone else got there first and did it for us."

There *is* no "us," Seb. It felt pointless to repeat it.

★

A Sunday morning heavy with the scents of August: privet hedge blossoms cut with Vydate, the pesticide sprayed on the potato fields. Edwina Scahill and Peter Grosvenor emerged from her bedroom and walked into the dining room holding hands and smiling like two bashful children.

"We're engaged, and we wanted you, our dear friends and elective family, to be first to know," Peter said in a plummy honk. "We're flying up to the Vineyard to tell the other family. Back in time for the Strike, of course."

Whatthe ... Where the fuck was JoBeth? ... The sorry bunch at the table, eyes tight in their skulls, maybe still hammered, could only stare, mouths ajar. They might have stepped out

234

of Brueghel's painting of sprawled revelers still cock-eyed the morning after.

Fred broke the silence. "I'm so happy for you both. We're kind of trying to catch our breath here," he went on in his most charming mumble, "you've taken us a bit by s-s-s-surprise. Peter, this has been quite the summer for you!"

So old Sebby Nye had been right about the dyke fling! Fred thought. Edwina had made a pivot back to camp hetero, even if her choice was not the most persuasive sample of hetero. In choosing Peter she'd rejoined her "people." WASPs married into their own tribe, Fred had noted, producing second rate, thinned-out intellects like Peter's, which produced mediocre work that found recognition only thanks to an Old Boy network of classmates from St. Paul's.

Fred suspected that Peter would quickly lose interest in that next book of his: *Penis Privilege and the Masculinity Trap*. The prospect added to his good spirits. Peter had likely cooked up the project to impress Edwina with his feminist credentials. Now that he'd closed the deal with Edwina, where was the impetus for the book? Fred felt ever more convinced that Peter was a ... a girly woman in a man-suit. He thought of the pre-Gilda Dark Ages: the moment a woman landed her guy, she ditched work. And along with it, she tossed her girlfriends. If Peter borrowed a page from *that* tired story Fred would not be surprised.

★

Nadine's hand pressed her middle, as if stanching a wound. She heard herself congratulate the new couple, thinking the while of the panda bear guy at her lecture ... *The life I should have had*. She felt a three-alarm "hot" about to land, frantically worked her little fan. What fresh hell? her upper arm was jiggling along for the ride! *Fogey alert!* Too late: she'd forgotten she couldn't do sleeveless. The other day she'd emerged from Kenneth (double process, highlights, hot oil treatment, blow dry – a time-gobbler she didn't exactly *advertise* to her radical sisters). She hit the streets, a vivid impostor, briefly visible again. She loved locking eyes with men, that lingering millisecond of mutual recognition. A genital salute. She was semi-tempted to mosey over to a construction site just to receive a little noontime ogling ...

Pathetic vanity. *Forgive yourself,* her friend would say. The other day she'd caught herself tottering around with a terrible smile, mouth slightly ajar like the beak of a sick seagull. She'd seen that smile on a woman during her talk "From Martin Buber's 'I-Thou' to today's 'I-Me'" at the Cosmopolitan Club. She'd vowed never to smile like that. Shoulders back; heart out; *don't waddle. To be both ageful and proud ...*

The movement offered no inspiration or guidance in these matters. The movement was for women who got periods. It had overlooked mothers and, God forbid, grandmothers; written off the hot flashes crowd who'd sucked up to the old boys and navigated the *patriarchal system,* as she had in the academy ... It turned a blind eye to skin tags, lactose intolerance, osteopenia. Last weekend she'd gone to a concert of chamber music at Islesfordd's House of God Inc. Hebrew Pentecostal Church and gotten caught in a geriatric traffic jam of walkers and wheelie things. She had no plans to join that party! If not for her work, she'd be as irrelevant as the aging population dismissed in that article in *Luce, Inc...* She and Gilda were working up a new slogan, "Aging is not 'lost youth' but a new stage of opportunity and strength." Nadine wondered if *that* dog would hunt ...

★

Nadine brightened at the thought of this morning's call. The week before, over a caffeine-and-dexie-fueled forty-eight hours, she'd whipped together a proposal for her new book on feminism and minorities and blue collar women, who, in all the fuss, had been left out of the equation. Her agent had phoned today, a *Sunday before nine* – too excited to wait – talking an auction, a bidding war ... Six figures ... The timing of her book was perfect! The advance would fund research across the country, travel to Europe, anywhere she chose ...

That she'd missed out on grand passion felt slightly less tragic. You had to factor in the larger picture. She'd escaped being born a pig in Smithfield Foods. She wasn't, to her knowledge, getting turned into stone – as if Medusa had shot you the evil eye – by that disease, whatever it was called ... Her books were reviewed in *The Beaver*, she had colleagues, the communards, most of her teeth ... Her son ...

Oy, her son. She heard herself groan. Ivan's life had imploded. From the start he and Maya had agreed that he'd hold the fort as house-husband and primary parent, freeing her up to pursue her art. Now Maya wanted out. He no longer turned her on, she said. He'd become emasculated by playing housewife, she said. He'd become a house-*eunuch*.

"Maya said to me, how can I have sex with a man who knits and talks recipes for Apple Crumble and sounds like all those park-bench yentas with strollers?"

Nadine sighed. Yes, Ivan had taken up knitting.

Worse, he wanted *her* to take up baby sitting for Fidel, their youngest, while he beat the bushes trying to salvage his professional life. She was expected to do this while researching her current book, teaching, working up a new graduate seminar for spring semester! – *Excuse me* ...

And she would do it. With children you were indentured for life.

If she ever surfaced from all this she might yet try to locate Panda-Bear. Failing that, the Well-Endowed – or was it Flatulent – Generalissimo ... With her lactose intolerance, they'd get a whole percussion section going.

★

Leora, tearing up, had thrown her arms around Edwina. For a long moment they held each other. "Thank you for loving my children," Leora murmured. Where had it come from, this love? The communards squirmed or looked away, unaccustomed to this type of emotional display ... at least when sober.

Leora was all but blubbering, when suddenly she remembered Peter's wife. He and the wife had been "on hiatus," in Peter's telling, he at the commune, she in the family's place on Chappy in Martha's Vineyard. They both enjoyed having their "space," Peter said. Leora doubted very much whether the wife had enjoyed having her space over the summer, or was enjoying having her space now, or enjoying much of anything. Why, as the happy couple rolls off in their pumpkin carriage, is there always some woman left on the roadside like one of Dean Moriarty's used condoms?

★

Gilda Gladstone beamed at the new couple. She'd lived in terror that Edwina might decide she preferred men after all. It turned out she did (though you'd never accuse Peter of machismo). Now marriage, blessedly, would take Edwina out of the running. The commune had finally shed any taint of the lavender menace. It was all good. The only *not* good? Another attractive man taken off the table.

238

CHAPTER 18

Crisis

*"I feel that 'man-hating' is an honorable and viable political act,
that the oppressed have a right to class-hatred against the class
that is oppressing them."*

– Robin Morgan

"Why were we so angry at the men? Were they truly our enemy?"

– Betty Friedan

"Could you get away for long weekend? I thought we could go
to gorgeous place in San Juan Islands. 'Rustic luxury,' they call
it, first-rate property. I have business in Seattle. We could meet
there and catch flight to the islands."

Leora propped herself up on an elbow. Kaz sat in a terrycloth robe on a gilded chair with faun legs that had cushioned
the asses of Borgheses, hair sticking up like Tintin's quiff. She
felt the slide of silk sheets along her haunches. Silk on the

outside, and on the inside, one great slidey delight. The genius who'd invented sex on silk sheets had gone a long way toward compensating mortals for all the rest.

"In Seattle there's great new coffee shop called Starbucks."

She dug his Puh-lish accent, front-of-the-mouth and flat, articles lost in translation. His sleepy eyes, compact body that fit just so. Toenails laid on hers. His smile when, scrunched up against the headboard, she was getting close. An ache radiated through her back, a cousin of labor pains ... She glanced at the tented lap of his terrycloth robe and heard Mae West, is that a gun or you just happy etc.? but Kaz wouldn't get it, and generally didn't go for raunchy humor, unfitting for a Polish bride. She said, "Why are you sitting way over there? Come be with me."

★

While the police disrupted life at the commune, Leora had taken to stealing away to Kaz Grabowski's place for love in the afternoon. Following their ill-fated lunch, they had finally re-consummated their re-union. It had not disappointed. Among the communards only Edwina knew about her and Kaz and had given them her blessing. Yes, Kaz was a bit crass, but under his umbrella Leora's children could enjoy a few more creature comforts. On his side, Kaz would acquire a ready-made family and move into the human fold.

Leora had made her peace with Kaz's bedroom decor: the pink marble fireplace he'd schlepped over from a castle in Scotland ("The owner wanted ten grand but I get him down to five. He was so broke, he was charging admission to tour his own castle!") The Swedish country chandelier with real candles that could torch the whole place ("A steal, that one"). The knight in a suit of armor worn by Henry II that Kaz had outbid some museum for. "Our very own voyeur," Leora called the thing all but *watching* them through slitty eye-holes, its armor shining when struck by afternoon sun. She'd come to feel almost tender toward the "hideosity," as Olde Islesfordd called it, of Dragon's Gate. She remembered Kaz telling her once about "mucking out" the stalls of his uncle's stables. All this mis-mated glitz Kaz had assembled must somehow neutralize the smell of horse shit.

"Y'know, this place in the San Juans sounds sweet – "
"First-rate property. Three room suite, fireplace."
" – but every time we plan a getaway, you have a business crisis that needs to be solved yesterday."
"Last time you had crisis," Kaz observed in his slow way.
"Yes, it's called looking after your children. I needed to take Cara to the pediatrician."
"And that other time ..."
"A deadline" ...

She had mailed her *The Kayak Caper* piece to the managing editor of *Gotham* and three days later, to her amazement, the editor called. Where had she been? The piece was delicious! Needed some minor revisions, but he wanted to publish it. She timidly asked when they might run it.

"Soon's you turn it around. We can still squeeze it in before Labor Day. After we close the current issue, you'll come to the office, we'll talk. See what else you got."

That was a Friday morning and she had too much riding on this to botch it. It kind of pleased her to be ducking out on

Kaz – with *her* "need-it-yesterday," for a change. Patrick took the kids to his fiancee's godmother's place in Oyster Bay. Leora hunkered down in the apartment, chloroformed by heat, sweat staining her pages. Changing commas to semi-colons, then changing them back to commas again. Scrounged around for 50 cents to buy a pack of Winston's. Leora felt a kinship with the dracaena plant by the window. Huge and ragged – it had grown an ugly extra stalk with freaky little shoots trailing – the plant had persevered and prospered through all the *sturm und drang* rocking the apartment, needing nothing, scarcely even water, a paean to survival.

Terry, Leora thought, it must have been Terry, calling on his contacts, who'd gotten her piece plucked from the slush pile ...

After she hand delivered her story to the editor, Kaz insisted they celebrate. Leora said it might be bad luck to celebrate before *Kayak* had actually landed in the pages of *Gotham*. Kaz waved that off as silly superstition and broke out his Veuve Cliquot Yellow Label. He held it aloft: "They get $55.95 for this stuff"...

★

Leora eyed the knight, who eyed her back through its iron slits. Remembering their little champagne celebration, it struck her that Kaz had seemed a bit subdued; preoccupied, somehow. He needed coaching in the new male supportiveness; he still had one foot in a world not far distant from his voyeur-knight ...

"I don't get why we have to *go* anywhere," Leora said. "Islesfordd in summer is heaven. What's wrong with right here? As long as we're together." A weekend getaway also meant the challenge of holding his gaze and civilly conversing while the urge to take a shit came on. Worse, didn't. *Try to act like a normal person*, she prodded herself, *just try, just for once, it can't be* that *difficult* if so many people do it ... She added,

"Anyway, when it comes to travel plans we might be jinxed." *Why was she shooting herself in the foot*, alluding to that sorry episode?

"Islesfordd is gossip mill," Kaz said, not missing a beat. "I treasure privacy. What is money for if not to buy privacy and keep the world's eyes off? You know that famous hairess, Marjorie something? She had to have her own private elevator in apartment building. She said she did not wish to be seen by anyone. Now *that's* what money is for!" A moment. "Okay, there's also Gilda Gladstone. She keeps pestering me to go with her to parties and yunkets (*junkets*, she translated). A conference in some place called Swaziland. Out of the question, of course, but she gets very dramatic and I don't want to upset her before the Strike."

"Do you think you might be, uh, leading her on, as they say?"

"She's very stressing about the Strike, best if I don't distract her right now."

Leora let it go. The afternoon's exertions had left her born again through all her body. She'd tired of spotting sabotage behind every bush; burned through her misgivings. "Well, no gossips right here – except maybe him." She shrugged toward the knight. "Specially since you laid off the old staff."

They say you can't change people, but Kaz was proving quite educable. She'd persuaded him to put Wilfredo, his former "domestic assistant," through cosmetology school. But it turned out Wilfredo had been gaming them all.

"I was just camping it up as the 'ditzy houseboy,'" he told Leora over drinks at The Spotted Dick. "Otherwise I would've been bored out of my gourd. I borrowed the character from

Vile Bodies, Evelyn Waugh's novel about London's 'bright young things' – you know, the randy servant who works at the Cavendish hotel? *Cosmetology* school? *nooo* thank you. I'd prefer a Creative Writing course. I've been working on a modern-day epic poem – sort of like *Beowulf* – about a gay hero from the Philippines."

Quick consult with Kaz, and he agreed to re-route the tuition to Columbia's School of General Studies.

For Quasimodo Leora had hatched a long term agenda. She hoped to pry him from the talons of Elsie van Otten. Leora considered that a grown man lying atop a station wagon like a dog while his employer hit the A & P disrupted some moral order in the universe. Quasi seemed to Leora one of Islesfordd's more benign spirits; she'd seen him at the ocean *feeding* fish – blues maybe – instead of catching them. He deserved nurturing. She'd push Kaz, a major donor, to approach the deacons of Islesfordd's House of God Inc. Hebrew Pentecostal Church about hiring Quasimodo as a bell-ringer. Eventually, Quasi could teach kayaking, weight training, and merciful fishing at her dream project: the Dragon's Gate Camp for inner city kids. Finn and Cara would be first to enroll. Leora hadn't yet found the right moment to broach this great undertaking of the summer camp to Kaz.

Next she'd press him to clean up his act and divest from those Asian sweat shops he denied he owned – under the rubric of Tramlaw. And maybe suggest he refrain from attaching a price tag to any object he'd acquired (was the makeover getting out of control again)?

Kaz came and sat beside her on the well-worked sheets. "You opened up the world for me." His sleepy smile. "I have to admit, *The Godfather* is more up my alley-way than Henry James." He lifted from the night table a glass paper weight she'd not seen before. It imprisoned an amber-colored scorpion. "Two grand Sotheby got for this." He replaced it. "I want to show you other worlds. The San Juans ... St. Tropez ... My beautiful Krakow. When I think of the way you've been living" – he shook his head in disbelief. "At the mercy of everyone. After I sold my first company for – well, lots of money – I never felt more peace in my life. I want to share that with you. My adorable girl," he added thickly.

Well, "girl" had gone the way of the dodo and she was inches taller than him. If no one but the knight/voyeur was listening, no harm done. In fact, Kaz's words had a retro appeal.

★

Kaz was right about the gossip mill, Leora thought, walking back to Cormorant Cove with her springy step. Wilfredo had let drop an intriguing conjecture about the identity of Elsie van Otten's one-time finance that cast the assault of Lester Annis in a whole new light. And convinced Leora more than ever that Lester had known his assailant.

Wilfredo himself was the object of gossip. After getting fired by Kaz, the Commodore of the Rottlesey – notorious for that "indiscretion" with his brother-in-law at the Ramrod Club – had jumped into the breach. He hired Wilfredo as weekend grounds keeper and installed him in his mother's gatehouse overlooking the Rottlesey golf course.

The juiciest gossip had set all Islesfordd chittering like sparrows in the hedgerows: Milt Merdle was getting blackmailed by a Malaysian hooker he'd met through a catalog. A New York City tabloid had pounced on the story and graced its front page with a head shot of Merdle and photo of the catalog's cover: *Meet Truly Beautiful Malaysian Girls*. She'd been seeing

Merdle for four years, the woman claimed, and had sold his love letters – which detailed his exotic tastes – to *The Town Babbler*.

Suppose Sophia dumped Merdle? Sophia would be in play, Leora reflected, snapping back to suspicious mode. She'd join Islesfordd's collection of wealthy widowed or divorced women who were manna from heaven for men reamed by alimony payments, business setbacks, tuition for Buckingham or Brearley, etc. etc. Kaz, like all the new money in Islesfordd, slavered over the Rottlesey; the more it shut him out, the more fiercely he wanted in. And Sophia was the ticket. How in hell did she know his name was Casimir?

He needs someone to show him how to spend his money, she'd said.

Of course, Sophia and Merdle might well try to "work through" the scandal of the Malaysian hooker. There was that much money at stake.

Okay, Monica, How does one feel sisterly toward Sophia Merdle?

★

"When I was young ... men were the main course, now they are only a condiment. I advise you to arrive at that same state as soon as possible. Life is doable only then."

– Vivian Gornick, quoting a friend

Nadine sat in the Adirondack chair in the lavender dusk looking out at Hooker Pond and paging through her life, a no-win business she'd indulged way too often in this summer of her discontent.

She'd once been proud of having a higher IQ than the smartest boy at Midwood High. Somehow all her smartness had got siphoned off into work. She couldn't remember when she hadn't sat down at her desk, switched on and humming, by 9 A.M. That she'd been less smart about recreation, for want of a better term, made her question the value, even *nature* of intelligence. She'd come to dread those fearful sink holes called vacations; the barren downtime between projects and deadlines, etc. that everyone else seemed to live for. She'd not been super clever with relationships either. Since Ivan's marriage had imploded, the bickering with her son had turned newly rancorous. After putting in time as house husband, he'd emerged to discover he'd somehow gotten aged out of his field.

Ivan accused her of taking a righteous "I-told-you-so attitude."

She had not said a word, she pointed out.

"I can *hear* you *thinking* it, which is worse. A guilt trip invented by over-educated Jews."

What she *was* thinking: *Don't expect me to babysit for Fidel and arrive at my Senior Colloquium wearing an epaulet of apricot upchuck.*

★

This time it was Edwina who'd set her off. She was accustomed to thinking of Edwina as a lightweight who took silly photos of silly people; a woman who existed in the world to receive sexual attention, and had slipped through the commune's back door on the strength of Fred's need to surround himself with pretty women. Yet Edwina turned out to be the smart one. She'd had the cleverness to engineer her own happiness.

The early arrival of dusk brought on a swelling chorus of peepers and crickets warning that the days of summer were numbered. The days left to be happy. The critters knew. It was the moment to fix herself a vodka hold-the-tonic (she no longer bothered to measure with a jigger), the better to blur out the evening's invitation to the dance. It had set up camp in her system, this longing that most people seemed to have worked into their resume in early youth. She thought of the couple in *One Summer of Happiness*, the dirty Swedish film they'd sneaked into as teens, impatient for their lives to begin. One happy summer out of a whole life? She'd take it. Hell, she'd take a few weeks – August through Labor Day! She hungered for rapture, madness, love that could stop the speed of light. Days of desire and faint nausea when every moment, waking and sleeping, was owned by images of *him*. He would gaze at her, head back, lost – and she at him. To exist on the planet in any other manner was to miss the goddamn point.

Instead of running its course like a head cold, the madness hung on. At 4 A.M. a soaking hot flash drove her down the stairs from her second floor bedroom/study to walk the cool wet grass behind Cormorant Cove. The word "unseemly" flickered like a broken neon sign. Whom could she tell? Fred, maybe, he could absorb most anything. Better yet, Leora, who went around saying she aspired to be a dirty old woman.

Back in her room she pulled her clammy nightgown over her head and inspected herself in the full-length closet mirror in the moonlight. White, lush, the odd bulge, rather inviting overall. A girl's modest chest. Dark pubic smudge. This would do. She felt not remotely *old*. She looked ... virginal – from dis-use. Fallow. She wanted to be fallowed. Before the dark tide rose. Her friend who'd liked to say, "vodka-hold-the-tonic," also liked to say, *Do not defer*. Then he'd checked in with the doctor for a "routine" visit ...

Her own malady was called Late Onset Adolescence.

★

Nadine had become convinced, on the basis of scant evidence, that Panda-Bear was her last best shot. She summoned up his largeness coupled with ... a certain shyness, Ivy-inflected speech (she was working with maybe ten words from their single encounter). She fleshed out this man after her own heart. He would be an academic, maybe in philosophy – wait, hadn't he said he was "in finance"? Divorced. Devoted to his grown-ish children, but not excessively. Not the way a guy she knew had bludgeoned his wife with his pervy devotion to their daughter, moved into her dorm at college, and gotten himself arrested ...

He'd be "first reader" of her manuscripts, this man. He'd call Fred on his bullshit. Travel with her to the Serengeti where Isak Dinesen had lived and loved. On the plane he would grasp her hand tightly during turbulence. He would not, like her husband, scrape the remaining margarine from his morning toast back into the container; leave soap in his ears; take the whole goddamn Sunday *Times* into the john. He would march beside her in the Women's Strike. She thought about this man while flossing her teeth, paying the Con Ed bill, looking out the car window at Islesfordd's sunflowers cocking their giant heads at the sun. He could be a polygamist, an ax murderer, a spook for the CIA. He would be her last chapter.

★

He turned out to be a global consultant. He was separated, not yet divorced.

★

She'd re-upped for the panel on "Miseries of Machismo" at Shitterton Grange, in the hope that his antennae would pick up her signal from wherever he might be. Inspired by Edwina, she'd gone so far as to buy a long red and white striped Marimekko dress at Handcock-on-the-Highway.

And there, impossibly – really, truly, he sat. Fourth row on the aisle. Her hand, spasmodic, all but knocked over her water. Luckily, she could reel out her spiel on automatic. His gaze the true North to which she kept returning. They shouted *Yes!* to each other, *Yes!* across the rows of blank faces.

A beat after the applause ended he was first to stand and was threading his way toward the little stairs and saying, "For godssake, how do I find you?" Pen and paper at the ready.

His name was Elliot Futterman and he consulted for international companies. He took her to dinner at the Old Sodom Inn. He worked for a firm with twenty-three offices in eleven countries. "We help businesses navigate the intersection between business, government ... " etc. etc. His light blue shirt and suspenders, eyes dark and watchful, with lavender half-moons beneath like a student who's spent the night cramming.

"I *recognize* you."

"Yes, we once met," she said stupidly.

"I mean as the person I've always wanted to know. It feels inevitable, meeting up with you. If it hadn't happened here it would have happened somewhere else, I would have found you. I never stopped thinking about you, since the first time at Shittington."

And I you. He was large and shambling and furry and she wanted to attach herself to his fur and ride around on him, marsupial style.

"I was slow to find you again because I was traveling for work – then a long-planned vacation. I looked up Peter Grosvenor, an old friend from Army Reserves.

I'd heard he was out in Islesfordd guessed you were both somehow connected with the famous – or should I say 'infamous' commune. I feel I know you from your books. "*Women start to see all men as The Oppressor, and pretty soon men are having to bear the brunt of their revolution,*" he said, quoting her. "*How did we wind up being the kind of scapegoats for all the things that women are objecting to in their lives?*" I said to myself, I need to know the woman who could write that. Who gets how the women's movement has hit men like a tornado so they don't know which end is up – while your fellow women writers dump on us like we're some sub-human species."

"I've taken a bit of flak for that book," Nadine said with a smile. Her glowy eyes, apple cheeks. She belled out toward him like a spinnaker.

"We speak the same language."

The same everything.

He ordered a second bottle of Sancerre.

The waiter carried away their uneaten appetizers and brought their *canard a l'orange*. Took up his post beside a Tiffany lamp. They barely touched their food. The waiter was not happy. Another pair of lovebirds, and worse for the wear. Actually, white boy lookin' fine ... actually, not so white – maybe a Brownie? Younger than the lady. Her gigalow? Not that he gave a shit, he just worried customers like this were a lousy testimonial for Old Sodom. Chiswick-on-Main was due to open on the main drag, and the competition would be fierce. He needed Old Sodom to thrive. He was about to put down money on the multi-level ranch in a section near the Islesfordd Town Dump that the Man called Lionelhampton, ha-ha. He had little patience with most Sodom clientele, honkies with black-face jockeys behind their gates – worse, the "liberals" who painted the blackface white. He particularly disliked when they failed to appreciate the house specialite *canard a l'orange* (crispy, never fatty) for which Old Sodom was famous. Especially as the Sodom had managed to pry loose the chef from the Rottlesey. Cat had it with making chipped beef and other crap for club members who wanted the shit they'd eaten in boarding school ...

The waiter stood beside the Tiffany lamp, head high, napkin draped over his arm, primed to respond to table four's least demand. He thought of his grandfather, his white wooly head, the deference, serving drinks to the young crackers at Harvard's Porcellian Club.

This couple tonight needed nothing he could give them.

★

The Old Sodom had rooms upstairs. They were determined to preserve a wisp of decorum.

★

Next date, decorum be damned, no dinner, no nuthin' – it was straight to Sea Breeze Cozy Cabins. Elliot couldn't stop apologizing. August, and everything was booked. The room smelled of mildew and a sampler on the wall read "You've got More Issues Than a Magazine," but worst was the ghastly awkwardness. Thank God for the bottle of Grey Goose. She needed to go easy on the booze, it brought on the sweats. Major flash coming on ... He went into the bathroom and she whipped out her fan. She heard him through paper-thin walls peeing for what seemed a very long time. There was black mold around the faucets and she couldn't pee at all. She hadn't anticipated these horrors. She'd pictured a night from when she was seventeen. Now what.

"Let's turn out the light."

"I want to see you," Elliot said, but didn't push it. He was purplish below and what about her belly folds?

He never got very hard, and she still had to pee, and he came right away in a kind of weak burble. Fuck, she heard him say over her head in the darkness. She feared it was her, her body, too old, it was her fault. Though she'd been plenty, um, ready, and if she was disgusting and old he wouldn't have come so fast, would he? She put him at ten years younger.

"I was nervous, it's always like this the first time

"I was nervous, too." She wondered how many "first times" he'd clocked.

"You'll see, next time will be much better."

She loved him, his wish to make it all good for them. His expectation of a *next time*. He'd left her mightily aroused. She could make love for both of them. The nights of perfect oneness were yet to come. "I'm so happy," she said, partly to reassure them both. "*Tu me fais du bien.*"

Jeanne Moreau had said that in a French movie.

★

They met the following week for dinner at High Petergate overlooking Megalomantic Harbor. "Listen, I know this has happened fast, bit of a whirlwind. Not too fast for you, I hope."

No, not too fast, she agreed, not too fast at all. The late sun had turned his skin copper dark.

"*Carpe diem* as they say. Think of the time we've lost already."

Her heart leapt at how he regarded moving ahead as a given. Clearly, he viewed their blurry encounter in Cozy Cabins as just a palate cleanser. She suddenly feared he'd registered her age – though he had to have known all along. Thank God for his big gut and hair in unexpected places, a fair trade for ripple-y upper arms.

"I'm leaving for Singapore in ten days and staying for a month. I have an apartment there overlooking Marina Bay. Come with me, Nadine, I'd love to show you around. Singapore's an economic miracle, now among the world's richest ... Mix of cultures ... Asia at its earthy best ... Have a blast ... "

She felt she'd caught a wave wrong and was getting churned under.

"I'd love to come with you but August 26 is the date of the march. The Women's Strike."

"Strike? What strike?"

She told him what strike.

"Oh, right, I read something in *Luce, Inc* about that business. Rather unkind. They said a few bra burners – 'unattractive and sex-starved' – were mounting an 'assault on American womanhood.'"

Nadine focused on the tall masts in the harbor. "'That business' will be the greatest demonstration for women's rights ever – and usher in the most important social movement of the 70s" (don't speechify, she cautioned herself). "The world will never be the same. I couldn't miss it for anything, especially as I'm one of the organizers."

"No, of course you can't miss it. An organizer, after all."

"Why don't you put Singapore on a brief hold and join us? Join the march? I would love that."

"Can't – I have the CEO's of five countries lined up to meet me the day after I arrive in Singapore, been in the works for months." He stroked an imaginary beard. "Suppose you fly to Singapore the week after the march. Some time after Labor Day."

"Oh damn, September I'll be traveling."

"Traveling?"

"I'm planning a sweep of the heartland to research the first section of my new book. I have a bunch of interviews set up." A moment. "Maybe I could come to Singapore for a long weekend," she said wistfully.

"Rather a long way to go for the *weekend*." He laughed, kind of.

The waiter brought a second round. Out beyond the masts in the harbor the sun had left molten creases in a pale blue sky.

Elliot swiveled ice cubes with his stick, gray eyes deep and wary. "You couldn't postpone this research for a month or so? That way you'll come back from Singapore all refreshed and rarin' to go."

"I can't, actually. I've signed a contract. I have deadlines. I've hired a researcher ... " How scout's honor and unsexy she sounded, with her deadlines and researcher. Like the boy they'd made fun of in college who put shoehorns in his loafers before sex.

"You can't be a bit flexible and switch the time around?" She heard, nesting dangerously within "you can't," "you *won't*."

"No, actually. Maybe you could come to *me*? Meet me in St. Louis?" she said, trying for lightness.

"Dear, dear Nadine, listen to me. We're neither of us so young any more. We have no time to play games."

"*Games*? This is no game – this is ... we're talking about my work. What I *do*."

"Of course." A little exasperated huff, she wasn't quite hearing him. "See, on my end, there's, well, a bit more, uh, compensation. Which would kind of give my schedule priority."

She wasn't getting enough oxygen. *Deep breaths ...*

"We can live well, Nadine. Very well indeed."

"Obviously, I don't pull in the money of a global consultant but – I already live well – in my fashion. I live in a way that makes me proud, because I've never taken money from any man. To me that's a way of 'living well.'"

"Whoever said 'living well is the best revenge' – well, I'm sure he pictured certain, um, material perks. Speaking of which, one of my partners has a place in Juan les Pins on the Riviera. Near where all those Fitzgerald types hung out? We could go this winter. Why are you looking like that?"

The air had gone super-still. Small black flies massed in the air, maddened. A zapper in the corner performed tiny electrocutions.

"I thought, reading your books, I could count on your empathy for the guy's point of view," he said.

"That was a book. Frankly, I decided to explore the male viewpoint because – well, with the women's movement getting covered from every angle, it was a great niche."

"A *niche*? So it wasn't your real thinking?"

Oh, there's nothing fake about the book. But life doesn't always imitate theory," she added, unsure what she meant but afraid she'd lost control of her story.

"Y'know, this reminds me of the crap I used to get from my wife, Libby. Though her 'work' – well, it wasn't clear what it was. Maybe origami or something."

"What 'crap'? We have a scheduling conflict, you and I, that's all." Try to keep a lid on it.

"Okay, listen, you of all people will understand. Libby gave me a really hard time with her accusations and rage: I was stunting her growth, her 'personhood.' Keeping her from fulfilling her potential.' These women are walking off into the blue expecting – who knows? Least of all, *them* – they haven't a clue what they want or where they're headed."

"Let me back up. We had a perfectly happy marriage. I was making plenty of money, she was there for me. We could talk about things, share our feelings, we had sex. Well, the sex ... with women's lib she began to *supervise* all the time. Do this, no, not like that, like this ... now do that. A little of that kind of thing goes a long way, y'know? Spoils the romance."

"Then she just ... up and announced she was leaving. It was handed to me in an ultimatum, unilaterally. I kept saying, let's explore this together, talk it over, get counseling. And her answer always was, No, I don't want to learn how to live better with you. I don't want to save the marriage. I want to be on my own and there really isn't anything to talk about. It was like nothing could stop her, it was life and death, like she's saying, I'll actually physically die if I have to stay in the marriage, I'll somehow vanish and be annihilated."

It struck Nadine that Elliot's aria uncannily echoed a case history from her book. That guy in Spokane, a near-identical story ... Her throat had gone dry and her heart lodged somewhere too high. She must salvage a piece of her own story. She cast about for a way back to the woman who understood the hearts of men.

"Partly you were dealing with the 'Me' generation," she offered. "On top of that, women who feel smothered are simply not going to let anything get in their way if they want to break out. Especially if they've never been on their own."

"And insist on taking themselves so goddamn seriously! So" – he put finger to his lip – "you're making a case for – *justifying* Libby's behavior. When the woman's flipped her lid. D'you realize she refused to take alimony and child support? Says she *prefers* to be on welfare? Maybe to make me look like a shit?"

"I'm not making a case for anyone, we were exploring why you got blind-sided. To be honest, I'd prefer not to talk about your ex-wife at all."

"Wife, actually." A long moment. "Why would I go to a march that makes men out to be little Hitlers, and validates what Libby put me through?"

They looked at their Dover sole, now lukewarm. He told her more about the glories of Singapore. Clarke Quay and the pedestrian mall. The vertical gardens. The Golden Palace. The Old Singapore Grand Prix. Of course, the cuisine. Nadine said she'd look into re-jiggering her schedule. Even as she'd gone dead inside. She would sleep lightly, assailed by useless, mildly tormented dreams, and coast into the next rest of her life.

Later that night she went out with Leora Voss to the Three Legged Mare and got very drunk.

By 9 A.M. the next morning she was at her desk.

CHAPTER 19

Beverly Baboon

"Biology will still set a few limits upon [women]; ... it might not be the best thing to have a Boeing 747, circling in the overcast, piloted by a woman during her premenstrual period."

— Morton Hunt

"Women will not simply be mainstreamed into the polluted stream. Women are changing the stream, making it clean and green and safe for all ... "

— Bella Abzug

Nadine was deep into her work day in her second floor bedroom/study when Cormorant Cove was rocked by a seismic disturbance, a likely seven on the Richter scale.

Monica Fairley had just *made the cover of Newsicle.* The magazine had christened her "the personification of the women's movement" and its leader and "unlikely guru." Gilda herself became a seismic disturbance, tremblors rattling the upper reaches of Cormorant Cove.

It was hard to pinpoint when and how it had happened, but over the past month the media had dropped *her*, *Gilda Gladstone*, the founder of the movement – ("and, for better and maybe worse, its face," a reporter had written); tossed her like so much hot contraband. Now it was Monica everywhere, all the time. The (mostly male) media slobbered over The Hair, the Ms. America features, the mini-minis, the gracious manner, pithy slogans. (So much nicer than dealing with the loud, ugly one, a cross between Ethel Merman and Hermione Gingold.)

Worse yet, it was now *Monica* liaising with the press over the march. *Her* march. Now, suddenly, *Monica's* march. The skinny *usurper* with zero credentials had slyly horned in from nowhere to steal *her* movement, *her* vision, *her* brainchild!

Then, in a one-two punch, news of a second putsch. Monica's people flat-out lied to the media, announcing that she'd been named head of the Steering Committee – to which Gilda had invited her! – and would preside at the march's closing rally to deliver the final speech. Monica was about to hijack the whole megillah!

★

It was a grim-faced commune that gathered around the refectory table at Cormorant Cove. Gilda occupied her usual Jesus position at command central, coming on like deposed royalty, lids at half mast, nose voguing floorward. Oblivious to the meat loaf and mashed potatoes Florence Luker had whipped up as comfort food. Reaching for, and overshooting, the neck of the Chianti. They couldn't make out what she was saying. No one had the heart to remind her she was up as Kaiserin of KP.

"It's not just about my supposed personal 'vanity,'" Gilda said, voice fading out. "Don't you see" – coming in stronger – "the ENORMITY of what's at stake? *Only EVERYTHING!* If Monica takes over, the whole future of the movement is compromised. This is more than just a power grab – it's about the course of history."

The communards were shaken to see Gilda, her negativity detector always at the ready, so despairing.

"Fucking media whores," Fred said.

"They want what's new, what's blue ... "

"This could simply be a Monica moment with no traction."

No one appeared convinced. They'd heard talk of another blow: the nomination of Monica Fairley as Woman of the Year at *Lady's Circle* – a supreme insult, since Gilda wrote a column for the magazine.

"My personal *'vanity,'* as the press likes to distort it, has nothing to do with it," Gilda said. "The Hair will drag the movement in a radical, negative direction that will alienate the mainstream, cancel all our gains. Monica's pushing man-hating. She and her followers knock marriage as 'prostitution'. Think of it: she's said no woman would ever want to go to bed with a man or get married if she didn't 'need to sell her body for bread or a mink coat' – that kind of shit."

"Or sell her body for heat when the temps drop below fifty-three," Leora said.

Puzzled glances; this Laura, or Leora, all these weeks at the commune – or, rather, dithering around its edge –- never failed to annoy.

"Monica's taking the movement in a wrong direction IT MAY NEVER RECOVER FROM," Gilda raged, "so how is that about my supposed 'vanity'? The movement was never about hating men. What a cop-out! It's so much easier to rant about the chauvinist pig in your bedroom and the missionary position than take the test for law school. We're about the complementarity of men and women! Men are not villains, they're fellow victims."

Somehow men managed to be both, Nadine reflected, reaching for her little fan. She couldn't stop mentally writing rebuttals to her own book about the beleaguered male. She'd come round to believing that certain beleaguered males richly deserved the beleaguering and maybe the Judas Cradle and rack as well.

"We want to rescue men from the pressure of being sole breadwinner, the nightmare of masculinity, we're about equal opportunity for women *without* savaging marriage and family ... "

The communards had heard the spiel many times over, but they let Our Leader vent.

"Monica's got more sympathy for lesbians. Homosexuals. They're basically sons who got screwed up by their overbearing mothers because the mothers didn't have work of their own – "

"Gilda, would you stop with that already?" Nadine said, flicking open her fan.

"To portray women as an oppressed *class*, like Blacks and minorities – what bullshit!"

"Bottom line, we don't want the press to get off on this as an ugly rivalry, they've had a blast mocking the movement as it is." Florence Luker, her voice so high all the stray dogs in Islesfordd must be streaking toward Midas Close.

The press was mocking no longer, Leora reflected; they were gaga over the new figurehead they'd help elevate, emblem of an un-strident, *inviting* style of feminism that even the president of Yale wanted to get into the hot pants of. What a windfall after the long season of ugly, erratic, bombastic Gilda, that ill-tempered witch.

"There must be a way to finesse this," Edwina said.

"How do you '*finesse*' this?'" Gilda snapped. "Monica assumes women have a moral and spiritual superiority as a class, and all men some brute insensitivity. It's male chauvinism in reverse. Female sexism."

"I'll thank you not to take that tone with me," Edwina said.

Gilda grasped the Chianti by the neck and seemed not to hear. "And the *most* galling thing? Monica preaches manhating – while *she's* .. *fucking* the 'oppressor'! Has the media mentioned they're all celebrities? Rich, powerful men who help advance her ambitions? The latest, an armaments guy, is giving her start-up money for some magazine. When has she ever been without a man for twenty minutes? She and her cronies are telling women they're 'traitors' if they love men. Urging women to avoid marriage and dump their husbands. Because Monica's got some phobia about marriage!"

"It's kind of ingenious, actually, to turn your own mishegoss into ideology," Leora observed. She drew the usual *what-was-the-stupid-girl-saying-now* looks.

"How many women are really prepared to give up men, marriage, family?" Gilda thundered, words leap-frogging over scraps of others. "Why in hell should they? And how many will actually go through with it – including the radical sisters whipping everyone on? Will they *stick* with it? The ones who do may find themselves standing alone out there wondering where's the sisterhood? While Monica, at some point – just watch – she'll up and get married. And by the way, while she's telling women not to waste their time and money gussying up for men – *she's* sitting at Kenneth getting her hair streaked. I saw her! – trying to hide under a dryer behind a copy of *Vogue*" ...

It *was* somewhat about her vanity, Gilda was thinking beneath her tirade, *of course* it was. Did they expect her to curtsy politely and depart the scene? Be relegated to a coin like Susan B. Anthony (Susan B. *Who*? Becca and friends would say). Hell, she'd invented the women's movement, named it, written it into being, fanned the zeitgeist into this force that on August 26 would prove *the fact of their revolution*. It was *her* vision, *her* labor, *her* baby. How could the – *the Hair* come out of nowhere to co-opt it? It was fucking unfair ... Fair had never been part of the deal, any idiot knew that ... But this was above and beyond ... She heard herself wheezing, in out, in out – Christ, an asthma attack? She reached for her inhaler ... Becca hated her, she'd failed her own daughter ... The men so disappointing ... If not for her fame what guy would even look at her? ... *No one* could steal the movement out from under her: she owned it, it was *hers*, the movement was *HER* and she was *IT*.

The old house seem to groan through its timbers in commiseration. From the darkening woods came the cooo-cooo of mourning doves.

"Y'know? the media's pretty canny," Nadine said into a silence, feeling her way. "The media's prescient – even when it's guys drooling over a beautiful woman. They have a sixth sense, and they're running with – maybe the female rage they smell in the air. By focusing on Monica they're betting it's sexier and more exciting to be radical and beat up on the patriarchy and tear it all down. Consequences be damned."

Nervous glances at Gilda. She never attacked Nadine, her loyal soldier.

Fred coughed and reached for a Lucky Strike. "I still don't get it. Last I looked, Monica was just a chick who wrote a couple of okay pieces."

"*I* get it."

The eyes of the communards grudgingly settled on Leora, designated dolt.

"I think it's futile and basically irrelevant to focus on any perceived 'hypocrisy' in Monica regarding men."

"Not *perceived*," Florence Luker squeaked, "it's out there for anyone to see – "

Everyone babbled over the other.

Leora pounded the table with the heel of her hand, glasses jumped: "Excuse me – *I believe* I *was speaking!*"

They looked at her, drop-jawed.

"First of all, Monica's selling feminism to women who were written off or ignored in the earlier wave. Younger women want to look like Monica – but more to the point, they want to *be* Monica. They want to live her life. Monica holds out the exhilaration of possibility. Freedom. Not just the message of equality – become a work-a-mommy and leave in the morning with a briefcase just like dad. Monica's selling the glamour of open-ended possibility."

Sort of what had set her in motion at twenty-one, minus the cheering section ...

"Monica's telling women, be anything or anyone, do anything, it's all up for grabs. Blow men off like I do cuz you have better fish to fry. The power of that! What could be more seductive? The reality, of course, is most women *can't* have her life – they don't have her looks, adroitness, sense of mission, the wind of history at her back. They're likely to pull in their horns, become lonely or tired or broke – or relax back into the old man-centric thing. But that's *now*. That's *today*. Nadine is right." She paused, sure of her audience, grudgingly listening, but listening. "Monica is what the future looks like."

A rush of voices. Leora held them off with her hand. "Monica's other not so secret weapon? She's pushing for more than just giving women a piece of the pie. She wants to change the pie. Change the terms, reinvent the culture from the bottom up." She was really into this. If she ever had a bit of money, she'd take one of those public speaking courses, maybe become a human potential coach like Werner Erhard with that est thing ...

"So where does that leave us? We can fight the future and get left behind. Or we can become part of the future. Nadine's right, there's no going back. The reality is that Monica is emerging as the movement's figurehead and galvanizer." No one dared look at Gilda. "What we need to do — even if we don't *entirely* buy her project — is *co-opt Monica.*"

They didn't dare look. Who could imagine Gilda stepping away from history, she who for so long had *made* history?

She's right. All eyes converged on Gilda. She looked restored to her old persona, armed for the next battle, she was bobbing her head in approval. "Leora's exactly right, we need to *co-opt the opponent*," Gilda said. "'Keep your friends close, and your enemies closer' — the better to move out ahead. Especially as no one realizes yet that the march is only *the opening salvo.*"

Someone might have flipped a switch, the war room brightened, swirled with energy. Even the damn mourning doves shut up.

"I *see the future.* I see *what has to happen next* — and I'm already planning the next stage, which I'll announce right after the march. We're going to expand to the political arena, we'll take the movement to a whole new front ... Recruit feminist candidates for the U.S. Senate ... I'm thinking of a run for the Senate myself ... I don't think another woman in America would muster more votes. You know how Joan of Arc heard voices that guided her? I think I hear voices sometimes. Like Joan of Arc, corny as it sounds. It's actually your own sixth sense telling you what's best."

The group exhaled in unison. Gilda talked and talked — let obsolescence try to fuck with her! They settled in for a long harangue.

Leora pictured Gilda storming the barricades like Delacroix's Lady Liberty Leading the People, sharp of elbow and short of breath, clambering over the competition, bosom bared in the red dress ... Back on top.

For the moment, anyway.

As Gilda talked, and talked, Leora attracted the odd admiring glance. She felt like the heroine of one of the books she read to Finn and Cara before bedtime. Some put-upon schmegeggy of a critter, maybe a skunk standing in for someone stinky or queerly colored or somehow *different*, finally wins, after many failures and trials, the acceptance of the hedgehogs and woodchucks and Beverly Baboon the librarian, and all the lovely creatures of animal town – and at long last becomes a member of the commune.

CHAPTER 20

Pox

He sounded tetchy and remote. "Can't we just talk now? On the phone? I'm not even sure I'll get out to Islesfordd any time soon."

"Terry, please, I absolutely must talk to you in person. Meet me at our beach, I'm asking you."

Over the summer they'd talked and walked and swum at Little Harbor, favoring cloudy days when, except for the odd fisherman or yachtsman angling his craft through the narrow channel, the dreaming cove was theirs. Their little ritual had worked to keep them honest. Over the past several weeks their sessions had slackened off, for no apparent reason. Perhaps she'd been less than honest. But this was no moment for niceties.

"My piece, *The Kayak Caper,*" she began, breathless – "it was skedded for this issue of *Gotham* – the one now on the news stands. And it's not in the magazine. The Managing Editor said he loved the story, the perfect late-August piece."

Terry shrugged. Squinted at her above his wire-frame glasses, its ear-piece still taped together: *I had to come here for this?* "Well, there's still a bit of August left." He considered a series of sand pellets at the waterline, slightly darker than the regular sand. "They're so ingenious, fiddler crabs. The feeding claw brings food to the crab's mouth, their mouthparts are able to sift out the good stuff – and then they spit out these pellets of cleaned sand."

"Why are you talking to me about pellets?"

Terry hiked his glasses on his nose: "Pieces get bumped all the time. Especially when there's a new owner." He picked up a flat rock and deftly skipped it into the bay and watched it stitch the water three, four times. The sun angled low on the bay spoke of autumn.

"New owner? What new owner?"

He picked up another rock; maddeningly, considered it. "Yah, *Gotham's* got a new owner. Hasn't been announced yet, but yah, a deal went through. And Clive's out, you know."

"*Know?* I don't know a thing."

"Editors get bumped, too. Once the new owner's in, it's his show."

"Who's gonna replace Clive?"

"Dunno. You might take that up with the soon-to-be new owner."

"You're saying the new boss would be like really eager to, like, *chat* with me?"

Terry cut her a sour smile. "Well, I would hope so."

"You *hope so?*"

"Seeing as how he's your boyfriend."

Her mind scattered in several directions at once. *Kaz had bought* Gotham? *Why hadn't he fucking told her? Don't panic.* There must be some explanation.

"Terry, you're obviously pissed at me and I don't get it. We had ... you and I ... we have an understanding. I've done nothing against you."

A beat. "No, you haven't, not at all," he said, fair-minded to a fault. He looked at her through smudged glasses, as if flipping through scenarios: "Funny, I assumed you'd know what was up at *Gotham*."

She grabbed onto a life raft: Kaz hadn't wanted to tell her till the deal was finalized. Official! So they wouldn't both be disappointed ... That was his way, he liked to spring surprises on her. *I wanted to surprise you and see your face*, he'd said about the George Sand ... *I felt such a burst of love for you ...*

"From what I hear," Terry was saying, "the *new owner*" – the words dripped acid – "might have a short tenure. Listen, I'm on deadline with an editing job." He nodded at her and opened the fingers of both hands: *we're done here, I assume?* "Gotta get back." He turned and headed for the path that wound through a bed of reeds to the cars.

"Waitaminute! You can't just drop these *bombs* and walk away!"

Terry kept walking.

"Why you being an *asshole?*"

He disappeared around the curve, flushing a piping plover which shot straight up, indignant, and jack-knifed across the sky.

The fact was, she knew why. But could focus only on a single idea: pieces get bumped *when there's a new owner.* There her known world ended. When she tried to connect the dots her brain polka'd madly around and slammed into a concrete wall.

★

On the drive back to Cormorant Cove Leora took a wrong turn and narrowly missed a smack-up with one of those battle-ready jeeps the local gentry affected. In good Islesfordd fashion the driver gave her the finger. She pulled over onto a grassy shoulder. *Once the new owner's in it's his show.* So her little boyfriend had killed her piece? She heard herself panting like in her old Lamaze class.

For a change, no cop cars in the commune driveway.

She found the communards hunched over the galleys of an article spread on the dining room table. Peter was reading aloud:

"*The latest fire in the Amor Fashions factory in Bangladesh killed at least 112 workers. The fire rapidly spread up the nine floors where garment workers were trapped due to blocked fire escapes. Many died inside the building or while seeking an escape through the windows. Workers said the exit doors to the factory, which had lost its fire safety certification months earlier, were locked, prompting some to leap to their deaths from the burning –*"

"Horrible," Gilda interrupted. "Why we reading this?"

"Let him finish," Terry said, catching Leora's eye.

"Where's it from, this piece?"

"*Left Review*, a weekly I free-lance for," Terry said. "Story's skedded for next week. *The Beaver*'s people are already all over the journalist who broke it."

"*Police ordered the building evacuated the day before, after fire hazards were identified*, Peter read on. "*But the authorities said the building owner had required the workers to come to work despite the safety violations* – Oh, here's why we're reading this:

"*The Amor Factory manufactured clothes for several western companies, chief among them Tramlaw.*"

"Why does that name sound familiar?" Gilda said.

"It's a company owned by Kaz Grabowski," Leora said.

Edwina shot her an alarmed look.

"God*damn*!" Gilda said.

"*The fire in the factory in Bangladesh has renewed questions over whether Western companies should be held accountable for lax safety standards in the factories where their products are made,*" Peter drawled on. "*Lawyers for Workers International plan to file a lawsuit on behalf of the victims' families in U.S. Federal court in Washington Friday against Tramlaw Stores Inc ...*"

"Well, there goes a huge chunk of funding for the Strike," Gilda growled. "He was paying for sound trucks, the coalition's office space ... We can't take dirty money."

And how could she now take Kaz to Swaziland? Well, politics was one thing, love quite another. She'd traveled with more scurrilous types. One had even been a Republican. Hadn't Hannah Arendt been in love with a Nazi sympathizer?

★

Kaz's secretary always put her through right away. Mr. Grabowski had left for Seattle the night before, she said. "He's expecting you at the Seattle Four Seasons – in a couple of days, I think it is. Friday, August 17th. Let me check on your flight, dear." A moment. "Arrives in Seattle-Tacoma Airport at 5:46 P.M. with the time change. Mr. Grabowski has to attend an important meeting that evening and feels *terrible* that he can't meet you at the airport. He'll be sending a limo."

★

On Friday, August 17th, Leora sat in her air-challenged apartment, packed suitcase standing by the door. Patrick was off with the children in Oyster Bay. Leora sat unmoving on the Queen

Anne chair disgorging its innards, staring out her living room window decked with strips of sheets.

It came time to leave for the airport.

She made no move.

Around 6:30 P.M., as if on auto-pilot, she picked up the phone and dialed The Four Seasons in Seattle.

"Mr. Grabowski is not taking any calls."

Sweat ran into her eyes, the salt made them smart. "Tell him it's Leora Voss and I urgently need to speak with him. I've arrived in Seattle but there's been a major delay coming in from the airport."

Silence, as the cipher on the other end presumably checked on something. Then he repeated the same sentence.

"Please tell him it's essential that Leora Voss speak with him."

"Mr. Grabowski asked not to be disturbed – he said *under no condition* – "

"He would want to know – "

"I'm sorry, Madam."

"It's urgent – in fact, it's a medical emergency – "

"The gentleman asked not to be disturbed – under any circumstances – "

" – a sudden seizure – "

"I do apologize – "

Bingo. One thing she'd gotten right.

★

Leora wasn't sure how she'd arrived in Tompkins Park from her apartment. She sat on a bench in a drizzle so fine you couldn't be sure. On the next bench a mother in a Peruvian hat shielded a baby with what looked like a music score, a pacifier dangling from her wrist by a dirty string. On the other side a couple was making out. Their dog lay, muzzle on its black-nailed paws, taking the philosophical long view of dogs.

At least she'd never boarded that flight to nowhere. A sliver of ... *something* ... salvaged. You take comfort where you find it. She rummaged for the first class ticket to Seattle in her bag. She eyed it. Her Ticket Out. She'd been evicted from the marriage plot with no Plan B.

She'd bounced off the ropes before, in venues ranging from l'Aeroport Nice Cote d'Azur, to 96th Street and Columbus Avenue ... You never got good at it. She thought of Monica Fairley. You'd never catch Monica bouncing off the ropes in the Nice Cote d'Azur. It was Monica who left the *suitors* bouncing. Her sinuses ached – impacted fury, she supposed ... She ripped the plane ticket into small pieces, then smaller pieces, till her fingers could get no purchase on the scraps. *There.* What had *that* accomplished? People yakked about closure. *What* closure? The shambles of Leora-and-Kaz would now blow kisses and depart? She must have groaned. The dog from the next bench had raised its head and eyed her, ears pricked, its black claws delicately laid out.

Lovers cruelly separated – at least there was a song there! You got no songs for getting caught pants-down. She was Fomushka the village idiot. She saw the drawing in Finn's book of Russian folk tales, Fomushka wearing a tricorne hat that mashed down his ears. His friend, Ivan the Imbecile ... Gatsby, a bootlegger and con man, forever golden in West Egg – it was all such innocent stuff. Gatsby's updated version was in the killing game. Kaz murdered long distance, corporate style. Then, the personal touch, stamped out her puny efforts at *Gotham*. She thought of the night of charades, how he'd ground his foot on the vole.

None of this had she factored into the marriage plot. No corporate killers roamed Jane Austen. Just bad boys and cads. A charming but unscrupulous officer, bounders in breeches, a spendthrift or two ... At worst, Darcy might act high-handed with a tenant farmer or whatever they had there that was lower on the food chain ... The crazy thing, Kaz *was* part Gatsby. He'd kept faith over the years, like Gatsby, with his obsession. Kaz was the flip side. Ugly Gatsby. Anger must turn him on – as the armored knight by his bedside could confirm.

How had he kept his dream of revenge simmering all these years? Truly, it took the soul of an artist, the glorious obstinacy.

"Think what you could have created, Kaz, if you'd channeled the power of all that hate into something that made the world a tiny bit better."

"It wouldn't have been as sweet as this."

"You could have made something magnificent. Like one of Gaudi's cathedrals. They look like dribbled excrement, anyway. You could have turned hate into towers of colored shit, and become a famous artist, at the very least!"

"Certain things a man doesn't forgive."

"C'mon, we didn't speak the same language, you and me. We were just dumb kids with our whole lives in front of us. How can you take yourself so seriously? You hang out with Gilda and talk the talk, but you're stuck in the old macho mindset."

"You know I never bought that libber bullshit. A man wants what he wants." *I get what I need ...*

Leora eyed the remains of the plane ticket turning to wet pulp on the pavement. She shuddered at the scenario she'd aborted, the ugly surprise that would have greeted her at the Seattle Four Seasons. *I'm terribly sorry, Madam, Mr. Grabowski asked not to be disturbed under any circumstances ...* She standing there *duh* gripping her suitcase ... *I do apologize.* So all these weeks Kaz had been working his plot –

It struck her, a rubber pellet between the eyes: Kaz had borrowed his plot from Henry James! The Master, no less! A script from *Washington Square* she herself had handed him ten years ago. He'd taken his cue from James' Catherine Sloper, the heiress who blows off her traitorous, money-grubbing beau after he comes crawling back and hammers at the door. Kaz had cast himself as Catherine! He'd sit high in his polished suite at The Four Seasons, while down below the girl who'd been his only story hammered away at *his* door. Leora almost wanted to compliment him on the symmetry! He'd gone one better than James's Catherine, doubled the payback by acquiring *Gotham*.

It offered a cold greasy pleasure to picture Kaz sitting in his suite at The Four Seasons, hearing the ice melt in the silver champagne bucket; checking his watch once again; maybe checking the arrival time of her flight to Seattle – *you say flight 702 was on time? You're certain there are no delays?* Understanding, finally, in a sludgy rage that Leora Voss would never push through the hotel's heavy revolving door, bellmen bowing, that she would never come ask for Mr. Grabowski at Reception, never hear what they'd been instructed to say, that she'd denied him his climax. Vindicta interruptus.

She could imagine Kaz venting at the poor limo driver he'd sent to the airport to fetch his no-show guest. The first night at Dragon's Gate he walked toward her over the lawn, stumbled on some ... *artwork godammit* – and she saw his anger, the swift flick of a lizard's tongue. Chose *not* to see it. The anger must reach back to the nights in his uncle's stables, to the master's *merde* in the outhouse.

What does payback do for you? she would have liked to ask. Where's the *fon?* Basically, revenge struck her as the ultimate futility, unless you were hunting down former SS guards in Argentina. The consummation, the big Fuck You – it would make her feel like throwing up. She'd sink into post-revenge depression. Medea? Please. Catherine Sloper? Hell, Catherine could climb those stairs into eternity while her lover pounded the door below – and where did that leave her? Hadassah would say it left her *empowered.* To hell with that! Henry James thought it a cool ending because, well, did the man ever get laid?

She sifted Kaz's words for missed clues: *You my only story ... couldn't move forward ... something gets choked off early ... you never recover ...*

I always get what I need ...

Fomushka in her tricorne hat had bought it. How readily we forgive ourselves! He'd neither forgiven nor forgotten ...

The hush of a snowbound morning when all the sounds outside are muffled, one of those New York Sunday mornings made for love. They might have heard the buzzer, she and Patrick, and maybe the pounding on the apartment door, and then the buzzer again, and more pounding, harder this time, but they heard these things from very far away. Toward noon she opened the door to see an envelope on the doormat. Dried white prints from his galoshes. Inside the envelope two plane tickets to Paris. An itinerary: from Paris the train to Bourges, rent a car, drive to Nohant – one hour and nine minutes – to George Sand's manor house. She'd forgotten all about it, how she'd once tossed out, with that whimsy they'd cultivated in college, her dream of visiting the place where Chopin had composed his most sublime nocturnes.

★

The following day – happily, a week day – Leora phoned Kaz's office and asked for his secretary. Could she please give Mr. G a message? "Tell Mr. G." – she was about to say – "tell Mr. G. I got what I needed."

Instead, she said, "I wanted to let you know about the Women's March for Equality on August 26th. We're meeting at 5:30, Fifth Avenue and corner of 59th Street. Join us, it's going to be amazing."

★

Leora slid out of bed the next morning feeling she'd kicked off iron leggings. She hadn't realized the massive effort she'd put into the Plot and keeping the novel of her and Kaz steaming ahead. She'd worn herself out doing double duty. Playing Jane Austen's Mrs. Bennet, hell-bent on marrying Lizzie and the other daughters to a rich squire – while also playing a daughter.

Of course she'd liked Kaz in bed, always. The body has its reasons.

Terry had almost pulled her off course. From the first, she'd been hot for him – *and* Kaz, true to the wondrous joys of sluttiness. Terry, though, was a comrade in arms. Terry was of her world. Terry was home – or could have been, if home weren't a mildewed basement. He'd perversely engineered his own poverty as penance for doing a number on his wife. She herself wanted no part of that trip. He was into the saint business, Terry – work as super and live rent-free among the spideys and black mold so he could write dispatches about famine in the Sahel in Africa for which he'd get paid in the high two figures. She was all for dispatches about famine in the Sahel! But Terry's poverty was bogus. Next, he could play flagellant, whipping his bare chest bloody with a knotted rope, in a one-man procession down Horatio Street. The male feminist was a creature in transition not to be trusted. So much for Islesfordd's better class of men that she'd envisioned that first night driving out in Fred's car to the commune! Kaz a felon in eggshell linen. Sebastian Nye a stalker. Lester Annis? The jury was still out on his attacker, but a crowd of suspects surely had excellent reasons for wanting him dead.

Maybe JoBeth Mankiller was right: there *was* something radically fucked up about men.

A pox on them all! She'd failed at the marriage plot and the plot had failed her. She was back to square one, when at twenty she'd sallied forth in pursuit of passion, art, Experience. Hell, she'd shake hands with her younger self, maybe take the old blueprint out of mothballs. The world had turned; she'd no longer be out there alone, making it up as she went; she could count on a whole movement gusting at her back. Women beyond number who'd discovered they wanted a life strangely like the one she'd reached for all those years ago.

Kaz: How did you *know*?

She: Trust a writer to conjure up the worst case scenario … Okay, seriously? Henry James and Catherine Sloper alerted me. But *The Godfather* could have done so as well. I'm sorry about what happened all those years ago, though I couldn't have known about the surprise trip to France. You always did like to surprise me. Especially this last time. We forgive ourselves so easily. You neither forgave nor forgot.

Kaz: silence.

She: We can't repair the past – the way fiddler crabs can replace a damaged claw. Oh Kaz, don't feel too bad, we had lovely times together …

She settled on the Queen Anne chair and flipped through the *Beaver* to Help Wanted. "Be the secretary executives fight for!" … "Airline Careers" – pilots were madly sexy, but she feared flying. "Be a Model" … "Female IRA fighter … " Those ads in the subway – hell, she could become a dental hygienist.

A corrections officer! Though she herself harbored impulses that might warrant a corrections officer. Something closer to home ... *I wanted your voice in the magazine*, Terry had said. A free-lance writer can't count on a reliable boiler – her standard for *haute* luxury – but she needed to start somewhere. As these things went, *Gotham* paid rather well. Terry was right: considering the Amor factory *scandale*, Kaz's tenure there might be brief.

★

Indeed, the unpleasant publicity that surrounded Kaz Grabowski over the role of his company in the Amor factory fire placed him in a revolving door that kept him ever reaching the mast-head of *Gotham*.

★

On a soggy afternoon Leora set the kids up with their sticky Fisher Price Junior Circus from Goodwill, and cold-called the new Executive Editor of *Gotham*. A long pause; then, amazingly, someone put her through.

"You wrote that *Kayak Caper* piece?" came a man's voice. "It's priceless. Don't know how it fell off the schedule. We plan to squeeze it in before Labor Day. What else you got?"

Leora pitched a story near to her heart: Libby Fenwick Futterman and *The New Welfare Moms*.

"That's a cover. Will she talk to you?"

"I think she will. Everybody wants to tell their story."

She replaced the receiver and smiled at her dracaena plant. The health benefits would have to wait; winters the kids would still sleep in snowsuits and ear muffs; as usual she was one late rent check away from welfare mom. Never mind, *you're on your way*. She'd make the kids proud.

She was heading for their huddle on the floor, when a sharp object stabbed her instep. She yelped and kicked it away.

"Ma, look what you've done," Finn said, "you've broken the dromedary acrobat!" Cara set to bawling, lips down-turned like the mask of Tragedy.

Leora limped over and kneeled to inspect the damage. "Look, the pieces fit, we'll put the dromedary back together with Crazy Glue and he'll be perfectly fine. Who are the finest children on all of Avenue A?" She pulled the kids against her.

The phone again – just moments after she'd hung up.

The editor had changed his mind and decided he hated her piece!

"We need to sell *now*," came a voice on the phone. "It's time to take the gain."

"Excuse me? Who is this?" The threatened rain suddenly let down; Leora was gratified to note the strips of sheets festooning the window were finally muting the drip-drip.

"Leora, are you there?" came the voice. Leora eyed the receiver. A crank call, surely. "It's me, Henry Lyman."

Henry? Christ, Gilda's finance whiz, the guy with narcolepsy. Couple of years back he'd absconded with her savings and blown them on some investment as nutters as he was. Something involving spinal surgery ... The children were loudly squabbling over who got to hold the dromedary. "Finn, give Cara a turn right *NOW!*" she called.

"Leora, this is a terrible connection, what's all that noise. Can you hear me? The stock has more than quadrupled and IT'S TIME TO TAKE THE GAIN."

"What stock?"

"Piece o' Cake. We got a home run here. Didn't I promise? But we should take the gain *now. And –* I've got the next home run for ya, the next big thing. I guarantee you it's a quadruple in the next twelve months."

A long moment. "Henry, about that *first* big thing. There was a gain?"

"I should say so."

"And I should take the gain now?"

"Abso-*lute*-ly, the timing's right. Sweet Jesus, it's what I've been telling you for the last several minutes!" Sigh. "You do have a financial consultant, I hope?"

"What was the gain?"

In one moment her world changed.

★

Kaz Grabowski hired a squadron of top tier attorneys who accused Workers International of a "witch hunt" and established, after a blizzard of shredded documents, that his company Tramlaw had never placed orders to the Amor factory in Bangladesh. He flew out to Islesfordd to see Sophia Merdle. They'd been in love since May and agreed that Sophia would confront her husband Milt by summer's end.

Sophia had been rethinking her affairs. She was far from pleased with the tawdry stuff that had surfaced about Milt and unleashed a perfect storm of gossip. True, she'd been sleeping with Kaz all summer; she could hardly expect Milt to be celibate. But to resort to Malaysian tarts in catalogs ...

And now a bad odor hung over Kaz for being mentioned in the same breath as the "tragedy" in Bangladesh. He'd been quoted in the paper telling a lawyer for Workers International, "I'm warning you, tread very fucking lightly because what I'm going to do to you is going to be fucking disgusting, do you understand me?" and saying other *wildly* unattractive things.

He'd likely be vindicated, but how could she take him to the Rottlesey? It was understood at the club that even *good* publicity should be shunned. In fact, there was no such thing as "good" publicity. Whatever might bring attention to the members' grand ocean front "cottages," the eight meter racing yachts, "camps" in Maine, "legacies" that greased entree to Yale, etc, etc. – must be squelched in a jiffy. If the lower orders knew what the Rottleseys and their peers had going – well, Sophia could picture an army of tumbrils mowing down golf carts and their occupants on the Rottlesey course to rival Gleneagles.

Hand it to Milt – her husband had exquisite antennae for picking up any threat of turbulence in his personal life. He announced he was ready to buy her the island off Virgin Gorda. Sophia had always wanted an island to call her own. Now she could construct that oasis nearby in the sea and plant it with three palm trees. Imagine, three palm trees waving their fronds in the middle of the Caribbean ... So sur*real*! Robert Smithson had just done his "earthwork" "Spiral Jetty." She would create "seawork." She'd get written up in *Art in America*! She'd have a show at a top-flight gallery on 57th Street – the Pace or Pierre Matisse. She'd create a line of clothing with a logo, call it Three Palms Sportswear. A makeup line, a perfume. A Three Palms restaurant right here in Islesfordd. She'd get written up in Style sections across the country as an artist slash entreprenew-uh!

It struck Sophia that she'd suffered from low-level depression all these years because she was an artist who'd never gotten the recognition she was due – *her* "problem with no name," as Gilda Gladstone had called it. She really ought to attend that parade Gilda was always going on about. It sounded like a celebration of women like her finally coming into their own.

★

Kaz sat alone by his moat-like pool, nursing a Maker's Mark, and wondered what he could get for Dragon's Gate. Only Gilda Gladstone still wanted to see him. He was keeping his distance. Earlier in the summer he'd promised her an answer regarding a trip to some place with savages with plates through their ears, and maybe cannibals, whose name escaped him.

★

The communards, who'd long ago rescued their money from Henry, were furious at themselves, and rediscovered the joy of disliking Leora. The sly ditz had put one over on them by passing herself off as financially illiterate. Obviously, she was some sort of financial genius. Only Edwina rejoiced for Leora. Those dear children could eat rib lambchops and – their favorite – shrimp cocktail – instead of chopped chuck diluted with hamburger helper; winters they'd sleep in their own little beds in jammies. The main thing, Leora could take Finn to that hotshot plastic surgeon in Philly.

Leora sensed herself undergoing a transformation. Possessing money was a chemical event, a drug coursing through her veins – this was how Frankenstein must have felt! She inhabited the world differently; she'd make a request and wonder, Why was this not done for me *sooner*? She heard her voice assume that silvery, guillotine-mongering lilt of Sophia's. Her tits and ass shrank – though they'd need to revert to pre-adolescence to do a full Sophia (rich men out here seemed to prefer the lads). She curated a super gracious demeanor toward underlings, sticking her butt out when inclining to address them, as she'd seen Sophia do. Her vascular system got the memo, blood pumped into her cheeks, she slept sounder, dreamt less of repo men hammering at her door, shat often and better. She stopped smoking and boozing. Now she, too, planned to live at least two hundred years, like the Greenland sharks, or Bowhead Whales, with their lipless smiles and knowing eyes.

She phoned the pediatric plastic surgeon. When the snippety secretary told her nothing was available till early '71, she wrote a fat check to the clinic's research arm and got an appointment for the following week. She arranged to meet with realtors (to their puzzlement her main requirement was a good boiler). She considered sitting on boards that could not dispense with her presence. Maybe she could serve on the board of The Critter Connection. Its stated mission was to "make sure no guinea pig got left behind."

Her beloved Stendhal named the self-regard of rich people *l'importance* and thought it not cool.

★

"Leora, you must consult a financial advisor," Edwina said. "Peter will find you someone he trusts."

"Got a good man for 'ya, super connected, who can make the right referral," Peter said. "Elliot's come through some personal crises. His wife walked out on him couple of years ago. She went and told anyone who would listen that he was the worst lay in New York. Can you imagine what that does to a man? Set Elliot back big time, I can tell you. Actually, the wife went to the same college as you, maybe you knew her? Libby Futterman. She's on welfare yet refuses to take money from him, go figure ... Well, never mind all that, Elliot's all squared away now and would know just the right person to handle your portfolio."

"This guy is Libby Futterman's ex-husband?" Leora stammered. "Uh, that might create a conflict of interest."

"Small world syndrome, eh? I'll ask one of his partners, then. Say, I just remembered: Elliot came to a couple of lectures Nadine gave out here and I think they had a thing. Went nowhere, I gather."

CHAPTER 21

The Marriage Plot Reconsidered

*"Love has always been the most important business in my life;
I should say the only one."*

— Stendhal, *La Vie d'Henri Brulard*

After a longish absence – which Leora embroidered three different ways – Terry was expected at the commune. She jacked up her nerve and phoned to ask him to meet her at their beach.

"What's up?"

Leora winced at this shorthand for "fuck off." Even if they'd fallen away from the days of acting as each other's sounding board, she expected nicer manners from Terry. He carried harm all over him and usually took care not to lay shit on others.

She needed advice about a writing project, she said. The usual place okay?

They set a time. Terry sounded as interested in meeting her as a bank teller eyeing lunch break.

★

The afternoon had turned bright, with a spanky little breeze. Already the sun of late summer packed less heat and autumn's crows were loudly bickering, clearly a domestic spat, in the scrub oak.

"Their beach" had been invaded. A family in a dinghy put-putted out to an anchorage. A boat came about violently several feet from Leora, as a sailor gathered in luffing sails to his chest like a hussard a reluctant bride. Some joker had driven his pick-up truck onto the sand and lay big-bellied on his towel, boom box blasting. The Carpenters, *We've Only Just Begun*. The sappiest songs, it never failed, triggered unbridled longing in Leora.

Her heart dove when she saw Terry approaching along the reedy path. Yellowed white tennis shorts with a dangling drawstring hung off his hips, troublingly narrow.

His lips brushed her cheek. "Been a while," he murmured. The Carpenters had only "just begun to live" ... *A kiss for luck and we're on our way ...*

They eyed the guy stroked out beside his radio, only the nostrils visible over his gut, and started for the familiar trail through the dunes. The bass beat from the boom box followed them, faintly thrumming even on the beach below.

"You wanted to run some ideas by me?" His flat line voice fallen below sea level.

Put a lid on it. She had no right to be angry. No right at all. It was he who had the right since the evening she'd silently let on that handing over everything to his ex and living in a basement – so he could feel good about himself – didn't work with the marriage plot.

"How 'bout I just thought it might be cool to touch base, now that summer's winding down. With such a coda as a bloody assault," she added.

He dropped to the sand – (the indifference a bit willed?) – and lay supported on his elbows, knees drawn up. A ribbon of white beyond the edge of his trunks. It struck Leora that Terry's chilliness seemed to cost him. It was the only encouragement she could muster.

"Terry, you once said I needed a murder to anchor my novel. Now that Islesfordd has delivered, well, what might be a *botched* homicide; you can't have everything – I thought it would be fun to brainstorm together about who dunnit." She folded down beside him. "Of course *The Commune*, as I'm calling the novel, is not constrained by fact. But several people around here had motives by the yard to get rid of Lester Annis that I thought might jibe with the motives of my characters. So far the cops have drawn a blank about who attacked him."

Something in his face woke up. She'd tapped into his book-ishness. "Top of the list, Sebastian Nye," Terry said. "Nye has the killer in him. Remember the time he swam out on Hooker Pond to 'rescue' Peter? And actually shoved his head under? Poor impulse control. Maybe a little rehearsal for murder."

"Yup, Nye's a prime suspect," she said, faux casual, as if afraid of scaring off a skittish creature.

"But why would he have it in for Lester Annis?"

"Listen, the first night I drove out to the commune with Fred I picked up on something ... Edwina made no secret of despising Nye, of course. But I think she may have hated another guy more. That night in the car, when Fred mentioned that Lester Annis had just been 'disbarred' for making it with his pa-tients in his nude encounter group – Edwina kinda freaked out."

"Mm hmm, of course, I just remembered: Fred, the Town Crier, once let drop she'd been 'in treatment' with Annis."

"Okay: suppose sicko Seb Nye decided to kill Lester Annis as 'payback' for seducing Edwina. I once heard Nye say he believed it was Annis and his abusive 'therapy' that soured Edwina on men. And made her 'decide to love a woman' – his words. Or, here's something twistier: Nye hoped that by killing Lester Annis he'd win Edwina's gratitude and they'd be an item again." A moment. "D'you suppose Edwina herself might have actually *asked Nye* to kill off Annis?"

"More likely, Nye could have *imagined* she asked," Terry said.

"Good, good, I like that! Unless" – she eyed a regatta way distant on the bay beating back toward Greenport – "unless Edwina herself *hired* someone to do him in. A yard man or someone desperate for money. I dunno ... doesn't have Edwina's prints on it. Anyway, I'm too grateful to Edwina for loving my kids to think badly of her."

"Unh, in the interests of your novel, you may want to set aside subjective bias. But we can work that out later."

Later, yesss ... She breathed out. "Even so, Edwina's an unlikely suspect. She's had so much mayhem in her life already. There's a rumor she ran off with her step-dad in college. She's been abused by Lester Annis – her supposed *shrink* for shit's sake ... Stalked by Sebastian Nye ... Then the breakup with Jo. Nah, the only tumult she could handle now is a colicky baby."

A long moment. "I hate to say this," Terry began, "but Fred – our Fred – "

"*Our Fred*," Leora echoed, moist-eyed. "Full disclosure: I'm certain it was Fred who made off with the manuscript of Annis's you were editing, the better to crib it."

Terry chuckled. "Didn't take Sherlock to figure that out."

"Our Fred takes envy and competitiveness maybe a tad too far. I mean, Peter Grosvenor gets Book of the Month Club, and he tries to drown himself?"

"Fred's kind of a clownish villain," Terry said. "Nadine saw him slinking about one morning with a stack of pages, then skiddooing off to his studio. Wouldn't surprise me if Annis found out about Fred's scheme to skim off his material. In that case, wouldn't Fred want him removed from the scene?"

"Okay, more subjective bias: Fred could bludgeon his own mother and you'd never heard a word from me. Friendship trumps justice and any compulsion to play righteous snitch."

Terry laughed low in his throat. "My concern is that you're kind of violating the genre of your own story. In any case, Fred is not a credible perp – he couldn't kill him*self*, much less try to kill someone else. He's such a softie, think of all the women he's married."

"*And* he's too delicately wired for physical violence. I mean, he once actually *passed out* on the kitchen floor from envy ... Fred would botch the whole thing by taking notes at the crime scene so he could write about it. Try to suss out his own motives, capture the smell of blood, include the brand of the sheets and all those details that anchor a scene. The cops would find him there, smoking over a cough and scribbling away. Mmm, there's someone, something else we're not seeing."

"The beauty is, of course, you can just make it up," Terry said. "But wouldn't it be cool if what you invent squares with the person who actually did attack Lester Annis?" He cut her a wolfish grin. "If you hit on the truth, you could slip the identity of the perp right into your pages. While Detective Neary – who by the way seems awfully taken with Gilda – is spinning his wheels."

"Have they found any clues?"

"I don't think so ... No, wait: the *Islesfordd Herald* mentioned a single clue, some sort of fish lure at the crime scene. But it's lead nowhere."

Leora flashed on a red flying fish lure nesting in Quasi's tackle basket and glinting in the sea-light. *Miss van Otten gave it to me as a good luck* charm. She envisioned doom crashing down on a soul who'd suffered more than his share of misery.

"You must swear you'll reveal nothing of what I'm about to say. Not even to the cops."

"Now you gonna make me an accomplice to attempted murder?"

"Don't go all boy-scoutish on me. I'll not say another word unless you swear – "

"Okay, okay. I assume we're talking about the *made up* plot in your novel?"

"And if I'm not ... ?"

"Just go *on*, dammit."

"Quasimodo carted around those fish lures because Elsie van Bonkers gave them to him for good luck. You may have noticed them dangling from her wacko head gear. *Shhh*, you promised. Quasi, of course, could have cared less about Annis. Elsie is another matter. Years ago Elsie was engaged to Dr. Lester Annis, who was a more conventional medic back then. Seems he had an eye for Rottlesey WASPs. Then, ever the bastard, he jilted Elsie at the altar. Moved upstate and started those nude bacchanals, or whatever."

"Where'd you get that piece of intel?"

"Uh, you hang around 'the help,' you pick stuff up," Leora said, evasive. Wilfredo, a purveyor of gossip second only to Fred, had shared that "intel" when he was working at Dragon's Gate. But Leora preferred to avoid any mention of Kaz.

"So Elsie van Otten," she went on, "may have been biding her time all these years – and then tapped Quasi to be the 'instrument' of her revenge on the no-show husband. There was reportedly a struggle at the crime scene, and Quasi, who's not the most graceful, could have dropped one of those doodads." She shook her head no. "My instinct tells me it would have been no-go. I've observed Quasi here and there. He's far too gentle a soul to bludgeon anything. He can't even hurt fish!"

"Mmm. From what I've observed, though, he'd do anything for Elsie. How you gonna play it in your novel?"

"Let them both off the hook, so to speak. The crime will remain unsolved, become woven into Islesfordd lore. Even if someone does eventually connect the dots, I'm willing to bet the perp will roam free. Elsie van Otten is Ur-Rottlesey. There's neither will nor muscle in Islesfordd to hold anyone from the Rottlesey to account, even for attempted murder. That crowd defines justice as something for *other* people.

"Well, you could give that ending a whirl in your book. But letting them both off the hook, I dunno, might piss off the reader. Maybe I can look at a draft," he added, vague. She feared the train was leaving the station.

Exhausted, suddenly, they both stretched out on the sand, hands clasped behind their heads, faces to the sun. These many days and weeks she'd kept any amorous thoughts of Terry on a tight leash. She closed her eyes, sensing the magnetic field of him along her arms and flanks and calves. A heaviness pressed up from between her legs and behind and all through her. The breeze delivered a post-tennis musk – had he played earlier with Peter?

★

She snapped upright and stared at the bay. Not far from shore a squall crimped a patch of water. "So ... " watching the squall – "I gather you've been, like, super busy in the city?"

"Yah, it's been crazy." He raised up on his elbows. She reminded herself to breathe. "Clive Monomark's replacement has offered me my old job back with an option to write a weekly column about politics. I suspect the columns would have to be 'centrist,' present both sides even when one side is blatantly wrong – you know, the both-siderism bullshit of Public Radio. But still – at almost double my old salary ... " He shrugged.

"I love it! You're the best and the new guy knows it."

"In fact, something else has come up." A chill wrapped her heart. He sat full up and clasped his knees. New magazine start up, she heard ... Pitched to the far left ... Funded by a do-gooder billionaire, owned wineries ... "I'd be editor in chief ... The thing would be mine to shape ... Publisher promises 'hands off,' though we know what that means ... Obviously, the pay would be lousy compared to *Gotham* ... The package is pretty tempting, though ... A lot to weigh ... "

"Yes, a lot to weigh." She exhaled mightily. She hadn't heard what she'd dreaded she might hear. She pushed on, throat tight. "Did you finish that, uh, editing job you mentioned?"

He scanned the bay as if trying to spot U-boats. "What editing job?"

"You know what editing job."

"You're talking about Meghan's book, I assume?"

"I don't imagine *Flavors of Scotland* would need much line editing. How many ways can you say, 'chop the fresh cilantro'"?

Terry muttered something about "a lot of text." "Meghan still needs to sort things out with Fred – but that hasn't kept her from launching ambitious projects."

He spelled out Meghan's ambitious projects. Leora wasn't interested in Meghan's ambitious projects.

"Y'know, we all underestimated Meghan, but I'm really into her," Terry said. A panicky fugue, like when she was trapped in the stalled cable car and they were rocking over a chasm in the Bernese Oberland.

"She's the true new woman," he went on. "Cut in the pattern of Monica Fairley. Meghan can't quite see the need for a husband-type guy and has no use for children – says she wants to create her*self*, not a baby. She's different from you and the other women in the commune. You've been imprinted, all of you, beneath the feminist party line, to put a guy – and family and children – at the center of your life. You're kind of dangling precariously between your generation and your rhetoric, uncertain where to set your feet. The wonder, the *genius* of Gilda is that she's desperate for a man – and thwarted at every turn – yet she gets up every morning mobilized to transform the world. She's a high-functioning contradiction. No desperation for a man in Meghan, I can tell you. I'm not sure she'd know what that is. Once she was on to Fred's catting around, she refused to play victim and simply waited for the opportune moment to split. Meghan's focused on this little career she's invented for herself – from *nothing* – and if a guy wants to join her for the ride, fine. Frankly, it's a little disorienting for a man to feel he's expendable, only one of 'several options,' as Meghan would say ... Also a big turn-on."

Leora's stomach had dropped to the chasm beneath the cable car.

"What makes it so arousing," he went on, brow furrowed in thought –

Oh yes, do tell!

" – if you're not responsible for her happiness in that clinging, needy way women insist on – and occasionally men, too, in all fairness – it's well, very liberating."

"I see, so you're borrowing a page from Fred's cradle-robbing playbook."

"Whaddayou care?"

In answer she shifted onto her knees and moved between his and roughly pushed him back so he was on his elbows

– "what's this?" he said, half laughing – and then she clambered on top of him, and down on the sand they went, she pressing her lips to his and greedily inhaling him and engraving herself into him, he responsive as a rock which aroused her more than she could have imagined but he was coming to life fast.

She rolled off him and they lay breathing on the sand. "What's all that about?" he said, sitting and righting his glasses. One ear piece still taped.

"You tell me."

"Talk to me."

"I once tried to tell my husband about an article I was writing, and he coughed a lot and then threw up. You're the first man who's ever taken the slightest interest in my work."

He laughed. "Glad I could compensate for the crimes of men." A moment. "So your felonious little friend wasn't a good listener?"

"The thing with Kaz was a head trip." This was only partly true. "I got caught up in some fantasy about Gatsby, with a dollop of Jane Austen, and the plot lines got tangled – Y'know the whole business has left so little trace it's like it never happened."

"It's left a trace on *me*."

"Well, as I remember, you yourself have been pretty tied up in knots over your ex – " She shifted to her knees, almost prayerful.

"You don't love Meghan, do you? Tell me you don't. I won't allow it! I couldn't bear it, I won't survive it, I'm an old-fashioned woman, you got that just right."

"I could use a cigarette." He looked around as though one might be offered. "Y'know, a woman Meghan's age," he went on, "bit of a generation *abyss* there ... We don't talk the same language. She's always 'psyched.' Things 'suck.' She says stuff like 'we need to explore if we have a common synergy' ... Luckily for Fred, he had all that surplus testosterone."

"Terry, we belong together, you and me, we both sensed it from the start. We could be a team."

"Yeah? What's changed since May?"

"Oh darling, I can afford you now!"

Henry, the windfall, the gain it was time to take – she told him all.

He whistled. He threw back his head and laughed. "That nutcase *Henry*? You gotta be kidding. Monopoly money."

She shook her head No. "Terry, I've *taken the gain*. It's a done deal. Listen, don't go with the *Gotham* job, you've said that place doesn't feel like the right fit and it never will. Run with this new magazine that you could shape to your own vision, lousy pay be damned. We won't need the money."

"*We*? Wait, this is much too fast."

She closed her eyes against the sun. Orange scorpions capered beneath her lids. "Alright, time's up, you had your moment. Take the job that really suits you. If nothing else, you'll be doing work you love."

"Whoaa" – the palm of his hand held her off – "I need to regroup. Considering I've spent the summer sort of hating you." A beat. "I just remembered how we swam here, in the harbor on the other side of the dunes. We *could* be a team. As synchronized swimmers."

She sat back on her heels and shaded her eyes with her hand. "You have the right to mock me, of course ... "

"It's just that" – he sighed out – "I'm slow to be happy. Give me time to be happy." He looked as though he might cry. "Leora Voss. You were such a brave little person that first night at the commune, with them all piling onto you. *Plucky*. I was an asshole to just sit by while Gilda did her number. Some communal spirit. Self-importance was running rampant, theirs and mine."

"Actually, you did extend a hand. Or waved your big claw." She mustn't feed his guilty conscience, which was already off the charts.

"I wanted to scoop you up and carry you off on a swan boat in Hooker Pond. Give me time ... I think I'm in love with you again."

"Imagine, we could hold hands after someone's funeral and shout to each other in our sleep."

"Bet no one's ever accused you of saying the predictable. Wait" – his eyes turned small and mean. "I am *not* going to goddamn live off you. Think how it would look."

"Who cares how it looks? Live off me! Live off me all you want! Women have done that for ages with men. As long as we can be together. I want to protect you" – she shivered to think she was echoing Kaz. "So you can go write about famine in the Sahel. We'll do our own thing, other people be damned."

She sat scissored against his groin, their lips together, his hands in her hair, her knees gripping his ribs – She tumbled off with a small groan. "Wait: I am *not* going to live in a goddamn basement with black mold."

"In fact," he gasped, "it's dry and clean. Kind of cozy."

"We can take a two-bedroom in your building. It's in a great school district."

Friction ensued. He liked being Super, Terry said; the company of the maintenance people who worked in the building "keep me real." He was intent on putting distance between them; he worried he'd capitulated to her so fast . Not until the fall would they agree that Terry would keep his basement lair as a writing studio ...

"I just thought of this," Terry said, excited, putting on his editor hat. "It's a little cheesy but – The publisher could embargo your novel – then create buzz by leaking that on publication date the book will reveal the identity of Lester Annis's assailant. Get a jump on Detective Neary. Naming the perp on pub date would make your novel an 'event book,' a literary crime *solver* and first of its kind."

"Oh, that's *bad*," Leora said, delighted. In fact, the ending is a work in progress. Here's the thing: as it stands now, the most plausible perp is Elsie van Otten's go-fer. But why make trouble for poor old Quasi? His life has been wretched enough. So, no 'event book.' Christian charity – and personal morality – will have to trump buzz." A moment, and she said,

"See, when I was playing out my summer of 'The Great Gatsby,' with Kaz miscast in the leading role – well, an aspect of that novel that's sometimes overlooked has always troubled me. Daisy runs over Myrtle Wilson in the yellow convertible. Myrtle is her husband Tom Buchanan's mistress – remember? – and the wife of that poor garage owner, George. And of course Daisy gets away with it. George Wilson kills Gatsby, then shoots himself, and Daisy and Tom Buchanan just carelessly destroy lives and move on. That's how it works for the rich. And here's the thing: Fitzgerald kind of *digs that*, he's into the *romance* of that, he had an unsavory love/hate thing going with the wealthy."

Mmhm, mmhm. "So now, in real life you get to symbolically vindicate poor George Wilson by protecting Quasi."

"At least in my novel. It's really a pity I have such an over-developed *private* moral sense. Because turning my novel into a literary crime solver would have been really kicky!"

"There's time to sort it all out."

"Actually, I just thought of a more plausible suspect – or, rather, *suspects* – that would make a cool ending. Lester Annis must have left behind a gaggle of women besides Edwina who he seduced under the guise of 'therapy.' Imagine a pack of vengeful Furies emerging at nightfall from the bays and dunes and wetlands of Islesfordd to bludgeon their tormentor. Enact their own sort of rough justice. A strike against abuser men for all womankind! It will make the perfect crime – and revenge – for the times!"

★

The Women's Strike for Equality, August 26, 1970

"It was, is, awesome – that quantum jump in consciousness."

– Betty Friedan

"And when it begins to get dark, instead of cooking dinner or making love, we will assemble and we will carry candles alight in every city ... and women will ... sacrifice a night of love to make the political meaning clear"

– Betty Friedan

"I was no longer alone; now there was a we—and we wanted to end the subjugation of women—now!

– Phyllis Chesler

At roughly 5:30, as if governed by a hive brain, the crowd powered on and began its journey down Fifth Avenue into a new era. Leora jumped to look behind: My God, the numbers, *beyond our wildest dreams ...* Marchers and their white placards stretched up up the avenue beyond sight, past the zoo at 66th Street, maybe clear to Spanish Harlem.

The mayor had granted them just one lane but no way could they keep to a little thin line down Fifth. The crowd swelled past the barricades. From the sidelines mounted police made gestures at containment but there were so many women. What could they do, mow the women down?

Gilda waved her arms over her head and yelled "*TAKE THE STREET!* EVERYBODY JUST TAKE HANDS AND STRETCH OUT ACROSS THE WHOLE STREET. THAT'S RIGHT, *THE WHOLE GODDAMN STREET!*" A bullhorn, then another, echoed the message through the ranks.

And so they marched, in great long swinging lines, from sidewalk to sidewalk, and the police on their horses got out of their way. From the side streets car horns blasted notes in varying registers in a furious chorale.

The route along Fifth felt electric, the avenue a giant party. WOMEN'S STRIKE FOR PEACE AND EQUALITY, read a placard. MEN FOR WOMEN'S RIGHTS. "Join us Now, Sisterhood is Powerful," marchers chanted – and passers-by on the sidewalks slipped into the ranks. Men looked on wearing an expression nesting between amusement-disbelief-fear. A fat horn-rimmed guy on the sidewalk hoisted a sign: THIS MORNING I MADE LOVE TO MY WIFE AND SHE LOVED IT. A small group of marchers fluttered Viet Cong flags. The woman walking beside Leora said she was Mrs. Ionella Church and she was seventy years old and she'd come in from Ossining with her daughter and granddaughter, both named Veronica ... A group came abreast yelling, "DON'T IRON WHILE THE STRIKE IS HOT!"

Women 20,000 strong – 50,000, who knew? – took Fifth Avenue, blocking the major thoroughfare during rush hour, Leora scribbled in her head. Material for a novel she'd call *The Commune. The sense of triumph and joy was contagious.* Remember the smiles: *radiant, post-sex, just-won-the-lottery smiles.*

Somewhere ahead of Leora, a fracas over a guy and his sign, MAN/WOMAN: VIVE LA DIFFERENCE! Women descended on him like Furies and dismantled the poster and him with it, almost. A teenage girl in a helmet putt-putted alongside on a motor scooter, a self-appointed honor guard. A bus! Somehow a bus was crawling down Fifth Avenue. Cops in the short sleeves of August wandered among the marchers, looking unsure they'd been invited to the party.

As the crowd approached 53rd street people leaned out of office windows and cheered and the crowd yelled, Join us!

"Join us sisters!" Leora called. The words tasted strange. She'd never joined anything. She got gooseflesh down the back of her neck like when she saw *Potemkin* in the Cinematheque in Paris and the sailors refuse to fire on their own. She thrilled to feel her walled, clenched self merge with the women all around, arms linked and soldered together, sparking off each other.

She spotted Nadine pushing her granddaughter Christabel in a stroller. The child looked large enough to be pushing *Nadine*. Baby Fidel rode happily in some sort of sling across Nadine's chest, dripping snot. Leora maneuvered over with Finn. She exclaimed over Nadine's new Parisian haircut – "very gamine."

"I almost didn't make it back from Paris – there was a strike of the baggage handlers at the airport, you know, the usual in France." She'd been "epically busy," Nadine went on – the meeting with her French publisher; interviews to hire a research assistant for the new book. Dinner tomorrow night at Sardi's with the producer Hal Prince, who was planning a musical based on *Damaged and Confused*.

He'd written her, Nadine said, voice dropping. Elliot was cutting short his time in Singapore. He wanted to see if they could put it back together, he'd said. He owed her an apology. It had happened so fast and he was still "dazed and confused" and "hurting" – she'd shuddered at the word – from the business with Libby, stuck in past acrimony, fighting past battles. With women's lib men felt caught between a rock and a hard place – she of all people would understand. Men were having to rethink all the terms. He himself was trying to recalibrate, etc. etc. He wanted a second chance.

Nadine was all for second chances …

He didn't want any rancor between them because he respected her so. Admired her so. He understood that her work came first and he *applauded that* but maybe it was too late for a fellow like him to make that sort of adjustment – It wasn't till then, mid-letter, that she suddenly got who "they" were. He was going back to Libby. Who was so helpless, running off half-cocked like that. And the children needed a strong parental figure, they were doing poorly with that step-aunt – or whoever the fuck she was – what a mess it had all been … Libby needed him, too. In a way Nadine never would. Which was precisely why he so *admired her*! She took pride in living well without a man's support. He'd never forget that. She was a class act! This was all so clumsily put, he apologized, he was not the writer she was, but he had the best of intentions and he hoped she would understand and think well of him.

"I wonder if Libby still calls Elliot Futterman the worst lay in New York," Nadine wound up.

"Nadine, I'm so sorry," Leora said. She was sorry in a different key to have to forfeit her cover story on Libby and the welfare mothers. The denouement was now too sodden and dispiriting for a magazine; editors would want a more uplifting wrap-up in keeping with the times, a woman starting a skin care empire, not a woman crawling back to her husband in defeat.

Nadine took her fingers to her temples and fluffed her new French coif. "Y'know? to hell *with* it. I'm fine. I'm wonderful!

Look at this" – her arms made parentheses to embrace the scene. "Do you *believe* this crowd? And *we* helped make it happen (kindly including Leora in "we"). "Compared to this, our sour little disappointments don't amount to much, do they? Don't amount to a hill of beans, as old Bogey said to Ingrid. Nadine smiled her lovely sad smile. Fidel started fussing and barfed something milky down her skirt. Nadine reached in a shoulder bag for a wipie.

A group of young women came abreast, lofting a banner and chanting HANDS OFF ANGELA DAVIS. Behind them Leora spotted – he looked familiar, could it be? Detective Neary, of the Islesfordd police! Bearing a placard, FREE THE FEMALE BODY.

Leora shot a little wave at Henry Lyman. He wore a seersucker jacket and suspenders and his glasses rode, as always, at the far end of his ski-slope nose. He was patrolling the marchers from the sidelines. He'd spot a matron in good tailoring toting a little satchel bag, and make his move. "Farmland in Adair, Iowa, they aren't making any more of it ... Got a quadruple for 'ya ... "

"I am not a Barbie Doll," a group chanted. BAN *COSMO* AND SILVA THINS ... LESBIAN MOTHERS UNITE. There was Hadassah Sarachild talking heatedly with JoBeth. They were trailed by Hadassah's consort and baby-carrier, beagle-faced and mournful, pacifier dangling from his neck. He tapped Hadassah's shoulder, gesturing at the infant on his chest in some sort of Snugli, his expression indicating a ripe diaper. She indignantly waved him away.

Becca Gladstone, where was Becca? She'd announced she was boycotting the march – but maybe she'd relented? Too cruel, Leora thought, if she failed to witness her mother's great triumph.

Edwina snapped pictures along the route with her new Leica 35MM. Peter Grosvenor walked beside her with his equestrian gait, strung with camera gear and tweedy as a country squire out for a stroll in his park. Edwina looked especially glamorous in a white taffeta jumpsuit, hair snatched up in a messy construction. "Bra-less traitor," a heckler yelled. "You're too cute to be a libber," a guy called.

Edwina would have liked to explain to the hecklers that while this march would always figure as a high point of her life, she was a bit of an impostor. She pictured Bryant Park after the speeches were over and the park stood empty except for a few placards blowing against the dark shrubs, and how the marchers would return on the subway to empty apartments and need to get up for their mission every morning of every day and recreate the world anew. She'd chosen a more easeful course. Feminism *was* about the freedom to choose, wasn't it? she thought, suddenly uncertain.

Lately she walked around in a haze of amazement that she'd survived her own life ... It was early to tell, of course, but this morning she'd woken with a strange metallic taste in her mouth, as if her insides were revving up for a major incursion, and noted a telltale tingling in her nipples. *Like that first time ...* She would love this child the way she loved Finn and Cara. She could weep with gratitude for Leora's children! They'd revealed her to herself. She looked forward to Labor Day with Peter at the Grosvenor's shingled ramble of a house on the Vineyard. Everyone would drink too much, of course; she would be careful, to protect the future. They'd teach their boy to sail on Lake Tashmoo. She'd design a perennial border worthy of the West Tisbury Annual Seaside Gardens Tour. She'd photograph gardens and publish a coffee table book and talk about doing flash portraits of flowers and how coyote urine keeps the deer off. How boring she would be! The prospect made her hum with contentment. At odd moments she would burn incense, figuratively, on some private altar in the shingled house to her great lost love. Peter would be none the wiser or wouldn't care; he was in a state of euphoria that nothing could puncture.

Edwina shot a wave at Fred, who traipsed along, pigeon-toed, beside Florence Luker. "Dutch women are marching on the U.S. Embassy in Amsterdam to demonstrate their support of their American sisters," Florence called.

Fred introduced his companion. Actionably younger; sculpted papaya-colored cheeks; head wrapped in a tribal print. Leora remembered a ruckus in the commune's kitchen: Meghan giving Fred what for over his affair with an African-American housekeeper on the staff of Sophia Merdle. It seemed a long time ago.

A reporter from ABC was working the crowd with a mike. "We have the right not to be viewed as a piece of meat," a young woman in shades said in forceful tones.

"Speaking of 'piece of meat', there's the editor of *Cosmopolitan*," Fred said. He nodded toward a small freeze-dried person with back-combed hair who appeared reconstituted from some original form. "Helen Gurley Brown a feminist? Who woulda' thunk it? Hope she doesn't see the BAN *COSMO* sign ... " He made a mental note to wend his way over to the reporter from ABC.

Fred was in excellent spirits. The infusion of new material to *The Future of Sex* added a certain gravitas. The book was due out in early '71. He'd push Cressida to approach Helen Gurley Brown about first serial rights in *Cosmo*. He could claim a great deal of credit for today, Fred thought, glancing with satisfaction at a rank of marchers with linked arms. He'd been instrumental in forming the commune, after all, the tap root from which Gilda had drawn to organize her great project – a detail that could figure in the jacket copy for his book. Fred had a premonition that this might be a kind of last hurrah, the apex of Gilda's reign as the figurehead of feminism; that a change of regime was not only in the works, but maybe already a fait accompli. The notion of Gilda forced to pass the torch was not pretty. They'd have to wrestle it out of her hands. Knowing Gilda, she'd find a new torch. Even so, Fred thought with a pang, the future that *she*, *Gilda*, had made possible was poised to leave her behind.

Terry Cameron had been keeping watch for them from the steps of St. Patrick's Cathedral. When Leora saw him she felt for a shivery moment she had *never not known him*. She'd not so much *met* Terry, as *recognized* him. He stitched his way over; the last of the sun glinted off his round specs. Terry praised the sign Finn had crayoned – WOMEN'S RIGHTS ARE HUMAN RIGHTS; ever the editor, admired the apostrophe. Leora walked, heart full, beside Terry and Finn. She'd bought Cara an obscenely pricey French romper –her first non-hand-me-down – for their post march celebration. That first ride out to the commune in May – could she have imagined this? A group of students fell into step beside them. "UPPITY WOMEN UNITE," Finn read. "Mom, what's 'uppity?'" "I'll explain later, promise."

Terry fired off a little military salute in the direction of Meghan. Her return greeting lacked warmth. Leora had always felt a solidarity with Meghan. She hoped she'd find someone her age. Better yet someone way younger, she thought, remembering Nadine going on about the indignities of aging. That way the guy could look after *her* when she was searching for her keys – or the glasses she was wearing on her head – and wondering what that sound of jingling change in her cervical spine was, and whether the tightness in her chest was from the chili oil in the Chinese takeout or a coronary. Leora linked her arm through Terry's. A banner rose high in the air: "*LIBERTE, EGALITE, SORORITE.*"

Leora startled to see Kaz some distance away in the press on the sidewalk. A newly minted feminist or just taking in the spectacle? Kaz either didn't see her or chose not to. Leora imagined herself old, not remembering if she'd slept with him ...

Kaz was hoping to "give back" by forming a fund to elect Congressmen who'd vote to crush the Commie gooks in Vietnam once and for all. Operation Ex-ful-iate could expect help from a new, super-efficient pesticide developed by his Tramlaw. Milt Merdle was on board. It was wonderful how shared patriotism could trump any hard feelings over the business with Sophia.

Of course the hearing loomed on that unfortunate incident at his factory. His lawyers and PR people planned to tie up the lawsuits with counter-suits and prevarications till people simply forgot or got bored. Ride out the clock, wear the bastards down ... You couldn't overestimate the short attention span of Americans. Back in the old country they never forgot, least not those goddamn Jews who kept coming around talking "restitutions," and pestering his uncle about reclaiming the farm he'd "stolen" from them ... He'd agreed to go with Gilda to Swaziland. She had political connections he couldn't afford to ignore. But did she still want him to come? Except for Milt Merdle, she was the only person in Islesfordd who would speak to him.

Leora caught Quasimodo's outsize head towering over the others. He carried a sign that read THE WOMEN OF VIETNAM ARE OUR SISTERS and kept to a deferential distance behind Elsie van Otten. Elsie beamed her gaze of a vampire at Leora and smiled as though they shared a secret. Swinging from her turban, a red fishing lure. It swung and winked at Leora in the drained light of New York at dusk.

Leora had been overjoyed to learn she'd been wrong in fingering Quasi as the assailant of Lester Annis. The week before the march, the trail of clues had lead to Lester's habit of joining the nocturnal revels on Bacchus Beach. He confessed, finally, that he had in fact known his assailant. The night of the assault Lester had threatened to expose the guy as a scammer who posed as gay in order to blackmail the scout leaders and fathers of five who'd discovered the action in the dunes. Things turned ugly; the guy followed Lester back to his house; there was a struggle, the perp grabbed a five pound weight on the night table; Lester slipped on the flokati rug by the bed ... It turned out the scammer had a lucrative racket threatening to "out" the high net worth married men who sneaked off to Bacchus or The Ramrod Social Club.

Monica Fairley and Gilda Gladstone, moving at the head of the parade, were mobbed by photographers. Shots of them, arms linked and smiling, would be mailed into the future. The sisters had come through and proved her right, Gilda exulted, they'd exceeded her wildest expectations. Reporters converged on Monica and Gilda, pelting them with questions. *Today women have marched in concert overcoming all their differences*, Gilda blurted, leaving stubs of unfinished words ... *This strike will continue as a political revolution* ... A recent magazine article had described Monica as "a virtual superstar in the field of women's rights." *She'll goddamn destroy the movement with the man-hating and the lesbians*, Gilda thought, smiling into the flash. She'd stick it to Monica *right now*: "The meaning of this strike is that we have no more time to waste in navel-gazing rap sessions, no more time to waste in sterile dead ends of man hatred," Gilda told the reporter. "Women want their families, women want to love men, this is not a war to be fought in the bedroom."

It was a pity she couldn't learn to be more manipulative, like Monica. But those were the breaks.

Leora had no regrets about missing the Labor Day parties in Islesfordd. She was flying Terry and her children out to the San Juan Islands to a little place known for "rustic luxury." There, a new chapter, Terry and the kids would knit together, learn to be a family. He'd bought Finn a kid's tennis racquet; "nothing like starting early." Leora looked around at the press of bodies and linked arms, thrilled to the banked power of all these uppity women, she just a molecule in a mighty being. The world in its forward churn had caught her up; she'd finally aligned with the moment. She would take some credit for this. Hadn't she tweaked the marriage plot to fit the times? *It is a truth universally acknowledged that a single mother of two in possession of a good fortune, must be in want of a partner.* A brief pause, and the marchers heaved forward again. "Join us, sister," Leora called. "Join us!"

The crowd swelled, an engorged monster, into Bryant Park, overflowed into neighboring streets. Gilda had never felt more on her game. Gripping the lectern, partly from exhaustion, she looked out over students, mothers, grandmothers, dads with kids, housewives, young girls, women with Afros, veterans of Nam and Civil Rights protests. Waiting on her words. From her visions and labor she'd *created this*, made the power of feminism visible to the world. "In our affirmation of ourselves as women, we have felt a transcendent joy tonight. We have had this great experience tonight of creating history, taking the torch from those great women who won us the vote fifty years ago ... " She looked over the crowd at all the beautiful women, all women were beautiful, so beautiful ... She was beautiful ... She'd argued so passionately for loving men, the love of a man would surely find her ... Kaz a disappointment but there was always the next invite, any evening now, just around the bend ... She saw the future, a kind of sixth sense, she'd stay ahead of the curve. After today's victory lap, the thrust would be political ... No more navel gazing ... As a Senator she'd make real changes ... Mingle with A-list men ... If only she hadn't screwed up with her daughter.

"Today we have witnessed the start of the most important social and political movement of the 70s." The crowd roared, a sea of faces turned up toward her as one. Gilda paused. She squinted into the dusk at the girl with dark hair and glasses on the lip of the crowd: *Becca?* The girl shifted position – no, maybe not, too far to tell. "Today," Gilda boomed ... "Today, I have led you into history." *Led you*, the echo bounced back, *into history*. "I leave you now – to make new history."

Acknowledgements

Thank you, communards of East Hampton, real and imagined, who inspired the story of *The Commune*. When I wake, laughing at my own characters, I take it as a good sign. I remain in awe of the women (and a few men) who helped launch the Women's Strike for Equality in August of 1970, which definitively put feminism on the map. In my research I drew heavily on works by Betty Friedan, intellectual founder of the women's movement, and the flood of books published in the 1970s that gave a freshly urgent voice to women's concerns. While working on *The Commune* I was spurred on by the mordant humor and satire of *Vile Bodies* by Evelyn Waugh. As always, I was buoyed by the spirit of Stendhal, who cuts through the cant while remaining romantic to the core. Maud, Neilson, Jasper, Otis, Stuart, Pat – thank you for keeping the faith. To Dick I'm grateful for the wonderful space to work and much else. Deep gratitude to my agent Richard Curtis for his savvy editing and unwavering support. And thank you to my publisher Stevan Nicolic for believing in this book.

Blurbs of previous works

WILD GIRLS

"Erica Abeel writes with an insider's authority and great charm about her "wild girls," who come vividly to life in this intelligent, compelling novel."

— Hilma Wolitzer,
author of *An Available Man: A Novel*

"Libidinous!" "10 Titles To Pick Up Now"

— *Oprah* Magazine

"A rollicking novel chronicling the exploits of female undergrads in the 50s."

— *Oprah* Magazine

"This libidinous period novel follows three budding feminists through an elite women's college, the New York art scene, and Allen Ginsberg's bed, as they redefine womanhood for themselves and future generations."

— *Oprah* Magazine

"Erica Abeel *is* a 'Wild Girl'— she lived the life, these are her friends, and this is an insider's peek into that world."

— Kevin Kwan,
author of *Crazy Rich Asians*

"A very funny, rueful and accurate recapture of things past. Erica Abeel's stylish prose delivers surprises and pleasurable shocks of recognition in every paragraph."

— Philip Lopate,
author of *Portraits Inside my Head*

"Erica Abeel writes with the eye of Margaret Mead and the soul of Tolstoy. In stunning and electric prose she gives us captivating – thrillingly flawed – characters and we embrace them, even when it might be wiser to flee. Along the way, she shows us the brilliance and devastation of love; the hidden geometry of complicated marriages; and the interwoven force fields of deep friendships."

— Grace Dane Mazur,
author of *The Garden Party*

"…Laced with gleeful, biting commentary. Toward her three protagonists, she is unsparing and compassionate in perfect proportion."

— *Kirkus* Reviews

"Finally, an examination of the female mind at the end of the Eisenhower era. The end of men's hats and ladies' garter belts. The pill displacing the diaphragm, and lust unleashed. A fine piece of literary anthropology."

— Amazon

"Ms. Abeel [is] a master of the sardonic voice ... Her prose is snappy, full of wit. The sentences, even when the characters aren't speaking, read like the quick back-and-forth dialogue of movies such as "The Apartment" and "How to Marry a Millionaire." The book is peppered with wry observations about the hypocrisies of men, of women, and of the consequences of attempting to carve out a career as a woman in a man's world ... "Men . . . used language as a kind of test drive to see how things might play out, but with no commitment to making them actually happen."

— *East Hampton Star*

"A fully absorbing and unfailingly entertaining read from beginning to end."

— *The Midwest Book Review*

"With literary finesse, the novel leaps through its wild moments with ease."

— Foreword Reviews.com

"*Wild Girls* will resonate with anyone who witnessed the cultural revolution of the 1950s and 60s, or wishes that they had. I loved it."

— HistoricalNovelSociety.org

"Young American women defying cultural expectations and inventing their own lives is one of my favorite subjects — and I am not alone. Erica Abeel's WILD GIRLS tells the delicious, page-turning story of three very different but equally thoughtful rebels from 1950s America, embarking on adventures that involve everyone from Allen Ginsburg to Yoko Ono ... This book will bathe the reader in a time and place in which female self-invention was never more important, exhilarating, and challenging. With feminism a passionate concern of today's young female journalists and Hollywood actresses and directors, I can hardly think of a timelier read."

— Sheila Weller,
author of *Girls like us: Carole King,*
Joni Mitchell, Carly Simon

With *Wild Girls* Erica Abeel tells a story very much in the tradition of Mary McCarthy, Rona Jaffe and yes, even Jacqueline Susann. What her smart and accessible novel shows is the underside of bohemianism: that it rarely has worked for women. *Wild Girls* brings us females who long for personal freedom, but who must struggle for it against both the mainstream *and* the counter-culture. This is the hidden story of the beats and the hipsters and it's one worth telling.

— Claudia Dreifus,
journalist, author

"Erica Abeel has written about the dilemmas that women face with wisdom, humor, and a wicked eye for the ironies of existence. Her message is timeless."

— A Literary Vacation

CONSCIENCE POINT

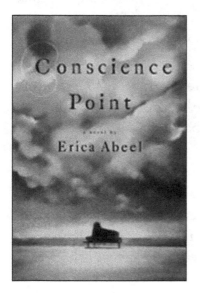

"Erica Abeel's Conscience Point is very sharp indeed...funny and sexy and smart... you'll fly through it."

— Alan Furst,
author of The Spies of Warsaw: A Novel

"An elegantly written, sharply observed saga, swirling with dark secrets and strong personalities. Conscience Point is a wholly satisfying read–enticing, suspenseful and difficult to put down."

— John Berendt,
author of The City of Falling Angels
and Midnight in the Garden of Good and Evil

"... an engaging read with plot twists and complex characters.... Echoing Evelyn Waugh's Brideshead Revisited...

— *Library Journal*

"I savored both the elegant prose and the page-turning story."
— Hilma Wolitzer,
author of Summer Reading:
A Novel and Hearts: A Novel

"…a rare novel, gracefully written, deftly unfolding its chilly secrets, exploding with witty little gems on almost every page. It's a gripping story that could have happened in real life."
— Marion Meade

Hamptons Gothic – "*Conscience Point*"
"Old Hamptons houses and their environs are rife with possibilities for melodrama, stages for scandals, and dark desires. Think Waugh's Brideshead, Dickens's Bleak House, and Bronte's Wuthering Heights ...

Ms. Abeel's writing features a savvy, satiric view of the back-stabbing publishing and broadcast industries, as well as the classical music world, offering many smart caricatures ... and colorful, apt asides.

Ms. Abeel is good at incorporating shrewd observations into a structure evoking the literary traditions of Waugh, Proust, Dickens, plus a touch of Stendhal, Nabokov, and Roth. A long-dead character is named a Brontean Linton.

Could more drama be packed into one book?"
— Regina Weinreich,
The East Hampton Star

"Contrived as a Yankee *Brideshead Revisited*, Erica Abeel's novel has as its center a Gothic fairytale castle ... Adolescent idealism, sensual satisfaction, and sexual awakening are a powerful mix."
— *The Boston Globe*

"The plot crescendos to a climax as ... dark secrets are revealed and various betrayals come to light. In the end, Abeel manages to tie together those strands in a way that's satisfying without being sappy. Maddy, whose ultimate triumphs are hard-won, is a highly appealing protagonist."

— *More.com*

"This genre-bending novel mixes heartbreak, Gothic atmospherics, and a satire of New York's high-stakes players."

— *Booking Mama*

"Abeel's prose is perfectly married to time and place, the New York intelligentsia, publishing, art, the music world and the gothic hideaway...The language is stunning, memorable ... "

— *Luan Gaines*

" ... a compelling story. All the characters in the book are carved out to perfection. The one liners ...reminded me... of *Sex and the City*.

— *Feminist Review*

WOMEN LIKE US

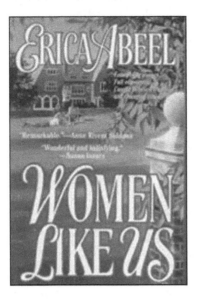

"Women Like Us" traces the lives of four women from their undergraduate days at Sarah Lawrence College in the late 1950's through the colorful and varied histories of their boyfriends, jobs, husbands, divorces, friendships, rivalries, failures, and successes to the present. The story of women caught between two generations — too restless for the pieties of the fifties, too early for the revolution of the sixties — it speaks to the hearts of women everywhere.

QUOTES

"A very engrossing, well-written piece of our romantic history – a generation of women who gave their all for love."

— Rona Jaffe

"A most welcome addition to that wonderful and satisfying Whatever-Happened-to…? genre. Wonderful and satisfying, a *Best of Everything* for the nineties."

— Susan Isaacs

"Erica Abeel has taken that hardy weed, the college reunion novel, and made it a flower. A funny, rambunctious book about what it means to be still alive and kicking at an age when women are supposed to be unseen and unheard."

— Erica Jong

"A remarkable likeness of women caught on the cusp between convention and change. Erica Abeel has perfect pitch when it comes to catching the soul of a generation."

— Anne Rivers Siddons

"I enjoyed *Women Like Us*. It describes the impasse faced by several generations of women with wit and humor."

— Marilyn French

"Erica Abeel's savvy, sexy, and fast-moving book deftly depicts a generation of women trapped by history." — Hilma Wolitzer "An old-fashioned good read…A Sarah Lawrence-based variation on Mary McCarthy's *The Group*…suffused with a persuasive and appealing 50's sensibility."

— *New York Times Book Review*

"By the end of this gritty but thoroughly readable and engrossing novel, it's hard to dispute that there is a lot about these insightful women that is just like us, just like women of every generation."

— *Christian Science Monitor*

"Marvelous writing… Abeel is a perceptive story-teller with a good eye for detail and a fine sense of the ridiculous … As her story unfolds, her true literary gifts as first-rate stylist and satirist emerge … The most remarkable thing about this book is the way it cleverly deals with the choices women make."

— *Minneapolis Tribune*

"Has everything I love in a novel; good story; interesting, believable characters, vigorous and vivid writing; fabulous descriptions of houses, parties, and clothes (Judith Krantz, eat your heart out); and tantalizing questions about Life."

— *New Woman*

"Every woman is sure to recognize something of her own experience in this compelling book."

— *Booklist*

"Vibrant and evocative…Abeel charts her principal's lives with energy and compassion."

— *Cleveland Plain Dealer*

"Intelligent … Genuine… Affecting."

— Scott Turow

"Smart, snappy, and compulsively readable … Writing with wit and perception, Abeel makes her characters' parallel lives an absorbing saga of heartaches and successes."

— *Publishers Weekly*

Women Like Us gets all the details right. In this rich, vivid, unforgettable saga, every woman will find something of her own life."

— Book of the Month Club

ONLY WHEN I LAUGH

"Pungent, acid, Hilarious, moving."

— Betty Rollin, *First you Cry*

"This is how it feels when your life falls apart. Erica Abeel could be the woman next door, telling her story with anger, pain, wit, irony – and the joy of a woman who survived it all.

— Gael Greene, *Blue Skies, No Candy*

"This is a book about beginnings and what it takes to get there. Irreverent, funny, devastatingly honest, and full of hope."

— Nena O'Neill, *Open Marriage*

About the Author

Erica Abeel is a novelist, journalist, film critic and academic. She has published six books. They include
- *Wild Girls*, a novel
- *Conscience Point*, a novel
- *Women Like Us*, a novel, Book-of-the-Month Club selection.
- *Only When I Laugh*, auto-fiction

Her current novel The Commune is a comic satire and roman a clef that takes us inside the Hamptons commune populated by the newly liberated women present at the creation of the seminal 1970 Women's March for Equality. The Commune's pioneering feminists can talk the talk, but find themselves whipsawed between the bold new ideals of the women's movement and the powerful tug of the past – and therein lies drama.

Based in New York and East Hampton, Erica frequently writes about women rebels of the 50s who defy their repressive period to chart their own course – a good decade *before* the upheavals of the 60s and second wave feminism. This makes them, in her view, true heroines. *Wild Girls*, her most recent novel, was featured in Oprah magazine's January 2017 "10 Titles to Pick Up Now," and touted as a "libidinous period novel [that] follows three budding feminists through an elite women's college, the New York art scene, and Allen Ginsberg's bed, as they redefine womanhood for themselves and future generations."

Erica's journalism serves as vehicle for her wide-ranging interests. She wrote the "Hers" column for the *New York Times*, personal essays which subsequently appeared in her collection *I'll Call you Tomorrow and Other Lies Between Men and Women*. Her book reviews and articles on "the sexes" have appeared in major national publications, including the *New York Times Magazine*, *New York Magazine*, *Esquire*, and *Ms.*.

Abeel is also a film critic. Her entertainment pieces have appeared in the *New York Times*, *Indiewire*, and *Huffington Post*. She was thrilled to participate in the great sprocket-fest that is the Cannes Film Festival, and feels privileged to have interviewed some of the great auteurs of contemporary cinema. She has also covered the Toronto and New York film festivals for *Indiewire* and the *Huffington Post*, zeroing in on the evolving portrayal of women in cinema.

A former dancer, Abeel majored in dance at Sarah Lawrence College at a time when few colleges credited the performing arts as serious subjects of study. In the early 60s she lived in Paris, studied at the Sorbonne, became fluent in French. Her novel *Wild Girls* recreates "the scene" with Allen Ginsberg and others of the Beat Generation who lived in Paris at the infamous "Beat Hotel." *Wild Girls* explores the joys and trials of rooming with Yoko Ono in New York, as Yoko was beginning her ascent in the avant garde.

Erica holds a Ph.D in 19th century French literature from Columbia University. After teaching at Barnard College, she joined the faculty of City University of New York where she is Professor Emeritus of French. Both her fiction and journalism are suffused with her appreciation and love of France. She feels that her training as a dancer and a scholar has given her the discipline needed for the long slog of writing a novel. Erica is a decades-long devotee of Pilates, and likes to hit "the zone" on swims in the bays around East Hampton. Most of all she cherishes time with her family.

Erica is active on social media. She keeps a website at ericaabeel.com, and frequently posts on Twitter, Facebook, and her Facebook Author site.

CPSIA information can be obtained
at www.ICGtesting.com
Printed in the USA
FSHW011150060721
82969FS

MORE THAN MY SCARS

THE POWER OF PERSEVERANCE, UNRELENTING FAITH, AND DECIDING WHAT DEFINES YOU

KECHI OKWUCHI

BakerBooks
a division of Baker Publishing Group
Grand Rapids, Michigan

Published by Baker Books
a division of Baker Publishing Group
PO Box 6287, Grand Rapids, MI 49516-6287
www.bakerbooks.com

Printed in the United States of America

Library of Congress Cataloging-in-Publication Data
Names: Okwuchi, Kechi, 1989– author.
Title: More than my scars : the power of perseverance, unrelenting faith, and deciding what defines you / Kechi Okwuchi.
Description: Grand Rapids, MI : Baker Books, a division of Baker Publishing Group, [2022]
Identifiers: LCCN 2021035423 | ISBN 9781540902054 (casebound) | ISBN 9781540901590 (paperback)
Subjects: LCSH: Okwuchi, Kechi, 1989– | Aircraft accident victims—United States—Biography. | Motivational speakers—United States—Biography. | Nigerian American young women—Biography. | Aircraft accidents—Nigeria. | Perseverance (Ethics)
Classification: LCC TL553.9 .O46 2022 | DDC 363.12/4092 [B]—dc23
LC record available at https://lccn.loc.gov/2021035423

The author is represented by the literary agency of The Knight Agency, Inc.

Baker Publishing Group publications use paper produced from sustainable forestry practices and post-consumer waste whenever possible.

22   23   24   25   26   27   28   7   6   5   4   3   2   1

If this book helps even one person,
it was well worth writing.

Contents

Foreword by Simon Cowell   11

Introduction   12

Prologue   15

1 The Day   19

South Africa

2 The Coma   33

3 The Dreams   40

4 The Fight to Survive   48

5 The Drive   55

6 The Itching   67

7 The Progress   80

8 The Truth   91

9 The Visits   111

10 The Ward   118

11 The Search for Me   130

Nigeria

12 The Return   143
13 The Little Things   148
14 The Grief   154
15 The Send-Off   162

America

16 The Adapting   171
17 Shriners and the Music   176
18 The School   183
19 The Surgeries   188
20 The Future and the Past   195
21 The Show before the Show   205
22 The Show   212
23 The Flight   221

A Final Word   231
Acknowledgments   233

Foreword

Kechi Okwuchi defines the word *champion*. And *courage*. Since meeting her on the set of *America's Got Talent* in 2017, I have loved everything about her. She isn't just a singer, she's an inspiration. She's made a big difference in my life, showing me the true meaning of courage and what it means to rise above adversity. When things are tough, she rises above it all. Never thinking about giving up. She's truly one of the bravest women I have ever met.

When I first heard that she was writing this memoir, I was thrilled. This is a story that needs to be read—a testament of what it means to not only deal with challenges in life that very few can imagine but to face them head-on and use them to bring hope to others. I've had the privilege of watching her grow over the past few years from a shy and timid girl to a confident woman ready to take on the world.

I've not only witnessed Kechi deliver many magical moments on stage but I've also been inspired by the work she's been doing behind the scenes. It's every bit as magical as her singing. From speaking to troubled youth to visiting hospitals around the world, she's brought hope to many just when they needed it the most. It's wonderful to know that her incredible story will continue to reach even more people with the publication of this memoir.

I can't wait to read it!

Simon Cowell

Introduction

*Tragedy is a tool for the living to gain
wisdom, not a guide by which to live.*

ROBERT KENNEDY

I'd like to say I picked up that quote from some article or book,
but I actually first heard it at the end of an episode of *Criminal
Minds*. Regardless, I was struck by its sheer profundity.

Tragedy: A tool to gain wisdom, not a guide by which to live.

My name is Kechi Okwuchi. I was twenty-five years old when
I first came up with the idea of writing this memoir, and twenty-
eight when I actually started to put that idea into action. I will be
in my thirties by the time it is published.

I would like to believe that I, Kechi, am the sort of person who
is actively trying to live her life by Robert Kennedy's wise words.

For years, I have been told by many that my story is inspiring.
While it brings me great joy to hear this, all I have really done, and
all I try to do each day, is to simply live my life. I do not think I have
done anything particularly fantastic or worthy of high praise. So,
I have decided to tell my story in its entirety, to hopefully give you,
dear readers, the chance to decide for yourself what to make of it.

I was born into an average, middle-class family in Lagos, Nigeria, on October 29, 1989. I was the cutest baby. I'm not even
bragging; I've seen the pictures. I was adorable.

Growing up, my family didn't have a lot, but I still remember being an absolutely happy and cheerful child. I was an only child for ten years, and my mom and dad were, and still are, fantastic. They fought and made up a lot, but I didn't mind that so much because it made them human in my eyes, real people. Because of them, I knew from early on that a marriage wasn't all good times, but they never once made me feel like they didn't love and care for each other. Together, they managed to find the fine balance between spoiling and disciplining me, and they did their best to make my childhood wonderful and fun. I believe they succeeded, because the good memories by far eclipse the bad.

My dad's great and I love him dearly. I'm a lot like him in many ways: super relaxed about most things and flexible, going with the flow and not taking life too seriously. My mom is the parent I grew more attached to. I remember relatives and other adults would joke around and say that I was her handbag, seeing as she carried me almost everywhere with her. When I was in elementary school, she would actually pull me from school in the middle of classes to accompany her on some trip. I loved that.

My little sister was born when I was ten, right before I started high school.[1] I was so thrilled to have a sibling, and considering the significant age difference, I had a feeling I was going to be something of a second mom to her.

I spent the majority of my childhood and teenage years with my cousins from both sides of the family, so a giant portion of my fond memories involve my extended family as well.

Then came high school, a boarding school system. Boarding school gave me my first taste of independence—within a controlled environment, of course. It took a while to adapt to this new type of life. My boarding high school, Loyola Jesuit College, was a mini world to us students, and it would be my world for the next six years.

1. In Nigeria, middle school, junior high, and high school are grouped together as high school.

13

I enjoyed my time at LJC. I had my first crush, my first boyfriend (not necessarily in that order), my first bad grade, and my first kiss all within the four walls of that huge campus. Most importantly, I made many lifelong friends during those six precious years and formed relationships without which I would not be where I am today.

I give this extensive backstory to emphasize how exceptionally normal my life was up until the day of my accident. Also, everything I have discussed so far plays a very critical role in what came after.

I was a high school senior at sixteen—Nigerian kids tend to start school early—and by then, I had been on multiple airplanes. Too many to count. For many in Nigeria, flying was a necessary part of life growing up. I've always loved flying. I still do. More precisely, I'm awed by the concept of it.

I was sixteen years old when the plane crash happened.

Sixteen years old when I was brutally ripped out of a comfortable reality with an admittedly predictable future and thrust into a brand-new one where not even the next hour was guaranteed.

Sixteen years old when my life went from choosing among multiple universities in the UK to wavering between pain, grief, and the incessant itching borne from third-degree burn injuries.

I do not share this story to garner pity. Rather, I write this because as painful and difficult as many parts of my journey have been, it was those very parts that have shaped the core elements of my identity today. The ways in which I, a burn survivor, chose to deal with physical and emotional pain borne from my severe injuries, grief and depression borne from loss, judgment from the world, and many other experiences that all human beings undoubtedly face in varying degrees. These experiences redefined me—body, mind, and soul. It is this redefinition that I feel compelled to share with you, readers, in the hopes that my words will serve as a guide to at least one person who encounters my story.

So here we go.

Prologue

I feel so much pressure, please make the pressure stop! My fingers feel like they're about to explode!

I drifted in and out of consciousness on the gurney, pain exploding through my body in enormous bolts, my scorched and swollen flesh oozing a steady stream of something that resembled neither sweat nor blood. My arms were swollen to more than twice their normal size. My flesh was charred, eaten away by something I did not understand at the moment. This couldn't be me. This couldn't be my own body betraying me this way, trapping me in this prison of pain.

I screamed and screamed again.

Darkness came and went, and I dived for it whenever it appeared, not caring if it meant death instead of unconsciousness. *Anything but this. Just . . . no more pain, please. No more pain. No more of this horrible pressure.*

But there was more of both. An overwhelming combination I would have never thought possible. It was so consuming that in those seconds and minutes and hours, it scorched my mind hollow, where nothing existed but its fury. Did I have a name? I didn't know and didn't care. Was someone yelling in the distance, telling me to try to stay still? It didn't matter. I'd been thrown into a propane-fueled oven and left to burn until I exploded.

Darkness came again. Then voices I did not recognize and occasional flashes of understanding that were like the setting sun, blinding me with their radiance but disappearing before I could get more than a glimpse of what they were trying to show me. I was lost and alone, unable to find myself.

Then the blackness came for good.

And I welcomed it.

Eyes slowly open to a reality I didn't recognize. A blitzkrieg of voices, noises.

I could barely move. Every inch of my body was stiff and numb, as if someone had pumped it with a gallon of Novocain before drilling into my bones.

Where was I? A hospital. But why? Had something terrible happened?

My head was foggy, as was my memory.

How long had I been gone? Hours? Days? *Weeks?* And where had I been?

Somewhere fantastic.

Away from this world.

But now I was back, in this rigid shell of a body.

Then an unfamiliar voice called my name: "Kechi? Kechi, can you hear me?"

Kechi. That's me. I peered at the figure in the corner. Then I squinted. Everything in the room seemed part of everything else, the walls and the bed and the woman calling my name. I squeezed my eyes closed and opened them again. And at last I could make out a nurse's face.

"Nod for yes and shake your head for no," she said.

I nodded.

"That's good. Okay, and do you know this woman? Do you recognize her face?"

I squeezed my eyes closed then opened them once more, and another figure leaned forward, close to my face. And even though she was wearing a face mask that covered everything but her eyes, even through my filmy gaze, I knew who she was before she spoke.

"Kechi, love? My darling, can you see me? It's Mommy."

I nodded as tears began to fill my eyes. My heart pounded with joy and relief.

My skin was shriveled and black and still oozing, but everything was going to be all right.

My mother was there, and that's all that mattered.

"Do you know where you are?" the nurse asked.

I nodded.

"Do you know what happened?"

Again, I nodded. Somehow, I remembered that I was in a hospital called Milpark in Johannesburg. I must have heard of it while I was in the coma. I'd seen TV shows where people wake from a coma in violent states, because they are confused and scared. But while I was in my coma, God had been working through my mother to prepare me for what was to come.

"Are you in any pain?" the nurse asked.

I shook my head.

The morphine in my system had made my body numb for the time being. And it would continue to do so for the immediate future. But I would know pain again. In the months and years to follow, I would learn the true definition of suffering.

Chapter One

The Day

The dormitory bell rang loudly on the Saturday that would change my life forever.

I got up from bed, grabbed my towel and toilet bag, and headed wearily for the dorm's public showers. I was not alone, of course. Several other students and friends who would be traveling the same route as me that day were also making their way to the bathroom, all of us blearily blinking sleep away as we shuffled like sheep in the narrow hallway.

It was the last day of the 2005 fall semester at Loyola Jesuit College, Abuja, Nigeria, the day we would all be heading home for the Christmas holidays. The last exams for the semester had ended on Tuesday, and the remainder of the week had been used to clean up the classrooms, hang out with friends, and pack up for the holidays. We would all be back on campus in less than three weeks. But it didn't matter; those last few days right before we headed home were always so much fun, not only because they were exam-free but also because we got to hang out with each other without the usual pressures of constant studying and strict schedules to keep to.

Freshly showered, I got dressed in my red checkered school uniform. I threw the remainder of my things into my open suitcase, including my self-written novel to show my mom when I got home, then headed out of the dorm toward the dining hall, luggage in tow.

Toke Badru, one of my closest friends and favorite travel companions, walked next to me, offering nothing but her silent company as we entered the dining hall and sat down for an early breakfast. I'm not a morning person so it wasn't unusual that I was a bit standoffish, but seeing as Toke and I were close, perhaps she could sense that the reason for my silence went beyond that.

"How do you manage to look so good in this stupid uniform?" she said, pulling at the waist of my dress.

I chuckled a little and batted her hand away. "You're an idiot."

"I'm just saying." She shrugged her dainty shoulders. "If not for my butt, I'd be a shapeless piece of string in this dumb dress."

I couldn't help but chuckle again, and she laughed her adorable laugh. I loved her sense of humor.

As I thought, she'd sensed something was on my mind but didn't want to pry. She was trying to cheer me up instead. Typical of her, really.

"Are you okay though?" The concern in her voice was palpable. "You're never this quiet, Kechi."

True. I'm not a quiet person, especially not on the last day of school, a day that every boarding school student looks forward to more than any other kind of secondary school student. After three long months away from home, in a few hours we'd be with our families, eating home-cooked food, sleeping in much more comfortable beds. Normally I'd be ecstatic and chattering nonstop.

But I was not going home under normal circumstances that day.

Before I could respond to her, the teacher on duty suddenly spoke. "Okay everyone," he said loudly, "as I call out your names, come up to get your ticket."

Later, we all stepped outside and started loading our luggage on the school buses that would be taking us to the airport.

I said goodbye to friends who had woken up early just to see us off: Womiye Ojo, Jude Igboanugo (Womiye's boyfriend at the time and also my good friend), and even Atuora Erokoro, who I usually said goodbye to in the dorms. They, like many others, were students who either lived right there in Abuja or had later flights and thus didn't need to be up as early as we did.

We all knew we would see each other again in less than a month—some of us maybe even during the course of the Christmas holidays—so there wasn't a lot of hugging. We never really said things like "have a safe flight" to one another. Obviously, everyone would get to their homes safely, not because plane crashes were rare in Nigeria—they unfortunately weren't—but because at sixteen, death is typically nothing but an abstract concept.

I learned a very big lesson that day: appreciate every single moment like it's your last. Hug your friends, wish them well. Tell loved ones you love them while you can.

I got on one of the buses and made my way to the first available window seat I spotted (my consistent preference on any mode of transport). Soon enough, the buses drove out of the LJC campus in single file.

I looked back, like I always did, to watch the school gates shut.

It always brought a smile to my face to see those gates close behind my bus with me on the outside. I was finally free, if only for a few short weeks.

Who could've known that the next time I'd set eyes on those gates would be at a reunion a decade later?

The airport terminal was packed. Girls in dresses, girls in uniforms, boys in suits, boys in flannel shirts. Many people in African print clothing. Folks in T-shirts and jeans scattered in. It was loud too. Way too loud. People shouted all over the place, as though haggling for ticket prices, which weren't exactly negotiable.

My schoolmates and I shuffled after our teacher in one large group of sixty-one. We were easily identifiable in our red, blue, green, and yellow checkered uniforms. We headed to the lounge area, only to discover our flight had been delayed. Typical. The students whose buses had left campus earlier than ours were still here as well, waiting for their own Lagos-bound flight.

We all filed into the lounge and immediately spread out. Our teacher disappeared, but I'd occasionally spot him scanning the room, most likely doing a head count. God forbid any of us go missing on his watch.

Toke and I found a couple seats together and sat, setting our backpacks down on the ground next to us.

My mood had improved significantly since leaving campus. It was only when I got a chance to step outside the confines of LJC that I was reminded just how much pressure that environment put on me, even more so now that I was in my final year.

"God, every single time," Toke grumbled. She was referring to the flight delay. "We might as well go home by bus!"

I laughed at her exaggeration. A three-hour flight delay followed by a two-and-a-half-hour flight didn't even come close to the twelve hours it would take to get home from school by bus.

Still, I understood her frustration. "It's so messed up that we spend pretty much one whole day traveling," I said. "Christmas holidays are already so short."

"I know! And this one won't even be fun 'cause I'll be studying throughout."

"Same here."

As seniors, the only things on our mind were the SATs, the WAEC[1], and of course, college applications.

"Are you gonna apply to any of the schools we saw at the college fair?" I asked Toke. Earlier that semester, the entire senior class had been taken into the city to attend a college fair that hosted more than twenty different foreign colleges.

"Yeah, mostly the UK ones," she replied.

"Me too. I really liked London School of Economics." I sighed,

1. The WAEC is a national exit exam that all students graduating from Nigerian high schools must take in order to qualify for entry into Nigerian colleges.

trying not to fall back into the slump I'd barely just come out of. That college fair had been the beginning of all my worries. I had no business aiming for a school of that caliber. I'd gotten a chance to look at LSE's academic requirements, and my grades were definitely not up to par.

"Will you talk about what's bothering you now?" Toke asked gently.

I looked at her patient expression and decided I would this time. But where to even begin? So much was on my mind, so many anxieties to unpack . . . "I just feel like my whole future depends on my SAT scores," I told her.

Toke nodded in understanding. "I know what you mean. It's so scary. It's the only way to get into schools outside Nigeria. And there's this vibe, like, if you don't get accepted into a college outside Nigeria—"

"You're a failure," I said, finishing the sentence.

"Exactly!" Toke made a sound of disgust. "What *is* that? I hate that mentality, like you're not 'cool' if you don't study abroad."

I hated that mentality too, so much. I hated myself more for buying into it.

Relief suddenly washed over me. "Oh my God, it feels so good to finally say all this stuff out loud!" I exclaimed.

"I know, right?" Toke said with a small laugh. "No one likes talking about grades, *sha*."[2]

She was right. It wasn't normal, even between close friends, to talk about academic grievances in depth, but I wished it was. It felt good to voice these thoughts to someone who not only understood but could also relate.

"But Kechi," Toke continued, "schools look at everything, not just SATs."

"I know, that's the problem." I shook my head. "My grades are nothing to write home about."

"What about me?"

2. *Sha* is a Nigerian expression for "anyway" or "though," depending on context.

"No, but you've been improving since last year, Toke. Steadily. The schools you apply to will take note of the improvement. They like that kind of thing, like when a student shows progress. Me, I'm just so . . . average. My grades are not the kind that a school like LSE would look twice at."

"Calm down, Kechi, it's not that bad *jor*."[3]

"I swear it actually is. Math alone is so horrible." I shook my head again. "My parents spent so much money, sacrificed so much to put me through this expensive secondary school, and for what? I'm such an average student. There're a few semesters where I excelled, but for the rest, I just never bothered applying myself more than I needed to in order to pass from one year into the next." I laughed self-deprecatingly. Now I was paying the price for doing the barest minimum.

"Kechi . . ." Toke leaned over and grabbed my hand. "Listen, we'll get home and study like crazy. We'll do our best with the time we have. I mean, what else is there to do?"

"Yeah, that's true," I said, huffing out a breath. "My mom is ready for me. She said she hired an SAT coach for me."

"You're not even home yet and they've already gotten you a lesson teacher?" Toke let go of my hand to pat my back in pity, making me laugh. "I hope they let you eat and sleep at least." She laughed with me.

"At this point, who knows," I said, still chuckling.

I felt so much better again. Toke had made me feel better. She didn't pressure me into talking, but in the natural way she had about her, she'd made it easy to open up about the stuff that had been bothering me pretty much all semester. And it turned out we were worrying about the same things.

"LSE, so you're thinking of doing economics?"

"Yeah," I said.

"But what about your writing?" she asked. "You have a whole book. That's, like, a big deal."

---

3. *Jor* is the Nigerian slang equivalent of "oh please."

Toke was right. I did love writing. So much so that I actually spent more of my time in school writing fiction than studying (sorry, Mom and Dad). Plus, my book got pretty popular among my peers.

"Yeah, but it's not like I can say I want to study writing in college. Economics is more practical." It certainly was the most conventional of all my interests, which, to me, made it the most suitable college major.

"I get you," Toke said. "Getting paid to dance would be so amazing." Her tone was wistful.

It really sucked that we both didn't feel like we could study what we were truly passionate about in college. Toke loved to dance, and she was good at it. She had charisma on stage, and she was so sassy with her moves. She'd be a great dancer if she chose to pursue that path. But I guess, like me, she felt she had to stick to something more societally acceptable.

Toke and I kept *gisting*[4], and there was lots of laughter and good-natured jabs, the kind only people who've been friends for years could throw at one another.

And Toke and I were nothing if not great friends.

"Is your brother gonna be picking you up from the airport?" I asked her.

"Yeah, why?"

"I'm just wondering." I shrugged innocently, humor dancing in my eyes.

Toke eyed me suspiciously. "Mm-hmm, and why're you asking?"

I laughed hard at her protective tone. "Is it now a crime to want to say hi to your brother?"

"Did I say it was a crime?"

"It's not my fault he's so fine."

"Ew, stop!"

I laughed again. It was so easy to tease her when it came to her big brother.

4. *Gisting* is Nigerian slang for conversing with a friend.

At some point the Lagos-bound students finally left. Meanwhile, Toke laid her head across my lap and tried to sleep a little, but she spent more time slipping and sliding on the perforated metal surface of the awkward lounge seats. It was hilarious.

Some time passed and she got up to use the restroom. As she stretched, she glanced at the Nora Roberts book in my hand and huffed out a laugh.

"You and this Nora Roberts."

"What?" I protested. "She's an awesome writer!"

"Whatever." Toke turned and disappeared into the crowd.

Another hour passed, but it seemed like only minutes as I got lost in the pages of *Homeport*. Toke returned with snacks to share, everything from meat pies to sodas to *chin chin*[5] and candy bars.

Then, at last, the arrival of our aircraft was announced over the speakers, and a collective groan of relief and exhaustion echoed all around the lounge. I put my book and foodstuff into my backpack and stood up to stretch, already so exhausted. My body ached from sitting for so long. Problem was, the plane seats weren't going to be any more comfortable than these god-awful lounge seats.

A uniformed woman opened the terminal gate, and the sound of the planes' engines echoed into the lounge.

I glanced at our aircraft through the windows. SOSOLISO AIR-LINES was written in bold blue-and-red lettering across its huge, shiny body.

Home. It represented home. Soon I'd be hugging my mom and sleeping in my own bed.

Or so I thought.

I walked with Toke to join the already forming line of fellow passengers.

"I'm so tired of sitting," Toke mumbled in front of me, and I groaned, sharing her sentiments.

---

5. *Chin chin* is a beloved Nigerian snack made from fried pieces of sweetened dough.

"At least it's a short flight," I said exhaustedly, rolling my stiff neck and trying to get the kinks out.

Toke rolled her eyes. "Since when is two hours short, Kechi?"

I huffed out a laugh. She was right, it wasn't. But it was better for me to think that it was, for the sake of my sanity. I just prayed I'd sleep for most of it.

It was finally my turn in line. I handed my ticket to the uniformed woman standing at the gate's border, who scanned it briefly before handing it back to me. I walked through the gate and was immediately assaulted by the excessive heat from the unrelenting Abuja sun.

My seat was close to the front of the aircraft, one of the first aisle seats in coach. *Why didn't Mom book me a window seat like usual?* I thought. *I'm definitely gonna complain when I see her. After hugging her.*

Another big lesson I learned from that day: God moves as He pleases, and He doesn't make mistakes.

Toke sat in the aisle seat next to mine, and we continued talking as the plane taxied, then picked up speed on the runway.

Then we were in the air.

This hour-and-twenty-minute-long flight had become a norm in my life by that time. A routine journey I made at least six times a year, for three consecutive years. There was absolutely nothing strange about that particular flight, nothing odd that had happened prior to boarding the plane that could possibly have hinted at what was about to happen while we were in the air. The flight itself was more or less normal. Right before things spiraled into chaos, nothing happened that would cause any passenger aboard to believe his or her life was in any danger.

I slept a little, rousing when the descent started. And I could always tell when that part of the flight began because it typically caused a lurching sensation in my stomach that left me feeling slightly nauseous.

I strained to see what I could through the window without imposing on my seat neighbor, but all I could see was the deep, dull gray of the skies. The pilot soon announced that we would be arriving at Port Harcourt Airport in about fifteen or twenty minutes.

Then the turbulence started.

At first it was nothing of note, just the usual jerking that happens when planes descend. But then it started to get increasingly forceful. I shifted uncomfortably in my seat because that kind of persistent, almost exaggerated shaking was definitely new. But even then, my mind hadn't gone to the worst possible scenario. Maybe it was just a particularly windy day in PH.[6]

Not a big deal.

Still the turbulence continued.

Tension started to grow in the air, but no one uttered a single word. No one wanted to be the first to admit out loud what we were all thinking.

The cabin lights flickered. The plane creaked and groaned. The jerking continued, then worsened, and tension was swiftly replaced by a thick, dark sense of foreboding.

This was the *exact* moment when *every single person* on board that aircraft realized, *Ah. Something is wrong with this plane.*

Then suddenly, from the back of the cabin, a lady screamed, "IS THIS PLANE TRYING TO LAND?"

Utter chaos.

Screams of terror.

"Jesus! Jesus! Blood of Jesus!"

"What is happening?! Oh God, what is happening?"

Frozen in my seat, everything slowed down around me. I was in a state of complete shock and awe. No one boards a plane consciously preparing for the worst to happen, even in a country like Nigeria where plane crashes were unfortunately not as rare as they should be. I had no idea what my thought process should be in that moment. I just stared at the back of the seat in front of me. I couldn't register the fact that this was my reality. I felt removed from the situation, as though I were watching it happen

6. PH is the local acronym for Port Harcourt.

in third person. In retrospect, I suspect that was the definition of an out-of-body experience.

Is this for real? Is this actually happening? What is happening? I started remembering random stuff for no reason.

Singing with my best friend Womiye Ojo during our last school trip with the HIV Awareness club.

Traveling by bus with my entire family three summers ago from Lagos to Abuja.

Singing Christmas carols on campus with the entire school during the candlelight service in the campus chapel just the night before . . . and what about my family? All the great times we'd had together? All the wonderful times that were no longer to be?

What did I even say to them that last time we spoke?

Sometime in the future, assuming I survived whatever this was, I would look back on this very day as the last day of my "normal" life. And I'd spent most of it worrying about grades.

What did grades matter now that everything was ending?

How would my mom survive without me?

It was like my brain was trying to focus on anything but the reality that I was currently suspended midair, trapped inside a crumbling airplane.

The plane just kept lurching, shaking, jerking up and down—all three hundred tons of metal reduced to a flimsy rattling box, at the mercy of natural forces that reigned outside. I sometimes wonder how it must have looked from the outside. Was the wind really tossing it left and right as it came down? Or did it just take a nosedive straight for the ground? It's a disturbing image either way.

I don't remember if any oxygen masks dropped down from the ceiling or if there were any other announcements over the plane intercom. I turned my head sideways and looked at Toke. Her eyes were two wide orbs of confusion.

I reached out as if in a trance and took her hand in mine.

Her fingers were ice-cold and stiffened immediately at my touch. Next instant, they were clamped around mine.

29

"What's happening? What should we do?" she asked, her grip tightening in desperation.

"I don't know." My voice sounded so far away to my ears, so foreign. "Maybe we should pray."

Those were the last words we ever said to each other.

One second, I was holding Toke's hand, then a loud, scraping, metallic sound filled the cabin, frying my brain. My whole body lurched forward as the world around me exploded into nothingness.

There was screaming.

So much screaming.

And then . . .

Darkness.

South Africa_____

Chapter Two

The Coma

Light drifted across the insides of my eyelids, and I awoke to a pain so great that it pushed all my senses into overdrive.

I was feeling so much. *Too* much.

Every single one of my nerves was charged, oversensitive. At the same time, numbness spread throughout my body. There was pressure in my arms and legs. So much pressure. I gasped for breath. My heart pounded.

What's happening to me?

I was feeling too much all at once, and my brain was overloaded. There was just too much going on inside my body for it to process at the same time.

I didn't understand what was happening. I had no memory of the plane crash or the events that had preceded it, and now I appeared to be in a room with lots of bright lights and lots of people hovering over me, around me, working on me, speaking all at the same time. It was all so disorienting, and I was crying and crying for my mommy.

As the seconds passed and more of my awareness returned, my body jump-started my brain, sort of kicking it into action, forcing it to break each overwhelming sensation into compartments so that I didn't go crazy from feeling everything simultaneously.

The most prominent feeling that shoved its way to the forefront of my mind was utter confusion.

I was so confused, and I wanted my mommy. Where was she? Who were all these people around me? I called and called for her. I needed her to come and make sense of what was happening, of all the chaos around me.

Why are all these people hovering over me? I thought. *What in the world is going on!*

Suddenly, miraculously, I heard a voice and I immediately zeroed in on the familiar sound. I cried out, "Mommy, Mommy!"

"I'm here, my baby. I'm right here, okay?"

I cried hard in relief at the sound of her voice. "Mommy, I love you."

"I love you too, baby. I love you so much. You're going to be okay."

Okay, Mommy's here. Thank God. Mommy's here, so everything is going to be okay.

Mommy.

My mom has always been there. She is in every single one of my most significant memories, from the moment I was born into this world to my very first memory after the plane crash. And she has shared every single memory with me since. I am convinced she is an angel on earth—at least, *my* angel. My special gift from God. It was because of the very specifically selfless, uniquely tenderhearted way God made her that she was able to be there for me the way that she was after my accident. But never mistake her kindness for weakness, for I have never met a stronger human being, and my dad will readily attest to that.

Lying there on that gurney, I heard my mom's voice, and just like that, I calmed down.

She stayed near my head, just at my periphery, probably because she needed to give the people around me—who I could now tell were doctors—space to work on me. Someone was squeezing bags of IV fluid into my body through a tube that was apparently inserted into my right foot. For all I knew, my leg could've been detached from my body; the numbing pain was everywhere, impossible to pinpoint.

Another person shoved a catheter into me. Now *that* I felt, and I was very vocal about it. They said my urine was coming out black due to all the smoke I had inhaled during the accident. Not a good sign at all. I didn't need the doctors' reactions to tell me that.

I still didn't understand what was going on or why I was in this situation, but my mommy was there so I didn't think too much on it.

At that point, the next most noticeable sensation made itself known: an insane amount of pressure in my hands and legs. My limbs and fingers felt like they were going to explode. Like someone had been pumping air underneath my skin and now they felt like balloons, ready to pop.

I raised my right arm above my head and started wailing at whoever could hear me. "I feel so much pressure, please make the pressure stop! My fingers feel like they're about to explode!"

I heard my mom relay this to the doctors, then she turned back to me. "I'm so sorry, sweetie. You have to stay calm so the doctors can work on you, okay? I'm right here. I love you, baby."

Her voice was soothing and just what I needed to calm down once more.

As I lay there with my arm still raised, I felt my entire body gradually go numb again. I guess, maybe because I wasn't panicking so much anymore, the meds that the doctors had been pumping into me finally had a chance to work their way through my system.

With the pain and pressure temporarily relieved, the next sense that kicked into gear was my sight. I was no longer disoriented, so now I could actually *see* the hand that was raised up, and all I was seeing was a lot of raw, red flesh. I could see literal *strips* hanging off my lower arm, palm, and fingers, and I stared in awe as my brain registered that those strips were my skin.

I just twisted my hand back and forth because I was baffled.

Why is my skin doing that? Skin shouldn't do that . . .

That was my last completely coherent, postaccident memory in that Port Harcourt hospital. My memories continued in full in South Africa, where I was flown the night after the plane crash for emergency burn treatment.

I do recall bits and pieces of moments and conversations that occurred before the flight to South Africa though.

For instance, I remember lifting my arms and legs when instructed to by nurses who were wrapping me in bandages and gauze. My mom said I even sat up when the nurses asked me to, and they praised me for being such a cooperative child.

At some point that first night, I asked my mom about the crash. Though I did not remember any part of it myself, enough people had told me what had happened, and naturally, my mind had gone to the other survivors, if there were any.

"Mommy, was I the only one who survived?"

"Survived what?"

"The plane crash."

She hesitated then answered, "No."

"So, what about Toke and the rest?"

"Toke is fine. They're all okay."

Mommy said that I heaved a huge sigh of relief and thanked Jesus before drifting back to sleep.

Whatever else happened between the plane crash and South Africa is steeped in darkness, though I was told I was conscious for most of that time. All I remember in earnest from that in-between is the darkness. For a long, long time, it was just emptiness.

A prolonged nothingness.

And then my consciousness slowly began to return, but in batches, in layers. My eyes weren't open, my body remained comatose, yet somehow I gradually started to gain a base level of awareness of my surroundings. This awareness grew to the point that I was eventually able to build a perception of my physical environment within my mind.

The bed I lay on. The music player next to my bed. The curtains that separated me from the rest of the room I was in. I saw it all in my mind's eye.

It started with music. The first time my mind roused, it was in response to faint music I could hear playing to my left. It was a song I had never heard before:

"Stand up . . . stand up . . . stand up!"

That was all I could make out—just a chorus of *"stand up!"* followed by a female vocal. Then *"Stand up!"* again and another faint vocal. Then it all faded away as my mind fell back into hibernation.

This started happening often. As more time passed, the frequency with which my mind woke increased, and in that brief interim of semiconsciousness, I would hear more music: Westlife, Women of Faith, Destiny's Child, many of my favorite artists at the time.

And then one day I heard more than music. One day, I heard my mother's voice.

She was talking to me, and I could hear her as clearly as if I had been fully conscious.

"Kechi, sweetie. It's Mommy. You were in a plane crash, sweetheart. And you were hurt really badly. But it's okay. You're now in South Africa, in Milpark Hospital, Johannesburg. And they're gonna take good care of you, okay? I'm right here, sweetie. You're gonna be okay."

I heard my precious mother's voice saying these things to me, and then she started to sing a hymn that was foreign to my ears:

> Wonderful and marvelous is Jesus to me.
> Sweeter than the honey in the honeycomb is He.
> Jesus is real, He will never fail.
> I will praise Him now and throughout all eternity.
> I will praise Him now and throughout all eternity.[1]

---

1. The author of this hymn is unknown, but my mother often sang it to me. It's called "Wonderful and Marvelous," and its lyrics are taken from Psalms in the Bible. Find a similar version at http://www.mission.net/england/bristol/songs.html.

Her gentle voice stopped, and the music from the music player returned. And for a while, it was just the music, which eventually lulled me back to an unconscious state.

Thus, the cycle began.

Whenever the music stopped, I would hear my mom's voice talking or singing to me, and when her voice disappeared, the music would return. When the music stopped again, it meant my mother's voice would return, telling me repeatedly about where I was and what had happened, or singing to me sweetly.

I began to use this cycle to keep time. I used my mother's voice to count the days. Each time the music stopped and her voice returned, it marked a new day in the cycle.

Her voice was my anchor to reality, and I held on to it with reflexive desperation.

At times, I would hear her so clearly, could sense her presence so distinctly, that I would respond in my mind to things she said, like imagining my mouth moving physically to say Amen when she would pray. I would imagine myself nodding when she'd ask me if I wanted her to sing or shaking my head when she'd ask me if I was in any pain.

It never occurred to me that I was actually physically moving my body in those moments until Mom confirmed this much later. She said I started getting increasingly responsive as time passed, even in my comatose state, and my blood pressure and pulse would even go up in response to her voice, or when I knew it was time for her visit. She called it my internal clock.

Nevertheless, it felt so bizarre to be fully awake inside a heavily sedated body. I'm a naturally talkative person, and not being able to express myself with words was unsettling. However, I was never really conscious long enough to worry about things like that.

Time passed like this until it was time for me to wake up. My mom later told me that I was in that medically induced coma for five weeks. I had been put under on December 11, 2005, and by the time I was awakened, we were well into January 2006.

It was because of the cycle that my mother formed and maintained, of talking, singing, and reading the Bible to me, that I roused from my coma calmly, with complete understanding of the state of things as they were. I knew what had happened and where I was.

Most importantly, I believed that come what may, I would eventually be okay.

I just had to be, because my mother had said so.

Chapter Three

The Dreams

Am I alive?

I'm standing in a field of green—endless green. It extends way past the edges of my vision. The blades of grass are tall enough to brush against my feet and legs, but I can't feel them. I can't feel anything. I seem to be wearing a white garment of some sort— unrestricting and flowing. I'm light and weightless and so very tired.

Where am I. . .?

I look down and realize I'm actually standing barefoot on a riverbank. There's a narrow river between me and the endless field of green.

The water is pretty and blue, and the river stretches to my left and right, again beyond the limits of my imagination.

A man stands right across from me, on the other side of the river. He, too, is dressed in white. But even though the river is narrow, I cannot make out his face, only his male form.

He raises his hand and with his palm, he motions to me to come to him.

Or to go back? I can't tell. The way he is gesturing, it could mean either.

To go to him I'd have to cross the river.

But to go back . . . there is nothing but infinite green behind me.

The still-gesturing man continues to look at me.
But I don't have a chance to decide, because suddenly there's a
nurse standing a few feet from me, next to a hospital bed.

I opened my eyes slowly and stared up at the now-familiar ceiling of Milpark Hospital's trauma intensive care unit.

What on earth was that dream?

A man in a field, beckoning me . . . was he meant to be Jesus? He certainly seemed very Christlike.

I remembered the nurse that appeared from nowhere at the end of the dream. How bizarre that it would end on that note, almost as if my subconscious was making sure I stayed connected to my reality.

Before the accident I did dream a lot. I've always had a very active imagination, and my dreams would often reflect this fact, though I never really remembered details.

This particular dream, however, I knew I'd never forget in my lifetime.

As time passed in the hospital, the dreams became more frequent, which made sense because even after I woke up from the coma, I spent most of that first month asleep.

The more frequently I dreamed, the more spiritual the dreams seemed to become.

I'm standing in an endless field of green, gazing upward with a smile on my face as thick, bright clouds descend and envelop me, pulling me into their gentle folds. My feet leave the ground and off I go into the air, still gazing up, my heartbeat quickening with an unexplainable excitement.

Then I look down and see that nurse, that hospital bed that all my dreams seem to always end with.

Suddenly I'm in the hospital bed I was just looking down at, and the nurse is tucking me in . . .

41

After a while, it became such that the contents of my dreams no longer surprised me. In fact, with each consecutive dream, it started to become clear that these weren't just dreams. Rather, they were some sort of representation of a life—my life—that was literally hanging in the balance. I was alive, but barely. And every time I closed my eyes, there was no guarantee I'd open them again.

Things didn't feel as urgent to me as they probably did for my mom and my doctors. But I did have a vague awareness of the fact that, in that moment, machines were keeping my damaged body alive, and that body was desperately trying to hang on to a wandering soul. This vague awareness came to me through my dreams, dreams that had me in cloudlike surroundings, like I was floating somewhere in the mystical divide between two worlds.

As more time passed, I began having new kinds of dreams with more realistic imagery and vivid details. Interestingly enough, most of them took place in my boarding school, and the experiences I dreamt about felt so real that for a moment I'd forget that the real Kechi was lying burned and broken in a hospital bed in South Africa.

I'm walking carefully down the stairs of a house I don't recognize. Everything around me is blurry and bright. I feel so tired and weak, but I'm also happy because I see my friends waiting for me at the base of the stairs, smiling and laughing and urging me to hurry down to them. But I know I can't hurry. Even though I can't see any injuries on my body, I know I'm hurt everywhere. I know I need to be careful.

I hold on to the banister as I carefully climb down. I'm wearing a floor-length, unrestricting Nigerian-style dress called a boubou, but it's much too long and I step on its hem and trip down the steps. . . . Luckily, though, my fall is cushioned by a bed of soft, cloudy pillows.

My friends laugh as they gently hold on to my arms and pull me to my feet.

I look up and smile.

I see Toke, Emmanuella, Sandra, Chinenye, a good mix of friends who were on the plane with me, and friends who weren't. I'm happy to see them all.

Suddenly we're all outside, on the grass fields behind the LJC campus clinic. The sky is a majestic blue, the grass is unnaturally green, and the white paint on the walls of the clinic is unusually bright. Everything just seems to be a little more than normal.

My friends are running ahead of me, talking and laughing, and I take my time walking behind them, smiling as I watch them running around and having fun. I can't join in, but I'm grateful for their company.

I look down and realize I'm barefoot. I can't feel the grass beneath my feet, but this doesn't surprise me.

I look to my side, and I see a hospital bed and a nurse standing next to it.

It's time.

Right on cue, I feel a severe bout of vertigo rush over me, and I lose my balance. The nurse catches me and helps me onto the hospital bed.

As she tucks me in, I turn my head to the side and I see my friends running toward us, and then—

I woke from my dream, though I didn't open my eyes. I had started having more conscious moments than not, moments where I was awake in my head and my mind but not my body.

I thought about this new dream for a while as I lay there, still as a corpse.

I supposed it made sense I was dreaming of school and friends. After all, school was the last place I could remember being before everything fell apart. I was on campus with friends and hours later I was inside a crashing plane.

Day in and day out, I'd have these weird dreams, always in some random location on my high school campus, always with a random mix of friends. They'd be laughing and running around me, and I'd just watch them and smile, knowing even in the dream that I was in no condition to run around with them. Then the nurse would suddenly be there, by the hospital bed, and I'd know it was time to go. Time to come back to reality.

One time I dreamt that my friends and I were getting ready to have barbeque, and then I woke up and realized *I* was the barbeque. Not that my friends were about to eat me, but the "barbeque" aroma I'd smelled in my dream was coming from me. *I* was the roasting flesh.

I laughed so hard on the inside when I realized this, but then my chest started to heave.

Oops, I guess I'd actually tried to laugh out loud and ended up choking on my own saliva.

"She's heaving!" I heard my mom say in a panic.

"I'll suction her," came another female voice.

The thing about these dreams about school, however, was that they unearthed all my anxieties about grades and college and a future that had, so far, been buried by the plane crash.

Growing up in a boarding school, I interacted with my peers more than anyone else in my life, even more than my family. I spent ages ten through sixteen with the same people. As such, I got to watch many friends and classmates develop a passion for many different areas of interest. Dele, at the time, loved math and already knew that it was going to be his major in college. Ijeoma loved to dance and was so amazing at making up original choreography and imitating existing ones. Womiye had a heart for helping others, and years after the accident, when we reconnected, she told me she'd actually won the prestigious Service of God and Others Award for our high school graduating class (this phrase was also our school motto).

But what about Kechi? What did she want to do with her future? Where did her interests lie? Her passions? What did she like enough

44

to focus on as an area of study? Because I could only choose one, right? I had to choose a major and build a career around it. That was the extent of my understanding of college. So what would that major be for me? I considered going into economics, but that was more of a practical choice than something I actually wanted to pursue. And that was my biggest concern all through high school. I didn't seem to have an interest in anything enough to commit to it completely.

I loved writing. In fact, I had actually started writing a book in SS2 (junior year of high school) that got incredibly popular among my fellow students. It was a work of fiction about a boy who moved to a new state with his family and met a girl who was a gypsy, and he would go on adventures with her and her people to secret areas of the world that common folk didn't know existed. I have no idea where the concept for the story came from, or how I was inspired enough to even make up a gypsy "language" for the characters in my book.

But the story extended from one notebook to about four, which I remember binding together with tape, and fellow students would get in line to read my chapter updates. The point is, writing was definitely a passion of mine. I remember I took my novel aboard the plane on December 10 so I could show it to my mom, from whom I got my love of reading. But when given the chance to submit literary pieces for writing competitions at school, I never took them. *Too much work*, I thought at the time.

I also loved talking. I always have. I don't know why; perhaps I had a lot to say as a child. My parents told me I did a *lot* of baby talk, and I recall that in primary (grade) school, while I would usually receive excellent grades, my report card would read, "Kechi talks too much in class." And "Kechi is always talking when the teacher is talking." Or, my personal favorite, "Kechi is a chronic noisemaker."

But it rarely, if ever, affected my grades, so I suppose my parents didn't see it as a serious issue then. Needless to say, I was often first to volunteer to read out loud in English, eager to take on roles with the most dialogue in school plays, and later on in high school, I was happy to be the representing speaker for any club excursions off campus. I memorized speeches with no problem and never shied away from speaking in public or during group presentations.

Because of this fact, I felt that whatever career path I ended up in, I would definitely love it if I could have speaking opportunities. I had no idea about the capacity in which I would speak, I just knew I'd like the chance to do it. Looking back, I'm certain that the Kechi of that time would never have been able to imagine how useful that skill would become in her future.

Another passion of mine was singing. My voice got better and better as I grew older, and in school I used to love singing with and for my friends. Still do. In fact, I had friends who would actually ask me to sing for them, like my friend Atuora. I thought nothing of it back then. I thought maybe she was simply indulging me because she knew how much I loved singing, or maybe it was because she heard something in my voice then that she liked way before my voice became anything special. I never asked her. I just sang. But when I was asked to join the school choir, I declined because it seemed like too much work, too much responsibility.

I seemed to find endless excuses to not do more of the things I obviously loved to do. Perhaps I didn't like the idea of doing those things, be it writing or singing, on someone else's timetable. Or perhaps it was simply a fear of commitment. I somehow believed that committing to one thing meant choosing that thing, and then that thing I chose would close off other choices and interests going forward. The concept of tying myself to just one possible path scared me more than I could understand as a child.

I now wonder if perhaps this fear stemmed from how restricting the Nigerian educational system was in my time. Or maybe it had nothing to do with our school system at all and everything to do with how my personal perspective on education and career paths happened to have developed thus far. Either way, *something* about growing up in Nigeria—*something* about my exposures to the world up until my teenage years—had led me to wrongly believe that once I chose an interest, a path, I could never deviate from it. I wouldn't want to be "a jack-of-all-trades and a master of none" as the saying goes. Therefore, as a lover of multiple art forms, I feared choosing one and losing the chance to explore the others for good.

Laying these thoughts out this way helped me understand the real truth of the matter. Clearly, I had interests: writing, speaking, singing. But in my young mind, none were *traditional* enough to pursue seriously. This brought me back to the Nigerian school system I grew up in. I, along with many of my peers undoubtedly, was conditioned to believe that certain fields of study were more valid than others. Therefore, if as a student you found yourself leaning toward more unconventional interests or skill sets, like singing or drawing, you became an outlier in a social environment that demanded conformity. Yet, as indecisive as I clearly was at sixteen—like most sixteen-year-olds, actually—I was supposed to be ready to make solid decisions about a future I had put no effort into investing in thus far. The idea terrified me.

So for many days after I woke from my coma, I'd dream of school, recall all my anxieties and fears and worries about my future, then I'd open my eyes only to be reminded of—*confronted with*, really—a reality where none of that mattered anymore, and wouldn't for a long while.

All I had on my mind, in the few waking moments where I wasn't too exhausted and numb to think, was my friends who made frequent appearances in my dreams of school.

I'd wonder about the ones that had been on the flight with me, especially Toke.

Where were they? Were they okay? How badly were they hurt?

Because obviously they were alive; I assumed they were since I was.

Were they healing up somewhere like I was? Were they here in Milpark Hospital? When could I see them? When would we be well enough to go back to school? Would we make it in time for senior prom and graduation?

It would take four months for me to realize the deep irony of my thoughts in that moment.

Chapter Four

The Fight to Survive

Around the middle of January, the doctors gradually started to reduce my dosage of the sedation medication until I was more awake than not during Mommy's visits. It took about a month for me to be fully weaned off the effects of long-term sedation.

When I wasn't sleeping and dreaming, I was staring at my mother's face and watching her talk. That was what I lived for day in and day out.

Mommy visited three times a day, each time for an hour, and just like when I was in the coma, my body clock was tuned to her arrival and departure. Every morning, I looked forward to her arrival and after she left each night, I fell asleep praying for the next morning to come as fast as possible so I could see her again.

I lived for her, quite frankly. Daddy had told her on the day of the accident, "Kechi is staying alive because of you, Ihuoma."[1] He was right. She *was* my reason to live.

Staying alive was exhausting. Especially in the beginning. It's hard to explain.

1. Ihuoma is her middle name, and Daddy usually calls Mommy and me by our middle names.

I had nothing to do with my *body* staying alive; the machines did that. The machines kept my body bound to this world, but me, I was the one in charge of keeping my essence, my *soul*, bound to my body. And it took all of my effort to do this. A body is just a body in the end. A body can be alive but empty, and I had to make the constant effort to make sure my body didn't become an empty shell. It wasn't because I was in constant pain, at least not at first. I was numb most of the time, everywhere, even on the inside.

But the one thing that I could feel with certainty was my love for my mother. It burned so brightly and incessantly inside of me, and that love was the reason I fought to stay present in this world. God knew I needed a reason to continue the constant struggle to stay bound to my body, and with my mother, He gave me one.

After I woke from the coma, I couldn't speak for the next few months, so I couldn't talk with Mommy whenever she came to visit. I could try, but no sound would come out. This was because there was a trachea tube that was breathing for me. It was inserted directly into my windpipe through a hole in my throat and connected to a ventilator. I also had a feeding tube inserted into my stomach through my mouth, through which nutrients were passed into my body.

It was such a strange feeling, not being able to talk. I would try to make sound, but it was as if I didn't even have a voice box. There was no vibration in my throat, just empty air. I couldn't talk with Mommy whenever she came to visit, but I wanted to hear her voice, regardless. Sometimes it was enough to just hear her speak, especially if I was drowsy or sedated. Then she would read to me from the Bible or from some of my favorite authors, like Francine Rivers and Nora Roberts. Sometimes she would sing to me too.

But other times I wanted her to just talk to me. Not read to me or sing to me but talk. The more awake and alert I became, the more this need grew. I wanted to interact more with her. I may not have been able to voice my replies, but I could nod and shake my head a bit. I could respond in the ways my body would allow.

I could look at her as she spoke. I could try to smile or laugh, maybe even mouth words to her.

"Are you in pain, Kechi?"

I shook my head no.

"Are you tired?"

No.

"Want me to read to you?"

Talk, I mouthed at her.

Mommy smiled. "Okay, you want me to just talk?"

I nodded.

"Okay."

So, Mommy would just sit next to my bed, decked out in her TICU visitor's gear of a long, disposable hospital apron and gloves, and she would start talking.

This soon became our standard form of exchange.

Talk, I'd mouth to her almost every visit. *Talk.*

And she would talk to me about anything and everything. She told me Johannesburg was beautiful. She talked about everyone I cared about.

"You know, your daddy came while you were in the coma," she said to me.

Daddy! I thought to myself. *I wish he was here right now.*

"He'll come again soon," Mommy said reassuringly, as if she could tell what I was thinking. She probably could.

She told me of other people who had come to see me—Aunty Dorothy, Aunty Chinyere. She told me about a wonderful lady named Betty who had been helping her since we arrived in Johannesburg. She showed me letters from my cousins, read me emails from Womiye, and told me that everyone was praying for me and couldn't wait to see me all better.

"Nduka said he wishes he could bear your burns in your stead," she told me, speaking of one of my cousins whom I loved with all my heart.

That shocked me to the point of tears. I was so touched that he would say such a thing.

"I know," Mommy said, understanding my tears. "It's so sweet." During some of our visits, Mommy and I would just stare at each other in silence. I was just so overwhelmed by my love for her and hers for me. I saw it in her eyes every time she looked at me. Her love strengthened me. I had so much I wanted to say to her. I wanted to tell her how much I loved her, how much I lived for her visits. I wanted to ask her so many questions too. Like, Where were the rest of the people who were in the plane crash? What happened to my friends and schoolmates?

In between our visits, I started to practice mouthing my words better. I wanted to surprise Mommy.

I practiced and practiced until one day during a visit, I turned to Mommy and silently mouthed the three words I'd been saying in my heart since I first opened my eyes from my coma and saw her face.

I love you.

Mommy's eyes widened. She looked so shocked and touched.

I love you, Mommy. I mouthed the words slowly, rounding my mouth so that she could see what I was trying so hard to convey.

"Kechi, have you been practicing?"

I nodded repeatedly, feeling triumphant. Of course I'd been practicing. It was so frustrating not to be able to talk to my mom properly and have conversations with her. I at least wanted to be able to tell her the most important thing.

"I love you more."

I shook my head at that. *Impossible,* I thought.

Mommy laughed. "Is this a competition now?"

I nodded with a smile.

"Okay, I love you more than the whole world."

More than the universe, I mouthed, making Mommy laugh again. I could feel myself getting emotional for some reason. *Mommy, I love you,* I mouthed to her again. I started to tear up. *Mommy, I love you. Mommy, I love you.* By that point I was full-on crying. Finally being able to convey my feelings to her had overwhelmed me.

Mommy, wearing her gloves and apron, stroked my exposed left shoulder, the only part of me she could touch for now because it hadn't burned.

How I wished I could hug her! Her gentle caress alone made me feel so loved and secure.

My machines started to beep as my vitals went crazy, and Mommy talked to me and soothed me until I finally calmed down.

I soon graduated from just mouthing *talk* and *I love you* to trying to form whole sentences, mouthing each word slowly so Mommy could piece together what I was saying. Before I knew it, she was interpreting my silent words as easily as if I were talking to her normally. It was wonderful to be able to communicate with her like this.

Mommy told me I didn't break any bones or lose any limbs in the accident, and that was just miraculous to me. I started constantly trying to move my arms and legs off the bed, just to make sure that I could still move and control them. I would lift my arms and legs one at a time, feeling reassured each time they responded. Sometimes I would overdo it, though, as was my MO with most things in life, and the nurse would have to give me some morphine.

In the first couple months after I woke from the coma, I was having surgery every other day, which was apparently less frequent than when I was still comatose.

I saw my general physician, Dr. Pahad, every single morning when he made his rounds in the TICU. He was a very friendly man, always full of smiles, and whenever he aimed one at me, I always felt inexplicably reassured, as if my lying in a hospital bed, bandaged head to foot, wasn't as bad as it looked. His sociable disposition and mannerisms made me feel like everything was going to be okay, no matter how bad things seemed. I guess that was what made him a great physician.

But visits from my surgeons were typically scarce. My main surgeon, Dr. Nel, rarely made his rounds when I was awake.

I didn't begrudge him that though. Dr. Nel's job as a trauma surgeon was restricted to the operating theater, where he was required to patch me back together while keeping me alive each time

I was wheeled in. He most likely had at least thirty other severe trauma patients, all probably in conditions as acute as mine.

If I were in his position, I would probably avoid making any unnecessary contact with my patients and their families as well, as a sort of coping mechanism.

Whenever it was time for surgery, the nurse on duty would detach all my probes and machines and wires and pile them on top of my blanket, then the theater nurses would wheel me from the TICU into a theater room.

The first time I remember being wheeled into a theater, my eyes darted every which way and the first thing that stuck out was how very white and . . . *stark* the room seemed. I was lying flat on my bed so I could only see the ceiling and some parts of the walls, and everything I managed to set my eyes on was very white and bare. It gave me the no-nonsense vibe of a room where serious things happened, nothing more, nothing less.

My bed came to a stop right next to a flatter, harder looking bed, then I was lifted, bedsheets and blankets and all, from my bed to the surgery table in one swift move. I was then lying beneath the strangest light fixture I'd ever seen: four wide, connected light orbs from which the harshest white light shone, all attached to a large, complicated-looking machine to my right.

Before I knew it, people in surgical caps and masks were hovering over me and gloved hands started reconnecting all my probes and wires to the weird theater machine.

"Kechi, are you okay?" a gentle female voice asked me.

I nodded.

"Okay, we're gonna take good care of you, all right?"

I nodded again, suddenly feeling very drowsy and lightheaded.

"Count to ten for me in your head, love. One, two, three, four . . ."

This was how most of my surgeries went. Soon enough, it became a somewhat reliable pattern. I'd be asleep before I saw any of my surgeons in the theater, and by the time I woke up, I was staring up at the familiar TICU ceiling or at Mommy's lovely face.

53

The South African trauma surgeons worked on me in batches. They did a little at a time so as not to strain my body too much or push me past my pain threshold. With respect to the latter, that ship had long sailed, to be honest.

Each time I went into the theater, they would remove dead skin from a burned part of my body and replace it with skin from another part that hadn't burned—typically my stomach or my back. They harvested skin from my stomach repeatedly until that area formed its own keloids[2] and became unusable. When that happened, they harvested from other parts of me, like the back of my right leg and my backside.

Mommy hated that they had to touch areas on my body that weren't burned, seeing as there were so few parts like that left on me, but she knew there was no choice. There were too many large surface areas on my body that needed immediate coverage, like my hands, thighs, legs, my entire head and face, and my neck. If they didn't cover me up quickly, I would get fatally infected. And so, every other day, I would be wheeled into the theater for another round of skin grafts.

Unbeknownst to me, my life was constantly hanging in the balance, even after two months of trauma care. As far as I knew, I was awake, I had good brain activity, I was communicating with Mommy and with my nurses, I was even moving my body. Meanwhile, I was developing fevers and high blood pressure, succumbing to sepses (contagious infections) that would lead to isolation care, and occasionally my breathing would halt for seconds at a time.

But I didn't notice when these things happened. From my perspective, it was all the same. I only knew that sometimes I was awake and sometimes I was asleep. There were times I slept longer than normal, but I always woke up. I was always going to wake up.

---

2. Keloids are an uncommon overgrowth of scar tissue that can occur where the skin has healed after an injury, especially skin with high melanin content.

Chapter Five

The Drive

As more time passed in the TICU, movement became increasingly difficult, and pain was beginning to become a constant companion. It got so strenuous to move that I wondered if I had imagined all those times from weeks prior when I was lifting my legs and arms off the bed with such ease.

"Her muscles are weakening from lack of movement," Dr. Pahad explained when Mommy asked him. "That's why it's getting harder for her to move. It might be time for Kechi to start physiotherapy so her muscles don't atrophy."

Physiotherapy?

Lying in that hospital bed and forcing myself to stay present inside my own body and allowing the machines to do their job to keep me bound to this world, these things already took such an incredible amount of effort that I could not explain.

If merely staying alive was taking everything inside me, how was I supposed to find the extra strength for physical therapy? As far as I was concerned, asking me for more was asking me for too much.

I looked at Mommy then. Her face was so full of worry. I didn't like seeing her like that.

If I were to obediently do my physiotherapy as the doctor

ordered, she'd be happy, wouldn't she? And I wanted Mommy to be happy. More than anything.

I was beginning to understand the importance of personal drive and its connection to basic human functionality. I thought about the motives behind every action I had carried out in my life so far. Studying to pass an exam. Buying specific brands and dressing in the latest styles so I could look cool to my peers. Being a good kid so my parents didn't get mad at me. Human beings can't function without drive, and behind all these actions combined is one overarching motive: happiness. At the end of the day, we spend our time on earth striving for happiness.

But then when your life gets derailed and everything is suddenly stripped away from you—be it beauty, fame, fortune, money, or even just the *promise* of all these things that arguably make life more interesting and worthwhile—when all you have left is just your life itself, what happens to your drive? What keeps you going when you have nothing left?

When I was stripped of everything but my very life, I lost that personal, inner drive.

Despite this, I wanted to live. But why make the effort to hold on when it felt so much easier to let go? What was my reason? Without one, I would fade away.

Since I had no inner drive or motivation, I searched for one *outside* of myself and latched my feeble life onto it.

At first, that drive was my mother's voice. Before I could open my eyes, the promise of her presence by my bedside was enough to keep me going, even in my comatose state.

Once I was awake and could see her, my motivation transferred from hearing her voice to seeing her face and her smile.

And so, physiotherapy became something I did only because I wanted to see my mom smile. She was my reason for living; therefore, her happiness became my only reason for going beyond any effort to simply survive.

I was soon going to realize that this wasn't sustainable long-term. Another human being should never be a person's reason for living. At some point, satisfying another person will not be enough of a reason for you to continue to live your own life fully. Inner drive becomes important at this stage, and by that point in my treatment, I hadn't found mine. Therefore, I did my physiotherapy because I knew my mom wanted me to. She dreamed and prayed incessantly for the day that my independence would be fully restored. I knew she believed with certainty that that day would come, and I knew that she believed physiotherapy played a significant role in that restoration. Her belief, while contagious at times, put a bit of pressure on me because it implied that I was partly responsible for the manner in which I came out of this ordeal. It was just the right amount of pressure though—not enough to make me resent her and just enough to make me want to please her. Even though I was lying down in a body that was so broken I couldn't even turn my neck side to side on my pillow, I believed in my mother's belief that physiotherapy was indeed my first step toward sitting, standing, and maybe even walking again one day.

Physiotherapy became a part of my everyday routine. Mommy had to leave the room once it was time for therapy. My physiotherapist Maya was a tough and frank woman, but also very positive. Anytime I allowed her to do my stretches, she would praise me and that was always encouraging. She would lift my legs and arms off the bed and stretch them, bending them at the joints. She would make me turn my head side to side in an attempt to loosen up the tightness in my neck muscles. It hurt so much and I would cry through most of the session, but I never told her to stop because I wanted to be able to tell Mommy that I did my stretches.

Maya showed me how my feet had bent forward with my toes pointing downward—a common occurrence among long-term comatose patients—so she would also bend my feet at the ankles and rotate them in an effort to encourage the muscles to loosen up. She'd even use me as an example to motivate her other adult patients in the TICU.

"If a sixteen-year-old girl like Kechi can do it, so can you," I'd hear her say. Yikes.

Maya told Mommy she was worried about my limited neck mobility. I had lain in one position for five weeks during my coma, with my head turned to my right, and now it was a real struggle to turn my neck to the other side.

"Kechi, you need to practice turning your neck to your left more," she said to me.

I pouted and looked at Mommy. *But it's so painful,* I mouthed to her.

"She said it's so painful," Mommy told Maya, who nodded in understanding.

"I know," Maya said, turning back to me, "but you're gonna have to try, okay? Better to fix what we can with physiotherapy now than with surgery later."

So every day after we did my hand and leg stretches, Maya would make sure to stretch my neck, no matter how painful it was and no matter how much I cried. After she left, Mommy would try to console me. I'd cry and cry, and Mommy would place her gloved hand gently on my exposed shoulder in a gesture of comfort.

I just didn't get why we had to do this now when everything still felt so raw.

"The thing is, it's so important that she stays as mobile as possible right now while the wounds and grafts are still fresh," Maya explained to Mommy, who was obviously distressed by my pain. "It's not just about her muscles. The more she heals, the tighter her skin grafts will get, and it'll be harder to manipulate her body. Therapy is only going to get more difficult as she heals."

So, basically as I got better, I would get worse?

I'd assumed that physiotherapy would get easier when my burns healed, so hearing Maya say the opposite terrified me at first. Luckily, I had no energy to dwell on a future that wasn't even guaranteed.

Days passed at a snail's pace in the TICU. Physical therapy continued with Maya, much to my dismay, and I started to call Maya a physical *terrorist* whenever it was just Mommy and me. Not that anyone else could read my lips anyway.

One morning, when Mommy came to visit, I opened my eyes and to my utmost surprise, I was staring up at my grandma's sweet face.

Grandma! I thought as I gazed up at that warm, loving, extremely familiar face. *It's Grandma!*

The second I saw her hovering above me, my lips pulled up into my very first smile since the plane crash.

"Oh, *shame*,[1] she's smiling!" said my nurse animatedly.

It was the first time since arriving in South Africa that I saw a human being other than Mommy whom I knew and loved.

"Kechi, my darling!" Grandma cooed, smiling down at me.

I loved my mom's mom dearly and had always been very close to her. She doted on me heavily as a child and even into my teenage years, probably because I was her very first grandchild. Seeing her then, at a time in my life when things didn't make a lot of sense, brought me a sense of security and assurance.

I thought about how hard it must be for her to see me like this and the thought made me burst into uncontrollable tears. My heart was suddenly heavy.

Unfortunately, my tears triggered hers and she had to leave the room briefly.

"Kechi, don't cry. It's okay, my love." Mommy quickly came to my bedside. "She's okay. You know it's her first time seeing you awake, so she's overwhelmed."

Grandma came back into the room and came up to me again. Her eyes were a little red, but she seemed fine now. She smiled down at me again. "Kechi, you're going to be okay, you hear me?"

I nodded.

"You've always been such a strong girl," she continued in the firm, encouraging voice I always knew her to have. "I know that God will restore you fully. You will be fine."

I just kept nodding and nodding to her every word.

Grandma was right. I was strong. I would overcome this, with God's help, with her help, with everyone's help. I had to.

---

1. *Shame* is a South African expression, similar to "aww."

———— ❦ ————

Some weeks passed after Grandma's visit, and Mommy said Daddy was coming next. I was so excited! Mommy told me he'd come twice already to be with her while I was in a coma, but this would be my first time seeing him since the day of the plane crash. As much as he wanted to, Daddy couldn't be here in South Africa with Mommy and me all the time, because one of them had to be at home in Nigeria with my little sister, Tara. I missed Tara so much too. I hadn't seen her since summer.

But it was January then; she was probably in school.

I would've been in school too, studying with my friends, were it not for the accident . . .

Speaking of friends and school, I briefly wondered where Toke and Chinenye were, and the rest of those who'd been on the plane with me. Mommy still wasn't bringing them up. I hoped they were okay and not suffering all the same hardships I was. I hoped their injuries weren't as bad as mine.

The next day came and I woke up to my daddy's voice.

My eyes shot open, and I saw him smiling down at me.

Daddy! I mouthed to him.

"Hey princess," he said with a wide grin. He was wearing the required disposable gloves and apron.

I smiled back up at him happily.

It must kill him to see me like this, I couldn't help but think, then I started bawling.

My father took pride in me, this I knew. Since I was a child, he always called me his princess. He always told me that I was smart and beautiful, and I grew up confident in my looks and my brains because my father took pride in these things.

My dad also took pride in the fact that he was a fixer. As far as I knew, there was nothing he couldn't fix and no situation he couldn't get his family out of.

But there I lay, body damaged and bandaged from top to bottom. I couldn't imagine the pain and helplessness he must have felt, looking down and seeing his princess in a state that was beyond his ability to fix.

Still, he smiled at me and encouraged me, and I took comfort in his presence throughout his time in South Africa.

I talked for the first time since the accident during Daddy's visit.

Over the course of the month or so before, my nurses had been turning off my ventilator periodically to slowly ease me into breathing on my own. Now, it seemed the doctors believed my lungs were finally strong enough to fully support my breathing without the machine's assistance. This was splendid news, a testament to the fact that I was definitely getting better.

I was full of nervous excitement the morning of the removal. They were going to pull out my trachea tube, so I could finally use my voice for the first time in months!

My parents had come to the hospital for the morning visit so I'd seen them both already, but only Mommy knew about the procedure. She wanted it to be a surprise for Daddy, and I was totally down for that. The TICU nurses and nurse aides were in on it too.

I couldn't wait to see his reaction to hearing me talk for the first time since the coma.

I wondered how I would sound. Would my voice come out different? Higher? Lower?

I guess we'll soon see, I thought. *I mean, hear.*

When they came back for the afternoon visit, Mommy sent Daddy away from the room with some excuse. I think she asked him to get her some coffee. He left the TICU, and once he was out of sight, the nurse drew the curtains around my bed and got to work taking out the trachea tube.

I was a little nervous because I didn't know what to expect from this process. As far as I knew, the tube was connected to my throat through a hole in my neck.

Would I feel it when they removed it? Would it hurt? I really hoped not.

"Okay, Kechi, you ready?" a nurse asked.

I nodded and braced myself mentally as she hovered over me. Her gloved fingers came up to my neck and soon I felt a strange pressure right in the middle of my throat. It was a bizarre feeling, like she was pressing down on my jugular. There was a firm tug right in the same spot, and then nothing.

The nurse straightened up, now holding a long, translucent tube in her hand. "Okay, it's gone!" she said with a smile, then she turned to open the curtains.

I felt my tense body relax with relief.

Well, that was painless. Thank God.

"You wanna try saying something?" the nurse asked.

I hesitated briefly. Suddenly I was nervous no sound would come out when I tried to talk. What if something had gone wrong in the trachea removal process?

I shook the silly thought away and looked at Mommy, then I took a deep breath and said the same words I'd been mouthing at her for the past few weeks.

"Mommy, I love you." My eyes teared up as soon as I said it out loud.

Finally!

And wow, my voice sounded so raspy and high-pitched! It sounded nothing like me, and it was such an intensely weird feeling to produce a sound from my own throat that was foreign to my ears.

Mommy's eyes immediately teared up as well. "I love you too, baby!" She laughed a little as she smiled down at me lovingly. "Your voice is so high!"

"It's so weird," I croaked out with an amused smile. This wasn't gonna be permanent though, right? My voice would go back to normal eventually, right?

"Her voice will go back to normal over time," the nurse said to Mommy and me, as though she'd heard my unspoken questions.

Another nurse came up to tell us Daddy was on his way back.

"He's gonna freak out," Mommy said with a chuckle, and I smiled wider in anticipation. Daddy was definitely going to freak out. He was a hard man to surprise, so I was really looking forward to this.

A few seconds later, he walked into the room. By that time, a few more nurses were hanging around my bed area, waiting to see my dad's reaction to hearing my voice.

"Hi, Daddy," I squeaked out into the expectant silence.

I will never, ever forget my father's completely stunned expression in that moment.

He whipped his head around and stared right at me with wide, shocked eyes. "What?!" he exclaimed in an uncharacteristically high-pitched voice (I could relate to that), and everyone in the room broke out into laughter, myself included.

"Oh, shame!" came a chorus of voices from those who had been watching the moment. We'd all hoped for a reaction like that, and Daddy didn't disappoint.

He eventually joined in the laughter, though his was more from disbelief than amusement. "Well, I certainly didn't expect that!" he said after he'd calmed down some, though he was still clearly trying to collect himself.

Mommy told me later on that Daddy had actually gotten emotional and cried a little. I wish I'd seen that.

"Is there a hole in my neck now?" I asked Mommy sometime after all the excitement.

"Yes, but they said it'll close up very fast."

"Wow." The thought creeped me out a little. I wondered if the inside of my throat was visible through the hole. It was a weird thing to imagine.

Once I could talk, it was all I wanted to do. This came as no surprise to Mommy or Daddy, seeing as I'd always loved to talk.

I talked to Mommy, specifically, about everything that came to my mind. I was like a faucet with no handle; words just spilled out of me unfiltered.

I told her about my boyfriend, Chimdi (though we were broken up at the time), when we'd started dating, our first kiss during junior high prom, and how we broke up. I told her I was still a virgin, just in case she was worried about that because I'd had a boyfriend, and I told her never to worry about me in that regard because I had no interest in sex yet. She laughed and admitted she was relieved to hear that. I told her to teach me some Igbo, our native Nigerian language, so we could talk smack about the mean nurses without being found out, and whenever we conversed in Igbo, she was surprised at how much I already knew. So was I, to be honest! I didn't grow up speaking Igbo, but I guess I picked up more than I realized by hearing my mom speak it.

Sometimes I wondered why I felt the need to share so much with Mommy all of a sudden. I suspect that something about a near-death experience makes a person more vulnerable and open. I think it has to do with the fact that, because you somehow survived what *should* have been fatal, something in your subconscious realizes how quickly and randomly everything can just be over. And you realize when you hold back or hold things in, you may never get the chance to express those things ever again. Tomorrow isn't promised, after all.

I also told Mommy that I loved her more than I loved Jesus. I asked her if she loved Jesus more than me, and I was so stunned and shocked when she said yes. I cried so hard that day.

How could she say that? I was her daughter! I almost died! I was hanging on to this life filled with so much pain because of her, and then she tells me she loves Jesus more than she loves *me*? I couldn't understand because I knew without a doubt that she loved me with her whole being. So how could she possibly love someone else more than she loved me? What more of herself did she have to give?

Little did I know that these questions were the true beginning of my own relationship with Jesus.

"Mommy, how bad was the accident?" I asked this question one day, out of the blue.

Well, out of the blue for her. I had been mulling it over in my

64

mind for a while, since before I could talk. I was sure there was a good reason why Mommy didn't want to bring it up. She probably didn't want me to relive any memories from that day. Or maybe she didn't want me to worry about my friends who had been on board the plane too.

Mommy visibly froze up at my question, though her expression didn't change.

"Did anyone else get hurt like me?" I pressed on, but my tone became tentative. Now that I'd brought it up, I wasn't sure what I was going to hear.

Mommy sighed and turned to me. "Kechi, remember how I told you that your schoolmates were fine."

"Yes?" For some reason, my heart started to pound. I stared at Mommy's face, trying to read her expression. She looked nervous, which of course made me even more nervous.

"I wasn't being totally honest."

What? I wondered to myself. *Did someone else get hurt, after all?*

Suddenly, my pounding heart halted as another possibility occurred to me and filled me with dread.

Don't tell me. "Mommy . . . did someone die?" My vision was already starting to blur.

Oh, God, please, please no . . .

Mommy hesitated. Then her face fell, and she nodded.

My heart broke into pieces. "What? Oh, God!" Tears rushed down my face, and I just stared at Mommy in shock.

What the hell? Someone actually *died*?

I thought about everyone I knew who had been on the flight, from close friends to classmates to other students I was familiar with.

Oh, God! Had it been one of them?

I just lay there in my bed, weeping. I was so devastated. I had hoped that I was the worst case out of all those who had been hurt by the plane crash, but someone had actually died? I couldn't believe it. I couldn't believe the accident had been bad enough to take a life.

I fought to take a deep breath and tried to talk through my tears. "Who was it, Mommy? Was it . . . is it someone I know?"

"No, I don't think so," she said, and she sounded as sad as I felt. "He was in JS2."[2]

I digested this and realized it didn't matter whether or not I knew the boy who'd died.

I could hear the machines above my bed beeping in protest because my pulse was going haywire with how much I was crying, but I just couldn't stop my tears. I kept thinking of the poor boy's family. If I felt like this, how much worse did they feel right now?

JS2. The boy would've been twelve years old at most. Twelve years old. He hadn't even seen his teenage years and he was already gone. It felt so unfair for someone so young to just be gone.

So this was why Mommy didn't want to bring it up. Someone had died. The plane hadn't just crash-*landed* like I'd assumed all this time. It had actually been a fatal accident.

I mourned the loss of that child's soul for the rest of the day, and I prayed with Mommy for him to rest in peace and for God to be with his family in this hard time. That was all I could do. It was all anyone could do.

2. JS2 is the Nigerian equivalent of eighth grade, the third and final year of middle school. In America, it is typically taken from ages thirteen to fourteen.

Chapter Six

The Itching

More time passed in Milpark Hospital's TICU.

Now that my trachea tube was gone, my feeding tube was next on the agenda.

I was gradually switched from my liquid-nutrients diet to semi-solids like ice chips and ice cream. The flavor of vanilla was so strong in my mouth that it blew my mind. I'd completely forgotten how sweet ice cream was! The texture felt so foreign to my tongue, it was delightful.

Finally, they took out my feeding tube and it was time for me to have my first real meal since the plane crash.

This was another huge day for me. I was super excited because I missed the sensation of real food in my mouth, the flavors on my tongue, the feeling of chewing and swallowing actual, solid food.

My nurse propped me up in bed and made sure I was comfortable, then a tray was wheeled into the TICU and came to a stop beside my bed.

Mommy thanked the kitchen staff who had delivered the food, and I watched as she lifted the metal cover off the main plate to reveal a very simple meal: grilled chicken breast and vegetables.

The scent of the food immediately filled the air. It smelled amazing to me.

Mommy carefully cut out a small piece of chicken and lifted it to my lips.

As soon as she slid the piece of chicken into my mouth, I was transported to plains of flavor I never even knew existed.

My taste buds came alive in response to the wondrous taste of that very first bite of food after months of IV nutrition. The burst of flavor on my tongue was so immediate that it startled me, and I just kept chewing, my eyes wide open in shock and confusion.

I was sure I'd never tasted anything as delicious as that chicken in my entire life, and that was saying something considering my mother is an excellent cook.

Mommy watched me in amusement. "Is it good?"

"Mommy it's so good, oh my God!" I said, my tone full of wonder. "How is it so good? This is literally the best chicken I've ever had in my life."

Mommy raised her eyebrows and laughed as she cut another piece. "Really?"

I could tell she thought I was exaggerating, but I really wasn't. "Yes! Have you tasted it? Taste it and you'll see what I'm talking about."

Mommy ate the piece she'd just cut and nodded in approval after chewing for a few seconds.

I was so confused at her lackluster reaction. "Isn't it amazing?" I urged.

"Yes, it's really nice."

Nice? Was she joking? How could she say something that tasted that good was just *nice*?

"Want some more?" she asked me.

I nodded emphatically. "Yes, please!" If she didn't like it, more for me.

Mommy continued to feed me small pieces of chicken, and I fell more and more in love with each bite. I ate until I was full and sleepy, which didn't take much; I was full before I'd gone through half the plate. Guess my appetite still needed work.

Mommy's reaction made sense much later because, in the end, it turned out to be just normal hospital food. However, because I hadn't tasted anything for months, my deprived taste buds were simply overly responsive to even the most lightly seasoned food. The human body is truly peculiar.

Three months passed in South Africa, and as I continued to heal, a new demon made itself known.

The itching.

It started with light, tickling sensations all over my body, originating at my scalp. God, my scalp itched so terribly. My head was always wrapped with bandages so it looked like I was wearing a turban, and I would press my head into my pillow and rotate it inside the turban bandage as hard as I could to create some friction against my scalp, just to get some relief from the itching. Of course, doing this was extremely unwise because the wounds and burns on my scalp would rub raw, but I literally couldn't control it. When it hit, the itching was a monster that consumed my every coherent thought, and as much as it hurt to irritate my scalp this way, I didn't care. The pain was so much more bearable than the itching, and the day I realized this was the day I knew that this itching would be the worst part of my entire experience as a burn survivor.

Eventually I started feeling like there were little pieces of lint—from people's clothes, from the linen on my bed, maybe from the very air itself—floating everywhere and landing all over my body. I'd ask my mom to please help me remove them one by one and she'd be at a loss. But she'd always try.

"What is this itching?" my distressed mother asked Dr. Pahad one morning when he made his rounds.

"It's the nature of burn injuries, especially when they're this deep," he explained. "Her damaged nerves are misreporting an itch at her burn sites. It's an 'internal itch,' so to speak, so scratching won't relieve it, I'm afraid."

My doctors explained that because all my nerves were exposed, I was extremely sensitive to even the lightest breeze. This helped me understand why I felt this way, but it didn't change the discomfort I felt every single moment of every single day.

The itching simply made me miserable, and in turn, it made Mommy miserable. Our lovely visits became marred by its awful presence, and there was nothing either of us could do to stop it. Sometimes it would be bearable. Most times, though, it developed into a full-body itch that persisted either until Mommy helped me scratch at every single part of me that felt itchy—which was all over—or until I was given Dormicum, a strong muscle relaxant that usually helped me sleep. Sometimes, we would spend the entire hour of a visit just scratching. And, of course, Mommy couldn't *actually* scratch my healing wounds or skin grafts. She'd just rub the area firmly until I got some measure of relief. I got to a place where my only respite from the itching was sleep. And then I got to a place where the only time I *could* sleep was with Dormicum. When the full-body itch (which I dubbed the Crazy Itch) started, it easily overshadowed any pain, and the discomfort kept me awake for hours at a time. But then sometimes the pain would escalate and add to the chaos within me, and I would get so overwhelmed that all I could do was lie there and cry and pray that I could cry myself to sleep. Sleep would be a temporary escape from the hell I was in.

I started to rely very heavily on morphine and Dormicum. I didn't see anything wrong with my reliance on these drugs. After all, I was a third-degree burns patient who needed them, plus my doctors were the ones who started me on them. But then those very same doctors believed I was developing an addiction to them and started to reduce my dosage. I couldn't do anything about that. But by that point, the drugs had become my only access to relief, so I started to plan everything around my doses.

The itching persisted and worsened, and soon we learned from the doctors and nurses that the morphine I so craved and depended on was actually making it worse.

I never thought I'd have to deal with addiction one day. Up until my personal experience with it, I'd always associated addiction with back-alley transactions and overdosing in abandoned buildings. Yet there I was, having developed a bona fide addiction to drugs inside a freaking hospital, one of the most drug-controlled environments to ever exist.

I wanted morphine *all the time*. I craved the brief feeling of sweet relief it brought me whenever my pain escalated, and when that sweet feeling faded, as it always did, I anticipated the moment I could have it again. I couldn't pinpoint the exact moment when it became more about experiencing that trance-like feeling the drug brought on than it was about my actual pain. What's more, just as my doctors said, the sweet feeling that came with it was swiftly followed by an intense itching that rivaled the itching caused by my burn scars. But I didn't care. I was actually willing to suffer the extreme itching as long as it meant I would get to feel that delicious, warm feeling that overcame me within the first few minutes after the morphine was administered.

It was scary. Itching was the worst part of my burn recovery journey, yet somehow my addiction to this drug had wired my brain to believe the itching was worth enduring if it meant I could get that next shot of morphine.

As I was slowly weaned off morphine, I came to understand how serious my addiction had been, and how lucky I was to have experienced it within a safe space. It occurred to me that this drug had the power to make me crave it even when I didn't actually need it. It caused me to trivialize something as horrible as my itching, to the point that I didn't even care when the drug intensified it. The thought scared the hell out of me. I still depended heavily on it while I was in the TICU, but since my daily dosage was gradually reduced, I tried to make sure my pain was real before requesting it.

My addiction to Dormicum, on the other hand, was for good reason as far as I was concerned, because this was the drug that gave me something that was consistently out of reach during my time in South Africa: sleep. I was so sleep-deprived that, to this day, I *still* feel like I'm making up for how little I slept during that period.

I already had insomnia before the accident—which I blame on my dad since we used to stay up watching kung fu movies together—but afterward, it became much worse. With the pain and discomfort coupled with the constant itching, sleep was always either fitful or distant. Ironic considering I'd spent the first few months in the hospital in dreamland.

Most nights, I lay awake in my bed, mulling over all sorts of thoughts while staring at the TICU clock and counting down to Mommy's morning visit.

So, for the first few months in South Africa, Dormicum was the only way to turn my mind off and allow my body to rest. It was a different feeling from the morphine. For one thing, it didn't have the terrible side effect of itching. For another, its effects were gentler and lasted much longer. After the drug was administered, I would feel myself sinking into unconsciousness in layered waves until I was suddenly awake again with no real idea of exactly when I'd actually fallen asleep. The feeling was very similar to the effect of surgical anesthesia.

I was weaned off Dormicum the same gradual way I was weaned off morphine. I suspect that, at some point, it was decided that I needed to learn how to let sleep come to me more naturally. I wasn't happy with the decision, and I cried a lot because of it, even though I also resentfully understood. Truthfully, my dependence on Dormicum was no different from my dependence on morphine. I craved both. But the morphine addiction felt more . . . violent by nature. More desperate and irrational.

Mommy started doing whatever she could to distract me and cheer me up. Aside from buying books by my favorite authors and CDs of my favorite artists, she bought me things that she felt I could look forward to enjoying after I left the hospital. She would buy them after every surgery and bring them with her to the hospital.

This was incredibly comforting for me, and for her too, I'm sure.

Doing things like that allowed us both to imagine a life that went beyond this particular hospital experience, a life where I would be well enough to wear normal clothes and live a normal life. Most importantly, it added back some of that happy glow our visits had been lacking of late due to the horrible itching.

She bought random things, from comfy nighties to cute bedroom slippers to silky bathrobes. I remember when she showed me these really gorgeous, colorful bras that she bought for me, and I was so thrilled because we *never* found cute bras in my size! I laughed with so much joy that day, and that was Mommy's goal. She just wanted to do anything that would brighten my days and make me laugh.

More time passed and we entered into April.

I started thinking more and more about my classmates back in Nigeria. Were they done with exams yet? Had prom preparations started?

What about my classmates who had been in the plane crash? Mommy never talked about them. Had their wounds healed already? Were they already back on campus with everyone else? It seemed so.

The semester before the accident happened, Emeka Iheme, a classmate and one of my closest male friends, had asked me to be his date to senior prom, and I'd said yes. I'd been looking forward to having a great time with him at prom, not just because he would have been a fun date but also because prom would've been the last chance to hang out with everyone before we each disappeared down the different paths our lives would take us on after we graduated high school.

For a time after the crash, even while lying in my hospital bed in the TICU, I believed I'd be well enough to go back to school and complete my final semester with the rest of my graduating class. At the very least, I believed I'd make it back to Nigeria in time for prom in May.

During one of Mom's visits, I tentatively asked her if I could talk to my friends.

"Okay, let me go ask if I can call them," she said to me.

My eyes widened. "Really?" I could feel my heartbeat quickening. I hadn't spoken to any of them since the accident, or heard their voices, but they were constantly sending me letters and entertaining emails, which Mommy read to me. Oftentimes while I lay in bed, I'd wonder how they were all doing. I knew from their emails that they were worried about me.

Mommy left the TICU briefly, then returned with the phone on speaker. She raised it and held it close to my face.

"Kechi? Kechi, OMG! Are you okay? Kechi, it's Womiye. I miss you so much!"

"Kechina!"

I smiled, staring at the phone. Womiye and Atuora. I could picture them both leaning toward the phone, talking into the speaker. I could picture them as vividly as if I were seeing them in person.

"Hey guys," I said, and my voice came out much weaker than I'd intended, devoid of any of the excitement I was actually feeling.

"Aw, Kechina, you sound so tired!" That was Atuora. "Are you okay?"

"I'm okay. They said I'm getting better."

"Thank God!"

"Kechi, Kechi—will you be back for prom?" Womiye asked excitedly.

"Ah, she has to come back for prom now. You want Emeka to cry?" Atuora said.

I heard a chorus of laughter on their end and chuckled myself. "I don't know. I hope so."

We talked awhile longer, then we said our goodbyes and wrapped up the phone call.

As Mommy took the phone away, all the happiness and excitement I had been feeling during the call started to seep out of me, and I could feel myself getting emotional.

Mommy, ever sensitive to my every mood, immediately picked up on this. "Are you okay?" she asked me.

For some reason the question triggered me more, but I didn't want to worry her, so I said I was fine. She obviously didn't believe me, but I insisted.

I was not fine though. I was not fine at all.

Hearing my friends' voices, while it had made me happy, had also filled me with an overwhelming sense of longing. I imagined them on campus, hanging out together, laughing and fooling around like they did in my dreams, except in my dreams I was with them too. But in reality, they were making new memories, memories I wouldn't be part of because I was here in this hospital room, going through a harsh recovery from severe burns. I hadn't talked to Toke or anyone else on the phone yet, but my guess was that they were back in school too. At the very least, they were not as badly hurt as I was, right? I seemed to be the only one going through all this.

I started to really wonder about the severity of my injuries. I had third-degree burns over 65 percent of my body. I knew this in theory, but what did it mean in reality?

"Mommy, are my burns really bad?"

She sat down next to me and looked at me. "Yes. Very, very bad."

"Was it my whole body?"

"Everywhere except your tummy, back, and butt."

"Even my head, right?"

Her gaze turned apologetic. "Yes, sweetie, even your head. They had to cut your hair to treat the burns properly."

That was why I had bandages on every part of my body, I noted. And why my scalp itched so much.

"How does that make you feel, knowing that?" Mommy scooted closer to me.

"I don't feel anyhow," I said, shrugging a little. "I mean, I'm not the only one who survived. Though, I guess I'm the only one who got this badly injured . . ." I had obviously never in my wildest dreams expected something like this to happen to me but that was life, and here we were.

Mommy seemed a bit taken aback by my response, for some reason. Then she said, quite seriously, "Well, if it were me, I would definitely be more thankful if the plane I was in fell from the sky and I lived to talk about it."

I was confused at that. "What do you mean, *fell* from the sky?"

"Yes, the plane fell from the sky," Mommy said. "What did you think *plane crash* meant?"

I gaped at her like a fish. "I-I thought the plane crash-*landed*. How else would you explain people surviving? Oh my God!"

I would never ever have thought that the plane actually fell out of the sky. I'd never have imagined something so dramatic. It was incredible that there'd been only one fatality.

My entire perspective shifted completely at this new revelation, which, I'm guessing, was exactly what Mommy hoped would happen.

Yes, I was always lying down, unable to move my body by myself, I was always medicated, I was always in some measure of pain, and now, I was always itching.

But my plane dropped out of the sky, and I *survived*. That was something worth holding on to.

Still, I considered what Mommy said about the severity of my burns.

Something told me I would not see my friends for a long while.

More time passed and my new perspective all but vanished in the wake of my exponentially increased discomfort. I was swimming in an ocean of self-pity. The more I healed, the worse the itching and my mood became.

It was a miracle so many people had survived a plane crash, but why was my own miracle full of loopholes? Why was I the only one this badly hurt? Why did *anyone* have to be this badly injured?

My naturally chirpy and positive disposition that the trauma care nurses liked so much got a little buried under the physical and mental difficulties I was facing during this increasingly difficult phase of my healing.

I remember liking specific nurses over others. It wasn't always because they were nice to me. I liked some simply because they were professional and did their jobs without bias. But, of course, I loved the ones who were great at their jobs and went the extra mile to be nice too, the ones who seemed to actually *like* me, Kechi. I loved Hilda, Rochelle, Maureen, Primrose, Maria, Mr. X, Mr. Z (everyone called them that). These people liked my lively spirit, and like my mom, they believed my personality played a big role in my survival. They called me a fighter and I believed it.

But there were some nurses who didn't quite like me. They thought I was spoiled.

One night, in the middle of a particularly bad itching episode, a nurse came up to my bed and reprimanded me. "You are stubborn, and you don't listen," she said sharply. "Why are you always crying? Why are you always feeling sorry for yourself?"

She went on and on, saying that I was not grateful enough to the people who were just trying to do what was best for me as a patient. I used to rub my head against my pillow to ease the maddening itching on my scalp, and that night, she strapped my head down to my bed to keep me from moving it.

"It's for your own good," she said, and then she walked away.

I lay there, tears streaming down my face in silence.

Stubborn? I wasn't gonna deny that. I might have been a little stubborn whenever she was the one on duty because I knew she didn't like me.

Ungrateful though? That was so untrue. I was nothing but grateful. For my life, for those caring for me, for those praying for me. It was just so hard for me to express it right now.

Besides, I could be grateful for the care I was receiving *and* also be unhappy with my predicament. They weren't mutually exclusive.

I knew she couldn't *literally* relate to my situation, but I wasn't her first burn patient. Could she really not understand how hard recovery was? Healing was a double-edged sword. The more alive I was, the more solid my foothold in this world became. With each passing day, my chances of survival increased until my life was no longer hanging in the balance—it was perfectly rooted to this side of reality.

But what does it mean to be alive inside a functioning body? Your senses come back. And as my sensations returned, pain became more apparent. Pain is one of the strongest indicators of life. In the beginning, everything was kind of faint and vague, I couldn't really see or feel things clearly or for long.

Now? Now, I felt *everything*. Pain became a constant, unwelcome companion. But even then, absolutely *nothing* was worse than the itching.

This nurse who reprimanded me, she made it seem like my feelings were invalid, like my mood swings didn't make sense. She made it seem like she'd deal with things better if she were the one living my reality and living inside my body in the state that it was. I knew this wasn't true. I knew I was dealing with things the best way I could, the best way *anyone* would, as far as I was concerned.

So why was she making me feel like I was acting like a spoiled child?

Better still, even if I was acting spoiled, *so what*? If a sixteen-year-old third-degree burn survivor wasn't allowed to act spoiled once in a while, who in the world was?

I cried so much more after her scolding, but I tried to be quiet about it. I felt so guilty. Then, during one of Mommy's visits, that nurse was on duty, and Mommy, as usual, sensed I was in a mood.

"What's wrong, sweetie?"

I immediately burst into tears. I didn't really want to say what was wrong, but it was so hard to have a filter or keep things buried, so I told Mommy everything that happened that night.

Great, now I was a tattletale.

As expected, Mommy was livid. She couldn't believe anyone would try to make me feel bad for feeling bad, and the strapping thing horrified her. She was so upset that she went to talk to the lady's boss, who was the TICU matron.

I don't know how that exchange went exactly. All I know is

sometime after, Mommy returned with the matron, who apologized to me profusely on the other nurse's behalf.

"I'll make sure she never attends to you again, Kechi," she said, looking very upset. Her gaze turned sympathetic. "I can't imagine how hard this whole thing must be for you. I'm so proud of you for enduring this long."

The matron not only apologized, she *empathized*, and that just got me crying again.

That was really all I needed from people then. Not to be coddled, just to be *understood*. I knew it couldn't be easy at all, from a caregiver's perspective, to deal with a person in my state, be it medically or emotionally. But even so, it helped if they tried to see my side too. I *couldn't* pretend to be happy, no matter how much I wanted to be.

Try to imagine how you would feel if our roles were reversed. And try to treat me how you'd like to be treated. That's all.

Mommy later told me that the matron said this wasn't the first time someone had complained about that nurse's bedside manner.

She was fired from the hospital a week later.

Chapter Seven

The Progress

Further into April, things were starting to get increasingly frustrating.

No one was telling me anything about the other survivors and none of them seemed to be in the hospital with me, so I assumed that, aside from the JS2 boy, everyone was recovering from injuries that weren't as bad as mine. As far as I knew, I was the only one suffering like this. I was the only one in this sorry predicament.

Little did I know how right I was, just not in the context I would've predicted.

The hospital started using this dressing called ACTICOAT on my burns; it's a silver-coated, antimicrobial dressing that protects wound sites while also helping them heal. All that was great, except that ACTICOAT needs to be constantly dampened in order for the medication in it to activate. So every few hours without fail, a nurse would come by to wet my dressings, thereby leaving me a shivering mess.

I hated the ACTICOAT dressing with all my heart. As if things weren't bad enough! I was in pain and itching *all the time*, and now I was wet all over in the freezing temperatures of the TICU.

On top of it all, my eyelids started contracting as they healed and wouldn't let my eyes close properly anymore. This started to affect my vision and toppled me over the edge.

"Mommy, I can't see your face. I'm tired. Why is all this happening to me?"

It was a useless, rhetorical question. Of course I knew exactly why all this was happening. I was a third-degree burns survivor; I knew nothing about this healing process would be easy. What I was really asking was, Why was all this happening to me *at the same time*? The plane crash was one thing but the pain, the surgeries, and the discomfort that came with treatment were another; the *constancy* of it all was its own demon entirely!

Why did I have to experience *all* these symptoms *all* at once? Why couldn't they take turns? Why did I have to itch, hurt, freeze, and lose my vision simultaneously? There was only so much one human body could endure at a time, for God's sake!

"I'm so tired of the pain and the itching, and I'm constantly freezing because they keep wetting my bandages," I wailed to Mommy one day. "And now I can't see your face properly. It's not fair. I wanna see your face!"

Mommy tried her best to comfort me by reminding me of all the things that were going right. "Remember, you're only alive and able to even experience any of these things because God delivered you for me. And it's that very same God who has brought us this far, Kechi. I believe that He who was able to pull you out of that wreckage can pull you out of this pain and itching and everything else."

When?! I wanted to scream. When *will He do it? How bad does it have to get before He sees that I can't take it anymore?*

I wanted practical solutions to my problems, and so far, I wasn't getting any.

As if on cue, the nurse came by to wet my bandages again, and no matter how much I cried and complained, she insisted that it had to be done. So I just lay there bawling my eyes out and wailing "it's not fair" over and over while she did what she apparently *had* to do. I was so, so cold. I hated everything at that time, and my one source of joy, my mother, was being stripped from my vision.

Seriously, why did I have to go through all that?

I was soon scheduled for my first eyelid surgery, and on the morning of the surgery, Maya asked me if I would like to try sitting in a chair. I was uncertain. We'd been working on my mobility for about a month, moving my arms and legs and my neck every single day, but sitting in a chair?

"We can try," I told Maya, but I might as well have said yes because she got this determined look in her eye that I had grown wary of. Maya never took no for an answer.

It took quite a bit of preparation. My nurse had to disconnect all my monitors to prevent the wires from getting tugged at during the move. Then with Maya's help the nurse began to move me. Immediately everything hurt. I could also feel the onset of the itching, like clockwork. I had such little strength in my leg muscles that both Maya and the nurse on duty had to heavily support me through the entire process. After a lot of careful maneuvering and moving of wires, we were finally able to get me seated in the sanitized armchair next to my bed. After that, the nurse reconnected me to all my machines.

"You did it, Kechi!" Maya beamed at me triumphantly.

I smiled, trying to share her joy, but my body felt so strained at its joints, even after all my physical therapy. Every movement was still met with heavy resistance. My body was still raw and trying to patch itself up, so it didn't take much for my thin, newly formed skin to break and bleed in certain areas. Plus, the itching was getting worse, and that never failed to spiral my mood downward.

Mommy came in for visiting, and as soon as she saw me sitting, her face lit up, she was so happy. "Kechi, you're sitting! You're sitting for the first time in four months!"

"I know," I said with the most genuine smile I'd sported all morning. "I'm itchy though."

Mommy launched into itch duty as soon as she set her things down, much to my relief. Honestly, left to me she'd help me scratch forever, but I knew that the itching feeling never quite went away, no matter how much we kept at it, so once I felt like it was at a stage I could endure, I would tell her I was okay, even though it really wasn't. Sometimes I'd have her on itch duty for over an hour before I felt any measure of relief. It must've been so exhausting for her, but she never showed it.

Later that day I had my eyelid surgery, and they taped my eyes shut while my eyelids healed.

It was the strangest, most disconcerting feeling, to completely lose access to one of my senses, albeit temporarily. For someone who already had very little sense of her surroundings, this was extremely difficult for me to adjust to. I had a newfound respect for those who were born blind, though I knew this was hardly an adequate comparison to their experience.

I couldn't see Mommy's face for a while longer. That really bummed me out, but I tried to remind myself that this was temporary, and that when I was finally able to open my eyes, I'd be able to see her even more clearly. Hopefully.

Ugh, it was all just a lot, honestly. I was here having eyelid surgery, while my friends were chilling in school.

"You're really taking this surgery well, Kechi," Mommy said when she came to visit the next day.

I attempted a smile, and in that moment, I was grateful she couldn't see my eyes. If we'd made any eye contact right then, I'd definitely have started crying in self-pity again. For some reason, my tears were easily triggered in Mommy's presence. I guess it was because she was someone I felt safe enough to vent my true feelings to, and those days, with the pain and the stupid itching, I was feeling very sorry for myself.

On that note, I was also grateful she couldn't hear my thoughts.

"I expected you to be way more impatient about not being able to see," Mommy said. She sounded pleased, which cheered me up.

"The anesthetist explained stuff to me and told me what to expect," I said.

A lot of people came to visit me during that time. I knew it wasn't easy for anyone to see me in such a state, so I appreciated every single one of them.

————— ✑ —————

After a few more days, the bandages finally came off my eyes.

They were quite sensitive to light for the first few hours, but only because they'd been covered for days. After a while they adjusted and I could see Mommy's face. No blurriness or anything! For a little while, it felt like all was right with my world.

I was propped up in bed, and Mommy was sitting next to me as usual. In that position, I was finally able to get a good look at my body for the first time.

I couldn't move much or lift or bend my head, so I just darted my eyes over every part of me I could see and . . . wow. I really was bandaged head to foot.

From my lower hands to my stomach to my thighs and legs . . .

My eyes zipped back up to my right thigh, and I felt my face squeeze into a frown.

"Mom. What's wrong with my leg?"

"What do you mean?"

"My leg, over here on my thigh . . ." I gingerly brushed over my right thigh with my hand, and my eyes widened because I realized I wasn't imagining what I saw.

I started freaking out. "There's a hole in my leg! Why's there a hole in my leg, what is this?" Panicked tears formed immediately and started to fall.

"Kechi sweetie, calm down, okay? It's okay, it's—"

"Mommy, there's a hole in my leg!" I wailed with tears running down my face. How was it okay? There was a literal hole, a *crater*, in my thigh, as if all the flesh and tissue and muscle in that area had been vaporized, and she was telling me it was okay?

I didn't understand what I was looking at, and I kept brushing my hand over the mighty dip in the middle of my thigh as the tears spilled out.

Was I missing a bone in my thigh or something? They'd told me I didn't lose any bones during the accident, so what was going on?

"Kechi, look at me." Mommy placed her gloved hand over mine. "Look at me," she repeated firmly.

I knew she would wait until I did what she asked, so I looked up and met her gaze.

"Nothing is wrong with your leg, love," she said in a reassuring tone I was wont to trust. "You remember the accident was very bad, right? Well, some areas on your body burned worse than others—like your thigh—so the doctors had to debride the area."

"Debride?"

Mommy explained that this was when the surgeons scraped off dead or infected skin cells and grafted new skin over the area in the hopes that the new skin would merge with the part of the body it was grafted onto or so that the skin would "take."

They had done this on different parts of my body so far, but this particular debridement had been a big one, performed on the front part of my right thigh, thus creating a "hole" there, as I'd called it.

I stopped crying at some point during Mommy's explanation. By the time she was through, I was less distressed.

"So . . . they basically had to remove most of the skin and muscle in my thigh 'cause it was infected," I said.

"Exactly, so that your leg could heal properly."

I looked down at my thigh again. "But will it ever go back to normal? Like, all the stuff they took out, will my thigh ever fill out again?"

Mommy hesitated, and that right there told me that I shouldn't hold my breath on that front.

Having moved past the initial shock of this new discovery, the thought of my leg remaining this way didn't worry me all that much anymore, especially when I learned that it was either that or potentially lose my entire leg to infection. But the bitterness inside of me was growing, and I started to cry.

"Why did all this have to happen, Mommy? Why did it have to happen to me? My friends are all in school, and I'm just here, suffering."

Mommy gave me this strange, sad look. I couldn't quite interpret it.

"Kechi," she finally said, "in the grand scheme of things, it's a small price to pay for your life, isn't it? You're alive."

She was right. I knew she was right.

But I wasn't the only one who survived, I was just the only one who survived with all these complications. I absolutely did not wish this fate on anyone else. But why was I the only one this badly hurt? If everyone else was more or less okay, why couldn't I have been okay too? I just wanted to go back to school and continue normal life with Toke, Yimi, Womiye, and everyone else. I wanted to go to prom!

I cried and cried, and Mommy did her best to comfort me, as she always did. When she returned for the night visit, I had more questions for her about the day of the accident.

Mommy told me about how Shell, the oil company, had completely taken over my medical care from the very beginning, specifically through the efforts of the managing director of Shell, Nigeria, who, incidentally, was my classmate Angela Omiyi's father.

"You know," Mommy said, "after we landed here in Johannesburg, the ambulance broke down on the way to the hospital."

I gave Mommy an incredulous look. "*What?*"

"I kid you not," Mommy said. "I just laughed and prayed silently. I refused to give the devil the satisfaction of seeing me panic. The driver had to park on the side of the road, and I sat inside with the nurse and doctor while we waited for another ambulance to arrive."

Wow. I couldn't imagine how scary that must've been for her.

The time finally came for me to try walking for the first time since the accident.

The mission was to get up on my feet and walk—with Maya's assistance, of course—from my armchair to the sink in the TICU, and then back to my bed.

The moment Maya got me standing, it already seemed like an impossible feat to me. First, merely standing was so exhausting. Second, I couldn't place my feet flat against the floor without bending over. My natural inclination was to stand on my toes. I guess my feet, which pointed downward when I lay in bed, had sort of adjusted to that position. With every step Maya had to remind me to walk heel first. It was so strange. What was once so normal now felt so unnatural to me.

With Maya's help, I made it halfway to the sink, which was about six footsteps from my bed. But I was too exhausted to go any farther.

Luckily for me, Maya seemed impressed with that much, so she walked me back to my chair and sat me down.

"Good job, Kechi!"

I heard clapping and looked up in surprise to see the TICU nurses and staff applauding my efforts. I smiled even wider, feeling encouraged.

It occurred to me at that point how much we take for granted as human beings. Walking is one of the most mundane, ordinary things a human body can typically do. A mindless motor function. But there I was, learning how to walk again at sixteen.

"So we're going to be doing this every other day from now on, okay?" Maya said while she and my nurse settled me into the chair once more.

My exhausted smile disappeared.

Crap.

My mood improved when Mommy arrived later that morning, and I told her I had walked halfway to the sink.

"Kechi, you're so strong," she said, gushing over me. "I wish I'd been here. I am so proud of you!"

Hearing Mommy say those words to me made it all worth it.

Truthfully, my attitude toward physical therapy never quite changed, even as I got better and better, although it did get more tolerable when Mommy was allowed to help out.

There was a time when I was moved to an isolation room because

I had developed a contagious infection and had to be kept away from other trauma patients so as not to spread it. One of those days Maya let Mommy help me up from my chair and walk me to the front of the room and back to my bed.

I was so thrilled to be held by Mommy after all those months of her just touching my shoulder. The absolute *best* part of that moment was that, after we got back to stand beside my bed, we were allowed to hug! It was our very first hug since the accident happened and neither one of us wanted to let go. I will never forget how it felt to be in my mother's gentle embrace that day. It was the best day of my life.

Another interesting situation popped up while I was in the isolation room. The surgeons had just finished surgery on my hands and fingers, so they covered my hands in ACTICOAT, then wrapped them in the standard bandages and wheeled me back to my room.

The trauma nurse in charge of me the next day was named Marie. She unwrapped one of my hands and shook her head in disapproval. It turned out that after my hand surgery the day before, my doctors had wrapped my whole hand in one long strip of ACTICOAT, probably for convenience, rather than wrapping the fingers in individual strips.

"If we leave it like this, your fingers will fuse together and heal that way," Marie said. "Then you'll have to do another surgery in the future to separate your fingers individually."

I was highly alarmed.

Marie decided to redo my dressing by rewrapping each finger individually.

Mommy was so upset that the surgeons weren't the ones thinking about these sorts of things, but Marie was quick to defend them.

"It's just faster for them," she explained. "When you have thirty surgeries a day, you don't really have time to think of the details."

When the time came for the dressing change, Mommy had to leave.

Marie wore her protective gear and laid an antibacterial sheet over the top of my blanket.

"I'll give you morphine and Dormicum now so you can—"

"No, please," I cut in, "I'd rather have it after we're done, if that's okay."

"All right." With that, she sat next to me and wet the ACTI-COAT to aid in the removal process.

I braced myself as she carefully started to unwrap it. The material stuck to my flesh like a Band-Aid, drenched or not, and pulled skin loose, causing it to bleed in areas. Removing it was such an agonizing and slow process.

Once the ACTICOAT was finally off, my hand was fully exposed.

And I saw that what we feared had already started to happen.

My fingers were clumped together, and my hand looked like a skinless lump of sticky, raw flesh. It was crazy to me that this was supposed to be a human hand—*my* hand. Looking at it as it was, I couldn't imagine any future when it would function as one ever again.

It was time to separate each finger. I took in a shuddering breath.

Should I just take my pain meds now?

No.

Considering what I was about to go through, I knew I would appreciate having my pain meds administered when it was all over. In my eyes, the morphine and Dormicum, which I was now getting only when it was deemed necessary, were the reward for my endurance.

Marie started the grueling process of separating each of my fingers, and the pain was infinitely more excruciating than I imagined. It felt like she was slowly peeling skin off my fingers, one by one.

I gritted my teeth each time she started pulling two fingers apart, telling myself to remember it was for my own good, that if I ever wanted to use my hands properly again, this was what we had to do. I blinked away ever-flowing tears and told myself I'd dealt with worse. But I hadn't. And without any pain meds in my system, I was feeling every single thing.

Marie had to stick strips of ACTICOAT between each finger once she'd separated them. ACTICOAT hurt to remove, but the pain when it came back in contact with my exposed flesh was even more violent.

"Almost done with this hand. You're doing so great, Kechi . . ."

I could barely hear her, I was in so much pain. I was so exposed and everything was so fresh and raw. And whenever my nerves reacted to pain, they tightened up and magnified the pain further.

After a long hour, both hands were rewrapped and redressed. I could tell Marie was extremely happy we had done this, and I was grateful that she seemed to care so much. She administered my medications, and I slipped into grateful unconsciousness before Mommy returned.

Chapter Eight

The Truth

Up until the day I was told the entire truth of the accident, I genuinely had not considered the possibility that anyone else had died. After Mommy told me about the JS2 boy, I closed the book on the topic of fatalities. One was already far too much.

I was still wallowing in self-pity more often than not, especially when my itching spiked. I could tell that Mommy was getting increasingly worried by the way I carried on and on about my plight, but I couldn't help how I felt.

That fateful day I learned the truth started pretty nicely, nicer than my past few days, at least. It was mid-April, approximately four months into my stay at Milpark.

It felt a little tense in the TICU that morning. Visiting hours hadn't started, so Mommy wasn't there yet.

A man suddenly walked into the TICU. I recognized him as the male equivalent of my trauma counselor, Cherie.

I liked Cherie. She was so sweet, and her cheery presence and melodic voice was always welcome in the otherwise monotonous, understandably serious atmosphere of the TICU.

Sometimes this other counselor was the one who came by to

check on me. He was a good guy too, but I didn't bond with him quite like I did with Cherie.

The counselor came up to the foot of my bed and drew my curtains closed behind him, which I found a bit odd. The nurses only did that when it was time for one of my daily procedures, like a dressing change or physiotherapy.

He turned and smiled at me. "How are you doing today, Kechi? How are you feeling?"

He and I talked for a little while and the weirdness faded away, only to return again when he lingered on after our chat naturally ended. He sat down next to me, looking like the weight of the world was on his shoulders.

Why did I get the strong feeling that weight was about to be transferred to mine?

My heart began to thump quickly in my chest.

"Kechi," he started. "Remember when your mom told you"—he paused for a moment before continuing—"about the boy who died in the plane crash? The JS2 boy?"

"Yes," I said warily, and I briefly wondered why he was bringing that horrible day up right now. As we looked at each other, I gradually realized where this may be going.

My pulse jumped painfully. I could already feel my pounding heart clenching like a fist. "What happened?"

The man hesitated. "There were actually only two survivors from the plane crash. And you're one of them."

My heart was racing. My blood pumping fast, too fast. "What do you mean? What do you mean by that?"

"The accident was really bad, Kechi."

I stared at him in utter confusion. He wasn't making any sense. What did he mean, only two people survived? What exactly did that mean? That couldn't be. It wasn't possible. There was no way *everyone else* died, like how, how could something like that happen? I just did not understand. I *refused* to understand.

I kept waiting for him to say something else, something more. Something *different*. I kept waiting for him to say *anything* else, but he just sat there silently, with this grave expression on his face. I felt like my world was spinning, sinking.

No, this can't be! No! No, no, no, no, no, no, no—

My vision blurred, my throat started to hurt, and I realized I was screaming and yelling. Suddenly, Mommy was by my bedside, holding me gently.

I quickly turned my wild, glassy gaze to her. Maybe she would give me some answers that made sense. Mommy would tell me the truth. She always did. I couldn't trust anyone else.

I looked at her, silently pleading with her to tell me the counselor had been lying.

But all Mommy did was shake her head at me, and her eyes, oh God, her eyes were so full of pain and a deep sorrow that I couldn't describe . . . and that was when I knew this was real.

I lost all my breath, like the wind had been violently punched out of my lungs.

"No." My eyes started to sting as I shook my head at my mother. "No, it's a lie, it's a lie! Mommy, what do you mean, what do you mean, now? What do you mean?" I wept and wailed. Hard. Just harsh, painful, gut-wrenching tears that had me heaving and coughing.

This wasn't happening, this couldn't be true. Mommy said that only one person had died! This wasn't adding up!

I felt like a heavy mass was pressing down on my chest. I couldn't breathe, and the tears refused to stop. My machines were going haywire, and my nurse came to try to calm me down. But I couldn't be calmed, I just couldn't. I could hear Mommy begging me to listen to the nurse, but how? I didn't know what to do with myself. I wanted to throw myself off my bed, but every movement exhausted me. Still I wept. I cried harder than I have ever cried in my life that day. My heart had simply shattered.

I thought about everyone. Chinenye, Waji, Chuka and his two sisters—all my friends' faces flashed across my eyes, as if someone were flipping through a photo book behind my eyelids.

"Toke?" I looked up at my mom, eyes wide with horror, silently begging her to tell me this was all a mistake "Mommy, you're telling me that Toke is dead?" I started to shake my head again, breathing hard as fresh tears formed and fell down the sides of my face. "Toke can't be dead! How can she be dead? We were right next to each other! I held her hand!" I suddenly remembered how small her hand was as I held on to it tightly while our plane fell from the sky. I remembered her eyes, wide with fear and confusion. Then I remembered her mom. I remembered her brother who loved her so much, and my heart, God, the pain was like a stab directly into my heart. I couldn't take it. "Mommy, Toke . . . Toke!" I wailed and wailed her name.

As Mommy tried to calm me down, I noticed she had started to cry too, and I stopped moving immediately.

Mommy is crying?

Something about that completely stunned me. My absolute shock at seeing my mother's tears actually stopped mine for a moment.

"Mommy, don't," I heard myself say. "You can't cry. I won't be able to handle it if you cry. Please, you can't cry." How could Mommy cry? She was my rock, my comfort, my strength. She was the strongest person I knew. She was all I had to hold on to. If *she* cried, if *she* broke down too, then there really would be no hope for me. As selfish as it may sound, I absolutely couldn't bear to see her cry. To me, her tears meant that all hope was indeed lost, and seeing as she was my sole source of hope in those increasingly hopeless circumstances, I couldn't bear to see her show any weakness whatsoever.

Mommy immediately wiped her tears and nodded at me reassuringly. "Okay, baby, it's okay," she said solemnly. "I'm okay. Don't worry about me."

I felt my body relax a bit when I saw she'd stopped crying, and right on cue, my own tears returned in full force. I cried and cried, wailing Toke's name. I kept shaking my head because there was no way. There was no way all those people—all my friends, my classmates, all those students—there was no way they could all be gone. This kind of thing just didn't happen.

That day, I cried myself to complete exhaustion and fell into a fitful sleep after the nurse gave me my meds.

I woke up hours later with an extremely heavy heart and within seconds of opening my eyes, I remembered the nightmare that my reality had become with the news of the accident. I remembered my friends' faces. I remembered Toke.

"Toke . . ." I felt a fresh wave of tears fall as the grief took over again.

Mommy reached for my shoulder. "Kechi . . ." The pain in her voice was audible.

"Mommy, she was so small and sweet. It's not fair . . . It's not fair, Mommy." I closed my eyes and wept for hours.

Jesus! Jesus!

For the first few days after I was told the truth, all I could think about was Toke.

Why was I so fixated on her? I didn't think it was just because she had been one of my closest friends; hers was literally the last face I saw in that malfunctioning plane before everything went dark. It was wild to me that that darkness had been the end for her. Our last conversation had been about our futures . . . and now she didn't have one.

How could life be this way? Who would've ever known that the last time I looked at Toke's face would be the last time ever?

It all felt so abrupt. I couldn't understand how I'd never see her again. Just like that, she was gone forever? All those people were gone forever?

So, this was what death was like. It was so mean, so harsh. So rude in the way it interrupted life and just . . . *snatched* people away, without regard for anything or anyone. It didn't care that you weren't done living, and when it happened, those left behind just had to deal with the fallout somehow. There was no other choice.

I could only pray that it had happened quickly and painlessly for Toke, for everyone who had died. I prayed with my entire soul that they had all transitioned seamlessly from this world into the next, without feeling any pain or suffering. After all, I couldn't remember the exact moment of impact from the plane crash. All I remembered was the moment right before, and then a few moments after.

Maybe it had been that way for them too. Maybe in that in-between . . . lay death.

I prayed so.

I struggled a lot, mentally and psychologically, after learning the truth of the plane crash.

I insisted on knowing everything I could about it, how the other parents were coping, how the other students were coping, how the country was coping after such a tragedy. Mommy told me it was all any newspaper had talked about since it happened. I asked her to show me, and she brought a newspaper to her next visit.

The first thing I saw was the school yearbook pictures of all my classmates who had been on the plane with me. The second I saw the first familiar face, Chinenye's, I broke down again. It was so agonizing to see. My classmates' yearbook pictures had become their obituaries.

Some nights after the revelation, I lay in bed, staring up at the ceiling and pondering about the accident and about God.

I had been learning so much about Him through Mommy and the rest of my family all through my time in Milpark. They said He was a good God, loving and kind, and He extended His grace to all those who loved Him.

But how did a good God let something like this happen?

I thought about Waji and Chinenye specifically, two brilliant people who had consistently excelled academically in all their years at LJC. Chinenye, especially, was such a good girl in school. An exemplary student. A devout Catholic. It was only just occurring to me, now that I thought about her, how much I actually admired her as a person. As far as I knew, she never gave any trouble to fellow students or teachers, never gave her parents cause for concern, rarely had detention; in my eyes, she was an all-rounder. An ideal to strive toward.

I, on the other hand, was an average student who cared entirely too much about her physical appearance, constantly had detention, and was no stranger to confrontation with authority. My Christian faith was a work in progress, more so now, in fact. Yet someone as good as Chinenye was dead and there I was. It just made no sense to me. Mommy said that God was fair and just. Where exactly was the fairness in this?

It wasn't that I felt like Chinenye deserved to survive more than I did, or vice versa, but I felt like if God could save someone as flawed as me, why not *also* save someone as good as Chinenye?

I shed silent tears as I thought about my friends. I couldn't wrap my head around the fact that they were no longer alive. And look at me, thinking they were all in school! I felt so thoughtless and ungrateful. I had complained so much about my predicament, thinking that no one else was going through what I was going through.

I remembered Mommy's words: *"You're only alive and able to even experience any of these things because God delivered you for me."*

I cried even harder, now understanding why Mommy said those things. To go through what I was going through, one would have to be alive in the first place. I had complained so much, not even knowing how privileged I was to be lying here!

I, lying battered and burned in this hospital bed, was the "lucky" one.

The irony cut into me, piercing deep into my soul like a jagged knife.

Oh, God . . .

I forced myself to take deep, steadying breaths and sought comfort in my mother's words. What would she say if she were here?

"God's ways are not our ways, Kechi. We cannot know His mind, but we pray for the Holy Spirit to grant us a greater understanding of who He is through His Word, the Bible, and through His revelations to us, His children."

Greater understanding . . . So that meant I couldn't use my human understanding of the concept of fairness to decide what was and wasn't fair to God. Okay, fine.

But, I thought to myself, *if God loves us as much as it says in His Word, He should want the best for us, right? So how could He allow so many people, so many children, to die? He is God! There's nothing He cannot do, no mountain He cannot move, so how was it that He didn't move this one? Because that's what we ask for when we pray, isn't it? For Him to move mountains for us, to intervene whenever He has to so that His will is carried out in our lives.*

I realized right then that I had reached a crossroads in my understanding of exactly who and what God is.

Was it in God's will, then, for all those parents to lose their precious children? For all those families to lose their loved ones? Was it part of some "grand plan"? Wouldn't that contradict everything the Bible says about God?

At this point I started to wonder, *Does He even exist?*

What if life is all just up to chance? I wondered frantically. *What if . . . what if there is no such thing as "God" and life is just a die toss? What if—*

My train of thought was cut short as I unwittingly thought back to all the humanly unexplainable things that my family and I had experienced since the accident. The stranger who found my body in the debris of the plane crash. The miraculous way Shell, Nigeria, stepped in and took over my treatment in its entirety. My ambulance unexplainably malfunctioning on the way to Milpark Hospital after my mom and I landed in Johannesburg. The music I heard and memorized in my comatose state. The strange, spiritual dreams . . . Too many incredible things had happened since the day of the accident for me to deny the existence of the supernatural.

Deep in my heart, I *wanted* to believe God existed. My very life should be proof enough of the existence of a power too great to be merely human. I had experienced more miracles in those past few months than in all sixteen years of my life to convince me of this.

But that confused me even further, because why then would such an allegedly good being allow something this terrible to happen? *Why do bad things happen to good people?*

I had all these questions about God, but I didn't want to bring them to Him directly. I barely knew Him, clearly.

I knew one person who knew Him well though. My mother. So, I decided I would direct these troubles to her. I desperately needed her to intercede for me, just as she'd been doing all those months prior. I desperately needed answers.

The nurse in charge of me that night suddenly hovered over me, pulling me away from my thoughts. "Time for your dressing change, honey."

I had a love-hate relationship with this part of my day because though it usually brought on a lot of pain, it also meant I would get my addictive drug combo of morphine and Dormicum, which ultimately meant sleep. I wanted nothing more than to escape into dreamless sleep, where my dark, complicated thoughts couldn't find me.

The nurse efficiently changed my dressings, then changed the bedsheets as well, which they somehow managed to do with me in the bed. It was interesting. They'd basically roll me over to one side and hold me in that position while they stripped off the old sheets and laid the new one down on the exposed side of the bed, then they'd roll me to the other side and pull the old sheets completely off, while pulling over the new ones to cover the newly exposed side.

By the time she was done, I felt roughly handled and everything hurt.

"You did great, love. I'll get your drugs now, then you can sleep."

Soon, an intense surge of lethargy overcame me. My eyelids grew heavy, and I sank into unconsciousness within seconds. My last coherent thought was of my dead classmates.

When I woke up, I could feel pain stirring as well, even before I had a chance to open my eyes. My whole body stung, and my nerves felt overly sensitive. I hadn't woken up with this much pain in a while, so needless to say, I was very upset. Moreover, my friends and my faith conundrum still weighed heavily on my mind. By the time Mommy arrived later that morning, I was sitting in the chair by my bed.

"Oh, you're sitting today, Kechi!"

It always made Mommy happy to see me in my chair. I knew this and usually it would make me smile, but I was not having the best morning. I still had a lot on my mind.

Mommy set her things down and looked at me, and as always, she immediately sensed something was wrong. "Are you okay, sweetie?"

I felt my mouth quiver as I shook my head no.

Mommy sat in front of me and leaned forward with a look of deep concern on her pretty face. "What's wrong?"

I took a deep breath and tried to coherently vocalize all my ponderings from the previous night. "I don't feel like I'm making any progress, Mommy. I've been doing well lately, but today I woke up in so much pain. And I keep thinking about my friends who died. I just don't understand. There's nothing special about me. I'm such a bad student, my grades aren't great. I'm always on detention. But Chinenye was such a good girl. Like, she was *such* a good person." I could hear my voice start to shake. "How can someone like her die? It makes no sense. God makes no sense. It's not fair, Mommy, it's just not *fair*." I was sobbing before I could finish, because that was what I was truly struggling with: the *unfairness* of it all. That was what was really at the crux of this entire situation.

It wasn't fair. None of this was fair.

I was just another human being. I didn't do anything special.

I knew that I didn't regret being alive. How could I regret a life that made my mother so happy? As painful as each day was, I was fully aware of the fact that I had been given a second chance to live, and I was grateful for it because it allowed me to see Mommy again. It just hurt me so much that no other classmate had been given that same chance, not even those I felt were more deserving of it than myself.

I didn't want to die in their place. I didn't feel like I didn't deserve to survive. But if even *I* survived, why didn't they? Why didn't we *all* survive?

"Kechi . . ." Mommy sounded so sad, and that made me feel even worse because I didn't ever want to be the cause of her sadness. All I wanted, all I lived for, was her smile.

"Kechi, listen to me," Mommy said, and I looked up at her with hope in my heart, knowing from experience that her words might offer some level of comfort and wisdom.

"It's not about who deserves life more or less, or who was a better or worse human being," she said. "Those are standards and rules created by us humans, so we can't use them to determine the way God moves. You're right. You aren't more special than any of those precious children who were on that plane with you. We may never know why things happened the way they did, but one thing we can be sure of is that you are alive because of God's grace."

"But . . . I don't feel like I've earned that grace," I whispered through my tears.

Mommy smiled understandingly and shook her head. "None of us can earn it, my love. It's something He freely gives us anyway. And I promise you that the parents of all those kids, even in the midst of their grief, are so thankful for that grace upon your life. They send prayers for you every day, and they send me messages asking about you."

My broken heart trembled upon hearing this. I don't know why, but the thought that the parents of the kids who had passed away were praying for me somehow made me feel a little better. I didn't expect them to resent me, but I had to admit that I had considered the possibility. I wouldn't have blamed them if they had either. I would've understood.

But Mommy said they were praying for me. Asking about me. Rooting for me.

I could feel something inside me soften.

"We live in a messed-up world, where messed-up things happen," Mommy continued. "But I want you to focus on the blessing and miracle that is your life and focus on getting better. Because, sweetie, that's what every single person out there is doing. We're all grieving for the lives that were lost, and are so, so thankful for the two lives that were saved."

Mommy and I kept talking for the rest of her visit. She told me that Nigerians all over the world were reaching out to our family with prayers and well-wishes. She showed me pictures of the crash site from a newspaper, and I saw that the plane had actually smashed into pieces and exploded. I marveled anew at how miraculous it was that two people had come out of such an experience alive.

Mommy said other LJC parents were hanging on to my life because it was the one light in all the darkness brought on by the tragedy. By the end of our conversation, I was feeling so much better about everything. Moreover, our talk had opened my eyes to a new perspective.

What if I found out the reason for the crash, the reason why all but two people had died in that accident? What then? What reason could I ever be given that would make me go, "Ah, makes sense"? What reason would ever satisfy me or justify the loss of so many lives?

Mommy suggested that we wrap up our conversation with a prayer and I agreed wholeheartedly. I felt all the love she had for me as I listened to her pray. She prayed for God to take away all my discomforts, all my worries and stress. She reminded Him that there was nothing He could not do, speaking of Abraham and how He gave him a child at an age that seemed humanly impossible, and of Noah and his family, who He delivered from the flood.

"Let's do what Grandma taught you, okay?" she said to me after praying, and I nodded. When Grandma came, she taught me how to meditate through controlled breathing and squeezing and releasing different parts of my body from my feet to my shoulders, one at a time.

I took a deep breath and squeezed my toes as hard as I could manage, then released my breath as I relaxed my toes.

"Kechi, I want you to keep your eyes closed and imagine a bucket," Mommy said as I continued to breathe and squeeze. "I want you to fill that bucket with everything causing you pain: your grief over your friends, your sleeplessness, all your doubts and fears. Just fill that bucket and imagine yourself walking up to the cross and dropping it at the feet of Jesus. Then just walk away. He told us to cast all our cares onto Him. I want you to do that right now."

I did as she asked and imagined the bucket. I imagined putting everything that was hurting me inside; my pain, my itching, my grief, my insomnia, my confusion about my faith. Gradually, I felt all the tension leave my body. I don't even remember when I fell asleep. That night, another miracle happened: I slept better than I had in a very long time, without the assistance of any medication.

I woke up a few minutes before Mommy arrived the next morning, feeling very refreshed and well rested. I had clearly slept well, and the heaviness I'd been feeling in my heart the night before was lightened.

I was a bit awed. Was it the conversation or the prayer that followed that had allowed me to sleep so well?

Mommy finally arrived and seeing me awake surprised her.

"Someone's feeling better," she observed with a hesitant smile.

"Mommy," I said to her once she'd set her things down. "I slept so well!"

I watched her smile bloom. "Really?"

"Yes." I looked down and put my hand over my chest. "I woke up feeling so much better, almost like a weight was lifted from my chest." I looked up at her and smiled. "I love you."

———— ✑ ————

After my meaningful conversation with Mommy, I had hoped I would finally be on a surer path toward recovery and the discovery of my faith.

As the days passed, however, the heaviness and confusion in my heart returned. The insomnia returned as well. I was starting to think that the relief I'd felt after our talk might have come from finally sharing my burdens with someone who understood.

Honestly, God still very much confused me, or the concept of Him.

All I truly wanted was to see Him the way my mother saw Him. Or more specifically, to experience God like she had.

My mother's faith in and love for God is beautiful. It is a gentle strength within her. I can say without a doubt that no matter what she faces on this earth, her belief in Christ is the one thing that is utterly unshakable. For goodness' sake, she said she loved Jesus more than she loved me. As far as I'm concerned, it doesn't get more unshakable than that.

Her faith was enough to create a derived kind of faith within me. Honestly, everything I believed about God thus far was what I had learned to believe through my mother's own steadfast belief, her and her family's.

But what did *I* believe, personally? For myself?

Long before the accident, my beliefs were something that was decided for me. I simply believed whatever my parents believed. We used to attend this place called the Grail Movement, when I was much younger, then when I was about eight, my family became born-again Christians.

My mother didn't change dramatically or anything like that. She was as loving, sweet, and kind as always, with the same gentle countenance. She prayed more often, though, and started taking church more seriously, so from then, being a Christian to me became going to church and attending fellowships with the family. I learned about God from my family, from church, even from elementary school where Christian Religious Studies was an obligatory part of the Nigerian curriculum up until high school.

That's where I learned that God was the source of all the things that most societies accept as just and moral and good. So, as I grew older, my approach to faith and Christianity was that—it made sense. Being a Christian made sense.

Then the plane crash happened.

After that, aside from my strange dreams, I still didn't have any definitive experiences that would serve to convince or convict me as a Christian. Dreams can easily be rationalized away, and I didn't want something as fickle as that to be the only proof I had that God was real. Mommy told me God had saved me from death on the day of the accident. Pretty much everyone who came to visit me told me the same thing. Because I had been raised Christian, I accepted this as fact. I knew it certainly wasn't anything *I* did that had saved me.

But I didn't have any *actual* proof God existed. Even after something as monumental as a plane crash had happened, He hadn't shown Himself to me in a way that would give me undeniable proof of His existence.

I wanted God to show Himself to me in a way that I simply could not deny. Until that happened, I looked to my mother for the strength I needed to survive, while she looked to God for her own strength. It wasn't ideal, but so far it had been working for me. It was a step in the right direction in my search for God.

Then I was told the truth about the accident. Everyone but me and one other lady died. Over *one hundred* people had died. Sixty of them *children*.

Whatever I believed about God so far had been shattered by this fact, and now I was left sorting through the pieces, trying to make some sense of them.

I was so confused.

How come He didn't save everyone else? I just couldn't escape this one question. I lied sometimes, I did things I wasn't supposed to, I disobeyed my parents a lot, I watched movies I wasn't supposed to in secret.

But I was sure everyone who had been on that plane could've said the exact same. No one is perfect. But clearly God wasn't looking for perfection. So, if being a saint is not an important criterion to God when saving people from death, what was? Was there even one? I was really beginning to believe that things happened at random in this world. If that was the case, where exactly did God come into play?

The Bible says that God is all-knowing. That implies He knew of the accident before it happened, right? So, how come He didn't simply stop it from happening?

My mind was whirling with countless questions about faith that I found very difficult to voice, even to my beloved mother. I feared it would break her heart to know the true direction of my thoughts. I feared my unbelief, or my struggle with belief at the very least, would throw a spoke in the wheels of her own faith, and I couldn't afford for my mom of all people to harbor any doubts of her own about Jesus, no matter how unlikely that sounded. I certainly couldn't be the cause of any such doubts, in any case.

From then on, I started to ask more questions about God and Jesus, little by little. As time passed, my questions grew more persistent.

"Being a Christian obviously doesn't exempt you from the pain and suffering of this world," I said to my mom one day.

She nodded. "Bad things seem to happen to everyone evenly, good or bad, Christian or not."

"But then, if believing in God doesn't improve your chances of surviving in this world or protect you from dying before your time, then what sets Christians apart? What's the appeal of the faith?"

"We don't believe in God because of the things He can do for us, love. We believe in Him because of who He is. Simple. Through His Word, we draw closer to Him."

"Why?"

"To learn what He expects of us, His creation. He wants us to love others the way He loves us. He wants us to live as good people. The way we live is far more important than death."

I thought about the accident, all those lives lost. "But death is scary, Mommy."

"True," she agreed. Her demeanor changed and she hesitated, like she wasn't sure about her next words, but then she went on. "When I thought you were gone, after crying my eyes out, I prayed, right there on that runway. I thanked God for giving me sixteen beautiful years with you, and I told Him that He better make sure I lived a good life so that when I died, I would see you again in heaven."

I stared at Mommy, speechless and in awe of her.

Prayed? Thanked God?

How could anyone *thank* God after losing their child?

My eyes welled up with unshed tears as I kept staring at my mother. What kind of strength did that require? What kind of *faith*? I just didn't understand. It didn't seem possible or realistic to me.

"We can't live in constant fear of death, or we will never truly live. Whenever death comes for us, what matters is the state of our souls in that moment."

There was a chance I would never understand all this, and it pained me to realize that I'd have to learn to live with that. Still, my lessons about God and faith continued throughout my time in South Africa. Everything Mommy taught me about God sounded so pleasing and filled me with a hope that was quickly and easily dashed by my predicament.

If He was as great as everyone would have me believe, why wouldn't He at least take away my itching? I was so *done* with the itching. Some days were better than others, but it was always there, like little ants crawling right under the surface of my sensitive skin, responding to the slightest agitation. Grandma's meditation method actually worked sometimes, but most times I was too far gone to put it into effect.

I admit it. I wanted immediate results from my prayers, and it confused me when I didn't get them.

One day, I was sitting by my bed when the Crazy Itch started. The visit with Mommy had been going so well prior, so this plummeted my mood entirely. After I was put back into bed, Mommy launched into itch duty, trying to rub every part of me that needed scratching. She was an expert by now, often knowing exactly where to rub with minimal direction.

Still, I had no relief. I started jerking from side to side, trying to use the friction my body created against the bedsheets to reach every part of my body at once. My nurse Rochelle decided to give me a shot of Dormicum to calm me down, and my body relaxed. The itching didn't stop—it never stops—but Dormicum sort of numbed my body and my mind a little, allowing my nerves to settle down.

I sighed long and low.

"What's wrong, love?"

I looked at Mommy. I was on the verge of tears, but what was new. "Mommy, I'm so tired of this itching."

She patted me soothingly, her eyes full of empathy. "I know, my love. I'm so sorry. It won't be forever."

I wanted so badly to believe her, but I didn't. It was so hard to believe in the promise of any kind of light when I was surrounded by nothing but darkness. Right then, my future looked so bleak to me. I couldn't imagine one where I'd be free of the horrific itching.

"Trust me, Kechi. Trust God."

Trust God.

I stayed silent. I'd heard that a thousand times.

Mommy leaned forward. "You know, one time when you were three years old, I was with you in the kitchen. I didn't realize you had climbed unto the dining table right behind me. Next thing I heard from behind me was, 'Mommy, catch me!' I turned around fast, and you were already airborne with your arms open wide!"

My eyes widened, and I couldn't stop my laugh. "Oh my God."

"Yup." Mommy nodded with a laugh of her own. "You had jumped off the table before I had even turned around, because you were 100 percent sure that your mommy would catch you no matter what."

I shook my head in amazement at the story. I tried to imagine little Kechi jumping off the dining table without hesitation or fear, and I smiled. The image warmed my heart.

"That's the kind of faith God wants us to have in Him, Kechi," Mommy went on. "He wants us to leap toward Him with arms open wide, in complete faith that He can and will pull us through any difficulty. Even when it seems impossible. In fact, *especially* when it seems impossible. The way I caught you that day is the exact way God will catch you every time you fall . . . if you let

Him. He pulled you out of a falling plane, Kechi. He will get you through this itching."

"But *how* do I let Him?" I asked. I so desperately wanted to. I wanted it more than anything. I wanted everything that Mommy had just described.

"You take every single problem you have to Him and just . . . stop thinking about it."

I was confused again.

Stop thinking about my itching? How? It was impossible. "How do I hand over a problem that my body constantly reminds me I have?" I asked, trying not to be frustrated.

"By giving it to God every single time," Mommy said, patient as ever. "Faith is like a muscle, you know. The more you exercise it, the stronger it gets. So every time you're faced with the problem, hand it to Him, over and over again. As many times as you need to."

I gazed at her in wonder, wishing with everything in me that I had just one *ounce* of the conviction she clearly had in her own words.

Mommy also told me about how her dad, my precious late grandpa, had been the pillar of faith and strength for the family at the time after the crash, when no one at PH knew if anyone had survived. The whole family had gathered at my grandparents' house, praying and waiting with bated breath for news from Mommy.

"Each time I'd call the family to tell them the death count," she told me, "Daddy would say with complete assurance, 'Kechi is alive.'" Mommy shook her head in awe at the memory. "Even after I'd been told that none of the survivors was a high school girl, he was undeterred. 'Kechi is developed, so they will think she's a woman. If there are any survivors, Kechi is one of them.' He just kept saying it. 'Kechi is alive. Kechi is alive.'"

I teared up as I listened to this incredible tale with wide eyes.

Wow . . . what must it be like to have such steadfast faith?

I couldn't help but wonder.

Mommy gathered her emotions and looked at me with so much love. "From the moment we found out you were indeed alive, it has been one miracle after another, Kechi."

109

Honestly, there really was no other way to describe all of it. It was an incredible miracle. And despite how rare they were supposed to be, my life, messed up as it felt right then, seemed to be full of them.

I decided to try what Mommy suggested. I would keep handing my itching and my pain to God. Over and over and over. I would just keep trying, believing each time that He would take care of it.

Based on Mommy's words, believing did not guarantee the immediate results I was praying for. I was not ready to accept the fact that being a Christian would require a lot of patience, since God tends to do things in His time, which, as I was quickly starting to understand, could be vastly different from mine. But Mommy spoke with enough conviction that I knew I wanted to unlock the truth of her words within me one day. Until then, I'd rely on my meds.

I will admit that that story from my childhood had a lasting effect on me from that moment on. It was such a perfect analogy for faith, a child's faith specifically, which the Bible does say we should work toward. God wants us to have faith like a little child's, the kind of senseless faith three-year-old Kechi had in her mother.

Would the sixteen-year-old me ever get there?

I had no idea, but it was clear there weren't going to be any shortcuts in this experience of mine. Be it with regards to my faith or my healing, it appeared I would have to plow through each and every difficult stage with as much help as I could get, maybe not from God, but from those He put around me.

How metaphorical, really, because after all, you appreciate the things you earn much more than the things that are handed to you. You cherish them more because you intimately remember everything you went through to achieve them.

God wasn't about to just *hand* me anything, plane crash survivor or not. I may not have known much about Him just yet, I may have been having some difficulties truly believing in Him, but He *did* exist.

I was certain of that much, at least.

Chapter Nine

The Visits

Toward the end of April, my six-year-old little sister, Chizitara, was finally able to come to South Africa to visit me.

I was so excited to see my baby sister, though I didn't know exactly when her visit would be. I just knew that she'd be coming soon and, frankly, I needed as many reasons as possible to stay positive those days. I liked having something new to look forward to that didn't involve my surgeries or itching or my unending concerns about God.

I wondered how Tara would process what happened to me. Mommy and Daddy had told her I was badly hurt and getting better in South Africa. I'd always felt like her brain was mature for her age, but at the end of the day, she was only six.

How much comprehension could I expect from a six-year-old? *Should* I expect any? Was it even fair to?

There was no way her little mind would be able to fathom the degree of my injuries until she actually saw me, and when she did, would she know she was looking at her big sister?

During one morning visit, Cherie, my trauma counselor, glided into the TICU, her singsong voice announcing her presence before anyone even saw her. She came into my line of sight wearing bright

111

yellow and orange, and she looked so much like a real-life Disney princess, I half expected to see a bunch of woodland creatures on her tail.

"Morning, Kechi!" she said chirpily. "I just talked with your little sister out there. She's so cute! Are you excited to see her?"

I stared at Cherie in utter confusion. What did she just say?

A chorus of sighs and groans immediately followed Cherie's shocking revelation, coming from the nurses all around the room. "Cherieeee!"

"What?" She glanced around the room, looking as confused as I was. I'd never seen her look so perplexed. "What, what did I do?"

"It was meant to be a surprise!" another nurse said.

"Oh my goodness!" Cherie covered her mouth with her hands, then she quickly turned defensive. "Well, no one told me!"

I was still trying to process Cherie's words. "Wait, Tara is here?" My head whipped toward Mommy, my eyes wide. She was shaking her head and laughing. "Mommy, Tara is here right now? For real?!"

Mommy nodded. "Yes, she is."

My heart skipped several beats, and I just lay there in astonishment while Cherie apologized profusely to Mommy.

Tara is here! In South Africa! In the hospital! Oh my God!

"I'm *so* sorry for ruining your surprise, love," Cherie said to me remorsefully. "Me and my big mouth!"

"I-it's okay," I managed to say, still in shock.

"So, are you ready to see her? She's out there with your aunty."

I hesitated a bit. Suddenly, I was nervous.

I caught Mommy's gaze. "Will she even recognize me?" My voice sounded unsure.

Mommy laid her gloved hand on my shoulder. "It'll be okay, sweetheart."

I looked into her reassuring eyes, and I believed her. Of course it would be okay. And as I thought about it, I realized I wouldn't actually mind if Tara didn't recognize me. In fact, I'd understand. I didn't exactly look like myself, after all, and she was just a child.

I nodded at Cherie, and the counselor smiled. "I'll go get them," she said and left my bedside.

As I waited with Mommy, my mind raced. I had no idea what to expect from Tara's reaction to the new me. My anxiety battled between excitement and nerves.

Would they let us hug each other? After all, they'd let me hug Mommy, albeit with her wearing full-body, protective medical attire. Since Tara would be wearing these things, I was sure they'd let her hug me.

But . . . what if she didn't recognize me?

"Here they are!" Cherie's voice interrupted my thoughts.

I couldn't turn my neck to the left toward the TICU entranceway like I wanted to because of how stiff it was, but I was propped up on some pillows, so I saw the exact moment Tara walked into my periphery, clothed in protective gear and gloves. All my nerves immediately turned into complete excitement.

"Tara!" I cried out in absolute joy, and before I knew it, I was crying. I had missed her so much.

As the small figure came closer and closer, I tried so hard to sit up even farther. I raised both of my bandaged hands and waved them in front of me, wishing my baby sister could run into my arms and hug me tight because that was all I wanted with all my heart.

As soon as she was close enough, Tara leaned up toward me without hesitation and opened her little arms wide for a hug.

I was thrilled beyond words. My own hands snaked around her shoulders, and she gave me the gentlest hug ever. Her tiny gloved palms touched my arms so very carefully, like she was hugging a delicate little flower with the most fragile petals. They must've told her to be careful when touching me.

I closed my eyes, crying at the tenderness. "Hi, my love," I whispered near her ear. "I missed you."

"I missed you too," she said. Her little high-pitched voice was music to my ears.

I heard a chorus of "Oh, *shame*!" around us as we pulled apart and wondered how she was processing everything.

I hugged Aunty Kechi (Mommy's older sister who came with Tara) as well before everyone got chairs to sit down around my bed. I was in a wonderful mood that morning. It felt good to be surrounded by so much love.

"Taraaa!" I cooed with the biggest smile on my face. My baby was finally here!

She smiled as she looked at me, and as I looked right back into her big, beautiful eyes, I just knew that she knew exactly who she was seeing. I was markedly different from the last time she saw me, yet she was looking at me with total recognition. She knew it was me, her big sister, Kechi. In the end, I had nothing to fear. My heart sang with gratitude.

"I can't believe Cherie, ruining the surprise like that." Mommy chuckled. "Well, it's my fault for not telling her beforehand, I suppose."

"I think I might have passed out from the actual surprise you guys planned," I said with a wry smile, "so maybe it's actually a good thing she ruined it."

Everyone laughed at that.

"Kechi, why are you so thin?" Tara suddenly asked me.

I laughed a little. I had expected curious questions from her. After all, she was still a kid, and kids are naturally inquisitive. "Well, I slept for a very long time," I said, "and when I was sleeping, I wasn't eating normal food. So I got thin."

"Are you in pain?" she asked, her big eyes full of childlike concern as they perused my bandages. "Does your face hurt?"

I smiled, touched. "I'm perfectly fine right now. Don't worry." My baby sister was in South Africa, and she recognized me. Right then, all was right in my world.

I'm standing in a room alone.

I notice a man standing across from me and he looks . . . strangely familiar. He looks like Harry Potter!

What in the world is Harry Potter doing in my dream?

"You and your mom need to stop what you're doing."
I stand there confused.
"What are you talking about?" I ask him.
"Your mom needs to stop healing you with her faith or you'll never learn."
I frown in annoyance. "Go away!"

I opened my eyes slowly, and I was lying in my bed as usual.

So . . . the weird dreams were back.

I recalled the man in my dream.

I'd thought he looked like Harry Potter, but now that I was awake, he was just a faceless figure. How strange.

"Your mom needs to stop healing you with her faith or you'll never learn."

I pursed my lips, feeling uneasy.

When Mommy arrived that morning, I told her about the dream, and she was surprised. She told me she'd pray about it. "If it was a message from God," she said, "He will confirm it."

To me, there was really nothing to pray about. The meaning was clear as day, and I resented it. Here I was, trying my best to understand God, to know Him, and He was telling me that my mother needed to stop praying for me? Why did she need to stop interceding for me while teaching me about Him? Why did it have to be one or the other?

I did not understand at all, and it made me upset that God seemed determined to see me suffer through my ordeal alone.

My itching flared up, and Mommy did her best as usual. Then she fed me and read to me from the Bible, as usual. I soaked up everything I could from the words she read out, more than usual that day, for some reason. Probably because of the chastisement I received from my dream earlier.

After she left, my nurse gave me my afternoon meds, and I dozed off.

I'm standing outside under an awning in front of Aunty Kechi's house. It's fellowship and everyone is standing and holding hands, eyes closed in prayer.

I open my eyes and look around, my gaze passing over each bowed head, and I notice a man staring right at me.

"Why are your eyes open?" he asks me accusingly. "Why won't you close your eyes and pray like everyone else?"

"Leave me alone," I say, and the man starts laughing at me.

I opened my eyes and stared up at the ceiling, comprehension flowing through my entire body like warm honey.

Mommy arrived for the evening visit, and I told her about the second dream.

"Two dreams in one day. What is going on?" she wondered in surprise.

I looked at her but said nothing. I was feeling a strange sense of conviction.

Her phone rang and she stepped out briefly.

As I lay waiting for her, I thought about the two dreams.

In the first dream, I had been so focused on the part about Mommy praying for me that I failed to see the main message, but the second dream had made things much clearer: I needed to learn to start praying for *myself* and trusting in the power of my own prayers. Because I clearly believed in the power of my mother's.

Mommy walked back into the room with a dazed look on her face. "Kechi, I just spoke with your grandma. Do you know what she said to me?"

"What?"

"She said she felt in her spirit that it was time for you to start taking some responsibility for your healing."

I looked at Mommy in surprise. "Did you tell her about—"

Mommy shook her head, preempting my question. "Nope, not until she was done talking." She looked at me knowingly. "What did I tell you this afternoon?"

I thought back to what she had said.

"If this is a message from God, He will confirm it."

My heart was beating wildly. Mommy didn't even have to say it because I hadn't doubted to begin with.

That night, I came to understand two very important things.

One, I clearly believed in God. If I didn't, it'd be very strange how I never once thought to question the source of my dreams. I believed in God for sure.

But I did not *know* Him.

And how can you trust or surrender anything to someone you don't even know?

The second thing I realized was one of my most significant realizations about my faith. I kept waiting for a big, dramatic revelation from God, but what if it never came the way I expected or wanted it to? Then would I refuse to believe because of that? Everything that had happened thus far—all the small and big signs through dreams, all the small and huge miracles we had encountered since the beginning of this recovery journey, starting with me surviving a freaking plane crash—would I just chalk them all up to luck or coincidence? And just how many "coincidences" needed to happen before I acknowledged the fact that there was, indeed, a divine presence in my life?

I had a lot to think about, but in that moment, I made a decision. I would start praying more.

I was still struggling hard with giving all my burdens to God and leaving them with Him, but one thing became clear to me with those dreams: He was trying to tell me that prayer was important.

Talking to Him was important.

So I was going to listen.

Chapter Ten

The Ward

Five months into my care at Milpark, the time finally came for me to be moved from the TICU to the burn care general ward.

This day was monumental for me, my family, and the hospital.

When I first arrived at Milpark in December, I had been given a 30 percent chance of survival by the first trauma surgeon who worked on me. Now here I was, five months later, moving from trauma care to the ward. This meant that my life was no longer in danger, and since patients like me rarely made it, the transfer was cause for celebration for everyone involved.

"You excited?" Aunty Uloma (I call her Aunty Ulo) asked me with a smile. She is Mommy's younger sister, and she had arrived in Joburg that morning, in time for the move. I loved having her around. I loved all of Mommy's siblings, but her two sisters were like my second and third moms to me. I was definitely the daughter they never had—they each have three boys.

I smiled back at her. "Kinda." It was a bittersweet feeling, and a bit nerve-racking, too, to be leaving a place I had grown so familiar with.

Hilda, Rochelle, Mr. X, Mr. Z, Maureen, and so many other nurses who had cared for me in the TICU came to bid us farewell.

It wasn't just them either; lots of unfamiliar nurses and staff came to say goodbye.

Everyone was happy to see me go because we all understood that this transition represented major progress in burn treatment.

In the ward, my surgeries continued, but much less frequently than when I'd been in trauma care. My graft sites were healing and my wounds were slowly covering up, so I was able to wear normal clothing like soft, sleeveless nightgowns and pajamas. My physiotherapy got more intense, too, with me walking almost every day now (not without a fight with Maya, though, which she almost always won).

I soon noticed, however, that the better I got on the outside, the worse I was starting to feel on the inside. I was now fully aware that the road to my recovery was going to be far longer than I'd anticipated while I was in the TICU. As the days went by, my mood fluctuated more erratically. I wasn't happy about the constant swings in emotion, but most times I couldn't control it. Sometimes it would hit me randomly, and I would get sucked into dark thoughts of a future filled with endless pain and uncontrollable itching. I would cry and cry and pray for peace. That was a new thing for me, responding to my own tears with my own prayers. But I still relied on Mommy's presence to make it all better. I relied on her much more in the ward than I did in the TICU. I wanted her with me at every waking moment, and for a while, I had that because the ward let Mommy sleep on the pullout couch in my room. It wasn't until Aunty Ulo divulged to me that Mommy wasn't sleeping well that I realized I had to learn to be okay by myself sometimes if I wanted Mommy to be okay too.

All this time I drew all my strength from Mommy, but she was just a human being like me. She, too, could run out of strength. And then where would that leave me?

It wasn't sustainable. I couldn't keep draining her.

Lord, how do I find strength for myself?

My mind went back to my last two dreams.

Mommy said to trust in the power of prayer and in the peace that would come from talking to God, if I let it come.

Lord, I prayed fervently. *Give me strength to cope when Mommy isn't here. Please.*

No matter how hard it was to be on my own on the nights that Mommy didn't sleep over, I had to remind myself that she needed to rest in a proper bed.

I slept easier when she was around though . . .

No, it'll be okay, I would tell myself. Whenever I couldn't sleep, I would occupy my mind with other things. Like my TV shows and movies. Now that I was in the ward, I had a DVD set, and I could watch all the movies I wanted at a good volume. I watched them when Mommy was here anyway, and they distracted me from pain and itching for long periods of time. I was starting to accrue a pretty respectable collection of DVDs. Then there was music. I stayed up long hours, watching music videos and listening to artists I loved. With the distraction and comfort that movies and music provided, books were long forgotten.

I wondered what would've happened if Aunty Ulo hadn't been there to handle things before they got out of control. Mommy would probably have fallen ill, then she wouldn't even be allowed to come to see me at all.

Thank God for Aunty Ulo, honestly. I felt like God had definitely brought her at this time for this reason, because I probably wouldn't have listened to anyone else.

Unsurprisingly, food was quickly becoming another source of distraction and comfort. I say unsurprisingly because I have always loved food, yet my appetite had not yet been fully restored to what it was prior to the plane crash.

When I was still in the TICU, Dr. Nel had told us it was unlikely I'd ever get back to my normal weight preaccident.

"The severity of her burns caused her to lose a lot of muscle mass in many areas of her body," he'd said. "Those areas are unlikely to ever fill out again."

How wrong he was!

When my appetite finally returned, it came back with a vengeance, as if it was determined to prove Dr. Nel wrong. I ate like a monster! My body was clearly trying to make up for all the months I hadn't eaten normal food. At every meal I felt like I was eating for four people at once. I had a bunch of favorite things I loved to eat, like scrambled eggs, *puff puff*,[1] and the candy Ferrero Roche.

Getting my strength back was an excruciatingly slow process, regardless of how much I ate.

My body was weak and fragile and prone to extreme exhaustion from the littlest effort. I was more awake so my mind was more active, but my body simply could not keep up with my mental, emotional, and spiritual progression, giving new meaning to the phrase "The spirit is willing but the flesh is weak." The routine in my days at Milpark that was once a source of security was now starting to become repetitive. I was growing restless. I wanted to see more of what was around me. I wanted to go outside. We asked the ward staff, and they said it was okay.

We were getting into Johannesburg's winter months, so they had me put on a soft pink robe and hat that Mommy had bought me before putting me into a wheelchair.

They wheeled me out of my room, and I sat there, hunched over in the seat, full of anticipation. I rarely left my room for anything other than physiotherapy or surgery.

We went down familiar hallways of the ward, then down an elevator and through the fancy lobby of the hospital.

Mommy wheeled me out the automatic glass doors, and before I knew it, we were outside, right in the parking lot of Milpark.

"Kechi, you're outside!" Aunty Ulo exclaimed excitedly from beside me.

I smiled and breathed the crisp air deep into my lungs.

It was so strange and bright. I couldn't look upward, but I looked

---

1. *Puff puff* is fried sweet dough balls, almost like donuts but denser. Aunty Ulo makes the best puff puffs.

straight out in front of me, above the sea of cars in the parking lot and far into the horizon. I saw the sky.

Wow . . . so the world was really still out there, huh?

It was a strange thought, but that was how I felt in that moment. Something about seeing that sky was so . . . reassuring. I realized that no matter how long I was in that hospital, no matter how many months or years this healing journey was going to be, the world would still be out there, waiting for me to come back to it.

"Kechi, how're you feeling?" Aunty Ulo asked, bending over to look at me. "You okay?"

"Yeah, I'm okay," I lied. I was freezing cold and I could feel exhaustion settling deep into my bones already, but I wasn't ready to go back inside just yet.

Mommy whipped out her camera and took a commemorative shot of Aunty Ulo and me.

Soon after that, my body decided it was done, and I found myself slumping lower in the wheelchair.

Of course, Mommy noticed immediately.

"Okay, time to go back inside," she announced.

As they wheeled me back into the hospital, she looked at me and smiled. "You did great, love."

After Aunty Ulo left, I despaired for a few days. I was never very good with goodbyes before the accident and now I was even worse.

But Daddy would be coming soon. He was coming with one of his sisters, my aunt Kate, who also made amazing puff puffs. I had many reasons to look forward to their arrival.

Meanwhile, itching hit its peak during my time in the ward. My burn scars started contracting rapidly. Severe burns like mine caused the skin to lose its elasticity as it healed. The burned skin around my joints contracted heavily, causing my arms, wrists, fingers, legs, ankles, toes, and neck to sort of fuse into curved positions. I lost a lot of the mobility I had while in the TICU, when my grafts and injuries were soft and pliable. I could no longer straighten my hands or legs and I couldn't twist my neck or lift my head up. My resting position was literally like that of a T-Rex: back hunched, arms and legs bent at the joints, and chin tightly fused to my neck.

Still, Maya came to torture me daily. Just as she had predicted, physical therapy became so much more painful while ironically becoming more important than ever. I progressed from merely walking to climbing stairs—with Maya's assistance, of course, and I hated every second of it. Some days I simply refused to do therapy. Some days, the physical discomfort was just too overwhelming, and it directly affected my emotional and mental state.

On the whole, I was doing better emotionally than physically. Music became a more potent distraction as I continued to heal.

Before I sang for the first time after the accident, I wasn't sure how my voice would come out. Singing was one of the most natural ways I expressed myself.

Would my voice sound different from what I remembered? Would it sound good? Or did the accident change that part of me too?

I'd have to test it to find out.

I opened my mouth and sang along to the next line of the Kelly Clarkson song that was playing.

Mommy whipped her head around to me, her eyes wide in surprise. "What was that?"

I laughed because she said exactly what I'd been thinking.

Something was different. Very audibly so.

I sang again, and as I kept singing, I started to smile.

I couldn't believe it. What *was* this, even? My voice sounded . . . clearer. Stronger. A little higher-pitched. There was just a certain *quality* to it that definitely had not been there before the accident.

Did the accident *do* something to my vocal cords? Something good?

It was such a weird thing to process. It was such an oddly specific part of me to undergo any sort of transformation.

The accident had caused so much tragedy. It had taken so much from so many people. It had taken so much from me. It was weird to think anything remotely positive could've resulted from something so horrible. I wasn't sure how to feel about it at first.

But as my time passed in Milpark, music became such an important part of my healing, and being able to sing along to my favorite songs brought me so much joy that I began to see this new development as a small but meaningful blessing.

Maybe God had granted me one gift to help me cope in this hard time, and He had chosen to give it to me in a form He knew I would truly appreciate.

Kelly Clarkson's *Breakaway* album will forever be imprinted with memories from South Africa.

One day in the ward, as the album was playing on my DVD, the song "You Found Me" started playing and the strangest thing happened.

When the song first started, the lovely melody captured my attention immediately. But then, as it continued to play into the chorus, my heart started to quicken for some reason. I felt as if I was on the cusp of a realization, an important understanding. I found myself drawn to the lyrics until the words of the song were all I could focus on.

> You found me where no one else was lookin'
> . . . I guess you saw what nobody could see cause you
> found me

The lyrics that followed, about someone breaking past all of my confusion to reach me, and staying with me through the hurt, gave me pause. I don't remember how I was feeling before the song started to play. I don't remember what I was thinking. But as it kept playing, the lyrics latched onto my very soul. I suddenly felt like a warm blanket had been draped over my heart. Lying in my bed, I felt a strange, otherworldly calm. An assurance within me that . . . that *I* had been found. As strange as that may sound. That from the moment I was born into this world, I had been found. And no matter what kind of pit I found myself in or how far into it I fell, I would *always* be found, I would always be pulled out, as long as I reached out.

Just as God had pulled me out of that plane crash on December 10.

Nothing made sense to me, not the random feeling of peace or the sudden assurance or the fact that all this had been invoked by a Kelly Clarkson song.

But then my mind went back to God and what Mommy said about His timing, and everything just sort of clicked into place.

The song, its lyrics, they painted the picture of a love that was so real and utterly beautiful in its completeness, the kind of love that Mommy said God had for us.

The kind of love He had for me.

I remembered the Harry Potter dream and the one after.

Was He trying to talk to me again?

Was He trying to reach me in a way He knew I'd notice, to show me that He was still here, and He still cared? Was He trying to show me that He hadn't left my side?

It may seem ridiculous to someone else, it may seem like I was reaching, but in that moment, that was exactly what it felt like to me.

I held in my tears. I didn't want to panic Mommy needlessly.

I was emotional, but for once, not because of pain or itching. It was because, as I lay there in my bed, I felt like I had been given a tiny glimpse into the depth of love I believed God had for me. And through a Kelly Clarkson song, no less.

If this was His weird way of showing me He was still right there with me, I would gladly take it.

My curiosity about my face grew gradually until the day I asked Mommy for a mirror.

My body had burned badly, this I knew well. My scalp had also burned pretty badly. But what about my face? I felt like I should expect the worst, considering everything else.

The bandages were gone now, and my face itched as much as any other part of me, so that had given me many chances to feel it. Some areas were smoother than normal skin should feel while some areas felt sort of rough and bumpy. It wasn't quite the same feel of the grafted skin on my hands.

How were my features? My eyes and nose and lips?

Days earlier, when I was talking to Daddy on the phone, I was looking at my reflection on the shiny phone screen before I even realized it. Well, a part of my face, at least. It happened so randomly, but before I knew it, I was looking into my own eyes.

My heart skipped a beat when I caught my own gaze. I didn't see much else beyond my pupils. The reflection had been a bit blurry, truth be told. Still, I'd seen enough to have my curiosity piqued.

Sometime after the call, I looked over at Mommy, who was sitting next to me. "Mommy, I have a confession."

She looked at me warily, which I always found amusing. "What?"

"I kind of saw my reflection on the phone when I was talking to Daddy."

I saw different emotions flitter across her face as she considered my words.

"I want to see my face properly," I said into the silence.

After a sigh, Mommy finally said, "Okay." Her tone was normal. Maybe too much so.

I guess she'd been dreading this moment. I understood why. She was most likely worried about how I'd react to whatever I saw in the mirror.

I was nervous too. I mean, the last time I saw myself in a mirror, I was as gorgeous as ever. And I liked being pretty. I liked being seen as pretty. It gave me a certain confidence.

Now I was burned. I knew I'd look different because of the scarring but how much so? And more importantly, how much of a change in my physical appearance would be enough to affect my personality? Because I liked that just as much as I liked my appearance. I liked the kind of person I was, give or take a few quirks. I liked that I didn't take things too seriously or hold things in my heart too long. I liked how easily laughter came to me. I liked being optimistic. Of course, there were things I didn't like about myself too. I was vain and self-absorbed, I procrastinated way too much, and not taking things seriously wasn't always a good thing, especially with school and grades. But ultimately, I felt pretty comfortable about the kind of person I was becoming. I didn't want the things I liked to change, and I couldn't help but wonder how much those good things were dependent on my looks.

Before Mommy raised the mirror to my face, she tried to prepare me by reminding me of the extent of my injuries, then she reassured me that I was still healing and that I still had many upcoming reconstructive surgeries.

I nodded as she talked, knowing she was just trying to lessen the shock of whatever I was about to see. Her intentions were good, but her words only served to make me more nervous.

Just how bad was it?

I braced myself.

Mommy handed the mirror to me.

I lifted it and finally looked at my full reflection for the first time since the accident.

Everything was very . . . *pink*.

It looked like someone had stripped off all the skin from my face. All I could see was raw, wet-looking flesh. Partly wet due to the thick layer of ointment they always put on me. I also seemed to have no eyelids. It was weird.

Wow. So, this was my new face.

It was definitely different. It looked *nothing* like me.

But somehow . . . "It's actually not as bad as I expected," I heard myself say. I turned my face left and right to get a really good look at everything. Then I looked directly into my eyes and held my own gaze for a moment.

It's hard to explain how I felt in that instant.

I was looking at a reflection in the mirror that looked nothing like I remembered Kechi to look like. Yet somehow, the person in the mirror felt familiar. It was eerie.

Moreover, the longer I looked, the more I noticed some unexpected things.

The shape of my eyes was the same. My nose and my lips were sort of the same too. Basically, it seemed like my facial features had pretty much retained their basic shapes; they were just all stripped of their skin. I hadn't expected this at all, considering the extent of my injuries.

I looked at my eyes again, and I smiled a bit. I'd always liked their doe shape. "Mom, I'm still kinda pretty!"

I turned toward her and realized Mommy had her head bowed in fervent prayer. She was just thanking God incessantly, and her voice sounded so emotional, I was certain she was crying. She must've been so nervous!

"Mommy, don't cry. I'm okay! It's not that bad. I'm actually relieved."

"I'm okay, I'm okay," she said as she wiped at her eyes. My heart went out to her because I couldn't imagine how scary this must've been for her as a mother who knew just how into looks her daughter was. She'd probably been more worried than I was.

Did I wish my face had taken less damage? Of course I did.

But I felt like it was best this way. It was better that my *entire* face had been affected. If I'd only gotten a few scars here and there, I felt like I would have been more likely to obsess over hiding them. But my whole face looked like one huge scar; therefore, to hide the scar would be to hide my entire face. And I wasn't going to do that. So, in a way, reality had forced me to choose between two extremes. I could either hide totally from the world or I could show myself totally to the world. There was a hidden parallel there, too, in reference to my identity, because I was forced to either completely accept myself or completely reject myself.

The fact that I could still see even a shred of Kechi in that reflection was something I knew I'd never be able to make sense of logically. It had nothing to do with the physical, even though, unbeknownst to me at that moment, I looked more like my old self then than I would later on. It was just a feeling in my spirit. The plane crash altered my face and body, but it did not take away the essence of who I was, and that essence had spilled out of Mommy's mirror that day.

Things could have gone very differently. I could only thank God that they didn't.

He gave me the ability to see the part of me that went beyond my physical appearance—the part of me that mattered most.

He had shown me Kechi through His eyes, and she was who she'd always been.

This was the very moment that birthed the phrase that went on to become my life motto.

My scars do not define me.

They were obviously going to be a big part of me from then on, but there was much more to my identity than that.

I am more than my scars. No one but God showed me that.

Chapter Eleven

The Search for Me

I was making so much headway in my tumultuous walk with God, but my erratic mood swings were getting even worse as my pain and itching persisted, especially when my pain meds were switched to pills. As it turned out, surgery without access to instant pain relief from drugs like morphine was a near-impossible feat. I didn't understand why I was expected to endure it.

My first neck surgery, for instance, was one such surgery. I knew from the first day the pain hit that I would never forget it.

"Is my neck open?! Did they slice it open? What's happening, Mommy? It burns!"

That surgery opened my eyes to new realms of pain. I felt like someone set a hot iron right across my neck, and it scared me to imagine what that area looked like. In my head, it was flaming red and dripping blood.

I screamed and screamed in agony after that surgery, and I knew they couldn't give me morphine anymore, but what about Dormicum? If I could just be put to sleep for the entire duration of the healing process, if I could just be granted the gift of blissful unconsciousness, would that be too much to ask?

Apparently. So they gave me pain pills that took forever to take effect, and even then, they never curbed my pain fully.

I was crying so much that my nurses thought I was depressed. It was a valid conclusion, given what I was exhibiting. I was restless, angry, and crying all the time. So I was prescribed an antidepressant.

But these feelings I was having, they came from a place of complete exhaustion from my repetitive physical predicament. It had been almost six months, and my pain and itching were ever present, no matter how much I prayed and meditated. The antidepressants did nothing to change the source of my mood swings, so it was no surprise they did nothing to curb my constant crying.

I was then assigned a psychiatrist, Dr. Ron.

During our first session he asked me to tell him all the things that bothered me.

"I'm in constant pain," I said in a low voice. Hell, I was in pain right then as we spoke. "I'm sad all the time because of the itching, and I can't sleep." I told him I didn't feel like myself, and I truly didn't. I wasn't this sad, weepy person. I didn't like that I was becoming her.

"Your TICU nurses said you're a very cheerful girl," Dr. Ron said.

"Well, it's hard to be cheerful lately. Everything is just so hard, and I'm so exhausted from crying all the time." I was happy the TICU nurses thought of me fondly though. I had given them their fair share of hell too.

After my first session with Dr. Ron, Mommy came back into the room and told me she'd talked to him briefly. He believed that I had a naturally cheerful disposition, and he didn't think I needed the strong antidepressants that were typically assigned for patients with my level of physical trauma. It turned out he was right because the antidepressants were actually a big reason behind my continued insomnia. Unfortunately, however, he also tried to reduce my pain med dosages, which really upset me. I thought he was meant to be helping?

At that point I was starting to believe there was a serious misconception about the *real* level of my pain. I was in a daily battle with everyone around me regarding how much pain I *should* be feeling versus how much pain I was *actually* feeling. Frankly, they believed my pain was more mental than physical. I could never understand this. I wept constantly because of the intensity of my pain and cried even more because I felt so misunderstood.

When the pain hit, I literally could not think of anything else. It took over my body and my mind, and all I could do to express how horrible I felt was cry and thrash about in my bed, which, of course, would make things worse. I was having these intense surgeries, but I was no longer being given the kind of pain meds that would easily deal with the level of pain caused by them . . . yet I was somehow supposed to be okay just as quickly as if I was being given something as potent as morphine? I honestly couldn't comprehend the reasoning behind that thought process, but it was my reality.

It was extremely frustrating to come to terms with the fact that the people who cared for me would never understand the daily horror of existing inside this body of mine unless they were in said body, and I would *never* wish that on any living soul. I was in permanent pain, and every day it felt like pain built *on top* of pain. Old pain was never fully managed before new pain made itself known. I was a mass of eroded nerves, and I was *constantly* uncomfortable.

Mommy told me to pray.

Daddy told me to take control of my body and my pain and itching.

It hurt to hear them tell me this, as if my pain was somehow my fault because I wasn't putting in enough effort to control it. I *was* praying. I was praying all the time. What other options did I have except to turn to God?

Every single night, I talked to Him. In the darkness of my room, in the middle of my pain. In the middle of my itching. Sometimes, the good times, I would fall asleep during my prayers. Other times, if I was lucky, I would cry myself to exhaustion. A night of peaceful sleep was a true blessing.

Sometimes, I would wake up and *decide* that day was going to be a good one, no matter what. Drugs weren't working. Crying only served to cause pain to myself and those around me. Prayers, despite how well they seemed to work with everything else, didn't do much good with my itching or pain. But one thing I was growing to understand was that I might have some control over how my days went *despite* my pain and discomfort. Somehow I had to decide that no matter what new obstacles my circumstances threw at me, I wouldn't allow it to affect my entire day. Somehow, I had to sort of . . . *will* a good day into being. If drugs weren't going to provide me with the relief I was searching for, I had to look for it elsewhere. Maybe the answer was in my mind. Maybe that was what "taking control" meant.

Such epiphanies usually came only after a string of days filled with nothing but tears and sadness. I knew what my crying did to my parents, and I hated it. I hated that I was this way, I hated that I couldn't seem to help it or control it. This was not me. They knew it; I knew it. I was not this miserable, tearful, sad person, and I *despised* that my circumstances had made me this way. I feared being this way forever. If not forever, how much longer? How much longer was I to be defined by my sadness? I was just so tired of being in pain *all the time*. I was tired of distressing my mommy, most of all. The Lord knew I wanted to be strong and positive for her, of all people. I prayed to Him to give me the strength to be positive, to overcome my pains and do what everyone promised me He could do, but He seemed content to leave me with my groanings. My freshly formed relationship with Him was already built on shaky foundations. I didn't need all this doubt too.

The doctors continued to prescribe me pain meds and dosages based on what they believed my pain level to be, not on what I told them it was.

Sometimes I would think maybe they were right. Maybe some of it was in my head. Maybe this was just a withdrawal symptom that would last until my body adjusted to the new pain pills. But most times I believed they treated my pain as if it wasn't real, and I resented them for it. I resented them all, and in my darkest moments, I resented God, who seemed just fine leaving me in this predicament.

God! Why did you save the life of someone too weak to handle this kind of survival? I don't understand. Help me understand. What do you want from me?

I didn't understand why God would think I could survive something like this. *He* made me, right? So He *knew* me. He knew I had the worst pain tolerance.

God didn't build me to handle this kind of physical pain. At least, I didn't think He did. Nothing in my life had equipped or prepared me for suffering of this magnitude.

Then again, I thought, *how would one prepare for something like this?*

I shook that thought away. That wasn't the point.

My body had caught fire, yet my soul had decided to hang on for reasons unknown. But every single day was extremely hard, and the nights were harder. I was alive, yes, but I was suffering for it.

Do I wish for death, then? Do I pray to God for a permanent escape from this living hell?

No. No, I was way too stubborn for that.

Besides, I had come too far in this journey. The time to quit had long passed.

So I just kept on turning my frustrations upward.

God, You saved me, right? And it looks like this pain and itching are an unavoidable part of surviving burns like this. If that's the case, then You're going to have to make me stronger because as I am now, this isn't working. I'm so weak, my endurance is so low. You saved me. You can make me strong enough to endure what I have to go through. So please. Make me stronger. Please!

Something inside me shifted gears when I began to pray this way.

134

I still prayed for relief from my pain, but then I started to pray much more for the strength to better *endure* the pain and itching. But I complained as much as I prayed. And whenever prayers worked without medication and I enjoyed a measure of relief for a time, I was quick to forget those moments of relief and answered prayers once my discomfort resumed—which it always did.

Then something incredible happened in the middle of my fervent prayers one night. My thoughts went off on a strange tangent.

Maybe I'm not meant to be rid of this itching in the way I want God to rid me of it. Maybe this is something that needs to run its course, for my own sake. Because if God magicked away all my problems, where, then, would growth happen?

I chose to live. I chose this struggle when death would've been so much easier. But at what point in my life will I gain the qualities I need to live this difficult life in this difficult world if I never experience difficulties?

God has already done the impossible for me. No one but He could have pulled me and the other survivor out of that burning plane alive. After that, He kept me alive, kept my soul connected to my body.

Is it now my turn? Is this my cross?

My heart was pounding.

I tried to reject this epiphany, to eject it from my mind, but I could not.

I then tried to bury it in the far, forgotten recesses of my mind, but it was too late; its roots had already wrapped tightly around my heart like curling vines, and I could not deny the truth of it.

That moment marked a turning point in my thinking, my perspective, and my vision for my future . . . indeed, it changed my very life.

———————— ✿ ————————

Weeks passed and my body slowly began to adjust to the pain pills and dosages. My pain felt better handled, and the constant crying it caused stopped. The itching remained a perpetual thorn in my side, but I was doing better mentally, despite it. I owed it all to that epiphany. It did something to me. It was strange.

Mommy started reading me letters and texts from the parents of the sixty angels, which is what the sixty students lost that day came to be called. And when I heard their prayers and encouragement, I felt like, of all the people in the world, I had to be strong for them.

"They hold on to your life like a lone light shining in darkness," Mommy said to me.

I thanked Jesus for that because many times, I felt I was holding on for them too. Just as they made my life their hope, I made their hope my life's ambition to uphold.

I decided then and there to live with purpose for the sake of the parents of the sixty angels. No more going through the motions like I did before the accident. The love and support I received from them was the foundation of my resolve to live in a way that would make them proud.

At that moment, I had no idea what I wanted to do with my life. I had no idea if I would even be well enough to live independently one day.

But if, by God's grace, I did get well enough, then whatever I chose to do with this life that God saved, I would do it as *excellently* as I possibly could. Because in my eyes, my life was no longer just mine. I was now living for at least sixty others, and I wanted to make them proud. I wanted to make their parents proud.

My sessions with Dr. Ron started to get very interesting when it became clear that my struggles with my situation were strictly physical, not psychological.

"Talk to me, Kechi," Dr. Ron would say. "How do you feel about the plane crash? How do you feel about your burns?"

Most times, I would just shrug. I had processed all that in the TICU. I was now in a place where I was heavily relying on my faith, the love from my family, and support from others to sustain me. "I'm fine, I think. I feel like things will be okay."

I suppose this emotional and mental recovery from the shock

of the accident was a bit too quick to be genuine or sustainable for Dr. Ron.

"It's only been six months," he told my mom. "There's just no way she can be fine this quickly. I believe she is in denial."

Well. I couldn't exactly blame him. The first time we met, I talked to him about my sadness and my insomnia, now I was saying I was okay.

But he wasn't there for all the stuff that happened outside of our sessions.

He wasn't there for all the talks I had with Mommy and my family after I was told the truth of the accident, about life and faith and strength. He wasn't there for all the cathartic weeping, for all the times when I talked and cried out to God. So I saw how it could all look *forced* to him, but I didn't really have any way to convince him otherwise. All he could go on was my word, and all I could say to him during our sessions was what I believed: that my family and my faith were really helping me emotionally and mentally, that I prayed for the families of the friends I lost, and that I was trying my hardest to trust that my doctors knew what they were doing and to trust God to pull me through everything. I told him I was lucky to have the kind of family I have, the kind that didn't give up on me because I cried too much or because I was hard to handle.

I guess I wasn't very convincing because he went ahead and prescribed all sorts of medications for me. Rather, I *was* convincing, just not in the way I'd hoped to be.

Mommy told me he was highly confused at my seemingly calm demeanor and was certain I was holding my emotions in, perhaps for her sake, even.

This really confused me because as far as I knew, I was having trouble with self-control.

I was a volcano of emotions, constantly erupting without warning, distressing those around me. People were always telling me to take control of my body and my pain, and I was trying. Now Dr. Ron was telling me I was holding things inside? Why, because I wasn't talking about the plane crash and the friends I lost anymore?

During our sessions, he would try to get me to express how I really felt about everything, and it was an interesting feeling, actively conversing with a person whom I knew my words were not reaching, who I could tell believed I wasn't facing reality.

Meanwhile, on the contrary, I was overly aware of my reality on every level. Finding out the truth of the accident and how all my classmates were gone, realizing I wouldn't make it back to school for prom or graduation, being in the hospital for months, my burn scars altering my appearance and disfiguring my body every single day . . . It was an overwhelming number of changes for one person to go through, and I wasn't made of stone. Of course, these things made me unbelievably sad. Of course, I cried when I thought too deeply about all of it.

But then, should I *stay* in that place?

Was there a predetermined amount of time for mourning one's plight that I wasn't fulfilling, a grief quota that I wasn't reaching?

I didn't understand why I was being compelled to talk about dark things when, by some miracle, I was already feeling such a strong pull toward the light.

But sometimes Dr. Ron's prodding made me feel like I *should* dwell a little longer on my dark and depressing feelings. And I knew he was just doing his job. I knew whenever he brought up the plane crash or my friends, it was because he felt I was being restrained, not allowing myself to fully feel and process the gravity of my situation and the fatality of the accident.

But oftentimes it kind of felt like he was unconsciously trying to *force* these dark feelings out of me, even when I was not currently experiencing them. It was like a battle between how he felt I *should* be feeling, versus how I *actually* felt.

This really seemed to be the story of my life lately. I was constantly caught in between what should be and what actually was.

What would be the point of allowing the darkness to fester? What would be the cost?

My life? This life that was incomprehensibly saved from a type of accident that typically had zero survivors? Who would that help? Why, then, was I saved?

I may live the rest of my life never knowing the answer to that last question, but I know for certain it was not to allow depression to win. Not after everything God had allowed me to survive thus far, not after everything my family and my doctors and nurses and therapists had been through to get me that far.

I was aware that my body and my reality were broken . . . but every day, I felt more and more alive inside this broken body. There was no way I could feel this way and stay in the dark. Hope was calling out to me.

I'd be a fool to ignore it.

Nigeria

Chapter Twelve

The Return

Around June 2006, my cousin Obichukwu Abii (I call him Bichu) came in from Nigeria to visit me. He is Nduka's younger brother and was the first of my cousins to see me in person after the accident.

I had a wonderful time with Bichu around. Visiting hours were always full of talking and laughter whenever I was awake, and we watched *Friends*, ate together, and just talked like we used to until he and Mommy left at night. He made me feel normal.

Tara and Grandma arrived while Bichu was still visiting, and honestly, having my family around played such a crucial role in my healing. At every stage of my time in South Africa, I had some level of support, and that was important not just for me but for my mom as well. My family made sure that neither of us ever felt like we were going through this hard time alone.

I couldn't have asked for anything better.

Bichu left Johannesburg after about two weeks, and I missed him a lot. But Tara and Grandma stayed right until we started making preparations to return to Nigeria in July.

Milpark in South Africa had done all they could do for me

medically. I had had over seventy-five surgeries there. Now, it was time to find a hospital that could handle the rest of my care.

August came and we said our goodbyes to Milpark Hospital, Johannesburg, South Africa, the hospital that had brought me back from the dead and kept me alive.

Everyone was justifiably concerned about the fact that I'd have to board a plane a mere seven months after being in a plane crash. I was neutral about it, though, and I think it was because I couldn't recall the actual crash.

I did remember holding Toke's hand amid the panicked screaming of fellow passengers on board, but my next distinct memory following that was opening my eyes in Milpark Hospital.

Now, if I remembered looking out the window as the plane hurtled downward, if I remembered the actual impact of the aircraft colliding with the ground, that would be a different story.

But the reality for me was that I boarded a plane one moment and woke up in bandages the next. Because I was spared the memories of the most horrific parts of the accident, I found that the thought of boarding a plane again didn't really affect me as much as I or others expected it to.

My memory of the flight back to Nigeria is covered in a haze, which makes sense considering I was drugged for most of it. Later on, Mommy told me I was actually awake for long periods of time during the flight. Not only that but I'd watched *V for Vendetta* and I'd even eaten prawns, which as far as I knew, I hated. It was hilarious!

When we landed in Lagos, I was transferred to a wheelchair, and we made our way to the arrival terminal, where the rest of my family was waiting to greet us, as expected. What I didn't expect was to see one of my good friends from LJC, Somachi Chris-Asoluka (now Somachi Osuno) waiting alongside my family. I was so emotional and touched that she went through the trouble to make sure she could welcome me home in person.

Somachi rode the ambulance to Shell Hospital, Lagos, with Mommy and me, and she even offered to spend the night with me in the ward. In the end, she wasn't allowed to due to hospital rules, but I knew I'd never forget how she was there for me that day. She'd never know how much it meant to me to have her present in that moment.

The next day, Mommy and I were flown to Port Harcourt, the city my family had moved to from Aba, and incidentally, the city in which the plane crash happened.

My days at Shell Hospital PH were extremely unbearable. The medical staff confiscated all the meds my South African doctors prescribed for me and never gave them back to Mommy. Without the right meds to manage my pain, I rarely felt any relief while I was a patient at Shell.

The Shell doctors there told Mommy I needed to be weaned off the meds for fear of dependency, which made absolutely no sense because, why would my South Africa doctors prescribe meds to me if they didn't think I *needed* them? I was only seven months into my burn treatment. These injuries were still fresh and so very painful when left mismanaged. Yet, the first time my pain spiked in the hospital, the nurse on duty gave me Paracetamol pills.[1]

They confiscated my meds only to replace them with Tylenol. For third-degree burns pain relief!

I later found out the hand-over letter from Milpark to Shell mentioned that a lot of my pain was psychosomatic. Honestly, I don't think my feelings have ever been more hurt in my life, especially considering Milpark gave me those meds to begin with. If I felt they weren't taking my pain seriously back in South Africa, they seemed to be making a blatant joke of it in Nigeria. They gave me Tylenol like my pain was as easily manageable as a headache. I would've been laughing if I wasn't too busy crying.

My mental state was much worse in Nigeria because I knew I was suffering so much more than necessary at that stage of my

---

1. Paracetamol is a common brand name for Tylenol in Nigeria.

treatment. I *knew* things did not have to be that hard. But somehow things managed to become generally more difficult while I was in Nigeria.

The transition could've been so much smoother. All it would've taken was the right meds given at the right time, and the crazy thing was, I *did* have the right meds until they were taken away. It was hard to believe anyone would think this pain was all in my head.

Nights in the hospital were definitely the worst, as most were filled with pain compounded with itching. The itching in some areas was so unbearable that no matter how bad the urge to scratch got, I did my best not to touch them, because if I did, the itching would *never* stop, and I would scratch until I bled. Sometimes I'd give in, though, and I'd always regret it.

After a while, the hospital started allowing my parents to take me home to our new place in Port Harcourt for a few nights at a time, much to the relief of the hardworking Shell nurses, I'm sure.

Meanwhile, I became more heavily scarred. Everything just tightened so harshly, and the keloids that had formed all over my body hardened and forced my joints into immobility, especially my fingers and elbows. My left hand was clenched shut, and my right hand was splayed open as the scarred skin tightened. The scar tissue on my elbows was so tight that I could not even straighten my arms. My face was a mass of bumps and hypertrophic scars that pulled at my eyelids and contorted my bottom lip. After my neck surgery, my neck had healed and formed new scars that kept it pulled downward so I still couldn't look up without leaning my entire body back.

I was a mess. As I healed and felt better, I looked progressively worse in appearance.

When I saw myself in a mirror, I saw the disfiguration as clearly as anyone else would. But I didn't take it to heart. I didn't find myself missing my old face or features. This was Kechi now. Simple as that.

I guess I just kind of . . . took it in stride. Maybe a little more easily than one would expect. My acceptance was enough to shock one of my closest friends into an awkward silence.

Womiye flew in from out of town to see me while my family was at a friend's guesthouse in PH. She was my best friend prior to the accident, so of course I was incredibly happy and excited to see her.

We were hanging out in my room when I passed by the mirror and stopped. "My face is like one of those horror movie monsters," I said with an amused chuckle.

Womiye went strangely silent, and when I looked over at her, I laughed long and hard at the expression on her face.

She was sporting the most awkward, confused-looking smile I'd ever seen, and her eyes were darting from side to side. "What am I supposed to say to that, Kechi?" she said, deadpan, humor dancing in her eyes as I continued to laugh uproariously. "Like, what the heck?"

It was honestly the funniest thing to me, but I guess that wasn't exactly fair to her. I could make such self-deprecating jokes easily because, well, if anyone had the right to make any kind of joke about my situation, it was me, but I couldn't expect anyone else to appreciate such jokes. Not yet, at least.

Chapter Thirteen

The Little Things

Our new home happened to be pretty close to the home of another fellow LJC classmate: Yimi Omofuma.

I considered Yimi to be one of my best friends. We weren't in the same friend groups in school, so our friendship was something that bloomed without any outside influences.

Yimi became a vital part of my healing during my time in PH. I grew extremely attached to her, and I wanted her around every time I came home from Shell Hospital. I couldn't really explain the reason behind the intensity of my need for her constant presence. It may have been because of what she represented.

School.

Mean teachers, study hall, school uniforms, and school dances.

She represented a phase in my life I never got to finish, a time period that I had a newfound appreciation for.

When she was around, talking with her took my mind off my plight for a time, and we would *gist* about anything and everything. Yimi also loved singing, and we would sing together too. She didn't ask too many questions about the plane crash or my appearance—not that I would have minded if she'd wanted to.

I felt like she didn't want to bring up the accident for her own reasons. The accident didn't affect me only, after all.

Living in Nigeria is hard because of the incessant heat. There is rarely power nationwide unless it is self-sustained, and for a burn survivor, heat is the enemy in more ways than one.

With more than half of my body covered in skin grafts and damaged pores, my body could no longer regulate heat properly. Without the feeling of cold air constantly blasting onto me from an air conditioner or a standing fan, I would feel like I was melting away, and that was what happened every time the power went out at home.

Of course, I could go back to Shell at any time. The power never went out over there since it was a private hospital, and I had a standing fan there too. But I wanted to be surrounded by family and friends whenever I could.

Frankly, if given the choice, I'd rather be miserable for a few moments at home with family, than comfortable all the time and alone in my hospital room.

While I was at Shell, Tara made friends with these two little girls, sisters, and they would occasionally come over to our house to play. I didn't meet them right away, but Mommy told me about them.

I was at home one day when they came over. One of the girls wandered toward my room, saw me, and screamed. Then she ran back out into the main hallway.

Startled, I stared into the now-empty space where the little girl had been standing, trying to absorb what had just happened.

I knew I looked very different now because of my scars, but was my face scary enough to warrant *that* dramatic a reaction? Did I no longer look human just because my face was burned?

It was a strange and new experience, and it roused strange and new feelings within me.

I tried to get back to my movie, but she came by again and did the same thing. Soon it became clear it had become a game to her to see me, scream, and run away.

I smiled wryly.

All of a sudden, my aunty Ogechi, our housekeeper, appeared in the hallway and yelled at the little girl to leave the room at once. After the girl left, Aunty Ogechi apologized profusely to me. She was very upset at the whole thing.

"It's okay," I said with a smile, knowing full well it wasn't.

Hours later, Mommy came rushing in, pushing open the now-closed bedroom door with a huge frown on her face. Aunty Ogechi had obviously told her what had happened. She was upset and hurt on my behalf.

"She's just a kid," I said, shrugging. I wasn't trying to excuse the little girl's behavior, and of course I didn't appreciate her exaggerated reaction or the little game she'd made out of the entire situation, but what was I meant to do? I'd feel ridiculous getting mad at a kid for being immature.

"It doesn't matter," Mommy said firmly. "She's not the first child that has seen you since the accident. They're not coming here anymore."

"No, Mom, they're Tara's playmates."

"Tara said she doesn't want to play with them anymore."

I blinked. "Oh." Tara's comprehension of delicate matters continued to surprise me.

I wanted to shrug off the entire thing, not linger on it. But whether I liked it or not, the experience did force me to become more acutely aware of perceptions of my appearance that may not always match the neutral reactions I'd received up to that point. Nobody had reacted as negatively as that little girl had to my scars, so I'd had no reason to concern myself with such thoughts. As such, I hadn't prepared for such a reaction either, so the whole thing caught me off guard. So far, I had encountered only friends and family who were happy to see me alive no matter how I looked, and strangers who, at the very least, knew how to behave cordially.

I learned that day that I couldn't expect every single person to be as easily accepting of the new me as my friends and family had been. That particular experience was just a little thing that happened with a child, but the world was full of all sorts of people. I needed to be prepared for people to react differently. At the same time, I had to remember, always, that my appearance didn't matter to those who mattered. Therefore, whatever kind of person I encountered in my life moving forward, I needed to remember that it was okay to be me, and that it was okay to present this me to the world. No matter what. And I also needed to remind myself that as difficult and uncertain as the future seemed sometimes, I knew sixty other children like myself who had lost their chance at *any* kind of future. It was a privilege to have one to worry and dream about. I had to remember that.

While I was at Shell Hospital, I had many visits from family members, friends of family, and well-wishers.

One day, Mommy informed me that the bereaved parents of the sixty angels, the ones who lived in PH, wanted to pay me a visit as a group.

"Is that okay with you?" she asked.

I thought about it, about how seeing the parents of friends and schoolmates who died in the plane crash would affect me. The first feeling that came over me was guilt. There I was, alive and healing, while their own children were just gone.

I tried to shake off that feeling.

I couldn't allow myself to think that way. I reminded myself that these parents were all rooting for me. I remembered their notebooks filled with prayers and letters of encouragement. These were the very same people who wanted to see me now, and though I knew it would be a difficult visit for both sides, I couldn't deny them the chance to see my progress in person, to root for me in person.

"Yes, it's fine," I told Mommy.

The parents eventually came by, and it turned out to be just the moms.

Tears were shared on both sides, but ultimately, they were thankful, hopeful tears.

There was one parent, however, who didn't come with the group: Toke's mother.

I had very conflicting emotions about seeing Mrs. Badru. Maybe it was because thinking of her made me think of Toke, and I tried very hard not to think of Toke or any of the sixty angels because it triggered my tears and I was so tired of crying all the time. But I couldn't ignore Mrs. Badru's noticeable absence.

My mind went back to Kairos Retreat in LJC, a time when all the eleventh graders (SS2) stayed on campus for an extra week after the fall semester closed, to meditate on our faith and bond with one another under the supervision of a few staff members of the school.

Toke and I were inseparable during that time. On the Saturday that the LJC campus officially closed for the holidays, the eleventh graders who lived in the city of Abuja were allowed to leave campus on that day alone, as long as they returned before 5:00 p.m.

Toke and I went with a fellow classmate and friend Cynthia to her home in Abuja to hang out until Kairos Retreat officially started. We had so much fun that day at Cynthia's. We ate huge homemade donuts, met Cynthia's wonderful mom, watched TV, and danced like maniacs to Ciara, Toke's favorite artist at the time. Toke mimicked some of her dance moves perfectly.

Now Toke was gone, I was a plane crash burn survivor, and her mom didn't come to visit me.

I shuffled about in bed, trying to get more comfortable.

Maybe it was better this way. After all, Mrs. Badru was the one parent who I wanted to see the most, while also the one parent I was most afraid to see.

I had no idea what I would say to her if we met. I was the last person to see her daughter alive, to look into Toke's eyes for the very last time. Mrs. Badru didn't know this, of course; I hadn't seen her since the accident.

If she came to visit me, would I tell her that I was with her daughter during her final moments? To what end? I had no idea what stage of grief she was in. What if I said something that caused her to backslide in her healing process? While I felt she deserved to ask me whatever she wanted to regarding her precious daughter, I absolutely didn't want to be the one to bring up things she may prefer to leave undiscussed.

But how could I possibly see her and *not* talk about Toke? She knew how incredibly close we were. It would be downright strange not to talk about Toke to her own mother, especially if Mrs. Badru brought up the subject herself. Therefore, I thought it best to prepare myself. I wasn't sure if Mrs. Badru would even want to see me—in fact, for all I knew she could have been pointedly avoiding me. Maybe she didn't want to see someone who would make her think of her daughter.

But if, just *if* she did come, I'd have to prepare for that visit. I'd have to make sure I at least didn't cry in her presence. I wouldn't want to incite the woman's tears with my own.

Well. All easier said than done.

Unfortunately, nothing in this world can quite prepare you for an impromptu visit from a deceased friend's mother.

No one told me she was coming.

No one *knew* she was coming, not even my own mother.

A few days after the other moms' visit, a nurse came around my curtains to tell me I had a visitor, and moments later, in walked Mrs. Badru, alone and completely unannounced.

So much for preparations.

Chapter Fourteen

The Grief

I looked up at her, and my eyes widened.

Before that day, I had met her only a couple times during the visiting days I spent with Toke, but I knew who she was the second I set eyes on her.

I struggled to sit up in bed, as it didn't feel right to be lying down all relaxed during such an important visit. She motioned for me to stop, shaking her head gently, but I sat up regardless.

Mommy wasn't there to act as my buffer that time. I was completely at the mercy of whatever was about to transpire.

I said a quick prayer to the Holy Spirit. *Please give me the right words. Please.*

I watched Mrs. Badru sit down in the chair by my bedside, her eyes downcast, and my heart broke for her. She looked . . . weary. Emotionally drained. Her countenance was that of a broken woman trying to hold it together, and I had to wonder how much effort it must have taken for her to come visit me. How hard must it have been for her to make that decision?

My mind raced with so many thoughts while my heart pounded with countless emotions. There were so many things I wanted to say to her, but I didn't know how to get them out without it all sounding like a jumbled mess of senseless words.

Where to even begin?

I'm sorry.

I hate this.

I hate that Toke is gone.

It's not fair.

I loved Toke so much.

I'm so sorry.

"Aunty . . ." I started, not sure where I was going, and that's when Mrs. Badru finally looked at me.

I looked into her eyes and saw grief. A deep-seated, heart-wrenching grief, the kind I knew I would never, ever understand. It emanated from her and permeated the room. The more I looked, the more I realized a light had left her eyes. I couldn't explain it, but it felt like something had died inside her when Toke died. I imagine it was the same for every single parent who lost their child or children that fateful day.

My mind flashed back to the mothers who visited me earlier in the week, and in that moment, it became clear to me that they had obviously decided to be brave for my sake, to put on smiles and focus on the promise of the future.

But this woman, Mrs. Badru, she showed me without reservations the painful reality of what it truly meant to lose a child forever. Her eyes revealed to me the bleak truth of what losing a loved one did to the person left behind, and even then, I saw just a glimpse. I probably wouldn't have been able to withstand the full extent of her sorrow.

In those eyes, though, I saw something else. I saw understanding.

And that was when I knew that no words were needed, because she knew everything I wanted to say. She knew I loved Toke. She knew that I, too, grieved her death. And she knew I was sorry.

"It's okay," she said in a very quiet voice that caused my heart to clench, my chest to seize up. "It's okay." She nodded gently, repeatedly. "It's okay, my dear."

My lips trembled, and I turned away, unable to hold her gaze anymore. I bit my lip, pondering my next words carefully.

Should I . . . ?

My brain told me not to, but my heart said I should. I thought about my prayer. Then I followed my heart.

"I was sitting next to Toke on the plane."

I heard Mrs. Badru's breath catch. I didn't look up.

Then I heard shuffling and movement, and soon I felt my bed dip on the side. I glanced up and saw that she was now sitting on my bed and looking at me, completely alert.

"You were?"

I swallowed and nodded. "We switched seats so we could sit next to each other. She was on the aisle seat next to mine, in the front of the plane." As soon as I said that, I regretted it. What if I just made things worse by telling her that Toke was sitting next to me?

If Toke was next to you, why didn't she survive too? I imagined her thinking.

I braced myself for this question, but she asked me a different one.

"Do you . . . do you remember what happened?"

Her gaze was so piercing, imploring, and again, I felt compelled to tell her what I remembered.

"Everything was fine for most of the flight," I said. "Then the turbulence started." I paused and stared down at my covers, my heart beating fast like it always did whenever I recalled this horrible memory. "Everyone was screaming, and I held Toke's hand. We looked at each other." I remembered Toke's wide, confused eyes. "I said we should pray. Then there was this loud metallic sound, then . . . nothing."

"Oh, Lord Jesus . . ."

I looked at Mrs. Badru. She had her head bowed and her hands clasped together.

My heart felt like it had squeezed into itself, and I slowly reached my hand out to cover hers. "I'm so sorry," I whispered, and when she turned her palm up to grab mine, the dams burst.

156

I cried uncontrollably. I don't know when Mrs. Badru started crying too, but soon enough we were both in tears. It was such an emotional moment for both of us, cathartic even.

The guilt hit me so much harder with her. I don't know why. Again, maybe because Toke was the last person I saw before everything went to hell. I held her hand. I looked into her eyes before the blackness came. I was the last person to see her in her final moments. And now her mom was here in my hospital room, sharing her grief with me. In that moment, it felt like she acknowledged Toke's death as a shared loss, and that moved me deeply.

Our tears finally stopped, and after a long moment, Mrs. Badru lifted her head.

"So . . . you were with her when it happened."

I sniffed and wiped my eyes with my free hand. "I was. I was right next to her."

"You held her hand."

"I did."

Mrs. Badru nodded several times in silence, as if she was forcing herself to come to terms with something. Then she gripped my hand tighter between hers. "At least she wasn't alone," she said. "She wasn't sitting next to a stranger. She was with someone she knew, a friend she loved. She wasn't alone." Mrs. Badru looked up at me with her tear-filled eyes. "Thank you for telling me."

Tears welled up in my eyes again at that. I didn't know what to say. I could only be grateful she saw things that way.

As we hugged, I thought back to my prayer and closed my eyes in eternal gratitude to God for how the visit had gone. I may never know why Mrs. Badru decided to visit me separately from the other parents. But then I thought about the alternatives.

What if she had come with the other moms? If that had happened, would we have been able to share this intimate moment? Not likely. Mrs. Badru would have been much more reserved in the presence of the other parents, undoubtedly.

And what if Mommy had been present for this private visit? There was no way Mrs. Badru would've felt comfortable being as vulnerable as she had been with me in the presence of my mother, who wouldn't tolerate anything that upset me to the point of tears.

I saw, then, that everything had happened just the way it needed to. I believed that this private visit was something we both needed, a part of our individual steps toward healing from the scars of this accident—internal and external scars alike. Because everyone has scars, that much has become clear. Some just aren't as visible as mine.

Thank you, Lord, I whispered in my heart when Mrs. Badru left. *Thank you for this visit.*

Mommy was taken aback by the news of Mrs. Badru's spontaneous visit. "She should have told me!" she said, looking slightly alarmed.

I shrugged. "I guess she didn't want to come with the other parents."

Mommy looked at me with concern, then she sighed heavily and put her arm around my shoulder comfortingly. "I wish she'd told me she was coming so I could've been here with you when she arrived."

Probably exactly why she didn't tell you, I thought to myself.

For a while after Mrs. Badru's visit, I couldn't get my mind off the sixty angels. I couldn't stop thinking about Toke.

Of course, Mommy was highly concerned about this. She didn't like me to linger on those kinds of thoughts because of the emotional toll they took on me, and she blamed my new focus on the visit with Mrs. Badru.

She wasn't altogether wrong, but it couldn't be helped. The visit had to happen. My current depressive state was a consequence of something that had been necessary, so I had no regrets about the visit.

I could picture Toke's face distinctly. Her short brownish hair, her bright eyes, her cute button nose. I remembered her as clearly as if she were standing right in front of my bed in her red checkered school uniform.

Then I remembered Waji, Chinenye, Zikora, Whitney, the Ilabor siblings, Ubani, and countless other children who had been on that plane with me and were now gone from this world forever.

My lower arm started to itch, and I rubbed it against the bed, jerking my body a bit to increase the friction. I suddenly felt a sharp twinge on my side and hissed in pain, stilling my movement immediately. As I waited for the pain to pass, I looked down at myself.

I wouldn't wish my burn experience on anyone, not even on my worst enemy.

Maybe. Maybe it was better that none of my friends and classmates had to live to suffer through this kind of ordeal.

I suddenly saw the faces of all the parents who had come to visit me, I saw Mrs. Badru's broken gaze, and I immediately regretted having such a reckless, foolish thought.

No matter how badly injured I was, I was *alive*.

What parent would not want their child alive?

Which of those parents wouldn't rather be in my mom's position, nursing their child back to health, than the one they were in right now? Had all the kids who passed away that day survived, their injuries wouldn't have mattered to their parents any more than they had mattered to my own parents. As long as there was life, there was always a chance, a hope for recovery.

But there was no recovering from death.

When you're gone, you're just . . . gone.

—————— &k. ——————

Almost three months had passed since we returned from South Africa, and Shell Hospital had started the search for the best reconstructive burns care for me. Shell, through one of their doctors, started to make contact with Shriners Hospital for Children (now Shriners Children's Texas), located in Galveston, Texas.

As assessments were being made on my behalf, I turned seventeen on October 29, 2006. It was an intimate celebration with friends and family.

One of the invited guests was Mrs. Mary Nkaginieme, who many call Aunty Mary. She lost two of her children in the plane crash and had become a pillar of strength and faith for a lot of the other bereaved LJC parents. She and Mommy became fast friends.

"This is a day that very nearly did not come," Aunty Mary said in her birthday toast. "Yet here we are, celebrating Kechi, against the odds." She looked at me and smiled fondly. "Our miracle child."

I smiled back shyly.

"So, I think I can speak for everyone when I say that you are a living testimony of what God can do. Happy birthday, Kechi."

In the midst of our joyous merrymaking, extremely unfortunate news reached our ears and blackened the cheerful atmosphere in an instant.

"...at 11:30 this morning, ADC Flight 53 crashed shortly after takeoff from Nnamdi Azikiwe International Airport, killing ninety-six of the one hundred and five people on board, including the flight crew. The Boeing 737 aircraft reportedly crash-landed and caught fire in a cornfield off of ..."

The woman's voice on the TV trailed off into the background as the ringing in my ears grew louder and louder. I stared at the TV in utter disbelief.

"Another plane crash," I heard myself say in a deadpan voice over the low muttering that had ensued in the room. Another plane had crashed just ten months after Sosoliso.

"It hasn't even been a year," Mommy said gravely as she stared at the TV, shaking her head.

Another plane crash. I couldn't believe it.

The grief of the parents of the sixty angels and everyone who lost loved ones on December 10, 2005, was still so fresh, yet here we were again. Same story, new lives lost. At least nine people had survived this one.

A raw mix of anger and revulsion flared up inside me.

Two plane crashes happening within ten months of each other meant that no lesson had been learned from the tragedy of Sosoliso. It meant that the loss of the lives of sixty *children*, a demographic that is typically so fiercely protected in any other country, meant absolutely nothing to the Nigerian government.

This ADC plane had also crashed for the *exact same reasons* as the one I had been on: pilot error and wind shear.

Even after sixty children had died, human life still meant nothing to those in power. They'd rather embezzle public funds than fix infrastructure. I would have expected that new airline safety measures would have been put in place to minimize further tragedy. At that moment, I hated the callousness of public officials for whom it was business as usual.

I will never forget my seventeenth birthday. A day my family and I were reminded that, just like the ninety-six lives that were lost on that ADC crash, my life, which we felt was worth celebrating, still meant *nothing* to those with the power to enforce necessary change in our airline industry.

Chapter Fifteen

The Send-Off

After much deliberation, it was decided that Shriners Hospital for Children in Galveston, Texas, would be the best fit for me for the remaining reconstructive surgeries I needed. Not only did they specialize in reconstructive burn surgery but they also specialized in treating children from infancy to twenty-one, regardless of their ability to pay.

Shell Hospital started making the necessary arrangements for my family's and my successful relocation to Texas. Dr. Moses, the kindhearted senior medical officer at Shell, was the champion of this move to America.

I had no idea how long we would need to stay and I knew we weren't exactly traveling for vacation, but I was excited, nonetheless. Nigerian media had done a fantastic job of painting America gold. To me, it was the land of endless opportunities and freedoms, where public, government-owned schools actually offered solid education, kids could wear whatever they wanted to school, burgers and fries were available at every corner of every city, and literally anyone could become a star overnight with the right luck.

It was also the land of hope. It was the place where I would receive top-notch burn care and possibly regain my independence. I couldn't wait.

Mommy, Tara, and I flew to Lagos toward the end of the year, and as a result, we spent Christmas and New Year's with Mommy's family. We stayed with Aunty Ulo briefly before moving over to my grandparents' house, where we stayed until it was time for our trip to America.

My time with my mom's parents was filled with lots of love, warmth, and happiness. I was constantly surrounded by family, especially my awesome cousins, who spent as much time with me as possible.

It was while I was in my grandparents' home that Bunmi Amusan, the only other Sosoliso plane crash survivor, came to visit me and my family.

Bunmi was a travel agent and had been the personal assistant of a renowned Nigerian pastor, Pastor Bimbo Odukoya, who had been on the Sosoliso flight as well. We'd never met, but Mommy told me Bunmi had actually ridden in the same ambulance as me on the day of the crash.

The day Bunmi came to my grandparents' house to see me, Mommy and Aunty Ulo were in my room.

Bunmi walked in wearing an arm splint, and she got teary the moment she laid eyes on me.

She approached my bed and gave me a gentle hug, and we stayed like that for a while, just holding each other, comforting each other. It was an emotionally charged moment, and I thought to myself, *Wow, here is a person, a complete stranger, whose fate has been linked to mine by the most inconceivable experience.* I did not know her, yet I shared an incredible bond with her, and it would last for the rest of my life.

"I've been looking forward to finally meeting you, Kechi."

"Me too," I said sincerely. Even though she wasn't nearly as burned as me, she was the only other living person in the world who could speak on that Sosoliso crash experience from a perspective similar to mine.

"I will never forget that day," she said as she shook her head. "I remember everything as if it just happened."

"Kechi doesn't remember the crash itself," Mommy told her. She was sitting right by me on the bed, by my pillow.

Bunmi looked surprised. "Really? Wow. So you don't remember the plane crashing?"

Nor do I want to. "I remember taking off," I said. "I remember when the turbulence started, but I blacked out before the impact."

"Ah, the turbulence was so bad. It was raining very badly that day in Port Harcourt. There was a thunderstorm, and everyone noticed that something was wrong. Then a lady at the back suddenly screamed, 'Is this plane trying to land?!'"

"Yes, I think I remember that!" My heart throbbed painfully in my chest at the mention of something familiar. It felt so spooky. For months I had been telling this story to others. I'd relive my memories of that day in my head and in my dreams. It was eerie to talk to someone who knew the things that happened *on* the plane that day without me sharing them. In a confusing way, it made me feel less alone.

"Then the plane hit the ground *hard*." Bunmi visibly shuddered. "My seat belt stayed on somehow. All I could see was fire. Fire everywhere! The flames, the smoke . . ." Bunmi's eyes turned glassy as she recalled the gruesome memories of that day. "Just bodies, so many bodies that had been thrown out of their seats, just all over the floor, burning."

My blood turned cold at the imagery in my head. As I looked at Bunmi, a surge of sympathy overcame me.

How horrific must it be to have such memories inside you?

"Then the fire engines came, and they didn't have any water in their tanks."

I wanted to scream. But to what end?

I was sick and tired of being shocked at the utter and irreverent inadequacy of Nigeria, because *of course* they didn't have water in their tanks. Of course they didn't. We will never know how many lives may have been saved had the trucks had water that day.

Bunmi took in a shaky breath and let it out on a deep sigh. "I don't know how come I wasn't very badly burned, honestly. Maybe it's because of where I was sitting? I was in front."

"Kechi was in front too!" Mommy exclaimed, and I nodded.

"Really?" Bunmi said in surprise. "I was actually supposed to be at the back, but somebody exchanged seats with me! And just imagine, the entire back of the aircraft burned the worst!"

So Bunmi and I were both seated at the front of the aircraft?

I had no idea whether that played a role in our survival, but seeing as we weren't the only passengers seated at the front of the plane, I thought it unlikely.

I sat back on my pillows, my mind in a million different places as Bunmi kept on talking through her grief. It was a miracle she did not sustain very bad burns, for sure. But as I gazed at her, I thought about the story she'd just told us.

This woman remembered the parts of the accident that I somehow could not. Only she remembered the worst parts of an experience we both shared. She remembered the fire. She remembered the smell of the smoke mixed with the smell of burning flesh. She saw it all, and she remembered it all. And now, listening to her, it was clear she was dealing with a huge amount of grief and guilt.

Somehow, in a grotesque attempt to create some sort of balance, it seemed as though I had received the bulk of the physical trauma caused by the accident, while Bunmi had been given the bulk of the psychological trauma. It was as though fate had decided the fullness of the trauma could not be handled by one person and had therefore split it between two people.

Bunmi's story opened my eyes to a brand-new perspective about the innate difference between physical and psychological trauma.

Physical trauma is painful and obvious, but if you survive it, it eventually heals. A living body will always mend itself, one way or another.

Psychological trauma, on the other hand? It is much less obvious to the eye, yet it seems to have the power to deal more lasting damage to the individual.

Bunmi's story made me realize I would rather deal with the burdens of my physical trauma than the crushing weight of her psychological trauma. I didn't even want to imagine how her mind was processing her experience and grief.

How would her mental state recover? How long would the recovery take?

I couldn't remember the plane actually crashing, and I believe that fact played a large role in why the idea of entering a plane again didn't quite faze me as much as one would expect it to. But with the kind of memories Bunmi had sustained from the crash, I was quite certain even before she ever affirmed it that she never wanted to board another plane in her life.

She and I talked a lot more. I told her of my time in South Africa. Then I asked about her shoulder, and she said she was frustrated at the slow healing pace.

I remembered the arduously slow process of my own healing in South Africa, and I smiled knowingly. "Don't worry. You will heal."

Bunmi gave me this strange look. Then she smiled beautifully back at me. "Amen."

I had a lot more visitors while I was staying with my grandparents.

Most people who visited would talk to me, try to encourage me, then pray with me before they left.

I appreciated the prayers and most of the encouragement, but there was one thing a lot of people said that gave me cause for concern: "God saved you for a reason, Kechi. He saved you for His special purpose."

At first whenever I heard this, I would just nod.

As I started to hear it more frequently, however, it got me feeling nervous and slightly uneasy. It occurred to me that, because I had survived an ordeal as terrible as a plane crash against incredible odds, people expected me to do equally incredible things with my life, and that put an insane amount of pressure on me.

I had already decided to live my life for the sixty angels and for the loved ones they left behind. But that was a self-imposed pressure. Pressure from the outside world felt very different.

What if they were wrong? What if there was no special purpose for my life? Or worse yet, what if I *was* saved for a special purpose but I never found out what it was? Would I then be considered a failure? If I didn't do anything special with my life after all, would people wonder what I was saved for?

It bothered me so much. Every time I heard that sentence, it made me feel as if I had to *earn* this life somehow.

One evening, I got a new visitor. Everyone called him Brother Chibunna, but he was Uncle Chibunna to us kids (as is the typical case with Nigeria's strict culture of respect for elders). He was a good guy, very wise, and I always felt like he had a real heart for God. I knew my family respected him.

Uncle Chibunna came into my room and sat at the corner of my bed, and I just knew it was going to be more of the same sentiments I had heard in the past.

"Kechi," he said. "I'm sure a lot of people have been telling you how God saved you for a special purpose and how He wants you to do great things, and I'm sure you're so tired of hearing all that."

Okay, I definitely did not expect that.

I huffed out a relieved laugh. "You have no idea."

Uncle Chibunna chuckled as well, then he waved his hand dismissively. "Pay them no mind, my dear. Because, you know what? God's plan in all this may just be for you to simply *live*. Just survive. And I want you to know that that is perfectly okay, Kechi. You don't need to worry about 'doing great things' or 'changing the world' and all of that. If it happens"—he shrugged—"great. But if it doesn't, still great. So don't worry about anything, and just live your life. You hear me? It's okay to just live your life."

After Uncle Chibunna left that night, Mommy came to me, all smiles.

"I bet you were happy to hear that," she said. I laughed, feeling like a weight had been lifted off me.

I thanked God for Uncle Chibunna's visit that day and for his perceptiveness. God definitely knew I needed to hear that, and He'd sent someone whose words He knew I would trust.

I just needed to know it was *okay* if I ended up being ordinary.

And honestly? *Any* kind of life, *any* kind of future would be extraordinary to me, because it would be a future I almost didn't have at all.

Toward the end of February 2007, Mommy, Grandma, Tara, and I flew to Abuja to meet up with Daddy. We were to visit the embassy there to get our visas for our trip to America.

The flight from Lagos to Abuja was only about forty-five minutes long. I didn't think much of it, really. One minute we were in Lagos and the next we were in Abuja. A few days after that, we were finally on our way to America.

I felt ready for whatever the next stage of my life had in store for me.

America

Chapter Sixteen

The Adapting

Mommy, Grandma, Tara, and I finally left for America in February 2007, a little over a year after the plane crash. I was delighted that Grandma was coming with us. Daddy, meanwhile, was going to stay behind to wrap up some business, then meet us in the States at a later date.

Our flight was announced at the airport, and the four of us boarded the aircraft.

It was my first time traveling in first class—that I could actually remember, at least. The trip from South Africa to Nigeria had also been first class, but since I didn't remember any of it, I didn't count it.

This sixteen-hour trip was actually quite pleasant. I slept for most of it.

We finally got to America, and we were welcomed very pleasantly at baggage claim by the Smiths, a Nigerian American family who was to be our host family.

Our time with the Smiths was tumultuous. It brought me head-on with childhood bullying, which perhaps explains my strong stance against any kind of bullying to this day.

The Smiths were a truly wonderful couple who compassionately let us into their home for a brief spell. Their nine-year-old daughter, Bella, however, wasn't so welcoming.

Tara, then seven years old, had already experienced some bullying back home due to family adjustments that arose from my accident. A family she was left with while my mom was with me in South Africa had older kids who turned out to be significantly unfriendly to her. When our family became whole again in Nigeria, I noticed that my typically active and self-assured little sister had become more hesitant and easily prone to tears. By the time we moved to America, Tara was all but herself again, but all her timidity resurfaced with the Smiths when Bella started bullying her. It was hell to witness yet another child prey on my sister's insecurities, and I was so enraged, perhaps more so by my inability to address the issue.

Long story short, we had to get our own place—which we wouldn't have been able to do so easily without Mrs. Smith's help, mind you.

I hated what this experience did to my little sister's self-esteem, which is a quality that should never be compromised in any human being. One might say Bella was just a child and she didn't know any better. That's partly true; she *was* just a child.

But I was nine years old when I developed early and kids in school started teasing me about my boobs. I got so self-conscious that I started to slouch in an effort to hide them. I knew that I was being teased, and it didn't feel nice. I knew the kids who teased me were wrong to do so.

I was also nine years old when a kid in class wet himself and all the other kids started pointing and laughing at him as the teacher escorted him outside. I watched those kids laugh at that boy, and I knew they shouldn't be laughing at another person like that.

At nine, you definitely know right from wrong. I did. Bella did. If she didn't, the bullying would not have been done in secret.

Bullies exist even at that age, and it's that kind of dismissive attitude toward childhood bullying that empowers tormentors and creates more victims. Childhood is the most impressionable time period of our lives. It worried me so much that Bella's behavior seemed to be left unchecked by the adults in her life, but I was even more concerned about how the experience would affect Tara long-term.

After we moved out of the Smiths' home, I genuinely prayed that Bella would eventually grow up to be a better person, for her sake and for that of those around her. I hoped she would change.

It would be a long road ahead, trying to ensure that Tara did not permanently internalize her experience with Bella or any other bully who came before or after her, but Mom and I were definitely up to the task. With God's help, we would make Tara bloom into the beautiful, self-confident person she was always meant to be.

We were able to fully find our footing in America after we left the Smiths' home and moved to Galveston, Texas. We moved into a cute little two-bedroom apartment, right off Galveston Seawall. It was five minutes from Tara's elementary school and about ten to twelve minutes from Shriners Hospital.

The transition from one country to another wasn't too bad for me.

Well, it didn't feel like much of a change for *me*, specifically. I was just moving from staying in a bed in Port Harcourt to staying in a bed in Galveston.

But it was a huge adjustment for the rest of the family, especially Tara, who had trouble coming into her own and finding the right type of friends. Daddy had to leave for Nigeria soon after the move to take care of his business, so Mommy had to learn and adapt quickly to so many new things while simultaneously taking care of Tara and me. She was like Wonder Woman to us.

After spending several weeks with us in Galveston, Grandma headed back to Nigeria as well. We were all sad to see her go, especially Tara, who had gotten very attached to her.

Then the time came for our first visit to Shriners Hospital. I will never forget the impact it had on me with the colorful, cheerful paintings and murals that decorated the walls on every single floor and even some of the ceilings.

When we stepped into the clinic lobby, I had a moment of shocking self-awareness.

For the first time since the accident happened, I was not the only burn patient in the room. For the first time since the accident, I was surrounded by other burn victims—and all of them were little children!

That day in the clinic lobby, I saw a kid wearing a sort of transparent mask over a face that was as heavily burned as mine. The mask had holes in it for his eyes, nose, and mouth, and it was held in place by multiple straps that went around his head. He could not have been more than three years old. I couldn't believe anyone that little had had to suffer through something painful enough to cause an injury like that.

I looked around as discreetly as I could and saw a little girl wearing a neck brace much like the one I'd worn in South Africa, and another little girl who was wearing a blue plastic-like mold that had been shaped to fit her tiny hand. All of these kids were running around the lobby, playing and laughing under their parents' watchful gazes.

As if in a trance, I just watched them in silence and awe.

Wrapped up in bandages, braces, and face masks, they were so carefree, like kids should be. So happy despite what life had done to them at such tender ages. It all felt so surreal to me, and for the first time since the plane crash, I turned my lens away from myself for a moment and pointed it out into the world around me. I acknowledged that I was not the only person that had gone through the kind of trauma I had gone through. But as I continued to watch those kids run around, I had an even more important epiphany: I didn't have to allow my trauma to victimize me more than it already had.

I realized that the plane crash—for everything it had already taken from me and so many other people, things that we could not help—did not have to take away my joy. Despite what happened to me, I could *choose* joy. I could choose to hold on to my smile, my happiness. Just as these kids had.

I found myself smiling at them.

So many painful things happened in this place, for sure. So many kids cried from the pain of their injuries, hurt from the strains of surgery and physical therapy. These walls definitely held the sounds of pain and suffering. One look at the kids in their therapy gear would tell you that much. But these walls held the sounds of laughter and happiness too. This hospital had chosen to give that to their patients. I hadn't even met my doctors yet, but I already felt like I belonged.

I hadn't really seen much of Milpark Hospital during my stay, but the little I saw was quite beautiful. While Shriners was also a huge, impressive building, there was something special about it, about the atmosphere inside. It went beyond the beautifully decorated surroundings, and it permeated the very air of the place.

It felt less like a hospital and more like a potential second home.

Chapter Seventeen

Shriners
and the Music

Suffice it to say that Shriners gave the best first impression *ever*. From that first day, Mommy and I knew we were in the right place.

In my first year with them, it was all I could do to keep up with the frequency of my surgeries. I spent most of my time sleeping and recuperating. I was having multiple procedures at a time, which would take a heavy toll on my body and test the limits of my pain tolerance.

My arms were one of my first surgeries at Shriners. They were bent at the elbows at almost ninety degrees due to extreme contractures, and my remarkable surgeon, (late) Dr. Robert Macauley, performed a skin release at the contraction points then inserted a skin graft to maintain the release. The majority of my surgeries were going to be similar in nature.

I was familiar with skin grafts by that point, but it still all sounded like magic to me. I had to wonder how in the world people realized it was even possible to move skin from one part of the body to another without the skin cells dying in transit. It was such an incredible concept.

Surgery at Shriners was different from what I remembered though. I had vague memories of the before and after of the surgeries I had at Milpark, but those moments became much more distinct at Shriners, especially the sensation of coming out of surgery.

I would be floating inside my head in blissful peace and quiet and sinking darkness, but then I would hear my mother's voice calling out to me as if from far, far away. The more she called my name, the more alert I would become.

As I waded up from the darkness, following her voice, other sounds from the outside world would begin to permeate my deep quiet: the beeping of machines around me; the drip, drip, dripping sound of an IV; the gentle, rustling sound of sheets and blankets. . . . Then I would open my eyes to the world once more. And after every single surgery, I'd get a stuffed animal, as per Shriners' protocol. I imagined their younger patients loved that, especially if I was so thrilled by it at seventeen.

Surgery was always followed with staple and suture removals, something I learned to despise very quickly. The sutures were tiny threads that the surgeons used to hold my grafts in place, along with silver pins called surgical staples. The thought of doctors using a needle and thread and some kind of stapler to literally sew a patch of skin into place, like my body was a patchwork quilt, amused me at first.

There was nothing amusing about the removal process of the staples, however. The sutures needed to be cut loose with scissors, but the staples needed to be pushed down in the middle with a staple remover to free their grip on my skin. Each one felt like a deep needle prick as it was tugged out.

The nurse always asked me if I wanted to take my pain meds before we started the process, or if I wanted to take breaks in between. As usual, I always declined. I just did not believe in delaying pain. I did, however, believe in delayed gratification.

After staple removal came the dreaded physiotherapy visit. My old nemesis.

Chris, one of my first physiotherapists at Shriners, tried to explain how important the splints and face masks were when he saw how averse I was to wearing them.

"All the surgery in the world won't matter if we don't control the contracting scars as much as we can, Kechi," he told me. "All you need to do is wear it for as long as you can stand to, then take it off when you can't. It's okay to take a break here and there. Try to keep it on longer than you keep it off, and try your best to wear it when you're sleeping. The longer you wear it, the straighter your arm will be, and I know that's what you want."

He was right. Of course he was right.

"I'll do my best," I said.

"That's all you can do!"

I could tell I would at least enjoy working with this guy. As hard as physiotherapy was going to be, it would be nice to at least like my physiotherapist this time.

But I hated the splints. Every single one of them.

I didn't understand how those little kids were able to wear them and play around like everything was okay.

As my grafts healed, the skin wanted more than anything to contract, to heal back into the same position it had been in pre-surgery, and the splints were there to combat that tendency. Every time I took the splints off, my elbows felt so loose, and I was able to stretch my arms out with virtually no pull. It was incredible.

The longer I *kept* them off, however, the quicker my skin started to pull tight again.

It was crazy the way my skin was so quick to do what it shouldn't. With third-degree burns, your skin can either form hypertrophic scars (the ones that itch the most), contraction scars (the ones that tighten, like my arm) or keloid scars (the huge, shiny ones that heal smooth). Naturally, my skin had decided to go for the trifecta.

As time passed, I did start to adjust. I mean, I had no choice. If these gadgets were to be a part of my life henceforth, I had to learn to adapt to my new reality and make them work for me.

Didn't you decide not to let your circumstances steal your joy? I reminded myself.

178

So I took solace in singing. Daddy bought me a karaoke machine, and it became my favorite distraction in the world. I could sing on that thing for hours every day I had the energy to.

Also, once my body had filled back out completely, I could more or less wear what I wanted, so I took solace in fashion too. I dressed up nice and made every hospital visit an outing. I had fun matching outfit colors with my shoes, and since I was now bald, I invested in every color and style of hat I could find. I basically decided that if I got to wear nice clothes and shoes, then wearing the splints and face masks wouldn't be so bad.

Months passed and Shriners really did become my second home. My nurses, doctors, and therapists became friends. Every staff member I encountered at every level, in every department, seemed to care about treating and catering to each patient as an individual, and I deeply appreciated the personalized care I received.

I think the people who worked with me appreciated my realistic attitude toward my treatment. I didn't have any idealistic expectations from my surgeries. Perfection was not the goal with these procedures. It couldn't be. I knew I would never look like I used to. All I could hope for was improvement with each surgery. And yes, every surgery had risk, but these procedures all had the potential to better my quality of life in some way or another. Each one was a *chance* at something better, not a *guarantee*.

My caregivers appreciated my realism, and it allowed them to relax a bit around me.

One day, I was at physiotherapy with Jenny, my other assigned physiotherapist. Just as with Chris, I had developed a wonderful camaraderie with her. During our physical therapy sessions, we would talk about many different things while I did my exercises, and on that day, we were talking about my hobbies. I told her I love to swim and read. By then, she already knew I loved to sing.

I told her about my karaoke machine, and she was so happy for me.

"It's all I ever do at home now," I said. "My dad keeps telling me I should sign up for *American Idol*."

"Yes, you totally should!" Jenny exclaimed. "You have such a great voice!"

I laughed off the idea the same way I laughed it off when Daddy mentioned it to me. Every time I recorded a cover of a song and sent it to him, his response was always the same: *"You know, Adaobi, you should consider signing up for one of those singing talent shows. You never know."*

Yeah, right. Like I would ever do something so scary.

"You know, I've been thinking," Jenny said. "The hospital has a music therapy program. It's geared toward the younger kids, but if you're interested, we can talk to someone, see if it's something we can add to your schedule."

My heart was already pumping in excitement at the mere prospect of music therapy. "I'm definitely interested!"

I soon met with Christine, one of the music therapists on staff, and she was a wonderful, warm human being. In many ways, she reminded me of my South African grief counselor. She was so talkative and sweet, and I could immediately see how little kids would love her.

"So, Kechi, what part of music do you like?" Christine asked me with a smile.

"I like to sing," I replied, feeling a bit shy for some reason.

"She has a really great voice. She's being modest," Jenny said from beside me, making me blush.

Christine took me to the music room the day we met. It was a small space, but it was well outfitted with pretty much every instrument I could think of, as well as several mics. It was incredible. The walls even had some colorful padding on them to improve the room's acoustics.

"So"—Christine looked at me—"how you feeling? Would you like to sing a little something for me, maybe?"

My eyes popped open. "Now?" I asked, startled. I hadn't expected we'd start so soon.

"Yeah, why not?" Christine walked across the room and pulled out a beautiful violin from its case. "Come on, I'll accompany you. Grab the mic over there. It's on."

I looked over at the mic she pointed to, and after a moment, I walked over and pulled it out of its stand.

I was very nervous. It only just occurred to me that I'd never sung in front of a stranger before.

"What would you like to sing?" Christine asked me. "We can do something simple."

"Um . . . I can pick anything?"

"Yeah. You never know, I might know the song you choose."

"Okay, um . . . do you know 'Breakaway' by Kelly Clarkson?"

"Sure! Okay, you wanna just . . . start?"

"Um. Okay." I cleared my throat and tapped the mic to make sure it was on. Then I started singing tentatively.

Christine started playing and as the beautiful, smooth sound of the violin strings enveloped my voice, I just knew singing karaoke would never be the same again. It could never compare to the feeling of singing with live, instrumental accompaniment. It felt so raw and emotional, like the sounds of the strings were vibrating inside my chest and enhancing my own voice, supporting it. It was my first time singing with a live instrument, and it felt wonderful. The more I sang, the more confident I felt.

I sang up until the second chorus and finally stopped.

I exhaled loudly and looked at Christine with a wide smile. "That was so awesome!"

"Yeah, it was." Her eyes were shining behind her glasses. "You have an amazing voice, young lady."

I laughed breathlessly, grateful for the compliment. It was definitely a different feeling to hear positive feedback about my singing from someone other than my family or friends, especially when that person had a musical background.

"Have you always been able to sing like that?" she asked interestedly. "I mean, how did you get into music?"

I looked at her, wondering where to start with my response.

"I kinda grew up with it." I sat down on one of the stools in the room. "My parents were always playing music in the house when I was a kid. But I didn't sing like this until after the accident."

Christine was easy to open up to, so I found myself explaining the crucial role music had played in grounding me to reality during my coma back in South Africa. Much like my mother's voice, it had been a lifeline, and I learned to appreciate the deep, almost spiritual connection between music, memories, and emotions. For instance, I knew that my soundtrack for South Africa would always and forever be that one Kelly Clarkson song that had opened my eyes to God's love for me.

"I loved singing before the accident," I told Christine, "but my voice changed after."

"That's incredible, Kechi," Christine said in awe. "I've always believed in the power of music. It's intangible but so very real, you know?"

I nodded, completely agreeing with her. Indeed, I would say that what medicine did for my body, music did for my soul, for it reached parts of me that medicine could not.

"I think it's incredible that you can play so many instruments," I said to her.

"Aw, you're so sweet, Kechi." Christine smiled gratefully. "We're going to have so much fun together!"

She was totally right. Music therapy became a huge part of my life. It brought me joy to share music with others who appreciated it as much as I did. Through music therapy, music had become an escape for me again, just as it had in South Africa. The Shriners Galveston music room became one of my happy places.

Chapter Eighteen

The School

My surgeries continued into the spring of 2008, as did physical therapy and music therapy. But I was starting to notice something new.

I was getting bored.

For the past year, I had done nothing but surgery and physiotherapy, so I had regained quite a bit of independence with the help of my many splints. This was great because it meant my surgeries were working. Though I was still having surgeries and physical and music therapy appointments, they were no longer enough to occupy me fully.

"Adaobi, maybe you're ready to continue school," Daddy suggested one day.

School? Hmm.

I thought about it for a long time, and it was interesting because for most of my life, the concept of school had never made me feel anything but resentment. I had only ever enjoyed school up to my middle school years. Everything that followed had felt like punishment. That was probably because school had always been presented as an obligation.

But being presented to me as a choice, however, seemed to make all the difference because for the first time in my life, I *missed* it. Maybe it was just a lifetime of conditioning at play, but I actually wanted to be in school. It was the strangest, most foreign feeling, missing school of all things, but I couldn't deny its existence.

Daddy's suggestion was absolutely perfect. The more I thought about it, the more I felt in my heart it was time. I felt ready for that step, for that new phase.

So in 2008, about two years after the plane crash, I decided to continue high school. I still had a long way to go with my treatment, but as my body was healing, my mind had been left idle for far too long, and it craved nourishment. Shriners liaised with LJC and got all the documents necessary for me to officially enroll as a senior at Ball High School in Galveston, Texas.

Being back at school was interesting. I entered Ball High as a part-time student because I still had surgeries and hospital appointments I couldn't miss.

The first week was difficult. It was a new school in a new country, an entirely new environment, and the semester had already started. Of course I wasn't expected to seamlessly slip into routine with students and teachers I'd only just met, but I had high expectations for myself. It took me a couple weeks to fully adjust. Once I did, I enjoyed the feeling of being back in a classroom setting, and I appreciated the opportunity to learn once again.

Though as time passed at Ball High, I found myself losing interest in my surroundings. I didn't really want to make friends. I didn't want to eat in the cafeteria. I just wanted to learn, ace my exams, do my assignments, and get out of that building.

Why? I wondered to myself, to my mom. Why didn't I want to interact with anyone? I thought this was what I wanted, to be back in school and immerse myself in the experience once more. It wasn't like anyone was being mean to me; as a matter of fact, those I bothered to interact with were really nice.

No one was rude or mean to me, at least not in reference to my burns. I was still wearing face masks and splints and all sorts of contraptions to help my surgery sites heal properly, and I had to wear all these things to school too. But no one seemed to care. It was wonderful.

It wasn't like I started at Ball High expecting to be harassed or bullied because of my appearance. I don't typically walk around expecting mistreatment from anyone in general. I just lived my life and minded my business, and consistent with my experience in America thus far, so did everyone else, for the most part. But Shriners had made it clear that experiencing such things was a possibility. My reintegration counselors told me to let them know if such a thing were to happen, but I was pretty confident it wouldn't. I had no basis for this confidence. I just believed I wouldn't experience harsh treatment due to my burns. Thank God I was right.

So, why was I so uninterested in my high school surroundings? One day I realized what it was.

All my friends from back home were in college. Even those who were grades below me at LJC had now graduated. Because of this, I had disengaged from my surroundings because I no longer felt like I belonged in high school. Circumstances had put me there, not choice. So I really felt like I was just playing catch-up.

This realization couldn't have come at a better time because it also turned out that my being a part-time student was no longer cutting it. I was missing too many classes because I'd often have to leave early for a hospital appointment. I needed a less conventional and efficient way to finish my final year of high school classes that would also be flexible enough to allow me to continue my hospital appointments without missing school lessons.

Thus, I was removed from Ball High and enrolled in Accelerated Independent Module. AIM was available to students who wanted access to accelerated learning so they could graduate as soon as possible, students who simply needed access to the education part of high school without all the other stuff that usually comes with it. Aka, students like me. It was perfect for me.

With its computerized program, I was able to focus on my classes with no forced interactions in any of them. I just did my work at my own pace, completed my modules and assignments, and voila. Done.

I loved the AIM program. I also really liked the teachers, and since the class sizes were so small, there was personalized learning too.

My math teacher, Mr. Richards, was awesome and patient. Math was my Achilles' heel at LJC, and when I started high school again in America, I had to start from scratch. It was that bad.

I decided to take it as an opportunity for a fresh start. Maybe if I took it seriously and didn't give up when it got hard, I could prove to myself and to all those LJC math teachers who gave up on me that anyone could pass math if they practiced it enough.

Well, I got so good that Mr. Richards started sending other students to me to help explain certain concepts!

The first time he did that, I laughed and thought to myself, *If my old math teachers could see me now, they'd faint from shock!*

Mrs. Moser, my English teacher, fell in love with my writing. Seeing as I always felt English—writing specifically—was one of my strong points, it pleased me greatly to see her appreciate my efforts. For some reason, she felt like I was an exemplary student, and honestly, I wasn't used to being seen that way by teachers, at least not since middle school.

I guess I never really gave a lot of teachers at LJC a chance to see what I was like when I took my studies seriously. The better I did in school, the more regretful I was about how lax a student I had been back home. But I guess the key difference between the Kechi then and the Kechi in AIM was that present-day Kechi had far less distractions to deal with, thus allowing her to focus entirely on school.

"You've been through so much," Mrs. Moser would say. "Anyone would understand if you decided not to go back to school, but you chose not to let what happened stop you from accomplishing your goals. You're amazing, Kechi, and I'm so grateful to God for your life."

I didn't feel like I was doing anything amazing. I was just doing what was normal. The way I saw it, I had no excuse. I was well enough, physically and mentally, to continue school and complete my high school education; therefore, I had no excuse not to.

Chapter Nineteen

The Surgeries

Of all the surgeries I had at Shriners, the most remarkable was the surgery performed on my fingers, the bones of which had curved into themselves and fused in that position. It was by far my most complicated procedure to date. It was also the surgery that changed my life the most with the results it produced.

I met the hand specialist, Dr. Charlotte Alexander, at Shriners Houston, where Shriners Galveston's patients and staff migrated after Hurricane Ike hit Galveston Island horrendously in September 2008. Shriners Houston and Shriners Galveston merged, and Dr. Charlotte performed this four-hour-long surgery with Dr. Macauley.

"What we can do is break the bones on your fingers and fuse them into a more practical position than where they're at right now," Dr. Charlotte told me before the surgery. "We'll use pins to fuse them into a sort of curved position, like so." She demonstrated with her own hand by bending her fingers into an open-palm, claw-like position. "This way, you'll be able to make a fist. The only thing is your fingers will be stuck in that fused position permanently, Kechi, so you'll never be able to straighten them fully again."

It truly dazed me to hear someone talk about breaking my bones in such a casual way, but I got over it and agreed to the surgery. I did want more independence. I did want to be able to do way more for myself so that Mommy could do less and rest more.

I was no stranger to pain, anyway.

Or so I thought.

Unfortunately for me, my IV got disconnected from my foot the day after the surgery, and once the numbing medication wore off my hands, what followed was the most excruciating pain I had ever experienced in my waking life.

It felt like my fingers were trapped inside the jaws of a vise and someone had turned the handle, clamping its iron grip until it could turn no more, and then just left my fingers in there to suffer permanently.

There was nothing anyone could do. The pain was literally bone deep. Since my surgery was on a Friday, there was no doctor available to reinsert my IV in order to administer numbing medication for the duration of the weekend, when my viselike pain was at its peak. The nurses rotated me on Vicodin and Oxycontin, which did absolutely nothing until much later in my recuperation.

This surgery was by far the biggest test of my endurance, patience, and pain tolerance to date. I was in a situation where I had no choice but to adapt. No one was coming to rescue me from this pain, and the nurses were doing their best with what they had.

Thankfully, the surgery was a huge success afterward, and combined with a lot of physical therapy, splints, and exercises, I got my grip back on both hands. Dr. Charlotte was a miracle worker. She was a gifted surgeon, and I was grateful to God that I was being treated by such incredible surgeons like her and Dr. Macauley. My fingers would never *look* normal—very few parts of me still did—but now they *worked* normally, and that was all that mattered to me.

Nothing of value comes easy.

Having the ability to make a fist on both hands is a gift that Shriners gave to me, but I had to do my part to earn that gift by making sure the surgery did not succeed in vain. The thought reminds me of the time in South Africa when God taught me the hard lesson that surviving the plane crash didn't mean the rest of my life was going to be smooth sailing.

Nothing was going to be handed to me, not in South Africa, and not here in America. I had to put in my own work too. I went through fire that tried to take my life and now . . . now, God was putting me through a different kind of fire.

A refining fire.

After we moved to America, many LJC alumni friends came to visit me in Galveston.

Honestly, at first I didn't think too deeply about how they would take my new appearance. A lot of Nigerians around the globe had been following my story and my journey through a Facebook page Mom had opened on my behalf, so I knew that my classmates knew what I looked like.

But then I thought about it more, and I stepped into their shoes.

At that point, I was in a place where I was fully aware of my situation. I knew I looked different. But with my awareness also came full *acceptance* of myself.

And I understood that it would be hard for others to go from awareness to acceptance as quickly as I had. In fact, it would be *unfair* to expect that of anyone who wasn't a close family member or a close friend.

So I decided that if they didn't know how to react when they saw me in the flesh and, through no fault of their own, didn't know how to break the ice, it was only right to afford my friends the same grace I afforded staring strangers. Because I did understand. A person might meet me and not know how to behave, especially if they didn't know how comfortable *I* was with my burns. Only I knew that I was okay with all of that. Only I knew that, despite the scars, I was the same Kechi on the inside.

How could I expect random people to know that? How would my classmates know?

So I prayed.

If there's a wall, Lord, please help me break it down. Show me how.

My only hope was that when they talked to me and saw that I was still the same Kechi, then they would also see that they could interact with me normally.

All I can do is be myself. I don't know how to be any other way, Lord. Please let that be enough.

I'll never forget when Chima Ebili came for my high school graduation, along with my friends Nosa, Chinedu, and Jude. Everyone but Chima had seen me in person already.

When we got to my house to continue the celebrations, we were all talking to each other and joking around excitedly, and that was when the magic moment happened.

Chima, out of the blue, just gave me this extremely bemused look and went, "Come, o!¹ This girl is still the same silly Kechi we know. I don't know what I was worried about."

Everyone laughed at that, including my mom and Tara, and really, I couldn't even begin to explain how I felt in that moment, but my heart was singing with joy.

All my friends' visits, Chima's especially, were extremely significant for me. They marked the moment I learned a most valuable lesson when it came to connecting with others: I can *help* people see past my scars. I don't have to be a passive participant in that interaction. I have a role to play there too.

Basically, I have the power to decide how much of "Kechi" other people get to see, to know, and to experience.

I also learned something valuable about myself that day: helping my friends see beyond this scarred exterior and get comfortable around me hadn't taken any extra effort on my part at all.

This was yet another gift from God, the fact that I didn't have to force my behavior around anyone I encountered or pretend

---

1. O is Nigerian slang, typically used at the end of sentence. It's a short phrase or word used for emphasis.

to be okay for anyone's sake. I really was okay and if I wasn't, it would show.

From that moment on, I knew the right way to interact with the world. I knew it would be my approach. When meeting new people, I would interact with them with the foreknowledge that I can help them see I'm a normal person just like them, even though I don't look very normal. I had to trust that God had given me a personality and an ability to allow people to be comfortable enough to be themselves around me.

This was the foundation of what was to become my brand a decade later: authenticity.

I could preach authenticity to others because I myself lived it.

It was really a miracle that I managed to make any new friends after the accident. Jennifer Gillis Harry and Sandra Ozuzu were definitely gifts from God. I didn't notice it for a long time, but the plane crash affected my willingness to form new relationships. I was content with the friends I had prior to the accident, and although we all lived so far apart, I was too wary to form new attachments to new people. It was a problem I became aware of but wasn't quite ready to address. Without Jennifer's and Sandra's own dogged efforts to create the bond we now share, I would be a different Kechi today.

I officially aged out of Shriners' system in 2010 as a twenty-one-year-old. Despite this, I was able to continue my procedures due to an incredible fundraiser my friends Yimi and Somachi organized for me back in Nigeria. The fundraiser raised enough money to fund my surgeries.

I was in a pretty good place at that point in my life, thanks to Shriners. If I'd been told I had reached the apex of what medicine had to offer me in terms of burn reconstruction, I would've been perfectly fine living as I looked because I was independent. My face was still extremely scarred, but I lived as confidently as ever, and I was grateful I still didn't have to pretend to be okay.

That was why when I was presented with the chance to reconstruct parts of my face, I was apprehensive.

During spring break of college in 2012, Dr. Macauley introduced me to his colleague Dr. Robert Spence, a reconstructive burn surgeon at Good Samaritan Hospital in Baltimore, Maryland, who performed the second most remarkable surgery of my life.

Dr. Spence talked about incredible, impossible-sounding things. Things like giving me back my wrist motion on both hands and rebuilding my cheeks and my nose—two features that were completely covered by heavy scar tissue and tended to scar many times over when they were worked on in the past.

"You have soft, untouched skin on your shoulders and on the left side of your hip," Dr. Spence said as he examined my face carefully. "We can remove the scar tissue on your face, then take a good layer of skin from each of your shoulders and sort of . . . flip them up to your cheeks, while keeping them connected to your shoulders to maintain blood flow." He made a flipping motion with his hands as he explained. "This way, the skin will heal and fuse with your face while maintaining the softness of natural cheeks. Your nose too." He brushed a finger over my nose, peering at it clinically. "We can excise the scar tissue and try to rebuild your nose with the skin from your hip. If you're up for it, we'll work on your wrists as well."

It just sounded so crazy. I did not want to hope for anything. I had learned to love myself, to accept myself as I was, and I didn't want anything disturbing that balance.

But Dr. Spence spoke with such confidence, and he gave me such a feeling of assurance, that I felt compelled to trust him.

This complex series of surgeries was performed in stages. First, they surgically inserted balloons underneath my shoulders and in the left side of my hip. Next, we were given syringes that Mommy used to inject saline water into the balloons over a period of two months. This gradually stretched the skin in those areas to the amount needed for the cheeks and nose, all while I continued to attend my classes and go about normal life.

Then the balloon on my hip ripped a hole through my skin, causing the balloon to stick out of my side.

Dr. Spence and Dr. Macauley arranged for me to have emergency surgery at Shriners Galveston to remove it. Luckily the skin on both shoulders was enough for the cheek surgeries.

When the time came, Dr. Spence did exactly as he planned and flipped my expanded shoulder skin onto my cheeks, and when I woke up, I had two giant skin shafts on each side of my face, connecting my shoulders to my cheeks. I literally looked like an alien.

The final stage of the procedure was disconnecting the skin shafts once the grafts on my cheeks had taken, and just like that, I had soft cheeks! Not keloids, not scars, but actual soft, plushy cheeks.

It was . . . marvelous.

After my successful nose and wrist surgeries, both of which used skin from my inner thigh, Mommy, Tara, and I returned to Pearland, where we now lived, at the end of that summer, in complete awe of God and all the gifted hands He had put in my path toward burns recovery.

I thought about Yimi and Somachi and how they were the ones who made all this possible with the fundraiser, and I was filled with gratitude for them both.

After a few more minor procedures, the surgeries stopped indefinitely. The way I saw it, there would always be little things here and there that could stand to be fixed on my body in order to make daily life easier. But even before I encountered Dr. Spence, I had long gotten to a place where I was content with staying the way I was, while simultaneously staying open to whatever opportunities presented themselves to better my life.

Until then, I would continue to focus all my energies on college.

Chapter Twenty

The Future
and the Past

After graduating with a 3.7 GPA from Ball High in 2009, I got accepted on an academic scholarship to University of St. Thomas, Houston, Texas, in 2010. My chosen field of study? Economics with a minor in marketing and communications.

My goals for college were simple and straightforward. I wanted to graduate with the highest possible honors so that I could stand on that stage proudly on behalf of the sixty angels and the loved ones they left behind. College was one more thing that death had stolen from the angels but that I could do in their stead, and I wanted to continue the trend of academic excellence that I had started here in America, for them. Just as I had vowed years ago in South Africa, anything I did, I wanted to do *well*. College would be no different.

My second goal was to get a well-paying job that would allow me to put Tara through college. Life after my surgeries had gotten a little difficult for the Okwuchis, and I wanted to take on some financial burdens for my family.

The first place I was taken was the disability services office, where I was presented with the option to sign up. I declined it. I was happy that my college of choice was accommodating, but I knew I didn't need the service, though I probably didn't look it, what with all my burns and splints and face masks. For me, accepting their service would be accepting special treatment, like access to alternative exam formats and extended time on tests—things I didn't deserve simply based on my burns.

Honestly, I just didn't want any handouts in life. I only wanted what I earned.

During my five years at UST I worked hard each semester, gathering my As and A-minuses. I kept my GPA high through each school year. But I was so focused on my grades that I forgot about the whole purpose of getting good grades in the first place—getting hired.

In 2015, the year that marked the ten-year anniversary of the plane crash, I graduated summa cum laude from UST with a bachelor of arts in economics. I won the award for Excellence in Economics for my graduating class, and I was even given the honor of delivering the student commencement speech for UST's class of 2015.

Receiving my diploma was one more milestone moment God had allowed me to reach. The diploma represented all my hard work, and most importantly, it represented a promise fulfilled to the angels. This degree wasn't just mine; it was for all of us. God had been faithful.

But there was scarcely any time to rest on my laurels, for it was time to embark on accomplishing my second goal: find a job and put Tara through college.

Unfortunately, I learned the hard way that I graduated completely unprepared for the job market, and I soon realized that, while I had thoroughly enjoyed college on the surface level, I had failed woefully on the level that actually mattered.

In all my five years at UST, I made no efforts to form lasting relationships with professors or fellow students, and I made no efforts to search for internships—at first because I was still undergoing surgery, and later on because I didn't want anything that would distract me from my schoolwork. Now that I had decided I was ready to work, I had zero prospects.

Undaunted, I put myself out there. I had faith that it would work out somehow. After all, I graduated summa cum laude. I had a 3.8 GPA! Someone would hire me for sure.

From the moment I graduated, I applied for countless jobs and positions, I went on endless interviews, but I learned rather quickly that the degree I had worked so hard for was a useless piece of paper to employers without the dreaded "work experience" in my résumé. All my As and distinctions meant nothing without work experience to back them up, and I had zilch.

Lord, please, help me. Please. I have worked so hard. Please, let one of these employers take a chance on me. I promise I'll work hard. You know I will work hard.

I continued to apply wherever I could. I wasn't getting offers for any paid positions, so I decided to keep myself busy with non-profit work. I also joined my church worship team, something I had been wanting to do since I was a freshman in college but had told myself I couldn't juggle with school. Now, I had nothing but time and no more excuses.

Truthfully, I was scared of singing on stage, even if it was for God. But then I remembered my first and only stage performance at Shriners Galveston years ago, when Christine, the music therapist, fellow patient Norma, other patients, and I put together a mini concert for the kids at the hospital. Although I was so nervous throughout that Shriners concert, it had become one of my most cherished memories, so I decided to give the worship team a try.

Unsurprisingly, worship soon became a sort of haven for me. Singing in general always made me happy. Singing for God felt wonderful. It filled me with joy and lifted my spirits, which was something I desperately needed.

Then toward the end of that year, a sequence of incredible things happened.

I was invited to speak at TEDxEuston: London[1] in November

---

1. TEDxEuston is an independently organized TED-like event dedicated to spreading the very best ideas and innovation from across Africa and the global Pan-African diaspora (https://www.ted.com/tedx/events/36077).

2015, an incredible honor that I really didn't feel like I deserved, especially given how standstill my life felt at that moment.

Then my Nigerian high school also wanted me to return for the milestone anniversary of the plane crash. It turned out they'd opened an affiliate high school in Port Harcourt called Jesuit Memorial College, and the ceremony was going to be held there.

Honestly, when the anniversary of the plane crash rolled around each year, I was always filled with complicated feelings. A keen gratitude for life juxtaposed with a sharp reminder of extreme grief and loss. I started making special posts on social media on that day every year in an attempt to express some of the confusing feelings, as well as to join my heart with the hearts of those who also lost loved ones that day.

Going back to Nigeria to be with them in person on December 10 would be an entirely different experience. I had to make sure I was ready for it.

And so, after speaking at the TEDxEuston event, I flew back to my home country for the first time since I left in 2007.

My aunty Ulo, who had traveled to London for my TEDxEuston event, was to be my traveling companion to Port Harcourt for the December 10 ceremony.

The day before the event, she and I were still in Lagos.

"Kechi," Aunty Ulo asked me, "how do you feel about flying into Port Harcourt tomorrow?"

Tomorrow? That would mean traveling on December 10.

I looked at Aunty Ulo for a second, then turned away and considered.

Flying to Port Harcourt on the anniversary of my plane crash, which happened in Port Harcourt . . . I could see Mommy in my mind's eye, shaking her head vigorously. Daddy probably wouldn't be crazy about the idea either.

But . . . "I'm fine with it," I said, and I meant it. "Objectively speaking, it's just a day. I don't want to give it any weird power over me."

Aunty Ulo smiled and nodded and went back to her phone. "I

knew it. Your mom didn't like the idea at all, and I told her you would see things differently." I could tell Aunty Ulo was pleased with my perspective, and I smiled too.

I ended up flying back to PH with Aunty Ulo and Somachi, who literally dropped everything she was doing in Lagos to be with me on such an important day.

When we landed, Daddy was waiting for us at the airport, and I ran straight into his arms. I had missed him so much! It was such a wonderful reunion for us, and I was incredibly happy to see him looking healthy and well.

We all drove straight to the ceremony, and the moment I stepped foot in Jesuit Memorial College, I knew I was meant to be there in person for this event.

The bereaved parents hugged me one by one, so obviously happy to see me.

"We're all so proud of you, Kechi," they said to me, and I knew they meant it.

I could tell it meant just as much to them as it meant to me that I came to share this important moment with them in person.

Nothing could've prepared me for the onslaught of emotions I experienced that day. I cried so much. We all cried so much. But we were there for each other, and it was enough.

Some days later, Daddy, Aunty Ulo, and I traveled to Abuja for an LJC reunion on the main campus. Yimi also flew in, so we all drove to the school together.

After hours on the road, the tall LJC clock tower came into view.

Something tugged at my heart the second I saw that nostalgic landmark. My mind drifted to Toke, and I pursed my lips in silence.

We finally arrived at the school gates, and as they slowly opened to welcome us in, I couldn't help but recall the last time I passed through them.

Minutes later, I stepped out of the car and looked around with a strange weight in my heart. I wasn't sad per se; I just felt . . . heavy. Still, I smiled a little as my gaze passed over the familiar buildings, the landscape, the Saint Ignatius statue at the center of the campus.

For six years of my young life, this had been home.

"Kechi! Yimi!"

I turned around at the sound of my name, and my smile widened into a grin when I saw several familiar faces walking up to us. A lot of LJC alumni who lived locally came for the reunion, and I saw so many former classmates I hadn't seen in person since before the accident. We spent some time getting reacquainted, then we decided to take a long walk around our former campus.

Being back at LJC a decade after the plane crash, walking those familiar roads and entering those familiar buildings . . . it filled me with a deep sense of nostalgia. Back in 2005, I had left so abruptly, not knowing that my last day on campus would be my last. Now there I was, ten years later. It was a little surreal to think of everything that had happened in the space between.

I thought about the sixty angels, who would never get this chance to come back and walk these roads. It was a bittersweet moment for me.

That's why I'm here. I'm walking these roads for all of you too.

The day's events ended with a nice little ceremony in the campus entertainment building, and then the most surprising, most wonderful thing happened.

Out of nowhere, a video started to play on the screen in front of the hall, and as I watched, I realized it was a video compilation of individual special messages from all my classmates, friends, and family! I was so shocked that I started to cry, and I think it moved even my dad to tears. Neither of us had expected this.

The second surprise took my remaining breath away.

All of a sudden, I was ushered onto the elevated stage by the principal, and all my classmates from my school year disappeared backstage.

I waited, wondering what was going on, then my classmates stepped out from backstage, each of them wearing their LJC graduation cap and gown.

My hands covered my mouth in shock. "Oh my God . . ."
Is this what I think it is?
One by one they filed out and stood as a group behind me, and
I could already feel my tear ducts gearing up for another grand
performance.

The principal draped a brand-new graduation gown over my
shoulders while Yimi helped me put on my cap. After saying a few
words, I moved my tassel from the right side of my head to the
left and the principal officially declared me a Loyola Jesuit College
graduate of the class of 2006.

I started crying-laughing as everyone in the hall cheered and
clapped, and we threw our caps into the air like it was a real graduation day.

This was the most thoughtful, most touching and caring thing
my classmates and alma mater could've ever done for me. They
gave me the graduation I never got to have. They gave me my LJC
graduation.

The entire moment was imprinted into my mind forever, and I
found myself thinking that despite the many disappointments I'd
experienced since graduating college earlier that year, 2013 ended
up being pretty amazing, after all. I may still have been uncertain about my future, but at least I had gotten closure from my
past.

Around April of the following year, I started to get heavily
discouraged.

*What are your plans for me, Lord? You've been with me since
South Africa. You're not about to let go now, are You? I need You.
Please lead me down the right path. I don't know what to do!*

More time passed with no answers from God or from any hiring
managers. The paranoia creeped in.

*Is it because of how I look? Do they not want someone with
such heavy scars like mine representing their brand? Is that what
is going on?*

I hated thinking this way, but it's where my mind went after a while.

Something's gotta give. Lord Jesus, I can't keep putting myself out there and getting nothing but rejections. At some point, something has got *to give.*

The weeks flew by, and I started to get desperate.

As an international student, I was not an American citizen or a permanent resident; therefore my time in America was limited to the duration of my college years and one work year thereafter. I graduated college in 2015, and I had until August 2016 to find a job or find the money to go back to school. It was now just months before my deadline.

Then a miracle happened.

One day in June, I was having a conversation about my future with Aunty Ulo, who was based in Nigeria.

"What do you think about creating a proposal, Kechi?" she asked me.

"What kind of proposal?"

"We'll create a proposal to raise money for you to start your MBA, and I will shop it around to some companies I know to see if they'd be willing to invest in you."

"Oh, I see . . ." I was very hesitant.

My life was a testament to the power of charity and human kindness, that much was true. From the miracles surrounding South Africa and Shell to the miracle of my fundraiser, I had seen the evidence of the goodness of humans with my own eyes.

But I did not want to appear as though I felt *entitled* to other people's goodwill simply because I had gotten so much of it in the past. I was afraid people might think I was taking advantage of their kindness and their sympathy toward "Kechi the plane crash survivor."

"I think there's no harm in putting yourself out there." Aunty Ulo shrugged. "The worst they can do is say no."

I asked for some time to think about it, even though I was running out of time.

Lord, is this okay? Is it okay to do this? I don't know. Please, if you don't want me to do this, tell me.

I kept waiting for God to give me a sign, but nothing concrete came to me. I told my mom and my closest friends, and they all said to do it. Eventually, I decided to hell with it. Even in the midst of my many fears, I would take the risk.

Okay, Lord, I'll just do it. If it doesn't work out, at least I'll know I tried.

I called Aunty Ulo and gave her the okay, then I set up a GoFundMe page and posted it on Facebook and Instagram with the title, "Tuition Campaign."

It was as if God had just been waiting for me to make a move.

As soon as the campaign went live, in His usual fashion, He completely took over.

In three days, I'd raised over three thousand dollars, and still it kept going up. I couldn't believe it. No one could.

Then Aunty Ulo called me with the most incredible news of all.

"Kechi, someone just called to tell me that she has about thirty thousand dollars to donate to your tuition fund."

I was speechless. I ran to Mommy and gave her the phone, and when Aunty Ulo gave her the mind-boggling news, she screamed.

Was this really, truly happening? My head was spinning from how fast God was moving.

"Kechi, God just likes to brag with you!" Mommy exclaimed, and all I could do was laugh in shock. A week before, I had no job with the fear of deportation looming over my head, and that day, I had enough money to start my master's program at my alma mater.

I was so thrilled. So grateful. So humbled.

For so many days I had prayed and prayed for God to tell me what to do, but all along, what I had secretly been asking was for God to give me a reason not to do this. I had been waiting for Him to confirm the doubts and fears I had in my heart.

But the moment I decided to step out in faith, to take the risk even in the midst of my fears, God gave me His answer.

A moment of clarity hit me when I realized there was a pattern in the way God moved in my life. He answered my prayers in a way that made it very difficult to deny His divine touch in every situation. From the plane crash to South Africa to Shriners to the fundraiser and now to my tuition campaign. The way things had unfolded in each of these situations, it felt like God was telling me He thrived in the most unlikely and desperate circumstances.

I internalized this and prayed that I would never forget it.

I started my master's program at UST in fall 2016, and that was the beginning of a new phase in my life that neither I nor my family could have ever predicted. Not in a million years.

Chapter Twenty-One

The Show
before the Show

It was October 2016, and I was in the middle of my first semester as a graduate student at UST. I was also working on campus as a graduate assistant for the Cameron School of Business. Needless to say, I was staying busy and working hard, trying to build professional networks and relationships, something I never did as an undergraduate. I did not want to make the same mistake twice.

Meanwhile, despite how busy I was, I couldn't get my friend Womiye to stop pestering me about signing up for *America's Got Talent*.

"You're always sending me videos of you singing one song or another, and I'm tired of you wasting your talent on me," she said over Skype one day. "Let's do something useful with these videos. Did you see the email I forwarded to you?"

I sighed, remembering her email. Apparently *America's Got Talent* was scouting for season 12 applicants, and they were currently accepting online applications.

Womiye has always been one of my biggest cheerleaders when it came to my voice. Over the last few years, she'd hinted at me

205

participating in music talent shows the same way my dad used to tell me to, but she'd never pushed the way she was pushing me toward *America's Got Talent.*

"Kechi, listen," Womiye said. "It wouldn't hurt to just apply. Just put yourself out there. Thousands of people sign up for these things. There's no guarantee that they'd even see your application. So there's no harm in trying."

I said nothing to that and took the conversation elsewhere.

It wasn't as though I didn't like my voice or think that it was good; I just didn't believe it was good enough for a competition. I watched a lot of those talent shows. I knew the caliber of singers who typically ended up on those stages. Even if I signed up, there was no way anyone was going to pick me to stand onstage. More importantly, there was no way they would put me on TV, not with all my burns and my scarred face. I was not being self-deprecating, just factual. I had never seen anyone who looked like me on TV, and I was not surprised. We live in a world that's very superficial, especially the entertainment industry. I knew the kind of people who ended up on TV in 2016, and none of them looked like me. My focus was entirely on school and work, and that was where it was going to stay.

A few weeks passed and I got another forwarded email from Womiye, only this time, I saw that she had filled out the *AGT* online application form on my behalf.

She opened an account for me, put in my name, number, date of birth, and even attached a video recording of me singing an Adele song, which I had sent to her some time back.

"Just submit it!" she said when I called her to protest.

After I hung up, I stared at the form on my screen for some time. I scrolled down and saw she really had done everything, even the "About Me" section.

Just do it, Kechi.

I hit "Submit" without thinking too much about it. I texted Womiye, telling her that I had submitted the application, and proceeded to forget about it all. I didn't bother telling my parents. I didn't even pray about it. I was confident *AGT* would never reach out to me. I was sure they wouldn't even see my application, and even if they did, that nothing would come of it.

Me, on a TV talent show? Give me a break. It'll never happen.

Besides, I was working on a trajectory in my life that had nothing to do with music. Singing on the worship team was already a step outside my comfort zone. That should be enough, right?

Two months passed, and I heard nothing from *AGT*. I was so busy with school and work, and I had no expectations anyway.

Then came the phone call that changed my life forever.

It was a Saturday morning in November, so I was sleeping in. Suddenly, I was awakened by a phone call that came in around 8:00 a.m.

"Hello!" said the chirpy voice on the other end of the line. "Am I speaking with Kechi?"

"Yes?" I was very groggy.

"Hi! My name is Destiny. I'm a talent scout for *America's Got Talent*, and I just wanted to talk to you a little bit about your application. We're really thinking about moving forward with you. We liked what we saw!"

Her voice faded into the background as I tried to comprehend what she had just said.

"So, we'll follow up with you soon, okay?"

I hung up and went straight back to bed.

Two hours later, my phone alarm woke me, and I sat up in bed slowly. For some reason, my heart was pounding in anticipation of something, though I wasn't sure what.

Did someone call me?

I grabbed my phone and looked at my most recent calls.

Yup, there it was. A call from a California number at 8:00 a.m.

Heart pounding, I called the number back.

"Hello?" said a female voice.

"Hi," I started. "My name is Kechi. Um . . . did I get a call from this number earlier, about *America's Got Talent*?" My voice sounded unsure.

The person on the other end laughed. "Yeah, I had a feeling you weren't quite there when we were talking," she said good-naturedly.

"I'm so sorry. I was half asleep!"

"I figured. But yeah, my name is Destiny, I'm an *AGT* talent scout. We're gathering potential contestants for *AGT* season 12 and . . ."

At the end of our second phone call, I was completely awake and completely stunned.

I had *not* expected this!

I jumped out of bed and raced downstairs to tell Mom and Tara the crazy news. They were so delighted but also confused since they didn't even know I'd applied.

We video-called Daddy and gave him the news as well.

"See, this is why you should listen to me!" he said with the proudest smirk on his face. "I've been telling you for *years* to apply for one of these shows, Adaobi, and now look!"

I could only shake my head and roll my eyes at the smugness in his voice.

"We'll just go with the flow and see what happens," I told the three of them, and I said the exact same thing to my friends later that day after telling them everything.

I definitely didn't want to get too excited prematurely, only to be disappointed later. I was all too familiar with the rejection process from my past experiences with job interviews. Something starts out looking like a great prospect and you clear several levels of interviews and then you receive that dreaded "Unfortunately" email in the end.

"I just got a bunch of emails from AGT?!" Womiye gushed on the phone one day. This was how I learned that she had put her own email in the application so that if *AGT* rejected me, I would be none the wiser. She'd thought of everything!

"I can't believe they actually called you," she went on. "*Oya*,[1] tell me everything!"

1. *Oya* is Nigerian slang for "hurry up."

The next few months were surreal. I stayed connected with multiple *AGT* representatives via Womiye's email all the way through Christmas and into 2017. They requested several clips of me singing all my favorite songs, trying to get a feel of my vocal range and singing style.

Their apparent interest in me stayed consistent, much to my confusion and surprise, and I eventually told all my close friends about this new development in my life. I still wasn't sure how to feel about any of it, and all the while, I had papers, exams, and work to do. These were concrete things in my life that I needed to focus on.

Then one day, Destiny said something that made it all very real for me. "We need to narrow down to two solid song choices for the actual audition."

"Okay, no problem," I said as calmly as I could manage, while my mind kept screaming the words *actual audition* over and over.

After that particular phone call, I clasped my hands together and closed my eyes. It seemed it was time to officially bring all this *AGT* stuff to God's attention.

Lord, I have no idea where this is going. You know I don't want anything that isn't from You. If this is a distraction, please don't let it go further than this. If this is something that You actually want for me, then please take control, and please let everything go the way You want it to go.

About a week after I said this prayer, Womiye forwarded me an email from *AGT* about travel dates and flight bookings.

I group video-called my friends in a daze.

Odinachi and Sandra just kept screaming about how we were about to be famous. It was hilarious.

"Um," Yimi said in a voice with barely restrained excitement as she raised her hand. "Permission to get excited now, please!"

Mom, Dad, and Tara had the same reaction when I gave them this update. I also told the rest of my family, who were just as much a part of this journey.

At that point, there was no denying it. This was happening.

I was, at the very least, filming an audition! Whether or not it actually aired on TV was a different story, but I wasn't going to bother myself about any of that. I wasn't hopeful, nor was I invested. Whatever this experience was to become, I was going to just enjoy every moment as it unfolded without thinking too deeply about it.

One day, I was walking on campus, and I spotted a flyer on the notice board in front of the student activities building. It read CELTS' GOT TALENT.[2]

I stared at the flyer, amused at God's timing.

I saw this flyer every year as an undergraduate, and not once did I ever feel inclined to enter because I was too nervous to put my voice in a competitive scenario. But things were different now. I was singing in church, and I was getting ready to travel to California to sing on the *America's Got Talent* stage, the very stage that this school talent show was modeled after.

Maybe I was finally ready for something like this. Maybe this could be a sort of trial run for me. A chance to practice being in a competition.

I took a picture of the email address on the flyer and when I got home that day, I applied for Celts' Got Talent.

I got an audition date and when I went in for the audition, I sang a pretty obscure song that I loved. The girls I auditioned for smiled and thanked me for coming, and two days after that, I received an email saying I didn't qualify as a contestant.

I felt a little disappointed about it, but I moved on.

A few days passed and I received another email from Celts' Got Talent. One of their contestants had dropped out and since I was apparently runner-up, they wanted to know if I was still interested in participating. What were the odds of that happening?

I went to the talent show with my friend Sandra, who came to support me, and wouldn't you know it, I ended up *winning* the whole thing!

2. Celts was the name of the UST sports teams.

I was so shocked and thrilled, not because I won but because of the circumstances. This was a show I almost didn't even qualify for, and in the end, I won it.

It wasn't like I felt this was a sign that I'd win *AGT* or anything like that. But it sure was a good motivator, one I didn't know I needed until I had it.

Chapter Twenty-Two

The Show

I flew into California alone the day before my audition taping. I had to take three days off work for it.

The next day, I got to the *AGT* waiting room, and I was blown away by the number of fellow contestants who were there already. There were cameras everywhere, capturing footage of every movement, every conversation. It was a whole new world to me. I noticed that there were people from all walks of life in the room, people of different races, ages, sexes, sizes. Some flashy, some ordinary.

Suddenly I realized that this was actually the perfect show for someone like me.

I thought I wasn't TV material, and maybe that was true in terms of appearance, but as a matter of fact, my burn survivor story was the kind of thing shows like this loved.

I didn't want to be here because of my story though . . .

"Kechi, it's time!"

I looked up, and it was my producer. I'd been corresponding with him over emails and phone calls for months already.

Minutes later, I was handed a mic, and a guy with a headset signaled for me to walk onto the stage.

I gripped the mic tightly, said a quick prayer, and stepped out onto the *AGT* stage in my blue dress and beret, amid the encouraging cheers of the audience.

It happened the second I stepped on the giant *X* right at the center of the stage.

I laid eyes on those four judges—Howie Mandel, Mel B, Heidi Klum, and Simon Cowell—and I realized in that very instant, that in my quest to be as relaxed as possible about this experience, I had done *nothing* to prepare for how overwhelming this moment would be.

Oh my God. I am about to sing in front of these four people who are going to tell me afterward whether my voice is good or bad.

The nerves kicked in, and my heart started to pound.

My track started to play, and I took a deep, steadying breath. Then I started to sing my Ed Sheeran number.

Immediately, it felt all wrong. I was singing faster than the track and my heart was pounding so hard that my notes were coming out too shaky.

"Stop, stop the track," Simon suddenly said into his mic.

The track stopped, and my heart stopped along with it.

Oh, God. I messed up. You know what, it's fine, I'm fine. This is why I didn't put any hope into any of this, this is why—

"Kechi, are you nervous?"

I looked at Simon and nodded my head several times.

"Okay, someone get her some water, please," he said, looking offstage, and before I knew it, someone was walking onto the stage to hand me a bottle of water.

"Just take a few deep breaths," Simon said into his mic. "Just relax."

I took several sips of water, breathing in and out, trying my best to calm my heartbeat. The audience started to cheer encouragingly again, and the other judges joined in. It honestly made me feel so much better.

"Start again whenever you're ready," Simon said.

I nodded, taking a few more breaths. *God, please. I just want to do my best.*

I opened my mouth and started to sing again, and seconds into the song, I could already tell it was going to be a much better rendition of "Thinking Out Loud" than whatever that first one had been shaping up to be.

I finished the song on as strong a note as I could manage, and once I was done, my hands started to tremble with utter relief. I was so thankful that Simon stopped me when he did. I was so grateful for the second chance to show what my voice really sounded like.

I looked up and realized that the entire room was cheering louder than ever. Not only that, but the judges were all clapping for me too!

One by one, the four judges gave me their opinions on my voice and when they were done, I had four yeses.

I was moving on to the Judge Cuts!

I flew back to California for the Judge Cuts episode a couple weeks after filming my audition, and this time, my mom joined me, so I wasn't alone.

My perspective on my *AGT* experience had changed a little since my first audition. I was now in a place where I was extremely grateful for the fact that I'd made it past the first stage. I hadn't expected that at all. I hadn't expected *anything*, so really, I was thrilled to have made it this far.

But that was only speaking generally. I was extremely anxious because I had come to California with a very bad head cold and cough. A cough is every singer's greatest fear, and mine was particularly persistent. We came to California with throat lozenges and cough syrups, but nothing worked to curb the cough.

Mommy and I prayed the night before the filming. We prayed that the cough would disappear by the time I woke up the next morning. We prayed for God to move.

As Mommy prayed out loud for my cough, I added my own silent prayer concerning something that had been gnawing at my mind since the first audition.

Lord, please send me home if I don't belong here. I don't want to be in a spot I didn't earn.

I prayed this prayer because I was getting increasingly concerned about the reason I was chosen as a contestant. I absolutely did not want to be there based solely on my story. This wasn't *America's Got Great Stories*; it was *America's Got Talent*. Mommy had tried her best to alleviate my concerns, ensuring me that it was definitely both, but it was hard to believe her completely seeing as she was my mom and therefore slightly biased.

Despite all our prayers, my cough didn't show any signs of stopping the next day, but Mom and I noticed, quite strangely, that no matter how much I coughed . . . my voice remained unaffected.

It simply made no logical sense. I knew what coughs typically did to my voice, but not this one. After every coughing spell, I would immediately test out my vocals, and they would come out sounding as clear as ever.

"How is this happening?" I wondered out loud.

"Don't jinx it," Mommy said, her hands raised in a gesture of submission.

Right up until I stepped on that stage that evening, I was *still* coughing incessantly.

Lord, what is this? I'm already nervous enough!

"Kechi, you're up!"

I closed my eyes and took a deep breath.

I don't know what Your plan is, God, but please walk out onto that stage with me.

I stepped out on the stage and . . . maybe because my nerves took over. Maybe because my celebrity guest judge was the incredibly talented Seal. I wasn't sure. All I knew was that the moment I stepped out in front of those judges and that audience, my coughing stopped.

"Good to see you again, Kechi," Howie said cheerfully.

The judges signaled for me to start singing, so I opened my mouth and sang Donny Hathaway's "A Song for You" better than I had ever sung it in my life.

215

As I kept going, drawing out the notes the way Autumn, my *AGT* vocal coach, had shown me, I knew in my heart that this particular performance would be the one performance I would willingly rewatch even after it aired.

I had an acute awareness in my mind that what was happening right then was a miracle. With the kind of cough I had, there was no reason for me to be able to sing that clearly. Once again, I was being reminded of the way God chose to move in my life. He could've taken away the cough, but I felt like He decided to show me that *even* with a cough, He could let my voice shine. He was telling me that as long as I left everything to Him, He would always take care of me. When I prayed, I needed to just let everything go and leave Him to do His thing. This was something I had struggled with since South Africa, and over a decade later, I still hadn't mastered it. I probably never would. I would probably need to remind myself countless times in the future.

When I finished singing, I opened my eyes to the humbling sight of all five judges, Seal included, standing and clapping for me. The entire audience was also on their feet, cheering and applauding, and I felt myself tearing up even as I laughed with joy. I was so overwhelmed by their response, by what had just happened with my singing. I couldn't believe the way God had pulled me through the performance. I knew for sure my mom was crying in that audience, which was just as well because I'd sung the entire song with her in mind.

I was so elated. It didn't matter to me if this was my last stop on this journey. No matter what the judges' decision was, I could rest easy knowing I had given it my all with this performance.

Seal came up on stage and gave me a big hug. I was so honored that he felt that moved by my performance.

Then Simon spoke. "What I can say for sure, Kechi, is that you deserve your place here tonight, not just because of your story, but because of your talent. That's the absolute truth."

My hand came up to my chest in shock at those incredibly validating words. Tears filled my eyes, and I just *knew* those words were from God.

How could this be? How could Simon have possibly known about the deep-rooted fears in my heart? He couldn't have. That was all God.

He had heard my prayer and He had answered.

I got back to Houston and resumed life as usual. It took a while for the giddiness I was feeling from my Judge Cuts filming to calm down. I fully immersed myself in work and exam preparations. I wouldn't have to travel again until September, so I was looking forward to working for the Cameron School of Business all through the summer.

CSB, unfortunately, did not share my sentiments. On the last workday of the spring semester, my supervisor fired me.

"I'm sorry, Kechi, but we won't be continuing your assistantship position after this semester. You're a great worker, but you missed too much work this semester and we need someone who will be here when needed."

The walk to my car that night felt long and endless. My legs were heavy like lead. I was so crushed. I really felt like I had been juggling everything well. When I'd told my supervisor about the trips and the reason behind them, she hadn't been happy, but she'd seemed understanding. Both times.

I drove home with tears in my eyes, and I realized they were probably right to fire me. How could I miss actual work for a chance to be on some talent show? A job that was helping me so much financially, no less. Working at CSB paid for one three-credit class per semester, which cost more than three thousand dollars. So far, the assistantship position had really been helping me stretch my tuition fund as far out as possible.

Now look at me, I thought. *Jobless, professional relationships probably destroyed. All for AGT.*

Was it worth it?

I cried so hard I couldn't see the road anymore, so I parked on the side of the expressway and bawled my eyes out in the dark. "Lord, I don't understand!" I cried into the silence. "I've been working so hard! Is this part of Your plan? For me to lose my job?" I felt so scared and confused about my future, so uncertain.

What if nothing came out of this thing with *AGT*?

What did I even want from this experience?

I was too scared to have any expectations or hopes, so what was the point of even going on the show? Did I want to pursue a career in music? Was it even possible? Would anyone even care?

These thoughts plagued me, and I vented until my tears finally stopped, then I reentered the highway. For the rest of my drive, I thought about things from CSB's perspective. To me, I was just trying to juggle the things in my life as well as possible. To my employers, I missed six days of work. The reasons didn't matter in a professional setting, especially if they weren't health related.

Classes were different. As long as I submitted my work on time and rescheduled exams with my professors, all would be well. But with work, I simply was not there when they needed me.

When I finally got home, I burst into tears again once I saw Mommy. "I feel so stupid," I said, amid my tears. "How could I have risked an actual job that was helping me professionally and financially over a TV show? I don't even know how far I'll get!"

Mommy rubbed my back and just let me cry it out. Then she said this to me: "Kechi, I know this sucks, and I'm so sorry. But just think about how all this started. You didn't even sign up for this show yourself, yet here you are, an actual contestant on it. This has God's signature all over it. I know it's scary. But let's put our all into this and see where it leads."

I looked at Mommy for a moment, then I huffed out a breath and nodded resolutely.

Originally I felt I'd be fine if *AGT* fell through, since I'd still have my job. But now I didn't even have that.

Might as well go for broke, right? I had nothing to lose anymore.

Might as well jump into this opportunity with both feet and see where I landed.

Fear seemed to be an unavoidable part of taking risks. As long as I decided to try new, open-ended things, like participating in a TV talent show, for instance, I would always feel fear.

I thought about the GoFundMe miracle that got me into my master's program. I had been so afraid to put myself out there. Even after I decided to do it, I was still so afraid.

If fear existed either way, wouldn't it be better to be afraid *while* doing something, than to be afraid *of* doing something? At least with the former, I would have fewer regrets.

I decided to take on this approach with *AGT*. No matter what kind of fear came my way, I would push on, even in the midst of it. If I gave it my all, then maybe, just maybe, I wouldn't have lost my job for nothing.

I moved on to the live shows with that Judge Cuts performance.

For someone who didn't expect to get past the first audition, everything that followed was the cherry on top. Every time I got past another stage of the live shows, I was stunned and immensely grateful to God for bringing me as far as He was bringing me.

As expected, my appearance on the show received mixed reviews from its global TV audience. The majority of the responses were positive and encouraging, but some were dismissive and disparaging, and most of the negative reviews revolved around my burns and my voice.

Throwing insults at me about my face or my scars had zero effect on my self-esteem. Anyone who knew me knew this. You simply cannot hurt me by insulting that which I have fully embraced about myself.

But at the time, a good way to get to me was to criticize my voice, because I was still building my confidence there. I was especially hurt when people said my story was why I was on the show because they were basically confirming my biggest fears about being on *AGT*.

But whenever I saw such comments online, I remembered Simon's words from the Judge Cuts, and I would feel so validated. Simon was someone whose opinion most people begrudgingly respected. If he, of all people, felt that my voice was good enough to be on a competitive show, then I felt like there was some truth to that.

I really had no idea just how much I would rely on Simon's words for the rest of my time on *AGT*. They allowed me to enjoy being in the live shows as much as possible, and by the time I made it to the finale, I embodied the meaning behind the song I performed that day, "Conqueror" by Estelle. I felt like God had truly allowed me to conquer this experience as best as I possibly could.

I was a top-ten finalist!

I didn't care about winning. I was just grateful to have made it to the end.

Chapter Twenty-Three

The Flight

Amazingly, people's interest in me did not end with my *AGT* appearance. God just kept on moving.

I built a sizable following on social media during the course of the show, which served as a fantastic platform on which to pursue the things I wanted to do. And boy, did I have plans! I wanted to give back to Shriners Hospitals in a meaningful way, and I wanted to become a bullying prevention activist. The response I received on the show made me believe in the possibility of a music career for the first time at twenty-eight years old.

The miracles did not stop.

Before the show finished airing, I was approached by an agency called The Grable Group, who wanted to represent me professionally. Tim Grable saw potential in my voice and my story, and through his expertise, I was exposed to the thriving world of music performing and inspirational speaking. I was born with a deep love for music, and I'd entertained lofty dreams of performing for as long as I could remember. Now, through an unexpected twist of fate, I was literally living my childhood dreams, performing on some of the most incredible stages across America and speaking on even more.

The trajectory of my life transformed right before my eyes. Suddenly, I was constantly traveling from city to city for performances and speaking engagements. My graduate studies, which had been the most important thing in my life prior to *AGT*, had to take a temporary back seat while I tried to navigate this new world to the best of my abilities.

In the midst of all this excitement, the most unexpected thing happened. I found myself in the position to continue my surgeries after nearly six years of dormancy.

With the help of ExtraTV's Sharon Levin and Laura Sharpe of Artists for Trauma, I had the privilege of connecting with two incredible California-based surgeons, Dr. Peter Grossman of the Grossman Burn Foundation and Dr. Andrew Frankel of Lasky Aesthetics.

"I watched you on *AGT*, Kechi," Sharon said to me when we met, "and I was just so moved by your story. Now, I'm not sure if you're still undergoing surgeries or not, but if you are, I wanted to see if there was anything I could do for you."

I spent the entirety of summer 2018 in California, working with these two great surgeons, though more extensively with Dr. Grossman. Having surgery again after six years of total independence was a very different experience. I was so much less patient during my recuperation periods because I was no longer used to lying in one place for long periods of time. I was living a much more active life, especially after *AGT*, and I had a lot more responsibilities, which kept me on the move. I found myself feeling idle and restless much faster during this time.

My surgeries in California were not something I could've possibly planned if I wanted to. This was yet another miraculous experience that God placed in this new path He had set me on, and I was once again reminded of the kindness that still exists in this world. I only pray that one day, I can give back the kindness I have received in my life in greater measure.

My new life as a traveling speaker and entertainer took me and my mom (my usual plus-one) to at least four different states a month. This meant we were on at least eight different flights a month.

Against the odds, I quite enjoyed flying. By some unexplainable miracle, the plane crash didn't take that away from me. Considering what I now did for a living, I was even more grateful to God for this fact.

But then, sometime in November 2018, Mommy and I had a flight experience that very nearly changed that for me.

We flew into Philadelphia for an event on the afternoon of this dreadful flight. It was going to be a quick turnaround. We had to head straight back to the airport once the Philly event was over so we could catch an evening flight to Dallas, where I had another event the very next morning.

Mommy and I wrapped up the Philly event and rushed off in our Uber. On our way back to the airport, it started to snow. It was the first snow of the season, and it was quite the downfall. All Southwest flights got canceled almost as soon as we arrived at the airport.

"What do we do?" I asked Mommy anxiously. "If we don't leave Philly today, we won't make it in time for the event tomorrow. It's at 6:30 a.m." I definitely didn't want to miss tomorrow's show because it was a music therapy event, and Christine, my former Shriners music therapist, was going to be there.

At that moment, my agent, Tim, called my mom. "There's another flight that's scheduled to leave for Dallas this evening," he said. "If you hurry, you can make it."

Mommy and I rushed to the terminal and booked the flight in the nick of time. We boarded the aircraft, thankful that we were still able to leave for Dallas that evening.

"Thank God," Mommy said as we made our way to our seats.

"Yeah." I let out a relieved chuckle. "Apparently this is the only flight that didn't cancel today. Lucky us."

But there was nothing lucky about it.

Mommy and I ended up sitting separately since the flight was booked last minute. I had a window seat in the middle section while she was seated all the way in the back.

I settled into my seat and prayed as I usually do at the start of every flight. Moments later, the plane started to taxi.

I looked outside the window at the falling snow. It looked so pretty. I briefly marveled at how planes could fly even in this kind of weather, then I put my headphones over my ears as the plane accelerated down the runway and lifted smoothly into the air.

It didn't take long for the turbulence to start.

Initially, I thought nothing of it. It was snowing pretty heavily, after all, so some gusty winds were to be expected. The turbulence got a little more intense as we gained altitude, but then it evened out after a while. Nothing to be concerned about.

All of a sudden, the aircraft jerked dramatically, like it had slammed into something thick and unyielding, and in the next second, we were engulfed in some of the densest clouds I had ever seen.

The aircraft jerked again and shook up and down dramatically, then it jerked left to right.

It got so bad that people all around me started raising their voices in alarm with every dramatic jolt of the aircraft.

"Whoa!"

"Oh my God!"

I had never heard Americans yell in fear inside an aircraft, no matter how bad turbulence got. This was an alarming first.

As the plane continued to lurch every which way, I sat up in my seat, observing the situation with a sort of detached awareness.

Is this for real? I said to myself. *Am I seriously in another plane that's trying to be funny?*

I laughed aloud and shook my head, then I settled back into my seat and turned the music up in my ears.

There was absolutely no way a plane I was in would crash. I was protected by virtue of my experience with this exact same scenario. God simply would not allow it.

The plane continued to lurch, and I stayed perfectly calm. Too calm. Even when it pivoted to the left so much that it forced the guy sitting on my right to lean into my shoulder, even while other passengers were screaming all around me, still I stayed as calm as ever. I was so sure we were going to be fine.

Finally, the aircraft burst through the other side of the thick clouds, and when I looked out the window, I could see we were above the clouds where the skies were clear.

The plane smoothed out completely in the air, and it was like the last eight minutes or so never even happened.

The relief in the air was palpable. Soon, the cabin was abuzz with noise and conversation. It was the noisiest flight I'd ever been on in this country.

The pilot's voice suddenly came over the intercom. "Hey everyone, this is your captain speaking. Uh, sorry about that. Only noticed how bad the storm clouds were when I saw the aircraft ahead of me heading into it, and by then it was too late for us to avoid it, so we just had to power through. Air control didn't notify us about anything like this, so again, deeply apologize for that . . . should be smooth sailing to Dallas now that we're above the clouds."

The talking resumed after the pilot was done, and I was almost positive everyone was discussing the ludicrous message we just received.

"Air control didn't notify us about anything like this?"

It was clear to me that our pilot's experience was what had saved us, because he himself had not expected any of that to happen.

I felt someone hold my shoulder and looked up to see Mommy leaning toward me, looking at me with extreme concern.

"Kechi, are you okay?"

I smiled and nodded repeatedly, putting my own hand over hers. "I'm okay, Mommy. Trust me. I didn't even panic. Don't worry. I'm fine." As I looked at her face, I realized she herself looked a little off. I squeezed her hand. "Are *you* okay?"

She drew in a shaky breath and let it out. "Well, I'm not sure. It got very bad back there."

I remembered that plane turbulence amplified the farther back you sat. "Oh my God. I'm so sorry, Mommy! That must've been horrible!"

"Never mind me. You're sure you're okay?"

"I am," I assured her. "I promise."

Well, I certainly *thought* I was fine. After all, I'd handled the situation very calmly as it was happening. Based on that, I thought I was unaffected by the flight. I was thankful for the calm assurance God seemed to have given me in those moments.

When we landed in Dallas and got to our hotel room that night, we called our family and friends one by one to deliver our accounts of what had happened to us, including the pilot's alarming message.

"I'll never fly that airline again!" I declared, and Mommy laughed.

I meant it though. I mean, there we were, thinking how fortunate we were that one plane was still flying that day, only for us to belatedly realize that there was a reason every single other airline had canceled!

After the event, we flew home from Dallas with no incident. Everything seemed fine and we put that horrendous flight behind us. Or so I thought.

The very next trip we took, I was in for the shock of my life.

The day had started out very dreary in Houston. We got to Hobby Airport and made it past security. By the time we got to our gate, it was raining heavily outside. Bad weather. That was my first trigger.

Sitting in the lounge and watching the rain beat against the wide glass panes of the building, I felt my heart start to pound.

Time passed, and I tried to distract myself with my phone. But I knew we were getting closer to boarding time and the rain wasn't showing any signs of stopping.

I looked at my ticket and stared at the seat number and wondered how far back in the plane we were. I remember Tim had said it was a small aircraft.

My heart pounded faster. I didn't really understand what was happening to me, but I didn't like it one bit.

Time to board.

We stood in line and eventually entered the plane

As we walked down the narrow aisle to our seats, my heart dropped to my feet when I saw that we were in the very last row, the middle and aisle seats. That was my second trigger.

I clenched my jaw and stood off to the side to let Mommy into the middle seat, then I sat in the aisle seat and put down my things.

I looked out the window to my left. It was still raining hard.

I silently put on my seat belt, and the second it snapped into place, my whole body went numb.

"Mommy, I don't think I can do this."

I was staring at the back of the seat in front of me, but I saw Mommy look at me.

"What?"

"I don't think I can do this," I repeated, and my breath started to come shorter and faster. I was hyperventilating.

"Kechi? Kechi, sweetie, it's okay."

I felt her hand come around my arm, and I shook my head vigorously. "Mommy, listen, we have to get off. I can't. I can't, okay? I can't, I can't!" I burst into tears and the next thing I knew, I was having a full-scale panic attack. It was my first one ever, but I recognized it for what it was.

I didn't want to fly in the rain. I didn't want to sit at the back of the plane. I didn't want to be there. Why did I have to be there?

The weird thing was that I wasn't even thinking about the shaky flight we'd been on just days before.

I couldn't pinpoint the source of all this panic and fear, but it wasn't that Philly flight. It felt like my body was reacting to something that my mind couldn't quite recall, a memory shrouded in mist and nothingness.

Did the turbulence on that flight trigger something in my memory? Something from the plane crash?

"Shhh, it's okay, Kechi. Shhh . . ." Mommy held me tightly in her arms. She started praying in a low, hushed voice as she rocked me in my seat. I felt protected in her embrace, but I was still so afraid.

As the plane took off, I panicked even more when I thought about how we were flying in the rain. Just like on December 10, 2005.

Mommy just held me tighter and rocked me, praying and praying.

In the midst of my panic, I felt a rush of anger and frustration edge its way into my turbulent emotions.

Why?

Why would I, of all people, have to experience something as triggering as that turbulent flight all these years after my accident? How was it fair? Had I not been through enough? Wasn't it a good thing that I couldn't remember what it felt like to be on a plane that was crashing? What was the point of making me fear flying *now*, after so long? *Now*, when I was flying more than I'd ever flown in my life?

For some time after that flight, I remained intensely traumatized. I didn't have any more panic attacks, but for months following that day, I got so nervous at even the slightest bump in the air, or if we had to fly in bad weather. Even Mommy was badly affected. When I had the panic attack, she'd just paused her own fears to help me overcome mine.

I hated it. So, so much.

I hated how I was now so hyperconscious of flying. Before that horrible flight, flying was the same to me as driving. Just another way to get around. Now I dreaded it.

It just seemed so unfair for a plane crash survivor to go through something like that. I felt like I was being punished for being okay with flying even after being in a plane crash.

For a long time after that whole experience, I considered getting prescription sleeping pills that would just knock me the heck out the second I got on a flight during bad weather. I'm still considering that, to be honest.

I considered therapy, but then I quickly dismissed it because I was afraid of mistakenly unlocking the plane crash memories that are buried inside my mind.

After my anger at God waned a bit, I prayed about the whole thing. Then I got the feeling I should just . . . wait it out and see if I could manually rebuild my confidence in flying. Before resorting to drugs, I would see if I could rely more on my support system, like I used to in the past, to get over this trauma.

So whenever I got nervous on flights, I held Mommy's hand, or Tara's hand, or the hand of whoever my plus-one was for a trip. If I was traveling alone and things got bumpy, I texted my family and friends, who were rock stars at being supportive. I did that for months and months, and eventually I mellowed. Flying didn't quite feel as laid-back as it used to, but it wasn't full of dread and panic anymore. And the more I kept flying, the better I got. The more *myself* I felt inside a plane.

I didn't know why I experienced something as triggering and traumatic as that flight to Dallas. There probably wasn't any reason. Just a bad day to be in the air.

But I knew one thing—I wasn't going to stop flying. That wasn't even an option.

How on earth would I make the impact I wanted to make or accomplish the things I wanted to with my life if I only went where I could drive?

If a plane crash didn't keep me out of the air, some bad turbulence certainly wasn't going to either. Simple as that.

Roughly one year after *AGT* season 12, I was invited back on the show to participate in the pioneer season of *America's Got Talent: The Champions*, where the show's most memorable acts and past champions came together to compete once more.

I was so honored to have been invited, and it was on this very show that I was awarded Simon Cowell's coveted golden buzzer.[1] Words couldn't describe how that felt.

1. When a contestant gets the golden buzzer on *AGT*, they move straight to the finale of the show.

Once again, I was overwhelmed by God's grace and the way He continued to convince me, through this man, that I was right where He wanted me to be.

Through *AGT*, God started me on a brand-new path that I never even dared to dream of. He used my friend Womiye to propel me toward His purpose for me, allowing me to inspire people through my voice and my burn survivor story.

In 2017, after I was on *AGT*, a literary agent, Travis Pennington from The Knight Agency, reached out to me to write my story, and now years later here we are. Full circle.

I find it so incredible how I am currently making a living doing all the things I was passionate about long before the accident: speaking, singing, and writing.

It took sixteen long years on a very twisted road.

I believe that the perseverance God gave me and the amazing support system He afforded me allowed me to defy the circumstances that the plane crash forced me into.

One might say that the accident deterred me from my purpose, or that it forced me to take the long way around via a path riddled with many obstacles, but consider this.

By slowly overcoming those obstacles on that twisted road, I was able to obtain the traits and qualities God knew I would need in order to be fully equipped to step into His purpose for me, which continues to unfold to this day.

Surgery didn't fix everything. It can't.

Even after three eyelid surgeries, my eyes still do not fully close properly, which has resulted in extreme sensitivity to light that grows more severe with age. I still deal with pain from my contracted skin. The itching appears to be a lifelong burden that I will continue to manage as best I can without letting it interrupt my daily life. And I may never know why the plane crash happened.

But I will never regret the experiences I've had since that accident. After all, they led me right here.

A Final Word

*"For I know the plans I have for you," declares
the LORD, "plans to prosper you and not to harm
you, plans to give you hope and a future."*

JEREMIAH 29:11 NIV

It has been sixteen years since the Sosoliso plane crash of 2005.

Since then I have used the incredible platform that *AGT* gave me to impact the world in the best ways I know how. I have become a performing artist, a recording artist, a songwriter, a bullying prevention advocate, a United Nations Ambassador, and now, a published author.

Sixteen-year-old Kechi, the one who had been innocently heading home for the Christmas holidays on December 10, 2005, could never have expected to end up on the path that would lead her to this very moment.

Life is so very interesting. We cannot stop it from happening to us. I couldn't stop the accident from taking so many lives and leaving me with these burn scars. I learned, however, that what I do have control over is how I choose to react to life when it happens to me. This book should show you that nothing about the process is easy or automatic.

231

If you made it to this point, then you have read my story in its entirety, and you have seen that there is nothing special about me. People tell me that they'd never have been able to handle the burden of my circumstances the way that I did, and maybe that's true. But that does not mean I am stronger or more enduring than any other human being. This was simply my own specific burden to bear, and I believe that when God made us, He equipped each of us with our own unique brand of strength that allows us to handle the individual burdens life will unfailingly throw at us.

So if you've read this book and you feel that you could not possibly have carried my burden, you may be right.

But I cannot carry your burden either. No other human being can.

We each have a well within us that life forces us to tap deeper and deeper into at different crossroads, and if we keep at it, we eventually tap into the next level of strength that will prepare us for the next life challenge. This is how we become more durable. I urge you to remember that.

Hopefully, you can also see that my story is still unfolding. I have so much more that I hope to accomplish with this second chance at life God gave to me. I want to perform my own music on the world's biggest stages, I want to try cuisine from all around the globe, I want to continue to use my platform to speak out against bullying, and I want to afford a comfortable life for my family, who have sacrificed so much to see me thrive.

I leave this story in your hands and in your hearts, with the prayer that something within its pages inspired you to keep trying.

Thank you for coming on this journey with me.

Acknowledgments

Subomi Aluko, you were the very first classmate to reach out to my mom after the accident happened. You called the very next day. I will never forget this.

Aunty Ngozi, you came to visit me in South Africa. I have always loved your wit and frank humor, Aunty, and the smiles I sported during your visit were some of my most genuine ones during those incredibly hard times.

Atuora Erokoro, the last friend I saw the night before I left Nigeria for good. Your visit was truly the best send-off I could have asked for.

Father Quickly, your visit coincided with my very first eyelid surgery, but I knew it was you the second I heard your grand voice.

My childhood friend Adanna and my former LJC classmate Onyinyechi, we may have lost touch over the years, but I will never forget the fact that you both came to see me in South Africa. Thank you.

Uncle Athan Achonu, your incredible generosity made it possible for me to restart my surgeries the period after I aged out of the Shriners system, and before Yimi and Somachi held a fundraiser for my surgeries. I am forever grateful.

Kechi Okwuchi is a Nigerian American recording artist and motivational speaker. One of two survivors in the Sosoliso Airlines Flight 1145 crash on December 10, 2005, she was a finalist on *America's Got Talent* in 2017 and has put out original music since her appearance on the hit TV show. As a burn survivor advocate, she became a national patient ambassador for Shriners Children's Texas in Galveston in 2017. She has since been active in events organized by WE Movement, a global youth empowerment organization, speaking and singing to thousands of students at WE Day events all over the country, the most notable being WE Day UN, which took place in New York in September 2019. As a bullying prevention advocate, she has teamed up with the organization Be Strong Global, as well as Instagram and *Teen Vogue*, to speak out against bullying. She hopes to use her story and her musical talents to ignite hope. Okwuchi lives in Pearland, Texas.

Stay Connected with
Kechi

www.KechiOfficial.com

Connect with

BakerBooks

Relevant. Intelligent. Engaging.

Sign up for announcements about
new and upcoming titles at

BakerBooks.com/SignUp

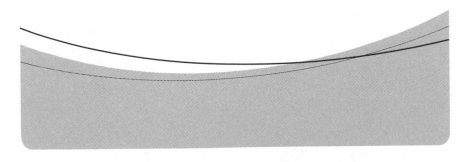

@ReadBakerBooks